GLEEFULLY
MACABRE TALES

A SHORT STORY COLLECTION
BY JEFF STRAND

DARK REGIONS PRESS
-2009-

FIRST TRADE PAPERBACK EDITION

Text © 2009 by Jeff Strand
Cover Art © 2009 by Frank Walls

Cover and interior design by David G. Barnett/Fat Cat Graphic Design

ISBN-13: 978-1-62641-067-1

"Really, Really Ferocious" *Small Bites*, 2004
"Socially Awkward Moments With An Aspiring Lunatic" Chapbook, 2005.
"High Stakes" *Planet Relish*, 2000
"Special Features" *Post Mortem #4*, 2006
"Sex Potion #147" *Funny Stories of Scary Sex*, 2006
"The Three Little Pigs" *Wicked Karnival #5*, 2005
"Everything Has a Purpose" *Scratching the Surface*, 2000
"Them Old West Mutations" *Trip the Light Horrific*, 2005
"Wasting Grandpa" *Scratching the Surface*, 2000
"A Bite For a Bite" *Small Bites*, 2004
"Glimpses" *Bare Bone #8*, 2005
"Common Sense" *Necon XXV Program Book*, 2005
"Gross-Out!" Transcript of live performances, 2006 & 2007, with commentary, 2007.
"Bad Coffee" Insidious Publications coffee mug, 2005
"Werewolf Porno" *Funny Stories of Scary Sex*, 2006
"An Admittedly Pointless But Mercifully Brief Story With Aliens In It" Previously unpublished, 2000
"Munchies" *Just Adventure* website, 2002
"Roasting Weenies By Hellfire" *New Voices in Horror*, 2004
"Quite a Mess" *Fusing Horizons*, 2003
"I Hold the Stick" *The Absinthe Literary Review*, 2000
"Scarecrow's Discovery" *Horrors! 365 Scary Stories*, 1998
"Howard, the Tenth Reindeer" Christmas card, 1996
"Howard Rises Again" Christmas card, 1998
"BrainBugs" *Eros & Rust*, 2004
"Cap'n Hank's Five Alarm Nuclear Lava Wings" 2007. Previously unpublished.
"A Call For Mr. Potty-Mouth" *The Horror Fiction Review #16*, 2007
"The Bad Man in the Blue House" 2007. Previously unpublished.
"Abbey's Shriek" *Beyond the Mundane: Unravelings*, 2004
"The Socket" *Deathgrip: Exit Laughing*, 2006
"One of Them" *Side Show: Tales of the Big Top and Bizarre*, 2002
"Secret Message" 2007. Previously unpublished.
"Mr. Sensitive" *Two Twisted Nuts*, 2005
"The Bad Candy House" *Hallow's Eve*, 2006
"Disposal" Published as a stand-alone novella by Biting Dog Press, 2007

DARK REGIONS PRES, LLC
6635 N. BALTIMORE AVE. STE 241
PORTLAND, OR 97203
UNITED STATES

TABLE OF CONTENTS

INTRODUCTION

Welcome to the Dark Regions Press edition of *Gleefully Macabre Tales*, brought to you in convenient paperback and e-book editions. They're both the same content—the only difference is what kind of virus they contain. It'll either erase your hard drive or give you malaria. Apologies in advance.

This is not a "Best Of" collection, because I really don't have enough short fiction out there to pick and choose only the gems. Nor is it a "Complete Short Works" collection, because I'm not at a level of popularity where I can justify including crappy stories just for their historical significance. So it's basically a "Most Of" collection: the complete short works of Jeff Strand minus the really bad ones (hopefully), the too-recently-published-to-reprint-quite-yet ones, and a few bits and pieces that didn't seem to fit.

As much as possible, I tried to make this a collection of stories that are...well, gleefully macabre. They aren't all funny—sure, there's humor in stories like "Abbey's Shriek," "One of Them," and "Glimpses," but I certainly wouldn't classify them as humorous horror. And they aren't all horror stories, especially "Howard, The Tenth Reindeer," which is shamelessly silly yet does have a slightly macabre ending.

Most of the tales in this book, however, fall into the category of "horror/comedy." Sometimes they're blatantly funny stories with a horror premise, sometimes they're comedies so pitch-black that they become horror, and sometimes they're horror stories with a tongue-in-cheek tone—a severed tongue, possibly forked, and hopefully not your own.

Within these pages, I want to make you laugh. I want to make you scream. (You probably won't, though—seriously, have you ever screamed at the scariness of a book? If you have, e-mail me to tell me about it. That would be pretty cool.) I want to disturb you. I want you to giggle while getting completely creeped out. I want you to shout "What a cruel injustice that Stephen King's *Just After Sunset* won the Bram Stoker Award for Best Collection while *Gleefully Macabre Tales* was merely a finalist! Does King's collection have an awesome wiener dog story? I think not!"

As a special bonus, this new edition of *Gleefully Macabre Tales* includes my novella *Disposal*, previously available only as a super-pricey hardcover limited edition. Had *Disposal* been part of the original edition of this book, it totally would have won the Stoker, I just know it.

Very special thanks must go to my elite team of test readers, who read the various tales and said "Why, yes, Jeff, this should be included!" or "No! Dear God, no! What the hell were you thinking?" So let's hear it for Mike Myers (not the actor, and not the serial killer), Nick Cato, Greg Lamberson, Jim Moore, Susan Bodendorfer, Linda Bleser, Moni Draper, Kenyon Charboneaux, and Tod Clark. Also Shane Ryan Staley and Dave Dinsmore. And Joe Morey and Norman Rubenstein.

I'd also like to thank all of the editors and publishers who gave these tales life for the first time, even the stories that appeared in anthologies that sold fewer copies than there were contributors. (However, I exclude the two editors who have yet to send me author copies. Bastards.)

Okay, enough of my incessant babbling. Enjoy the stories!

Jeff Strand
Tampa, Florida
Wayyyyyyy past deadline

REALLY, REALLY FEROCIOUS

"Get off my property, or Silas here will tear the flesh right off your bones!" shouted the old man, angrily tapping his finger against the *No Solicitors* sign next to his front door. "He'll rip out your throat and lap up your blood, then he'll bury your mangled corpse in our backyard with the rest of 'em!"

The teenager looked down at the animal lying at the old man's feet. "But he's a wiener dog."

"Don't you call Silas a wiener dog, you son of a bitch! He's a *dachshund*! And he'll shred your disrespectful ass into Alpo if you don't get off my porch!"

The dog panted happily.

"He's kind of cute," said the teenager, bending down and scratching Silas behind the ears. "Hi, Silas. Are you a good boy? Yes you are, yes you are!"

"Are you freakin' insane? For the love of God, pull your hand away before he bites it clean off!"

"Noooo, Silas wouldn't bite me, no he wouldn't, no he wouldn't! He's a gooooood boy. Yes, I just wuvs my Silas. He's the best wiener dog in the whole wide world!"

The old man hurriedly scooped the dog into his arms. "You're living dangerously, son. Don't let his loving eyes and cylindrical body fool you...this animal is really, really ferocious. Now get off my porch."

"Are you sure you're not interested?" asked the teenager. "Because for only three dollars and fifty-eight cents a month you can—"

"*Kill!*" shouted the old man, thrusting Silas at the teenager. "Bite his nose off! Claw his eyeballs out!"

"Okay, stop poking me with the dog."

"Kill him, Silas! Kill, kill, kill!"

"I mean it; you're starting to piss me off."

The old man shifted so that he gripped the dachshund by the hind legs, and then bashed the animal against the teenager's face. The teenager stumbled backwards a few steps, taken by surprise.

"Rip him apart, Silas!"

The old man swung the dachshund again, smashing it into the side of the teenager's head. The teenager fell to his knees and held up his hand to defend himself.

"Ow! What the hell are you doing?"

The old man hoisted the dachshund over his head and then brought it down upon the teenager as hard as he could. There was a "*Yip!*" from the dog, a "*Shit!*" from the teenager, and a spurt of blood from each. He struck the teenager with the dog over and over, screaming with rage, until the teenager lay motionless, not breathing, his face a ruined mess.

"Aw, jeez, Silas, look what he did to you," said the old man, cradling the dead dog in his arms. "But you were a good dog. You fought bravely. I'll make sure you get a special memorial."

He wandered into the backyard, past five or six memorials and an equal number of unmarked graves.

Maybe now Denise would finally let him get a pit bull.

Socially Awkward Moments with an Aspiring Lunatic

Question of the day: What is insanity? Is it tying a woman to a bed and giggling with maniacal glee as you slice off her extremities with a chainsaw? Or is it simply taking ten minutes to decide what you want to order at McDonalds?

The chainsawed extremities thing is probably a better example, so we'll go with that one. Keep it in mind because we'll get back to it in a bit.

Anyway, on the day that I turned thirty, I decided that I wanted to be insane. I'd tried three decades of sanity and it just wasn't working out. I was bored with my tedious, intellectual, clear-focused existence. I wanted to lose my mind.

But how to do this? I thought about hallucinogens, but that would just turn me into a druggie. That had no appeal. Any cretin off the street could be a druggie. I wanted to become a lunatic through natural means.

I'd always had a spider phobia, so I drove around to all of the pet stores in town, bought out their tarantula stock, and then lay on my living room floor and let them crawl all over me. What I realized is that spiders aren't so bad. They're kind of soothing, actually. I only squished one.

I spent an entire weekend watching the goriest films ever made, back to back, stopping only for a bathroom break every other movie. I even watched *The Evil Dead* twice because it was so cool. But that didn't work, either. Being able to separate fantasy from reality was a real bummer.

I tried a bit of self-mutilation but it hurt too much.

Even when I simply practiced expressions of insanity in the mirror, none of them were convincing. I could successfully look like I was confused, frightened, sleepy, or suffering from testicular distress, but I couldn't look crazed. I remained completely, miserably sane.

Depressed, I went for a long walk to figure out what to do about my healthy mental state. Didn't electroshock therapy mess up your mind if you were sane when they zapped you? I thought I'd read something about that somewhere, but I also didn't have access to an electroshock therapy device. The best I could do was stick my finger in a light bulb socket. That didn't seem like the answer.

What did insane people do?

Well, for one thing, they tied women to beds and giggled with maniacal glee as they sliced off their extremities with a chainsaw. I wasn't insane enough to want to do something like that (yet), but maybe if I did it *before* I was insane, the insanity would follow. It was certainly worth a shot.

The first thing I needed was a victim. Maybe a prostitute; after all, that was good enough for Jack the Ripper. Of course, if she turned out to be an undercover cop, I could end up getting arrested, and while I didn't mind going to jail for committing gruesome cold-blooded murder, going to jail for hiring a hooker would be way too embarrassing. My mom would freak.

Prostitutes were out.

So was stalking a potential victim. I'd always been a major klutz, and I'd probably end up tripping or doing something else stupid that gave away my position, and then she'd blast me in the eyes with pepper spray or something like that. I'd been hit in the eyes with pepper spray once, during an ill-fated self-performed experiment to find out what it felt like to get hit in the eyes with pepper spray, and I had no desire to repeat the experience.

No, the best way to find a victim was to go on a successful date, invite her back to my place, knock her out with chloroform, and then begin the chainsaw festivities. My friend Tracy had spent the last few years constantly trying to set me up on blind dates, so I gave her a call.

"I'm in the mood to go out tomorrow night," I explained. "Got anybody you could hook me up with?"

"Probably, yeah," she said, amused. "Let me think..."

"Do you know anybody who looks like my mother?"

"Excuse me?"

"My mom. You've met her, haven't you?"

"Uh-huh."

"Do you have any friends who look like her? Not that old, of course, but the way my mom would look if she were our age."

"You're kidding, right?"

"No. I just thought it was time to date somebody who looks like my mom. Everybody's doing it these days. Oedipus Complexes are in."

"Well, my friend Sandy is a blonde. Is that close enough?"

"That works."

"She broke up with her boyfriend a few weeks ago and I think she's looking to start dating again. Let me find her phone number."

After I got the number, I called Sandy, chatted for a bit (about non-insanity-related topics), and arranged to pick her up at her apartment the next evening.

I looked around my own apartment. So many things to do to prepare!

Now that I'd committed myself to this act of atrocity, it was clear that the whole chainsaw idea had to go. Chainsaws made way too much noise and the neighbors would complain. I'd have to go with an axe. I didn't own an axe, so I added it to the shopping list.

I'd also need duct tape to put over her mouth, handcuffs to bind her to the bed, plastic covers to keep blood from soaking into my mattress, something to shield the walls from any excess spray, chloroform, mood music, and scented candles. Insanity was going to be expensive, but hopefully worth it.

The hardware store had several varieties of axes to choose from, and I ended up going with the standard woodcutting model. I wasn't sure that I could take off an entire limb in one chop with this thing, but two or three would get the job done. Because the cashier forgot to offer me a receipt I got a five dollar discount, which was nice.

Have you ever tried to find chloroform? I see it used in movies all the time and kind of figured that I could get it at Wal-Mart or something, but it's really not easily available. I decided that I'd have to replace the chloroform with a good solid whack to the back of the head with the dull side of the axe.

I finished my shopping and went home to get a good night's sleep.

«« — »»

I woke up the next morning pissed off at myself. A *bad* night's sleep was conducive to insanity, not a good one! If I didn't get with the program I'd be sane for the rest of my life. But there was nothing I could do about it now, so I got up and spent the day preparing for my pre-insanity activities. I sat on the couch for about twenty minutes, staring at a picture of my mother and thinking about how much I hated that bitch. It was a bit tricky, because my mother had always been loving and supportive and even a friend to me, but still, there had to be *something* about her that I despised.

Her fettuccini alfredo sucked.

I stared at her photo. *You bitch. You crappy fettuccini alfredo-making bitch. You've ruined my life.*

At five o'clock, I showered, dressed, primped, and then drove to pick up Sandy. She met me at her front door, looking absolutely radiant. She didn't look anything like my mother (her hair was dishwater blonde, while my mom was more of a bleach blonde), but she did get the same little crinkle in her nose when she smiled, sort of.

We drove to the restaurant, joking and laughing and enjoying each other's company. We got an excellent table, ordered drinks, and spent a moment perusing the menu. When the waiter arrived, I stared at Sandy, mentally pleading with her to order the fettuccini alfredo to set me off.

"I'll have the lasagna," she said.

I ordered the lasagna, too. A guy at the next table had it and it looked pretty good.

As we talked and laughed, I realized that I didn't really want to kill her. We'd had an instant connection, and it seemed like a waste to murder somebody who was such excellent girlfriend material. Of course, once I was insane I wouldn't need a girlfriend, but still, I really liked Sandy and there was no reason to chop her up.

I decided that for tonight, I wouldn't worry about trying to become insane. I'd worry about trying to get laid.

The lasagna was delicious, and the portions were so generous that we both had to ask for to-go containers, not that it stopped us from ordering dessert. After lingering in the restaurant for another hour or so, we finally left and got in my car.

"I'm really having fun," Sandy told me with a smile as she fastened her seat belt. "I'm glad you called me."

"Oh, me too," I said. "It's hard to believe that the only reason I invited you out tonight was to murder you."

Faux pas.

Sandy frowned. "I beg your pardon?"

Oooooh, this is awkward. "I'm just kidding," I assured her. "Sometimes I have a sick sense of humor."

"Oh," she said, but she didn't sound convinced.

I thought about what I'd said. Confessing my original intentions seemed like a pretty silly thing to do, but was it *truly* silly...or was it insane?

Slip of the tongue or insanity?

Maybe I was on the brink.

Or maybe I was over the brink! Maybe Sandy was a figment of my imagination, a vision created by my mother-loathing subconscious.

I reached over and poked her in the side to test that theory.

"Ow!" she said.

"Sorry."

This was interesting. I certainly *felt* sane and more than a little foolish, but my actions seemed to indicate that my mental health was rapidly deteriorating. Perhaps after I took Sandy home for some hot sex I could give the spiders-crawling-over-my-body thing another shot.

Instead, I grabbed her by the neck.

She let out a gasp and grabbed my wrist.

I squeezed.

I stared into her eyes as I squeezed, my thumb pressing into her throat. She was struggling too violently, so I began to squeeze with my other hand as well.

She punched and clawed at me, but I didn't feel it. Her eyes bulged and rolled up in their sockets. Her face took on a purple hue.

I kept squeezing for several minutes after I knew she was dead.

Finally I released my grip and let her body slump against the door. I did a quick glance around the restaurant parking lot, but nobody seemed to have noticed.

I regarded her body with interest. I'd never seen a dead person before. It was strangely beautiful.

Then I sighed and cursed. I'd strangled a woman to death in my car and I didn't feel even one bit insane. No voices in my head, no urge to curl up in the fetal position and cry for my mommy, nothing.

Damn.

I started the engine and drove home.

I carried Sandy's body up to my apartment. I didn't really have a good cover story for if somebody saw me walking around with a dead woman in my arms, but fortunately nobody saw me and I didn't have to ad-lib. I carried her into my bedroom, placed her on the bed, and arranged her body spread-eagle.

Despite all the blotchy parts, she was still gorgeous.

I picked up the axe, swung it high above my head, and brought it down upon her wrist. It was a good, solid hit, and it got the job done.

Still, I didn't feel insane.

I chopped off her other hand.

I felt fine.

I decided to try going completely nutzo. I brought the axe down again and again, not even caring where I hit, keeping my mouth open to hopefully catch some of the splatter (insane people did that sort of thing), and chopping until my arms were so sore that I lost my grip on the axe and it dropped to the floor.

No reaction.

Not a goddamn thing.

I stared at the unrecognizable mess on my bed, hoping that maybe I'd see something terrifying in it, sort of like a Rorschach ink blot test. But no, I just saw the remains of a woman I'd dismembered with an axe.

What a freakin' waste.

I wasn't going to give up, though. If there was any insanity in my mind, any at all, I'd find it. I'd sleep in my own bed tonight.

Some musings on sleeping with an extremely mutilated corpse: The blood is warm and pleasant at first, but when it gets cold it's sticky and very uncomfortable. Because the pieces are scattered, a chopped-up body is quite the bed hog. Rolling over on a protruding bone while you're half-asleep wakes you up *real* quick. And brain matter makes a crappy pillow.

But did I feel like I'd lost my mind when I got up the next morning? Noooooooo. I didn't even have a lousy nightmare.

The most disturbing part was when I woke up in the middle of the night and briefly considered following through on my desire to get laid, but decided against it because it seemed too icky. That's right; I couldn't even handle a bit of necrophilia. I was an absolute disgrace.

I was sane, I would always be sane, and I was just going to have to deal with it.

Sometimes life sucks.

«« — »»

I know what you're thinking as you read this. You're thinking "But, sir, you're *clearly* insane! You just chopped up some chick with an axe and slept in a pool of her gook! You're like the narrator in 'The Telltale Heart' who gives the whole 'Very, very dreadfully nervous I had been and am; but why will you say that I am mad?' speech when he's quite obviously a total whack-job!"

So let me clarify some things. First of all, there's a huge difference between my own actions and those of the guy who got bent out of shape over the old man with the funky eye. I feel sympathy for people with eye problems. One of my uncles has one blue eye and one green eye, and he's very sensitive about it, and when I was a kid and my cousins made fun of him, I never once joined in the ridicule. In fact, I thought it was in remarkably poor taste and told them so.

Second, the gentleman in that story was a fictional character, and should not be held to the same standards of sanity as a real person such as myself.

Anyway, as I stood in the shower, washing off Sandy's blood, I decided that to achieve my lofty goal, I needed to embark upon a killing spree. Not something where I went berserk with a machine gun, but rather a series of individual victims, serial killer-style.

To boost my insanity potential, I set some rules. First of all, all of the murders had to be committed with a bladed instrument. No guns, no rope, no automobile tires, and no bare hands (I'd just think of Sandy as a practice kill). Each murder would take place on the same night of the week, preferably within a one-hour window, although I'd relax that rule if it became too inconvenient. And I had to leave some sort of calling card. Maybe I'd take a finger from each victim, but it would be a different finger each time, so that I'd take the right thumb of Victim #1, the right index finger of Victim #2, and so on until I had ten victims and ten fingers.

No, no...I'd start with the right pinky and move to the left (assuming you were looking at it from the victim's point of view; otherwise, I'd be moving to the right). Maybe if things went really well, frightened people would start cutting off their own fingers that were next in the rotation just to keep themselves safe from my trophy-collecting! Unlikely, sure, but if my reign of terror was scary enough, anything could happen.

That was it. Every Friday night at midnight I'd claim a new victim, and I'd cut off a finger. If I were ever caught, I could do an interview where I said "Society gave me the finger, so I decided to take it back!" Well, that wouldn't be the exact quote, since I wouldn't need to take back a finger that I was given, but I could certainly figure out a way to connect being given the finger by society to slicing off the fingers of my potential victims. I was creative.

Maybe I could even eat the fingers. Now *that* would be the actions of an insane person, no doubt about it. I could fire up the grill, add some Cajun spices, and—

The phone rang.

I cursed, quickly rinsed the soap out of my hair, and ran wet and naked into the kitchen and picked up the phone on the fifth ring.

"Hello?" I answered.

"How was your date?" asked Tracy.

"She never showed up," I said, sadly.

"I thought you were picking her up at her place."

"Uh, no, we changed the plan."

"But I was on the phone with her and she heard somebody knocking on the door and she said 'Oh, that must be him.'"

"Ah."

"Was it a bad date?"

"No, no, it was rather pleasant."

Tanya's voice took on a "You're such a naughty boy" tone. "Is she still there?"

"Yeah, actually."

"So it was a really *good* date."

"Yeah."

"Can I talk to her?"

"She's still in bed."

"You wore her out, huh?"

"No, I strangled her and chopped her up with an axe."

Faux pas again. I froze. This could be bad.

"You're sick," said Tracy with a laugh.

"No, really," I insisted. "I chopped her up and slept with her dismembered corpse."

I quickly hung up the phone and slapped a hand over my mouth. Curse my loose tongue! I hadn't given much thought to the possible repercussions of murdering a human being in cold blood, but now I knew I had to flee. Hide out like a common criminal.

Oh, if only I hadn't said "No, I strangled her and chopped her up with an axe," how differently my life would have turned out!

The phone rang again but I ignored it. I knew what I had to do. I'd drive to Florida. A state already filled with whackos might not notice one more. (Well, technically I was a whacko poseur, not a real whacko, but I'd still blend in.)

I grabbed a change of clothes and some snacks from the refrigerator, threw a sheet over Sandy, turned out the lights, and hurried out of my apartment. I drove to the nearest ATM but in my nervous condition I entered the wrong code three times in a row, so the machine ate my card. I uttered many an expletive. I got back in my car and drove far, far away.

Well, not *that* far away, since I only had half a tank of gas. I could've used a credit card, but if Tracy had gone straight to my place and seen the mess, she might have already called the police. Or she might have called the police before going to my place. Who knew how the female mind worked? Either way, I couldn't risk alerting them to my whereabouts by using a credit card.

Wow, I thought, *I'm really screwed.*

Damn, I thought, *it sure would be nice to be insane enough not to realize just how badly I'm screwed.*

I left my car in the parking lot of a 24-hour supermarket and walked down the sidewalk, sighing loudly and frequently. I had no money. No transportation. No fake beard. And still no voices in my head.

What was I going to do?

A lot of homeless people were insane, so wandering the streets might be effective…but to be perfectly honest, that sounded really unpleasant. No, I had to kill somebody and steal their cash. Which sucked, because if you were killing people for financial gain, there was really no insanity involved. I mean, sure, I could always mutilate the body beyond all recognition and *then* take the money, but I would always know deep inside that the murder had been committed for practical reasons.

Still, a man's gotta eat.

«« — »»

I'm going to elect not to discuss my first attempt at a murder for cash in great detail, because it involved me getting my ass kicked by somebody who, in theory, should not have been able to kick my ass with such ease.

«« — »»

I'm also going to skip my second attempt, although in this particular case the ass-kicking was much more justifiable.

«« — »»

The third attempt was a rousing success. The elderly gentleman put up very little struggle after I poked out his eye with a stick. I tried to poke out his other eye, but instead the branch went up his nose and got stuck, which caused problems for him when he fell forward and the stick hit the ground first.

He had $181.76 wadded up in a small change purse with "World's Greatest Grandpa" stenciled on the front. He sure couldn't be the world's greatest grandpa with a poked-out eye and stick in his brain, now could he? Heh heh heh.

Was that an insane laugh?

Nah.

I dragged the old man's body behind a dumpster and then walked until I found an affordably crappy motel. I paid for a week in advance, raided the vending machine, and decided to just hang out in the motel room until this all blew over.

How long did it take for a dismemberment to blow over?

That evening, I sat on the bed, watching the news and eating stale peanuts (I didn't realize that peanuts even got stale; this whole thing was a learning experience). The chief of police was on-camera, addressing a group of reporters.

"Obviously, we're dealing with a madman," he said. "A very disturbed individual."

"Bullshit!" I shouted, flinging some peanuts at the television screen. How could somebody be chief of police and not be able to tell that I was completely, frustratingly sane? Who hired this dork?

I immediately regretted throwing the peanuts, because they'd probably have to last me for a while. And I wasn't nearly insane enough to want to eat them off the floor of this particular motel room.

To be honest, I was starting to wonder if this whole "losing my mind" thing was such a good idea. Maybe I'd been too anxious to become a lunatic and hadn't weighed the pros and cons carefully enough. Was I really so unhappy being sane? My life had actually been pretty decent. And now here I was, a fugitive in a foul-scented motel room having a food fight with an inanimate object.

I slept poorly.

««—»»

I spent the entire next day in bed, pouting. I was already getting stir-crazy, but it wasn't safe to venture outside in the daylight. I watched TV and played Tic-Tac-Toe against myself (3 wins, 297 draws).

When night fell, I snuck outside to refill my ice bucket. The ice cubes screamed in terrified agony as I scooped them up, which was odd. They were screaming so loud that I didn't realize until it was too late that a man was standing next to me, regarding me with great interest.

"I know you," he said. He looked about fifty, had a thick beard, and wore filthy jeans and a t-shirt.

"No you don't."

"I do! You're the guy who axed that chick!" He stuck out his hand. "*Nice* work, buddy!"

I shook his hand, not wanting to seem impolite in the presence of somebody who was in favor of mutilating people. "Uh, thanks."

"I mean it! I've read all about you! I keep wanting to do something like that, or at least the voices in my head tell me that I do, but I've never been able to work up the nerve. You're an inspiration, man."

"You hear voices?" I asked.

"Oh, yeah, all the time. Right now one of them is telling me to bite off your left nipple. I won't, though."

"When did you start hearing voices?"

"Around the time I quit drinking."

It wasn't fair. Why did this guy get to hear voices and not me? He probably didn't even appreciate them!

I wanted to kill him. I wanted to bash him over the head with my ice bucket and shatter his skull. Only the certainty that he would deliver a rousing ass-kicking before my goal could be accomplished kept me from giving it a try.

"You're looking kinda twitchy there, pal," said the man. "Don't worry, I'm not gonna report you. I want to be your friend. I want you to teach me."

"I'm not sure if I can," I said. "I really don't have any mentoring experience."

"I learn quick," he insisted. "And I've got a nice big black van that we can use to lure unsuspecting victims, and it's filled with knives and stuff. Please. We could be partners."

I stared at him for a long moment. "Do you think insanity is contagious?"

He shrugged. "I don't see why not."

"Then you've got yourself a deal."

《《 — 》》

I never did ask the man his name, which seemed kind of strange. Although not as strange as his habit of suddenly disappearing while I was talking to him, and having his beard change colors, and sometimes appearing in multiples of three. But, as I said, I'd slept poorly the night before.

He had to be real; otherwise, where had the van come from? And who had put the tied-up teenage girl in the back?

"It's important that you hold your hacksaw correctly," I told the man. "You've gotta have a tight grip. And you should cut straight down, not at an angle. Let your arm do the work instead of your wrist."

Yeah, I was bullshitting, but he didn't know that. As long as I kept pretending to offer nuggets of homicidal wisdom, I could continue to hopefully soak up his lunatic aura.

"What if I want to saw off her hands?" the man asked.

"Now that's a problem area, because she's got her hands bound together. If you saw them off, that frees what's left of her arms, and she might be able to injure you with her stumps."

"I see."

"What you would do in that case is compromise. Saw off her fingers, but keep her wrists tied together. Here, I'll show you."

The girl shrieked so loud that I wouldn't have been able to hear the voices in my head even if they existed. It was so annoying that I stopped cutting off fingers after seven of them dropped to the floor.

"Does the same thing work with toes?" the man inquired.

"Absolutely. What's so cool about toes is that you can play the 'This Little Piggy' game with each one before you cut it off, which makes you sound really sadistic."

"And when the little piggy has roast beef, you could feed her that toe!"

I shook my head. "No, no, no, you haven't been paying attention."

"I'm sorry, sir."

"It's okay."

"Is there something we can do about that screaming?"

"Sure. Get rid of the tongue. But tongues are slippery creatures, so you'll have to be quick."

"Should I cut it out or rip it out by the root?"

"Try to rip it out. See what happens."

"I can't hold on to it."

"Yep, that ties into what I said earlier about it being slippery. You'll have to cut it out."

"Maybe I should give her a forked tongue first."

"That would be cool."

"She's squirming too much!"

"So make her less squirmy. No, not that hard, you don't want to kill her. Good. Okay, now try the tongue again."

"Oh yeah, this is much better."

"Quit playing with it. Just cut it out."

"I got most of it."

"Good job."

"She's still screaming."

"Yes, she is. So what lesson have we learned?"

"Uh...that screaming comes from the lungs and not the tongue?"

"Lungs? Or vocal cords?"

"I don't know! You're the fucking mentor!"

"Now, now, take your frustration out on her, not me. Wait, too much frustration. Look what you did."

"Sorry."

"You don't sound sorry."

"Well, I'm not. I don't think you know what you're doing. I'm leaving."

"No...don't go!" I followed the man out of the van. "You were doing fine! Really you were! I give you an A+! That's the best grade there is! C'mon, you can't just—"

Something hit me in the face very, very hard. As I fell to the ground I realized that it was a fist. The fist was followed by several shoes belonging to several different people. Another guy climbed into the van, and when he came out he didn't look happy.

"You son of a bitch!" he screamed, with tears in his eyes.

I tried to explain that I hadn't done anything, that I'd merely been instructing the man, but it was difficult to speak coherently with his fist smashing into my jaw over and over. I quickly lost consciousness and slept well.

I woke up in a small, barren room. My whole body hurt, especially the parts that had been punched and kicked. I'm not completely sure how long I was in there. I'm guessing about two days, but it might have been two hours instead. Hard to say.

Finally the door opened and the gentleman who'd called me a son of a bitch entered. He said a lot of things to me, but he wasn't enunciating clearly and I couldn't understand most of it, although I figured out that the teenage girl the man had killed was his sister, and that he'd decided not to involve the police. I thought that was remarkably generous of him and offered my gratitude. Then I realized that he planned to punish me himself. To give me what he called "a sneak preview," he removed my shoe and sock, and cut off the little toe on my right foot with a butcher knife. (He didn't play the "This Little Piggy" game.)

He told me he'd be back soon and then left.

He came back with a glass of water, explaining that he didn't want me to die of anything as painless as dehydration. I have to admit that I did a lot of begging at this point. He did a lot of laughing and said he'd be back with his friends.

And so I'm waiting. I have been for a long time.

I'm scared.

This wait is almost driving me insane.

But not quite.

I wish to God that the wait *had* driven me insane, because now I can hear footsteps outside the door. Bad things are going to happen to me, and if I'm out of my mind, maybe they won't hurt as much.

HIGH STAKES

After losing his entire gambling, hotel room, nudie show, and food budget in just under three hours, Jeremy was down to his last quarter. He stood in front of the heartless slot machine, silently cursing Margaret for making him leave the credit cards at home with her.

He wiped his sweaty palms off on his jeans and breathed deeply, in and out, in and out, preparing himself for the crucial mission ahead. He had to win. It didn't have to be a big payoff—two quarters could turn into four, four could turn into eight, eight could turn into sixteen, and then he'd be well on his way to not having to sleep outside amidst the pornography distributors for the next three nights.

Jeremy inserted the quarter into the slot and cracked his knuckles. He squeezed his eyes shut and tried to become one with the machine. *Jackpot...jackpot...jackpot...*he thought, hoping that sheer force of will or some previously unlocked psychic abilities would encourage the machine to give up its bounty.

He pulled down the arm.

Cherry. Bar. Bar.

Meaning he just got his quarter back.

He reached into the coin return and frowned. Instead of his quarter there was a red token, with "One Free Try at High Stakes" engraved upon it. The address was on the back. Great. Just great. Now he had to go and find this stupid place, and probably just lose the token for his efforts. Next vacation he was going someplace where he could shoot animals and relax.

«« — »»

High Stakes was off the main Vegas strip, a comparatively tiny, non-descript place without all the flashing lights and gimmicks of the other casinos. Jeremy walked into the main entrance and found himself surrounded by a fairly typical display of slot machines, though there couldn't be more than twenty or so. There were no other patrons, just an elderly man in a tuxedo who sprung to attention as he entered.

"Good evening, sir," said the man. "Welcome to High Stakes. First I must ask if you have one of our special tokens."

Jeremy nodded and held it up for him to see.

"Ah, excellent. Then feel free to use it in any machine you wish, and good luck to you."

Jeremy strolled around, checking out the machines. They all looked about the same to him, though he noticed that all of the displays read bar, bar, bar. Maybe that was a good sign. He stopped at one on the far end, inserted the coin, sucked in a deep breath, and pulled down the arm.

Bar. Bar. Bar.

A soft bell rang as dozens of dollar coins fell into the coin return. "*Nice* place you've got here," Jeremy told the man, smiling.

The man smiled back. "Definitely."

Jeremy dropped one of the coins into the slot and pulled the arm. Bar. Bar. Bar. Another big payoff. "Yes!" This was what gambling was all about!

He cracked his knuckles, kissed the coin for luck, and tried again.

Bar. Bar.

And a picture of a finger.

He leaned forward to look at the display more closely. Finger? What was that supposed to mean?

An iron claw swung out from a hidden panel on the side of the machine, latching firmly onto his left wrist. "What the hell—?"

He tugged as hard as he could, but his wrist wasn't going anywhere. Another claw swung out of the machine, attached itself to his little finger, and neatly pinched it off. Jeremy shrieked as the claws swung back into the hidden panels, taking his finger along with them.

The man stepped over to him, balancing a tray. "Would you care for a drink before you try again?"

"Are you *crazy*?" Jeremy demanded, almost in tears, falling to his knees in pain. "That thing ripped my *finger* off!"

"Well, sir, perhaps some white wine would dull the pain. We have a splendid Zinfandel."

"You sick freak!" Jeremy wailed. "Why would you possibly think I'd ever want to play again?"

"Why, to win your finger back, of course. We're living in the age of laser surgery, my friend. It can be reattached."

Jeremy stood up shakily, his right hand clenched over the stump where his finger had been. "No way."

"The stakes are high, but the odds are in your favor. You don't want to walk out of here having lost a finger for good, do you?"

No, he didn't.

But this was absolutely insane.

Still, in the time it would take to call the police and have them raid the place, it might be too late to reattach his finger. He'd be permanently disfigured.

Jeremy thought for a long moment, then dropped another coin into the slot and pulled down the arm.

Bar. Bar. Finger.

He turned and sprinted down the aisle, but the claw telescoped forward and snatched his wrist. As it pulled him back to the machine, the second claw pinched off his index finger. Jeremy screamed.

"You can still win them back," said the man. "The odds remain in your favor. Your life will be much harder with two missing fingers, don't you think?"

Jeremy gritted his teeth, forced the pain out of his mind, and tried again.

Bar. Bar. Hand.

He almost quit after that.

SPECIAL FEATURES

"Hi, this is Dale Marshall, director of *Draining*."

"And I'm Craig Marshall, producer of *Draining*."

"I guess the first thing we should talk about is the opening credits, or, more specifically, the lack of them."

"Right. Actually, it's pretty common these days to save all the credits for the end of the movie and just open with the title and nothing else, but we didn't even want to have the title at the beginning, we just wanted to jump right into the story."

"If I remember correctly, we sort of bounced back and forth about that idea, but really, when you see a title on the screen it screams '*This is only a movie!*' and we were going for total realism."

"Yeah."

"Anyway, the title *Draining* is on the DVD itself, so people aren't going to sit there thinking that they're watching, y'know, *Josie and the Pussycats*."

"I actually liked that movie."

"Well, maybe you should take a good, hard look at yourself in the mirror and figure out if there are personal changes that need to be made." [*Laughter.*]

"Here we are in the garage where we shot most of the film. Again, we were going for total believability, so we didn't want to do a lot of set design. We added a couple of things, but what you're seeing here is pretty much the real-life garage."

"And we couldn't afford a set designer."

"Yeah, that too."

"Great pan here by our director of photography, Gary Lawson. We didn't have access to a Steadicam—"

"We didn't even have a dolly track."

"Right, no dolly track or anything like that, so it was just Gary scooting along on his knees to get the shot."

"Although we did sweep up the floor so he wouldn't get any nails in his legs."

"Because we *care* about our crew, damn it!" [*Laughter.*]

"And there's our lead!"

"The amazing Lee Newman! He was great to work with."

"Oh, definitely. A real trooper."

"He wasn't getting paid and he was in almost every scene, but you never once heard the guy complain."

"I heard him complain a few times."

"He didn't like the food we served, that's for sure. But if you're on a Hollywood set, it's just one egomaniac after another, and we didn't have anything like that here."

"Hard to be an egomaniac when you're working eighteen-hour days and getting paid in Ramen Noodles."

"That is true."

"But he was really awesome to work with. We couldn't have found a more talented lead."

"Should we talk about how this project started?"

"We came up with the idea, what, five years ago?"

"Five years, yeah."

"We'd been doing little movies since we were kids. Nothing major, just filming bugs and frogs and neighborhood dogs and stuff like that."

"We should probably mention that we're brothers."

"I think they got that from the last names."

"Yeah, because 'Marshall' is *so* obscure!"

"No relation to the other sibling team of Garry and Penny Marshall, of course."

"Of course."

"And, hey, the first shot of Trish!"

"Patricia Damon."

"She really looked great in this film."

"Yeah, she did, and she was so wonderful to work with."

"She was one of the easiest casting choices. We basically just happened to see her shopping for groceries, and we looked at each other and said 'That's the one!'"

"She had this innocence about her that made her perfect for the part. And amazing talent for somebody who'd never been in a film before."

"Yeah, absolutely. Now, because she had no on-camera experience, we wanted to make sure we got the most authentic reaction possible. So we didn't tell her what she was going to see. I don't think we told her anything, did we?"

"Uh...no, we did tell her that it was going to be frightening."

"That's right, we did. We wanted to get that build-up of terror before we even started shooting. We pretty much forced our cast to become method actors." [*Laughter.*]

"Now what you're seeing here is actually a mix of two different takes, because when she was struggling she hit Lee a lot harder than we'd anticipated. She didn't hurt him too badly, but his reaction was out of character. If you watch carefully, you can see that there's extra tape around her wrists in a couple of the shots."

"Freeze frame geeks, have at it!"

"We did have quite a few continuity problems during the editing process, but I think we covered most of them pretty well. Nobody never really said anything. If we were smart we'd shut up about it and not give away all of our failings as filmmakers!"

"Oh, I love this shot."

"Great shot. How many takes of that one?"

"Jeez, I don't even remember. At least ten."

"Essentially, Gary was lying on his back with the camera, while Lee and Trish stood over him. But of course Trish was kicking and struggling and she kept kicking Gary and wrecking the shot."

"We're lucky she didn't break the camera."

"Yeah, we would've been screwed. But look at that. We move back, we pan up (and this is just Gary standing up) and see that she's chained to the wall. Fantastic."

"But it took us all night to get that damn shot. We weren't quite as ambitious as we got further into the shooting schedule." [*Laughter.*]

[*Long silence.*]

"I think we're supposed to be saying something." [*Laughter.*]

"I haven't watched this in over a year. I forgot how gripping some of this early stuff is."

"Okay, we've *got* to talk about that moment!"

"The blood in the mouth shot! That, ladies and gentlemen, is the genius of Lee Newman. So he slices her arm with the straight razor, and we get this unexpected arterial spray that goes right in his mouth! We knew that once we got into the actual cutting scenes, it was going to be tough to do more than one take, so I'm watching thinking 'Oh, crap, he's gonna vomit and ruin the shot.' But, no, he turns to the camera and wiggles his bloody tongue! Those moments can never be scripted."

"It's all in the casting."

"He was pissed, though. Look at the way he's cutting her leg. When he carves *Whore*, that wasn't in the script, either."

"That part was. It was in the shooting script."

"Are you sure? I thought it was *Bitch*."

"Oh, right, I just meant that cutting a word in her leg was in the script."

"I think *Whore* works better."

"I remember Lee explaining it afterwards. Because when you look at Trish, obviously you can tell that she *wasn't* a whore. I wouldn't necessarily say that she looks virginal, but she's at least not whorish."

"I think she looks virginal."

"Do you?"

"Yeah."

"Okay, I can see that, I guess. Lee's point, though, was that she's definitely not a whore, so when he carves that on her leg we can really see how disturbed the character is."

"And when you trust your cast, you get these wonderful moments."

"The hand part. That wasn't originally going to be a saw; it was just going to be a knife. But Lee couldn't get through the bone."

"That'll be one of the outtakes. He's just sitting there cutting and cutting and cutting and the goddamn hand won't come off!"

"So the part where the saw starts cutting her wrist, that's actually an insert shot we did later of him cutting her *other* wrist. And the sawing we're seeing now is actually him sawing in the groove made by the knife."

"The magic of cinema!"

"Should we talk about soundproofing?"

"Oh, yeah. We spent an entire weekend soundproofing this stupid garage. Testing it was a lot of fun. I'd go in there and scream at the top of my lungs, and you'd stand outside to see if you could hear me."

"But the funny part is that Trish was screaming *so* loud that we were sure the cops were going to show up!"

"Thus...the tongue scene!"

"Oooooh, even I cringe at this part."

"Gotta hand it to Lee, though. One take."

"The pliers are in...in...in...*oooh*, there goes the tongue!"

"Ouch."

"Now *this* is interesting. That shot right there of the tongue hitting the floor. That's not Trish's tongue."

"It's actually a prosthetic tongue. We bought it from a Halloween shop for, what, ninety-nine cents?"

"Ninety-nine cents before tax. We had a shot of the real tongue hitting the floor, but it didn't look real. The real tongue looked fake, and the fake tongue looked real. Isn't that weird?"

"And there go her eyeballs!"

"You've gotta have an eyeball moment in a movie like this. It's, like, the law."

"The fans would boycott us forever if we didn't have a good old fashioned eyeball scene."

"This scene was tough, though, because we've all seen so many eyeballs come out. How do you make it original? We were brainstorming ideas back when we were writing the script, and I thought, what about a frozen eyeball pop? So we just had Lee spray CO_2 on her. We had to sharpen the Popsicle stick so it would go in, but you can't really tell."

"We did cut out the part where he severs the stalk because it interrupted the pacing of the gag."

"And now the big death moment!"

"We had to get this in one take, for obvious reasons. We'd originally settled on a decapitation, but I think two days before that we changed the plan."

"Well, that was around the time when the news was filled with stories about hostages being decapitated by terrorists, and we were worried that if we paralleled real-life horror too closely, we'd lose some of our audience."

"Also, Lee was getting into his role so much that we wanted to give him a chance to really cut loose. So we gave him the axe, and just told him to go nuts."

"And he did, as you can see."

"Look at those pieces fly."

"The one that hits the dartboard...wouldn't it have been cool if it hit the bullseye?"

"If we'd had a CGI budget, we could've digitally altered it."

"Maybe for the *Super*-Special Edition of *Draining*."

"Oh, man, I just love watching this scene. Look at Lee's face while he chops away. He was just so great to work with."

"Is she dead yet?"

"No, I think she dies right...*here*."

"Right in the throat."

"But not a decapitation." [*Laughter*.]

"Do you want to talk about cleanup?"

"God, no!"

"When we do the sequel, we're going to hire a janitor."

"That took *forever*."

"I still slip on blood occasionally."

"You do not."

"No, but I do see a dried speck here and there."

"Look at Lee's face while he stands there. A perfect combination of excitement and remorse."

"Yeah. You know that the guy feels bad about what he's done, but you also know that he'll do it again."

"And we cut to...the lovely and talented Rebecca Fredell! Now *that* is a whore!" [*Laughter*.]

"I can't believe you said that!"

"We'll edit it out."

"Seriously, though, she was great to work with..."

SEX POTION #147

The elderly Gypsy woman gazed intently at Melissa Tucker's palm, tracing a line with her fingertips. "Ah, yes…I see it now…the truth is right here…I see it most clearly…"

"What do you see?" asked Melissa, leaning forward.

"Your sex life…your sex life is…crap."

Melissa shook her head, offended. "It's not *crap*."

The Gypsy tapped Melissa's palm. "Says so right here. Crap."

"Yeah, well, my hand is wrong." Melissa pulled her hand away. She'd paid twenty bucks for this? So what if she wasn't getting laid every freakin' night? It was perfectly normal for a single woman in her 30's to go through a dry spell every once in a while. It didn't mean there was anything wrong with her. It wasn't like she was a hermit or a leper or something like that. Well, maybe there was a trace of hermit in her current lifestyle, but she wasn't a leper. Definitely not a leper.

"Actually, from what I saw, your hand has been your only source of sexual gratification for a long, long time," said the Gypsy.

"That's a lie! I've got a dildo!" said Melissa, approximately 350% louder than she'd intended.

"I see," said the Gypsy with a knowing smile that made Melissa want to smack her over the head with the dildo.

"And you know what? It isn't even an actual dildo…it's not male-shaped or anything like that. It's a vibrator. I bought it to soothe my sore shoulder. And you know what? It worked damn well on my shoulder. And why am I justifying my vibrator to you?"

The Gypsy's expression turned serious. "All is not lost for you, Melissa. I look into your palm, and I gaze into your eyes, and I know why your vagina remains eternally vacant. You feel unattractive, Melissa. You feel like...like a..." She grabbed Melissa's hand and checked out her palm again. "...fat pig."

"I do *not!*"

"Look for yourself," said the Gypsy, holding Melissa's hand up in front of her face.

Melissa yanked her hand back and rested it in her lap. "I'm not a fat pig."

"I didn't say you were a fat pig, though your palm says that you could certainly stand to visit the gym a bit more often. I said that you think of yourself as a fat pig. It's your poor self-image that keeps your sex life dry and barren, like the windswept deserts of Egypt."

"That's not true. I just don't feel the need to slut around. I suppose you have a hot stud muffin waiting in the back room?"

The Gypsy nodded. "Pedro. He's yours for another twenty bucks."

"Seriously?"

"No. But your desperation is evident in the way you perked up."

Melissa sighed. "Okay, so, I don't feel attractive. Guys just aren't into women who look like I do. They want those thin models who couldn't eat a whole sandwich without it bulging out their stomach like a snake. You know, when a snake eats a rat and its stomach bulges out? Or, not its stomach, I guess, its whole body, but you know what I mean. It's in nature documentaries all the time. Those kinds of women."

"You are mistaken, Melissa."

"No, I'm not. Women who look like me don't get laid."

"You have no idea what a man will screw."

"Well, it's not me."

The Gypsy looked Melissa in the eye, her gaze intense. "I see frightening things in you, Melissa. I see a woman who is ready to snap. Your pent-up sexual energy could explode with dire consequences to those around you. People could *die*, Melissa."

"Maybe I'm happy not being in a relationship."

"You're not happy. If you don't have sex soon you're going to kill somebody. Trust me."

"So what do I do?"

"I'm glad you finally asked," said the Gypsy, reaching under the table and retrieving a briefcase. She popped open the lid. "I have a wide assortment of potions that will solve your little problem. I've got nine different love potions, but that's not what you're looking for...you need a sex potion. I've got one hundred and fifty of those. Let's see...no, not potion #14...maybe #27...or #40...no, wait, I've got it, you need Sex Potion #146."

"What does that one do?"

"It…oh, wait, I'm out. Sex Potion #147 works the same; it just doesn't have the mint flavor." The Gypsy took a small red vial out of the briefcase. "One drop of this and you will be sexually desirable to every man who sees you. Men will want to leave their wives for you. Politicians will want to destroy their careers for you. Homosexuals will…well, I've never tested it on a homosexual, you might be out of luck there, but mark my words, this is a powerful potion."

"How do I know it isn't water?"

"All of my potions are real." The Gypsy took a blue vial out of her briefcase and unscrewed the cap. "This is Sex Potion #79. Try a drop…but only a drop."

Melissa took the vial from her. She lifted off the lid, which had a small dropper attached to it. Figuring that one drop of anything couldn't hurt, she tilted her head back, lifted it to her mouth, and let the blue liquid fall onto her tongue.

She screwed the cap back on the vial. "Nothing happened."

"Wait six seconds."

"So what's going to happen in six…OH MY FREAKING GOD!!!" Melissa gasped for breath as she was struck by a wave of horniness beyond anything she'd ever experienced in her entire life. "OH…OH, SHIT…GET ME SOMETHING TO HUMP!!! IT'S AN EMER-GENCY!!!"

"Feeling a bit frisky, are we?"

Not caring about the fact that this was extremely impolite, Melissa began rubbing herself through her pants. Her eyes crossed and she could feel a bead of sweat running down her forehead and she knew that her hand wasn't going to be enough, she needed two hands, she needed a whole *legion* of hands…

"OH MY GOD I CAN'T TAKE IT ANY LONGER I NEED TO—oh, wait, it's gone."

The Gypsy nodded. "Sex Potion #79 doesn't last very long. We experimented with doubling the dose but the results were messy."

"So these things really work," said Melissa. "I can't believe it."

"They do indeed. But you must be responsible with Sex Potion #147. Enjoy yourself, but don't go trying to create adulterers or convert homo-sexuals."

"How much is it?"

"It's quite affordable, actually."

"How much?"

"Remember, when you tried the other potion, you wanted to start humping things in front of me. You came very close to going at it with my table leg. This is potent stuff."

"It's a lot, isn't it?"

"You have to put it in context. In a cost-per-drop sense, yes, this potion is a bit pricey. But can you really put a price on the boost in self-esteem?"

"I'm betting that *you* can."

"A thousand bucks. Cash."

Melissa glanced at her hand. "My palm says 'Fuck that.'"

"A thousand bucks for a vial with ten drops. The potion works, Melissa. Men will be crawling at your feet, pleading with you to open your legs and allow them to pleasure your silken femininity with their tongues. They'll do anything you ask. *Anything.* Anyplace you want licked, they'll lick. If there's anything especially kinky you've ever wanted a man to do, like dress up in a…well, I'll let you brainstorm those ideas yourself, but a world of sexual adventure is yours, Melissa."

"Oh, well, gee, I always carry a spare thousand dollars in my purse, so let me just hand it over."

"Sarcasm boosts the price. And there's an ATM two blocks down."

"Sorry, but no." Melissa pushed back her chair and stood up. "Thanks for the information that my sex life is crap. That was very helpful."

"I see that a deal is in order," said the Gypsy. "I'm going to raise the price to fifteen hundred dollars…"

"Ooooh, that makes all the difference."

"…and I'm giving you a free sample." The Gypsy took a very tiny red vial out of the briefcase. "Use it wisely. The effects will last for exactly six hours. I'll see you *very* soon, Melissa."

Melissa took the vial and dropped it into her purse. "I don't think you will, but thanks anyway."

"*Very* soon."

«« — »»

"*Die, bitch!*"

Harold Tiberius Chaumley slammed the claw hammer into the young woman's skull for the eighth time. She'd quit struggling after the third blow and quit screaming after the fifth, but Harold wasn't yet finished.

"*Die, bitch!*" he repeated as he struck her a ninth time. He wasn't good at murder-talk and truly admired those killers who could eloquently taunt their victims, or at least rant incoherently. Harold felt self-conscious about speaking during the process, but he wanted to say *something*, so he stuck with...

"*Die, bitch!*"

And one last "*Die, bitch!*" as the claw hammer damaged the girl for the eleventh time. That was enough. Eleven blows for his eleventh victim. The next one would get twelve. This pattern had been pure coincidence at first; it simply took one blow to kill his first victim, two to kill his second, and three to kill his third. But when the news started reporting on this, he'd decided to embrace the pattern and add one new blow for each successive victim. Victim #5 had been tricky, because the first four blows hadn't killed her and she almost looked like she'd survive a fifth if it wasn't a damn good one, but he'd gotten her between the eyes with the claw end of the hammer and finished her off.

Harold, now out of breath, stared at the bloody mess of the girl. She deserved it. The filthy slut deserved it. Freely giving of her filthy body to that filthy college student. They were all filthy sluts these days. Tramps. Whores. Loose women who thought that a condom made it safe to allow disgusting diseased appendages into their body...if they even *used* a condom. He knew darn well that these kids weren't using dental dams.

It made him physically ill to think of the vile activities she must have been doing in her bed. How could people do those filthy, dirty, depraved, wretched things to each other and still look other human beings in the eye?

Harold knew that he would never give in to that temptation. He'd sliced off the offending body part months ago, right after his first murder. He kept it in a jar in his bedroom as a reminder of his purity. And he was going to purify the world, one slut at a time.

《《 — 》》

As Melissa drove home, she considered the possible implications of the Gypsy's potion. There was a definite moral dilemma here. If this potion worked, it probably wasn't much different than slipping a drug into somebody's drink at a bar.

Of course, if she'd thought to slip a drug into somebody's drink at a bar, she might not have had this dry spell in the first place.

Her neighbor James was hot, muscular, and unmarried. He brought home various women on a semi-regular basis. Would it be so very bad if she used the potion on him? Would it kill the bastard to give her a bit of pleasure?

She could do this.

This was something she could do.

Maybe.

She tried to think of the potential downside. For one thing, he might wake up next to her and start screaming and crossing himself. That would be uncomfortable, but probably worth it. And she might feel horrible guilt for taking advantage of him in his potion-possessed state. She'd get over it.

Well, that pretty much covered the situation from all possible angles. Yep, nobody could accuse her of acting without thinking. She'd just go home, freshen up, swig the potion, and finally end this goddamn dry spell.

She got home, took a quick shower, put on her "Yes, you may touch" panties, dressed suggestively but not slutty, and fixed her hair. Then she paced around the house for about twenty minutes.

This was a bad idea.

The potion probably didn't work, anyway.

Of course it didn't work.

And since it didn't work, there was nothing morally wrong with walking three houses down, knocking on Jim's door, and asking to borrow an egg, right? She needed an egg. Can't make cupcakes without an egg.

She primped a few more times, left her home, walked three houses down, stepped onto James' front porch, primped again (to make him more amenable to parting with the egg), swallowed the drop of potion, and rang the doorbell.

The door swung open, revealing James wearing naught but a pair of red shorts. His tanned chest was slick with salty perspiration. His jaw dropped as he saw her. "Melissa! Hi!"

"Hi."

"You...you...wow! Won't you come in?"

"I'd love to," said Melissa, trying not to trip as she stepped inside.

James couldn't seem to keep his eyes off her. "Can I get you a beverage? Snack? Anything?" The distorted shape of his red shorts made it perfectly clear that the potion worked.

Screw the moral dilemma.

"Could I borrow an egg?" she asked, sweetly.

"Oh, can you ever! How many do you need? I can go get more if you need more."

"Just one. So what have you been doing?"

"Working out."

"I can see that."

"Just showing my brother my new equipment."

James' brother stepped into the living room, also shirtless and covered with sweat. "Well, *hello*," he said.

Melissa tried not to lose her balance. "I didn't know you had a twin."

"Yeah, Mike's in town for the weekend."

Mike took her hand and gently kissed it. "And what can we do for you, sexy lady?"

«« — »»

Four-and-a-half hours later, an exhausted Melissa staggered out of James' house, doing a mental inventory of all the possessions she was going to sell to get more of the potion. She hardly ever used the toaster, and she could always get a smaller TV, and the refrigerator was more of a luxury item anyway...

«« — »»

Harold finished cleaning up after his Cleansing and walked out of the house. He inhaled deeply; the air always seemed fresher after a good murder. One bitch down, many more to—

He gaped at the woman who was walking on the other side of the street.

She was a filthy, disease-ridden skank, but she was the most beautiful filthy disease-ridden skank he'd ever laid eyes on. Dear God, the wretched whore was absolutely gorgeous.

He wanted her.

Not to kill, but to ravish. To make sweet love to her syphilis-infected body. To throw her onto his bed and thrust his—

Damn. He didn't have that anymore, and if he drove home to get the jar, he'd lose her.

Who was she? Where had she come from? If he were to caress her breasts, would he see the handprints of many a drunken miscreant? If he were to kiss her lips, would blisters on the inside burst, spewing forth a delicious concoction?

She would be his.

He would love her, worship her, erect a shrine to her glory. He would kill for her. In fact, he *had* killed for her, retroactively. He would follow her home and show her his true devotion. They would be together forever, in this life and the next, and the next, and the next, and the next...

《《 — 》》

Does doing two guys at once make me a slut? Melissa wondered as she walked up onto her front porch. She was pretty sure it did. She tried to feel bad about it. That didn't work. She gave up.

Maybe she didn't need any more of the potion. Maybe having those incredibly hot twins worship her body (which they had done, literally, with James even making up a hymn on the spot) was just the boost of self-confidence she needed.

Maybe the potion *didn't* work, and she was just one damn hot babe. Maybe the drool stains on her back had nothing to do with any shriveled old Gypsy woman.

Or maybe she was going to stick with the original plan of selling off all her possessions.

She reached her house, went inside, and happily collapsed upon the couch.

《《 — 》》

Harold walked up to the slut goddess' front door. Knock or break a window? He decided to knock.

The front door opened and it was all he could do to resist leaping upon her.

"May I, uh, help you?" she asked.

"I want our bodies to join as one," Harold informed her.

She suddenly looked very uncomfortable. "Oh, shit, I'm sorry. There's been a misunderstanding. It's all my fault."

"I wish to ravish your body as a canine ravishes another canine."

"I'm going to have to ask you to leave."

Harold considered that, then punched her in the face, knocking her to the floor. He stepped into her home and shut the door behind him.

《《 — 》》

When Melissa woke up, she was lying on her bed, spread-eagle, with her wrists and ankles cuffed to the bedposts. He'd found the fur-lined handcuffs in her bottom drawer, the ones her ex-boyfriend Geoff had bought her three years ago and they'd only used once (and with minimal success).

She tugged as hard as she could, yanking until it felt like her arms were going to pop out of their sockets, but the fuzzy cuffs held.

She'd been gagged with a couple of tube socks but tried to scream anyway. No good.

The threesome with hot twins was *so* not worth it.

She heard her front door open, and then close again. A moment later, the creepy guy walked into her bedroom, with a jar tucked under his arm. He was breathing heavily.

"I love you," he said, gazing at her.

She shook her head violently. How could she have been so...?

She noticed the clock. 8:24. She'd taken the potion around 2:30. So it only had about six minutes left. If she could keep this creepy guy from expressing his love for six minutes, he'd realize his mistake and leave.

He unscrewed the lid of the jar. Something was floating in the cloudy liquid.

"This is no longer part of me," he said, reaching into the jar and fishing around. The object was slippery and he seemed to be having trouble getting a good grip. "Now it will be part of you."

He proudly held up the item.

Hell no. No way. Absolutely not. Not a chance. Not gonna happen. Nope. Uh-huh. Not in this or any other universe. There was no possible way Melissa was going to let herself be raped by a severed dick.

The man grinned.

The penis popped out of his hand and landed on the floor. The man cursed and bent down to retrieve it, as Melissa let out muffled scream after muffled scream after muffled scream.

He stood up and wiped it off on his shirt.

I'll be okay, Melissa thought. *There's no way he'll get that floppy thing inside me.* Still, the thought of being prodded with it was one of the less appealing mental pictures she'd experienced during her lifetime. And who knew what that liquid was in the jar?

She shouted at him to leave her alone.

He tilted his head, confused.

She repeated the request.

He walked over to the side of the bed and removed her gag. "Don't scream," he warned her. "I can still do this if you're dead."

"Please, just let me go," she pleaded. "This is all a mistake. It's not really you doing this."

"It's not?"

"No, it's not." *Just keep him talking for another three minutes.* "It's

Sex Potion #147. I took it, and it turns men crazy." She was pretty sure that it didn't cause them to store genitalia in mason jars, but she'd worry about that later.

The man's face darkened with rage. "Are you calling me crazy?"

"No, I meant—"

The man clenched his fists, and the penis popped out of his hand again. This time he didn't retrieve it. "How dare you say that I'm crazy? If you weren't my soul mate, I'd turn your skull into a bloody splintered mess!"

"I take back my comment."

"I am *not* crazy!" He raised his fist as if to punch her again.

"I know you're not!"

"I don't believe you!"

"Shouldn't you pick up your appendage?"

"It'll be fine."

"I've got cats."

The man frowned and bent down. Melissa struggled some more with the cuffs, hoping that they'd notice just how dire her situation was and let her break free.

"Damn, it rolled under the bed," the man said.

The fuzzy cuffs refused to break.

The man stood back up...and then gasped. His lip curled up with disgust. "You...you diseased tramp! What did you do to me?"

"I'm sorry! It was the potion!"

"I can see the viruses squirming all over your rotting flesh! They're circling in the air all around you! Whore! Unwashed whore! I left something in your living room!"

The man hurried out of the bedroom, still clutching the privates. Melissa screamed for help, figuring that the whole "I can still do this if you're dead" threat was pretty much a moot point at this time.

The man entered, holding a claw hammer.

Melissa said "fuck."

Several times.

"That's right, bitch," said the man. "A dozen blows for you. Each strike of my hammer will Cleanse your soul."

Psychology, Melissa thought. *There's gotta be some kind of psychology you can use on him.*

"I'm your mother!" she shouted.

The man stared at her. "I beg your pardon?"

"I'm, uh, your mother."

"No, you're not. My mom lives in Schaumburg. I talked to her this morning. What are you babbling about?"

"Nothing. Sorry."

The man raised the claw hammer. "Die, bitch!" he said, slamming the blunt end against her head.

The pain was so intense that Melissa thought her eyes were going to burst out of their sockets. She'd turned her head at the last instant, so the hammer didn't break through her skull, but she'd taken a hard hit on the side of her temple, and she could already feel blood trickling from the gash.

He turned the hammer around, claw side down.

Melissa screamed again, desperately wishing that her neighbors weren't so respectful of her privacy.

He slammed the claw hammer toward her. Again she twisted her head out of the way, and the claw slashed across her cheek. She cried out from the stinging pain.

"Keep moving, bitch," said the man. "I've got another ten hits to kill you with."

Her vision was starting to blur, but not enough that she wasn't perfectly aware that the man was raising the claw hammer high over his head.

"There's a wart on the dick," she said.

The man turned his attention to the penis, which again popped out of his hand.

"*You there! Help me!*" she shrieked as loud as she could.

The man quickly turned around to face her non-existent savior. He slipped on something—Melissa had a pretty good idea what—and fell to the floor.

He let out a moan.

Melissa screamed yet again as he reached up and grabbed the mattress. He pulled himself up.

The claw hammer was imbedded in his chest.

He wrenched it out.

Raised it over his head.

Then fell back down.

He didn't get back up.

«« — »»

Somebody *finally* came to investigate her screams ten minutes later. Melissa tried to explain the situation to elderly Mrs. Graham, but quickly gave up and just asked her to call the police.

This was my comeuppance, she realized. Using the Gypsy's potion had been wrong. Even though James and his brother had seemed to enjoy themselves immensely, it was wrong to rob somebody of their free will. If she had to suffer another sexual dry spell, she'd do it without complaint. She'd almost died tonight, and let it never be said that Melissa was not a woman who learned from her mistakes.

«« — »»

Melissa crouched on James' bed, trying to keep her balance. His brother was no longer in town, but that was okay, Melissa didn't need twins to be satisfied. Not when James' cute friend Gary was around, anyway.

The goddamn Gypsy woman had raised the price to two thousand dollars, but Melissa had paid it. Happily.

She was a woman who learned from her mistakes, but the *real* mistake was not robbing innocent men of their free will. The mistake was leaving James' house with a full two hours left, so that some whacko on the street could be affected by the potion.

She had three hours left in this session.

She was going to enjoy them.

THE THREE
LITTLE PIGS

Once upon a time there lived three little pigs. Oh, these pigs had a merry life! They sang and played games and danced around the meadow and took six naps a day. But for all little pigs there comes a time when they must set out on their own, and so one day the pigs kissed their mother goodbye and ventured out into the big, beautiful world.

The nights were cold and the three little pigs knew they needed shelter soon. As they walked, they passed a vendor who was selling straw. The second little pig and the third little pig laughed and went on their merry way. But the first little pig, who was the laziest of the three pigs, stopped.

"If I purchase this straw, I could have a house built within an hour," said the pig. "Then I'll have plenty of time for singing and games and dancing and naps!"

And that's exactly what the little pig did!

But as the little pig napped in his new straw house, the Big Bad Wolf was watching. Waiting. His stomach rumbled with a torturous ancient famishment, and vile black saliva bubbled in his throat as he fantasized about sweet, succulent pig flesh. His ravenous hunger had gone unsatisfied for far too long, and there would be much bloodshed this day.

Oh yes. Yes indeed.

The Big Bad Wolf silently approached the straw house, licking his lips in anticipation of the grisly feast. He could barely control his giddy laughter as he crawled over to the front door, which was barely a door at all, and breathed deeply of the porcine scent inside.

"Little pig, little pig, let me in," he said, the words stinging his parched throat.

"Not by the hair of my chinny chin chin!" cried the pig.

The pig's mockery amused the wolf. The spectre of Death was scratching at its door, and this feeble attempt at ridicule would not save it. The Big Bad Wolf narrowed his eyes, and then he huffed.

And then he puffed.

And then he blew the house in.

The pig squealed in surprise and terror as his straw shelter scattered into the foul wind, leaving him naked and vulnerable. The little pig tried to flee, but the Big Bad Wolf was upon him instantly, pinning the pig against the hard ground with his oversized paws. Sharp claws dug deep into the pig's flesh, and suddenly nothing existed for the little pig except a dark, twisted universe of fear and pain.

Pain that had only just begun.

The Big Bad Wolf drooled and gnashed his teeth, savoring his glorious victory. The pig struggled beneath him, sobbing and begging to be released, but the pig's mockery still echoed in the wolf's ears, and there would be no mercy.

The wolf opened his jaws wide and then tore a long strip of flesh from the little pig's shoulder. Blood spattered against some remnants of straw on the ground as the pig shrieked. The wolf licked the glistening wound, inhaling deeply of its coppery scent, and then ripped a second strip from the same shoulder, exposing bone.

"No! *Dear God, no!*" the pig screamed.

The wolf's hunger became too much to bear, and he clamped his jaws over what remained of the pig's ruined shoulder. He bit down, severing the pig's entire front leg and swallowing it whole.

The pig stopped struggling. "*Please…*" he whispered. "*Please kill me.*"

In response, the wolf bit off the pig's other front leg, catching a delicious spurt of blood on the edge of his tongue. He could feel his strength returning. His *life* returning.

The Big Bad Wolf stood up on his hind legs and howled.

The little pig tried to crawl away on his gory stumps. This amused the wolf even more than the "not by the hair of my chinny chin chin" taunt, so he watched as the pig continued his feeble attempt at escape, painting twin lines of crimson upon the ground.

The wolf's stomach rumbled.

And then he dove upon his prey and gobbled the little pig right up.

«« — »»

As the second little pig and the third little pig made their way through the big, beautiful world, they passed a vendor who was selling wood. The third little pig was momentarily intrigued but quickly decided against it, while the second little pig looked more closely.

"If I purchase this wood, I could have a house built before night falls," said the pig. "Then I'll have plenty of time tomorrow for singing and games and dancing and naps!"

And that's exactly what the little pig did!

But as the pig slumbered, the Big Bad Wolf crawled through the night air, lit only by the full moon. His muzzle was still stained with the blood of his previous kill, but his hunger remained. With great stealth, he approached the house of wood, absent-mindedly playing with the new necklace he wore...a necklace made from the first little pig's ears and teeth.

He could still taste the pig's curly little tail.

The wolf knocked on the door. "Little pig, little pig, let me in!"

"Not by the hair of my chinny chin chin!"

The wolf frowned. He'd expected mockery, in fact he'd hoped for it, but he hadn't expected *identical* mockery. Had the pigs been plotting against him? Toying with him?

It didn't matter. The pig was doomed.

The wolf huffed...and puffed...and blew the wooden house in.

The little pig's eyes shone in the moonlight, wide with fright. Didn't he realize that there could be no sanctuary from the Big Bad Wolf?

This pig was not going to receive the quick, merciful death that his brother had been granted. This pig was going to suffer. This pig was going to learn the true nature of agony.

Before the pig could flee, the wolf picked up a jagged strip of wood. With his astounding wolfish strength he slammed it all the way through one of the pig's legs and deep into the ground underneath, pinning him there. The pig screamed and frantically tried to pull himself free, but his efforts were for naught.

The wolf traced a single claw through the bloody wound and then held it to the pig's snout. "Breathe in deeply," he snarled. "This is the scent of your demise."

"*Please*..." the little pig begged, "...you don't have to do this..."

"Don't I?"

The pig shook his head. "You don't! This isn't you!"

The wolf growled. "You dare to speak for me? You think you *know* me? You think you can look *inside* me? You're nothing, little pig...*nothing*. I'll show what you what you are."

The wolf slashed at the pig's fat tummy with his claw, making trickling red letters that formed a single word.

Meat.

"What do you think of that?" the wolf asked.

The pig spat in his face.

Anger flared through the wolf, but he kept himself under control. If he lost his temper, he'd end the life of his prey too soon, and that wouldn't do at all.

Instead, he carved more words onto the pig's flesh. *Pork. Bacon. Ham. Sausage.* The pig squealed and squealed, thrashing back and forth, and the creature's misery was blissful music to the wolf's ears.

The words were becoming difficult to read, so the wolf greedily lapped up the excess blood.

The pig stopped squealing and struggling. Its eyes glazed over and it stared vacantly at nothing.

Was it dead? Had the wolf lost control after all?

The wolf placed an ear to the pig's chest and listened for a heartbeat. No, it was still alive. Just catatonic. The pig had retreated into a safe place in its mind where there was no blood or death or wolves.

The wolf raked a claw across the pig's cheek to encourage it to return to reality. The pig didn't react. It was gone.

Cursing under its breath, the wolf slashed open the pig's belly. One of its claws caught on the intestines, yanking them out like thick rope. The wolf burrowed its face into the pig's open stomach and gobbled away, devouring the pig from the inside out.

When there was nothing left but teeth and ears, the wolf added to its necklace.

«« — »»

As the third little pig made his way through the big, beautiful world, he passed a vendor who was selling bricks and mortar.

"If I purchase these bricks and mortar, it will take me a long time to complete my house," said the little pig. "There will be no time for singing and games and dancing and naps, but I will have a sturdy shelter!"

And that's exactly what the little pig did!

As the pig slept for the night, the Big Bad Wolf approached. "No brick house can keep me out," he said. "I will blow it in just as I did the house of straw, and just as I did the house of wood!" He pounded on the door. "Little pig, little pig, let me in!"

"Not by the hair of my chinny chin chin!"

The wolf chuckled at this insolence. And then he huffed...and puffed...and blew with all of his might...

...but the house still stood!

Undaunted, the wolf sucked in another deep breath, filling his lungs with air, and then he huffed...and then he puffed...and then he blew with even more of his might...

...and yet the house still stood!

How could this have happened? His huffing and puffing had never failed before. Was he past his prime? Did this spell the end of his reign of terror? Would the name of the Big Bad Wolf be a source of laughter for little pigs throughout the meadows of the world?

The Big Bad Wolf felt helpless.

Impotent.

No. There had to be another way to get inside.

And then he saw it. The chimney. The foolish pig may have built a house that could withstand the force of the wolf's breath, but he'd neglected to completely seal off the structure, and that would be his tragic downfall.

The wolf climbed onto the roof of the brick house and then leapt down the chimney, just as quickly as you please!

He plunged into a pot of boiling water, howling as his flesh blistered and bubbled underneath his fur. Before he could leap from the death trap, the pig slammed a lid on top of the pot, trapping him inside.

In the darkness of the pot, the wolf renounced his canine gods. His fur came off in bloody clumps and the bones in his paws shattered as he slammed them against the lid. Slowly, ever so slowly, the Big Bad Wolf boiled to death.

His corpse floated in the water long after the fire died out.

The next morning, the little pig removed the lid and laughed at the dead wolf. He decided to go fetch his brothers and show them the body of the wretched creature that had...

The pig froze in horror.

The wolf's belly had split apart, and his last meals, undigested, floated in the water. Though they were well-boiled, the little pig recognized his brother's snout and his other brother's severed leg.

The little pig collapsed into the corner. He closed his eyes and screamed in anguish. He screamed and screamed and screamed, his entire world collapsing around him as his brick house stood firm.

Everything
Has a Purpose

The handwriting on the note was terrible, but "or your wife will be killed" stood out nicely.

Harry Stearns was going to turn forty in two weeks. He'd been dreading that particular birthday for the past nine years, yet now the idea of being over the hill didn't seem so bad, as long as he didn't have to be over the hill alone.

He'd get Joanne back. Of course he would. He'd obeyed orders and would continue to do so. He hadn't called the police, he hadn't told anybody what had happened, and he hadn't let anybody follow him. He'd play their game, do whatever they wanted.

What scared him the most, though, was that the kidnappers hadn't asked for any kind of ransom. He'd brought Joanne's jewelry box just in case.

«« — »»

Despite having lived in Bodenwolf, Indiana his entire life, Harry didn't know the numerous back roads very well and got himself thoroughly lost. If he hadn't given himself so much extra time to reach his destination, he probably would have missed the meeting altogether, but the third time he passed the same overturned Volkswagen he got back on track and reached the rendezvous point only ten minutes late.

He shut off the engine, but left on the headlights as he waited. He was on a short, unpaved dead-end road, in the middle of a heavily wooded area. When he rolled down the window he could hear that there was a stream nearby. Hopefully the ten minutes he'd been late weren't enough for the kidnappers to get impatient and take off.

Harry sat there for a while, whistling badly to calm his nerves.

After fifteen minutes he was horrified to think that he might have missed them, but then something tapped against the passenger-side window, making him flinch. A man in black denim jeans, a black leather jacket, and a black facemask stood by the window. He'd tapped it with a revolver.

"Kill the headlights, then get out of the car," said the man, moving a few feet away from the door and pointing his revolver at Harry's head. "Slowly." He sounded fairly young, but the facemask made it difficult to be sure.

Harry shut off the headlights as the kidnapper turned on the flashlight, focusing the beam on Harry's face. He carefully opened the door and eased his way out of the vehicle, trying not to make any sudden movements. After he got out, he stepped away from the car and raised his hands in the air.

"I brought some jewelry," Harry said. "The box is in the back seat."

"Thanks. Maybe I'll pick it up later." The kidnapper slammed the door shut, then kept the gun aimed at Harry while he dug a set of keys out of his pocket. He selected one and scraped it along the driver's side door, leaving a zigzag pattern all the way across it. "Doesn't that just piss you off?" he asked.

Under other circumstances it would have, but for now Harry had much more important things to worry about. "Where's my wife?"

"Don't worry, I'll take you to her. We've got a pretty nice hike ahead of us, so we'd better get started. You don't mind if I keep this gun aimed at your back the whole time, do you? Didn't think so. We'll be going through some rough area, and I'll have to shoot you if you pull anything sneaky, so try not to trip."

«« — »»

Harry snuck a glance at his watch every so often, and noted that it took about forty-five minutes to reach their destination. The kidnapper was a regular chatterbox the entire time, sharing numerous vivid descriptions of what would happen to Harry and Joanne should he become even the slightest bit annoyed.

Finally they emerged from the woods into the side yard of a large two-story log house. Far from the cobweb-laden shack Harry would expect kidnapper scum to reside in, from the outside it was a perfectly maintained home with a second-floor deck that looked to have been recently repainted. The outside was fairly well lit, and the man shut off his flashlight.

"Here we are," he said, tucking the flashlight into his inside jacket pocket. "Not bad, huh?"

"Very nice."

"I'm glad you like it. Keep walking."

They moved around to the front yard. The house was completely surrounded by forest except for a small driveway that curved out of sight. The man forced Harry up onto the front porch, and then pressed the barrel of the revolver against his neck.

"Wipe your feet," he said.

Harry wiped his feet on the "Welcome Friends!" mat.

The man reached past him and opened the door. "We're here!" he called out as they stepped into the foyer. There were two sets of stairs, a tan-carpeted one leading up and a wooden one leading down.

"You're late," said an elderly but forceful voice from upstairs.

"Hey, your friend here was late. Not my fault."

"Well, that's not surprising. Bring him up here."

Still at gunpoint, Harry walked upstairs and found himself in a spacious, immaculate living room. The walls were decorated with framed pictures of beach scenes, and the furniture was all the color of sand. An old man, probably in his seventies, was relaxing in a recliner, reading something by Hemingway. Though his body was slender, it was obvious at a glance that there was nothing frail about him. He placed a bookmark inside the paperback and set it aside on an end table, then regarded Harry with a warm smile.

"Welcome to my home," he said. "Do you know who I am?"

There was something vaguely familiar about the old man, but Harry couldn't place him. He shook his head.

The old man shrugged. "You never did have much of a memory. Would you care for a drink? I'm afraid I don't keep liquor in the house, but you're welcome to a glass of orange juice or water with lemon."

"I just want to see my wife."

"Of course." The old man nodded to the man in the facemask. "Alex, please point your gun at our guest again."

"Don't use my *name*, for God's sake! What's the matter with you?" Alex demanded.

"Relax, relax. Ulcers are nobody's friend. Now let's go visit his wife in the basement."

The cement-floored basement was just as immaculate as the upstairs. Neatly stacked cardboard boxes lined the walls, and there was a tool bench with several unfinished projects resting upon it. There was a small desk in the corner, and an uncomfortable-looking wooden chair in the center of the room.

But what really caught Harry's attention was Joanne, tied to a chair against the far wall, grotesque streaks running down her face where the absurd amount of makeup she wore had mixed with tears. Her eyes widened as she saw Harry and she tried to say something, but her mouth was gagged, muffling her words.

"There she is," said the old man, gesturing dramatically. "You'll be pleased to note that she's unharmed."

"*Mostly* unharmed," Alex corrected.

Now that Harry had found Joanne, his thoughts turned toward figuring out a way to get them out of here. If he could just get a hold of the gun...

"I want to talk to her," Harry said. "Take the gag off."

Alex casually walked past Harry, then spun around and punched him in the stomach, doubling him over. "Excuse me? Did I miss the part where the balance of power shifted in your favor?"

"I just want to hear her say that she's all right," Harry groaned, standing back up, arms wrapped around his belly.

"Tough. Remember who's in charge here."

"That's enough," said the old man. "Lead our guest to his seat."

"Sit," said Alex, pointing at the wooden chair.

The feeling was seeping out of Harry's legs. There was no way he could lunge for the gun without getting shot, and if he spun around to attack the old man, Alex probably wouldn't hesitate to fire. Basically, he had to cooperate and pray that a window of opportunity presented itself.

He sat down on the chair, which was just as uncomfortable as it looked. Alex gestured toward the chair leg with the gun. "See those handcuffs?"

Harry looked down and saw them, one bracelet wrapped around the leg of the chair, the other lying on the floor. "Yes."

"Lock the free end around your leg."

Harry picked up the bracelet and snapped it around his left ankle. Alex dragged the desk across the floor of the basement, creating an ear-torturing screech, until it was in front of the chair. Alex bent down and squeezed the bracelet, making sure it was on securely, then, satisfied, walked over to a position behind Joanne and began to stroke her hair. She whimpered at his touch.

The old man began to pace slowly around the room. "So, Mr. Stearns, I am now going to give you a chance to save your wife, as well as your-self. I hope for both of your sakes you'll be able to give me what I want."

"Anything I've got, it's yours," Harry insisted. "I've got a couple thousand dollars' worth of jewelry back in the car, and I'll empty my bank account, anything you want."

The old man shook his head. "Unfortunately, I don't want money. I want answers."

Harry gave him a confused look. "Answers? What, are you trying to get the inside scoop about the merger? If so, you've got the wrong person."

"No, no, nothing like that. The answers I want come from far in your past." The old man picked up a stack of papers from the top of one of the cardboard boxes and set it on the desk. The stack was at least an inch thick, and the front page was blank.

Alex walked over to the tool bench and grabbed a pair of metal garden shears. He opened them as wide as they would go, then approached Harry and snapped them shut an inch from his nose.

"Here's how this is going to work," the old man informed Harry. "You're going to answer all of my questions. For every question you get wrong, my associate is going to cut off one of your wife's toes. After that, he'll begin removing fingers. After that, he'll get creative. Then he'll start on you. Is that clear?"

"Yes," Harry whispered, barely able to breathe.

"Good." The old man handed him a pencil. "You may begin."

Fighting the urge to vomit, Harry turned over the blank page. What he saw on the next page was both hopelessly foreign and frighteningly familiar.

An algebra test.

And suddenly he remembered exactly where he'd seen the old man before. An hour a day, five days a week, for a full year. "Oh my God...Mr. Shadle!"

The old man smiled. "You always said you'd never use this stuff. Don't you hate being wrong?"

THEM OLD WEST MUTATIONS

Now, the citizens of Spittin' Hollow had got themselves all worked up to see a good gunfight, so when it was interrupted by giant cockroaches they were none too happy. You see, the Halloran triplets had come into town not two weeks ago, shootin' and hollerin' and overall causin' a ruckus. Spittin' Hollow was a rowdy enough place on its own, so most of the locals didn't pay 'em much attention. But then Bob Halloran, the one who still had both his eyes, went and questioned the decency of Miss Jenkins, who everyone knew was just as pure as an unopened bottle of sarsaparilla.

Sheriff Mason, he wasn't gonna put up with that kind of behavior in his town, so he challenged Bob Halloran to a gunfight at dawn. That was a mite earlier than the sheriff was happy with, since he liked sleepin' late almost as much as he liked lockin' up drunks, but he reckoned that was the proper way to do it. Bob Halloran accepted the duel, havin' some honor despite the fact that he was lowlife scum.

So at dawn the locals who weren't too tired gathered 'round Main Street to watch Sheriff Mason plug that Halloran boy a good one. Earl and Frank Halloran were there, sittin' on their horses and tryin' to look sinister. Sheriff Mason and Bob Halloran exchanged some fightin' words, then they stood thirty paces apart and got ready to draw.

Which was when those cockroaches showed up.

A dozen scurried out of Doc Rollin's pharmacy, each one of 'em a good ten feet long. A couple of Madame Paula's workin' girls were unfortunate enough to be standin' there at the time, and some of those things started crawlin' right over the women. They fell to the ground just screamin' as loud as you please.

So Sheriff Mason, he turned around and got ready to put a bullet or two into those creatures, seein' as how Madame Paula was prone to givin' him a freebie when she was inebriated. But before he could do anything,

Bob Halloran shot him in the back. The Halloran boys didn't have *that* much honor.

Havin' a dead sheriff would've been a bigger deal to the rest of the locals if they hadn't been so preoccupied with the roaches. One of the bugs took a huge bite out of one of the workin' girls, lowerin' her askin' price drastically. About six of the other roaches started runnin' down the side of the street, sendin' those townspeople scattering.

"Hot damn!" shouted Howie the bartender. "It's Armageddon or somethin'!"

Bob Halloran, he was generally as yellow as they come, but instead of takin' off he started shootin' his last five bullets at the roaches. The first bullet missed entirely, the second bullet missed the roaches entirely but hit Howie, and the last three hit the back of a roach that was runnin' after Miss Jenkins. But the bullets bounced right off like they'd been shot at steel, one of 'em hittin' Howie again.

That roach turned to look at Bob Halloran, and while scientific theory's got nothin' to say about a roach makin' a sound like a lion roarin', that's just what that critter did. Bob Halloran, he went all white 'cept for the crotch of his pants. Then that roach leapt right at him, and without a speck of exaggeration, that thing jumped thirty feet. He threw up his arms to protect his face, but that roach knocked him to the ground and just started munchin' away. A couple seconds after that Bob Halloran was only fit for a cheap pine box.

Now everybody was just screamin' and runnin' for their lives when those roaches suddenly took off down Main Street, tramplin' poor Howie in the process. They moved so fast that it was only 'bout twenty seconds before nobody could see 'em any more.

For a few moments nobody said anything, 'cept those who were wallowin' in pain. Then Tim, the blacksmith, pointed at the swingin' door of Doc Rollins' pharmacy with white-hot fury in his eyes.

"That Doc Rollins—I knew he'd be the death of some of us! Those experiments he's been doin' in his makeshift laboratory have gone *too far!*"

The townsfolk shouted their agreement.

"Let's get him!" Tim cried out.

The townsfolk shouted their agreement.

"What if he's got more o' them roaches in there?" asked Howie from where he lay bleedin' on the ground.

The townsfolk looked questioningly at Tim.

"I say we risk it!" Tim cried out.

The townsfolk shouted their disagreement.

"Listen to me," said Tim. "We've gotta stop that quack before he causes any more big bugs! If we leave him alone, who knows what's next? Giant termites? Giant leeches? Madame Paula, what's gonna happen to you and your girls if next time Doc comes up with giant *crabs*?"

The townsfolk were silent. Tim was one of the braver folks in Spittin' Hollow—he was the only one to actually drink an entire mug of Howie's special Devil's Drool brew—but he didn't much relish the thought of goin' in there alone.

"Somebody's gotta come with me," he said. "It's only fair."

Fair is one of those relative terms, and it doesn't much apply when you've got a group of folks who don't wanna get consumed by large cockroaches. So Tim, he had to go by himself into the pharmacy, after borrowin' a couple six-shooters just in case.

"Doc?" he called out as he walked through the center of the shop. "Hey, Doc, are you around?"

The first thing to catch his eye was a metal cage, 'bout six feet long and six feet wide, with the bars on the front bent wide open, like somethin' had forced its way out.

Suddenly a door in the rear of the pharmacy swung open and Doc emerged, his glasses fogged and his hair all messed up. "I did it!" he shouted. "My experiment worked! Pretty soon the name of Doc Rollins is gonna be known around the entire...say, *that* ain't good..."

Doc glanced at the cage, then at Tim, then began lookin' around the pharmacy. "Say, Tim, I don't reckon you've seen some cockroaches runnin' around, have you? They'd be big fellas, 'bout a foot long each."

Tim took a purposeful step forward. "I saw your roaches, but they weren't no one-footers. Those things I saw creatin' a disturbance were a good ten feet!"

The Doc's eyes widened. "Then it worked...too dang well! What have I done? What fearsome enemy have I wrought upon humanity? Hell, all I wanted to do was create a bigger, better breed of cattle to make up for what the rustlers were stealin', that's all, and now this!"

"Doc, you're rantin' and ravin'!" said Tim. "I need your help. We have to destroy them bugs before it's too late!"

"I reckon it may already be too late! Because before dark you won't be dealin' with cockroaches that are ten feet long, they'll be a *hundred* feet long! And soon they'll have all of mankind in their grasp! Oh, why couldn't I just stick to sellin' hair tonic like my father?"

"Your father did sell high quality hair tonic, that's for sure, but that's neither here nor there," said Tim. "So what made these roaches so ample-sized and vicious?"

"They're mutated," said Doc Rollins. "I mutated 'em myself with my own special recipe. But I didn't know they was gonna break out of their cages and start killin' the Spittin' Hollow populace like that, I swear I didn't."

"Considerin' that I ain't told you 'bout any populace bein' killed, I reckon your story ain't the God's honest truth," said Tim.

Doc Rollins frowned. "You've got me there."

"So what're we gonna do 'bout this predicament, Doc?"

"Hell, I dunno. I s'pose I oughta start formulatin' an antidote."

"Sounds good. I'm gonna go keep the townsfolk informed, seein' as how Sheriff Mason is now departed, and I'll be back to check on your progress."

So Tim, he told the citizens of Spittin' Hollow to get in their homes and lock 'em up tight. But it did no good because when those roaches came back, lo and behold they were a hundred feet long if they were an inch. One of 'em broke right through a stable door and carried away two of Jake Smith's best horses. Some folks with no sense stayed at the saloon, gamblin' and drinkin' just like there weren't any giant cockroaches around, and ten minutes after the sun went down their death rattle was a-rattlin' just as loud as you please.

Why, nearly half of the Spittin' Hollow populace was deceased when the sun come up the next morning, an' Doc Rollins was no closer to formulatin' his antidote than he was to growin' a second nose.

"Look, Doc, we do have somethin' of a time constraint here, seein' as how nearly half of the Spittin' Hollow folk are swimmin' around in them roaches stomachs," said Tim, tappin' his foot impatiently.

"Now, now, you can't rush science," said Doc Rollins. "What if I were to administer this here formula and it made those roaches even bigger? We'd have a mighty heap of a problem on our hands, let me tell you."

"I reckon you've got a point," said Tim, "but damned if I can't help but feelin' a bit antsy."

Well, Tim sat there feelin' antsy for a good long while, durin' which time those cockroaches went and devoured enough members of the populace that Spittin' Hollow was gettin' dangerously close to havin' less than twenty-five percent of its residents still alive. And those roaches, they just kept gettin' bigger and bigger, until they was nearin' two hundred feet in length.

"Hell, Doc, why'd you have to go and do such a thing?" asked Tim. "I thought a medical professional such as yourself was s'posed to know the dangers of messin' with science."

"I already explained my reasonin' and I don't reckon I need to go repeatin' myself," said Doc Rollins, holdin' up a test tube with some greenish-blue gunk in it. "I do believe, however, that I've got the solution to our problems."

"That's a mighty small test tube for such mighty large cockroaches," said Tim.

"Never you mind how big it is. This oughta react with the mutatin' serum in them roaches and kill 'em up right nice. I reckon you don't need more than a single drop per roach, but they've gotta swallow it."

Tim took the test tube from Doc Rollins. "And just how do you figure we're gonna get those mutants to ingest it?"

Doc Rollins looked around as if to make sure that nobody was 'round to overhear. "Well, Tim, just between you an' me, if those roaches are eatin' people anyway, I don't see any reason why we can't fix some of the townfolk up with a drop o' my liquid beforehand."

"Now, Doc, that's just plain diabolical. Still, I reckon I see your point."

So Tim, he went and asked the townsfolk that was still livin' to drink a drop of Doc Rollins' roach-killin' potion. He had to be a mite deceptive 'bout the whole process, considerin' that he was plannin' for 'em to get eaten, and it didn't sit on his conscience none too well, but a man's gotta do what a man's gotta do in times of hardship.

Well, those roaches, which was now up to three hundred feet in some cases, kept on eatin' the Spittin' Hollow townfolk, and damned if the potion didn't work. A cockroach scooped up and started chewin' on pretty Miss Bianca, and that thing was dead in eight seconds by Tim's pocketwatch. Why, within the hour, eleven of those creatures was just lyin' dead on the streets, not botherin' a soul.

"Doc, we've got ourselves a problem," said Tim, walkin' back into the pharmacy. "There's still one roach left, the biggest and meanest one of 'em all, and we ain't got no populace left to feed 'em your potion."

"Well, seein' as how I'm the one who went and formulated it, I reckon the honorable thing would be for you to sacrifice yourself," said Doc Rollins.

Tim shook his head. "I can't abide by that line of thinkin', considerin' that it was you who mutated them things in the first place."

"Aw, hell, I was hopin' you wouldn't go and bring that up. Yeah, seein' as how I'm the one who done created this catastrophe, I'll accept my just desserts." Doc Rollins took the test tube from Tim and swallowed down that last sip.

At that very moment, the last roach busted right through the wall of the pharmacy and it ate Doc Rollins right up.

"Ha!" Tim shouted at the roach, not knowin' whether or not it had the word "ha" in its vocabulary. "You're in for a world o' death now, you damn fool critter!"

But unbeknownst to Tim, that roach had attained a size of sufficient mass that just one drop wasn't gonna do the trick, and before he knew it that roach had made Tim a meal.

Well, that roach died of starvation not too much later, seein' as how when you're three hundred feet long it takes a lot of nutrition to keep you goin'. But that was about it for the town of Spittin' Hollow. With no populace left there wasn't anything to do but just let the dust settle.

And that's the story. I reckon you may be wonderin' how I know all of these details, considerin' that nobody survived to tell the tale. I guess, if you want to narrow it down, I'm either the ghost of a dead mutant cockroach or a liar, and I ain't sayin' which.

WASTING GRANDPA

Before you start thinking I'm a total jerk, I want to preface things by saying that I was in Grandpa's will for almost ten years before I decided to kill him. That's ten years I was perfectly willing to let the old man die a natural, peaceful death in his own home, surrounded by those he loved and who loved him in return.

Am I such a bad person for getting a little impatient?

Now, it wasn't like the guy was having an especially productive life or anything. He was on crutches and hardly ever left the house. Grandma had died eight years earlier in a car accident that had nothing whatsoever to do with me. I mean, what did he have to live for besides sitting by the fire, telling boring stories to his boring friends?

I needed the money. I was getting married, and Pauline wanted a big wedding. Her parents refused to pay for one the third time around, so I had to take care of it. I was making decent money selling magazine subscriptions over the phone, but Grandpa had a huge fortune that he wasn't using. Even divided among myself and my cousins, my share would be more than enough to get married in style.

And so, on my twenty-fifth birthday, I invited myself over to Grandpa's house for our own private celebration. He supplied the birthday cake and ice cream, and I supplied the cyanide.

We sat in his annoyingly tasteful upstairs den, started a fire, and began to chat as we ate. He'd bought a vanilla cake with coconut all over it. I personally can't see any reason why somebody would destroy a perfectly good cake by smearing it with that repulsive pseudo-fruit, but I was polite and said nothing.

After Grandpa finished sharing an "amusing" anecdote about my youth, the one about the dead chicken I kept in my room for two weeks when I was six, I got up from the vibrating recliner. "You know, I think a cake like this calls for red wine. There's some in the refrigerator, right?"

"Always," Grandpa told me. He leaned forward and reached for his crutches. "Here, I'll get it."

"No, no, it's my birthday, I'll get it." I left the den, went down a short ugly hallway, and proceeded down the spiral staircase. I crossed through the living room into what an adorable little sign on the refrigerator informed me was "Grandma's Kitchen."

Grandpa knew me too well. The red wine rested in an ice bucket on the counter, with two glasses next to it. The ice had apparently melted and then been refrozen, because the bottle appeared to be enclosed in a bucket-shaped block of ice. With a bit of strain, I withdrew it and poured us each a glass.

I took the cyanide vial out of my pocket and poured some into Grandpa's drink. Then I added some more. And a smidgen more. I put a thumbprint on my own glass, just in case I got nervous and mixed them up.

"Here you go," I said, returning to the den. I handed Grandpa his glass, and he took a nice big sip. I sat back down on the vibrating recliner and encouraged him to share another hilariously stupid thing I'd done as a kid.

"This wine is exceptionally good today," he told me. "I don't suppose you'd care to get me some without poison in it, would you?"

I froze. This was, you might say, not good. "I beg your pardon?"

"I know you put something in my drink. I've been drinking wine almost my entire life, and I know when there's something wrong with it."

I'd been under the impression that old people had vastly inferior taste buds.

He sneered at me. "You haven't wanted to spend a birthday with me since you were ten. I figured you were just here to brownnose your way into a bigger piece of the inheritance, but no, you're trying to knock off the old man to get your cash faster. Well let me tell you something, you little bastard, you've *never* been in my will. The whole thing is going to Regina, because she can make the best damn sauerkraut I've ever tasted!"

"I don't know what you're talking about," I said. Okay, it wasn't much of a cover, but I was flustered.

"I want you out of my house," Grandpa said. "And then I never want to see your adopted face around here ever again. Do you understand me?"

"I wasn't adopted," I protested.

"Well, you *should* have been."

"Grandpa, you're tired. How about a nice long nap, and then we'll talk about this later?"

"If you don't get out of my house this second, I'm calling the police."

Now, I didn't know whether or not he really intended to let me just walk out of there and keep it a secret. Maybe, if only to protect the family name. But maybe not...and being accused of attempted murder would certainly put a bit of a strain on my marriage plans. Besides, I had a feeling he was lying about the will just to save his life.

I did know one thing. The phone was well out of his reach.

I looked him in the eye. "Okay, Grandpa, I don't want to hurt you, and I guess there isn't a reason to now. Come downstairs with me so we can talk."

"I've already said what needs to be said. Get out."

"Grandpa, you can do what I say, or I can go into your kitchen, get one of those big carving knives out of the drawer, and demonstrate a total lack of respect for my elders. Understand?" I tried to sound sinister, and was pleased that at least my voice didn't squeak.

"You little—"

"*Understand?*"

He glared at me, then nodded. I gulped down my entire glass of wine in one swig. It didn't make me feel any better.

"Use your crutches. We'll go downstairs, have a pleasant talk over a cup of hot cocoa, and hopefully part ways on good terms. Sound okay?"

"You were an accident," Grandpa said. "Your mother didn't want you. She called me up in tears when she found out your dad had knocked her up."

"Do you want me to kill you right now?" I asked. "I'll do it. I just forced myself to choke down that crap you tried to call a cake, so I'm in the mood to hurt somebody."

Without another word, Grandpa picked up his crutches and got to his feet. I watched as he walked out of the den and toward the top of the spiral staircase. Normally he'd sit and scoot all the way down on his rear, but I had a speedier alternative.

I walked up behind him as he reached the stairs.

Bye-bye, Grandpa.

I gave him a violent shove, causing him to drop his crutches and fall forward. He cried out, struck the stairs, and tumbled all the way down. *Thump, thump, thump.* He hit the floor with a *crack* that made me cringe, then lay at the bottom and was still.

For several moments I just stared at him, trying desperately not to hyperventilate. I certainly wasn't going to have any problems sounding panicked when I called the police.

"You little shit!" Grandpa shouted at me, his voice surprisingly strong for a guy lying face-down on the floor after a fall down a flight of stairs. "You rotten little bastard! I hope you burn in hell for this!"

I immediately rushed down the stairs, almost falling myself, and stood next to him. Grandpa lashed out with his right arm, trying to grab my ankle, but I moved my foot out of the way.

"I'll kill you!" he shouted. "I'll break your rotten little neck! Help me, somebody! *Heeeeeelp!*"

"Grandpa, not so loud! It was an accident!" Grandpa lived in a fairly remote area, a farmhouse surrounded by cornfields, but he did have neighbors across the street who were possibly close enough to hear.

"Help! Help! Somebody help!"

"Be quiet!" I whispered. "Grandpa, shut up!"

"Heeeeeeeeeeelp!"

So, I jumped on his back. I had no choice. I leapt into the air as high as I could, and came down on his back with a *crunch* that made me cringe more than the previous *crack*.

Grandpa shut up, except for a soft moaning.

I did it again, just to be sure.

I stepped off his back and surveyed the damage. Certainly there had to be some sort of believable explanation for Grandpa falling down the stairs and then having somebody jump up and down on his back. Over-enthusiastic CPR?

No, no, I was screwed. Utterly, totally, completely, 100%, nice-knowing-you-buddy screwed.

Unless I hid the body. I'd be a suspect for sure, but if I could get rid of all the evidence, maybe I wouldn't be charged with anything. I just had to find a good place to store him, a place nobody would ever look.

I had begun to brainstorm possibilities when I glanced over and saw Ms. Rawmet peering in through the living room window.

The seventy-five year-old woman's horrified expression indicated that she'd just witnessed an ample helping of homicide.

She ran off.

I bolted into the living room, but instead of heading for the front door, I went for the gun rack. Grandpa kept them loaded—at least that's what he'd told me as a kid when he was giving me strict instructions not to touch them. I smashed open the glass case with a couple of solid kicks, retrieved a rifle, then rushed over to the front door and threw it open.

Ms. Rawmet had made it across the street. Though she had always been a grouchy old hag who made me pay for each and every window I broke, I didn't feel good about what I had to do.

JEFF STRAND - 67

She looked back at me. We were about a hundred feet apart. I raised the rifle, peered through the sights, and took aim. Then I pulled the trigger.

And missed. Big-time.

She took off running toward her house again, though her mild limp kept her from moving very quickly. I fired again. Missed. Fired once more. Missed, but put a nice hole in her mailbox.

I lowered the rifle and ran after her. She finally found her voice and began shrieking. "Harvey! Call the police!"

This would have worried me, but Harvey was her pug. She hadn't lived with anyone besides a dog since she was eighteen. As she hurried onto her front porch, I raised the rifle again, fired, and missed yet again. Her window shattered. I sure as hell wasn't paying for that one.

Aside from Ms. Rawmet, the nearest neighbor was at least half a mile away. The stretch of road between the two homes was rarely used. I know it was rarely used. I'd spent many afternoons playing kickball and soft-ball and Red Rover on that stupid road and we could play for *hours* without anybody driving past. In later years, during my less and less frequent visits, we could sit outside most of the evening and only be interrupted once or twice by a car driving by.

So, yes, I was surprised when a car came into view at the exact moment that I finally succeeded in shooting Ms. Rawmet in the back.

She cried out and fell. I immediately dropped the rifle and tried to look nonchalant. The car was about two hundred feet away and driving fairly quickly. Maybe they'd look at me, smiling and waving, and not notice the bleeding woman on the opposite porch.

The car came closer. I smiled and waved. The driver, a man about my age, smiled and waved back.

The woman with him screamed.

The car braked to a halt. Now I could officially say that I was getting frustrated and more than a little pissed. I grabbed the rifle and took aim.

The man ducked down and floored the gas pedal. The tires shrieked as the car sped past me.

My first shot kept up with my tradition of lousy aim. The second shot blew out the rear windshield. The third and fourth shots missed completely. But it didn't matter, because the driver was paying more attention to not getting shot than to steering accurately, and the car went off the road, plowing into the cornfield.

I ran toward the car. The driver's side door swung open, and the man got out, hands in the air.

"Don't hurt me!" he begged. "I won't tell anyone!"

Yeah, right.

I aimed the rifle at his chest, pulled the trigger, and was rewarded with a *click*.

The man turned and began to run, not even glancing back at the woman he'd left cowering in the automobile. I swung the rifle behind my head like an axe about to chop wood, then hurled it as hard as I could.

My throwing aim was a lot better than my shooting aim, and the rifle struck him in the back of the head, knocking him to the ground. I hurried over to his fallen body, picked the weapon up by the barrel, and finished him off with several solid blows to the head. The wood didn't even splinter. Grandpa bought good guns.

I was feeling really sick, and my arms were sore, but if I still wanted to be married by a Justice of the Peace rather than a prison warden I had to finish the job. I went back to the car, where the woman had finally opened the door and was pushing her way through the cornfield. Her high heels weren't making the process easy. I caught up to her and got ready to bash her skull.

And then I did it.

The next hour or so was not particularly enjoyable. First I went over and finished off Ms. Rawmet. Then I covered her with garbage bags to keep the mess to a minimum, and dragged her body into Grandpa's house and put it down in the basement. I carried Grandpa and the woman in the cornfield down there as well, storing the bodies in a corner for the time being. The man wasn't exactly skinny, so he took longer than the others, but eventually all four corpses were out of sight. After gunning the engine a few times, I managed to get the car out of the cornfield and parked it out of sight behind Ms. Rawmet's house.

I got a broom and brushed the broken glass off the road, and adjusted the rug on Ms. Rawmet's front porch so that it covered the bloodstains. Then I returned to Grandpa's house, closed the curtain so nobody could see inside, straightened everything up as well as I could, sat down on the couch, and fell asleep.

Falling asleep is generally accepted as a poor tactical choice in situations such as these, but I couldn't help it. One moment I was sitting there trying to figure out what I was going to do, the next I was having that dream where you're naked in school. I'd always kind of liked that dream. Just call me a sicko.

I was awakened by the doorbell. I sat upright, and a glance at the clock told me I'd been asleep for over an hour. I didn't move.

The doorbell rang again. Then again. And then I heard Pauline's voice: "Is anyone there?"

I got up and hurried over to the door. Pauline certainly had seen my car parked outside, so I couldn't pretend that I wasn't here. I had to get rid of her.

No, not kill her, just make her leave.

I opened the door.

A group of approximately two dozen of my friends and relatives stood outside, holding presents and party favors. Pauline stood in front, holding a cake with twenty-five burning candles.

"Happy birthday to you.. happy birthday to you..." they sang in energetic tones. Pauline had that wide grin she always got when she felt she did something wonderful. I think the fact that I was able to force a smile and keep the urine inside my bladder is worthy of knighthood.

I basically just stood there, stunned, as the uninvited guests moved past me into the house, patting me on the shoulder and wishing me many more happy birthdays in the future.

"Is Grandpa upstairs?" my mother asked, giving me a kiss on the cheek.

"Umm, no, actually. I don't know where he is. Nobody was here when I arrived."

"Really?" Mom looked a bit concerned. "That's unusual."

"I know. I guess one of his friends picked him up." I feigned an expression of disappointment. "He must have forgotten about my birthday."

"Well, he is getting up there in years, and he probably just thought you were trying to brownnose your way into a larger share of the inheritance." She smiled.

For some odd reason I found myself unable to have fun at my birthday party. The chocolate cake was probably delicious, but I couldn't taste a damn thing. Everyone asked me about Grandpa, but I just told them what I'd told Mom. The guests were in almost every room of the house, but I stayed in the kitchen, making sure nobody tried to go down into the basement for any reason.

After about half an hour, Pauline thrust a large glass of sparkling fruit punch into my hands. "Are you feeling all right?" she asked.

I shrugged. "A little worried about Grandpa, I guess."

"I'm sure he's fine."

"You're probably right."

She put her hand on my shoulder. "Sweetie, it's something else. You look like you're feeling sick to your stomach."

"No, really, I'm fine. Never felt better." I took a huge gulp of the punch to show her just how fine my stomach was.

"You need to relax." She leaned forward and whispered in my ear. "You know, I bet we could have some privacy in the basement..."

I drank some more punch to give my mouth something to do besides let out a terrified yelp. "We'll be missed," I said. "Not a good idea."

"Mr. Ever-Ready turning me down? Should I be offended?"

"No, of course not, it's just...well...there are too many people around."

"That didn't bother you during the six other parties we snuck off at."

"I know, but...look, I really am feeling kind of bad. Maybe it's a virus or something."

"Want me to drive you home?"

"Nah, I'm gonna hang around and wait for Grandpa to show up."

She kissed me on the mouth. "You really do need to relax. And I have a really good way to relax you..."

"I'm sure you do."

"I've been naughty, sweetheart." She gestured to my punch. "I spiked it with a glass of wine I found upstairs in the den. You really do look like you need something to calm you down."

So, anyway, this explains why I've been such a party pooper.

A BITE FOR A BITE

"How many zombies outside?"

"Not sure," said Scott, peering out the window of the apartment. "Thirty, thirty-one, maybe."

Rick sighed. "Sorry I threw away my gun after it ran out of ammo. I had no idea you had more in your backpack."

"That's okay."

"I just didn't want to carry it around, you know? But I feel bad letting you do all the shooting. Maybe we'll find another gun somewhere."

"Maybe."

They sat in silence for a while.

"Know what I'd like to do?" Rick asked.

"What?"

"Eat one of those things. The same way they're eating us. Just take a great big bite out of one, to show 'em what it feels like."

"Why don't you?"

Rick shrugged. "Dunno."

"I'd like to see that."

"Nah."

"I'm serious." Scott stood up. "I'll drag one of them in here and hold him down while you dine away."

"Yeah, right."

Scott opened the door and peered outside. "Ooooh, there's a nice big fat one! He looks scrumptious!"

"What the hell are you doing, man? Close the door!"

"Sorry, you were watching your cholesterol, weren't you? Here, this one—" Scott stepped outside and returned a moment later holding an elderly zombie by the back of the neck "—looks perfect."

"Get it out of here!"

Scott kicked the door shut and threw the zombie to the floor. "Mmmmmmmm. Tasty."

"You're gonna get us killed!"

Scott knelt on the zombie's back, pinning it against the floor. It opened and closed its mouth, teeth scraping against the tile. "Get over here," Scott demanded.

"You've gone completely—"

"Get over here!" Scott shouted, pointing his pistol at Rick.

Rick slowly walked over to Scott and the writhing zombie. "Scott, c'mon, this isn't funny."

"You don't have to eat the whole thing if you don't like it," said Scott. "Just take two bites and I'll let you have dessert."

"But—"

"Eat, you incompetent piece of shit, before I put a bullet through your face!"

Rick knelt down, his entire body trembling, tears beginning to pour down his face. "I can't do it."

"Yes, you can. Just take a bite out of its arm."

"I'll get diseases!"

"Tough!"

Now sobbing openly, Rick opened his mouth and pressed his teeth against the zombie's upper arm.

"Bite it!"

"I can't break the skin!"

"Yes you can! Don't be such a fuckin' coward!"

Rick bit down harder. A gout of blood sprayed into his mouth. He gagged, spat it out, frantically wiped his mouth off on his sleeve, and scrambled away from the creature.

"That wasn't a bite."

"Fuck you, you sick—!"

The bullet pounded into Rick's forehead and exited through the back of his skull, taking plenty of brain matter with it.

Scott shot the zombie in the head as well, then stood up. He wandered into the kitchen to find a meat cleaver. He certainly wasn't enough of a freak to eat a zombie, but Rick would provide plenty of nourishment in the upcoming winter months.

GLIMPSES

Patricia stared at the odd new visitor. He was her size, which was a nice change of pace, but wasn't very communicative. He just sat on his mother's lap, bouncing a bit, staring at Patricia with a blank expression.

She tried again to speak to him. Nobody else seemed to understand her, but maybe he would.

He didn't.

Patricia's own mother made a loud sound of displeasure and carried her into the bathroom to change her diaper. It was about time.

«« — »»

"WAAAAHHHHHHHH!!!" sobbed Dennis, rushing through the back door, pants around his ankles. "Patti pulled my pants down! She did it on purpose!"

"I did not!" shouted Patricia from the backyard.

"Yes you did!" Dennis shouted back. "She did, Mom! An' Bobby was there an' Stacy was there an' the lady who sells us milk was there an' Kyle was there—"

"Kyle was *not* there," shouted Patricia.

"Calm down, honey," said Dennis's mother, crouching down beside him. "Did you really run all the way home from school with your pants down?"

"Uh-huh."

"Didn't you trip?"

"Uh-huh."

"Why didn't you pull them up, and then run home?"

"'Cause she pulled them down! On purpose!"

"I did not!" shouted Patricia.

Dennis's mother smiled. "You know, she only did this to you because she likes you."

"I do not!" shouted Patricia.

《《 — 》》

Dennis cracked his knuckles and waited for his prey. Soon she would arrive. Oh yes, very soon indeed.

"Admiral Tim, is the ammunition ready?" he asked his second-in-command.

"Aye-aye, sir," said Admiral Tim with a salute. "I have inspected all of the snowballs and they are ready for throwing, sir."

"Good work, Admiral. Give me three of the ice ones. No, make that two ice ones, and one with a rock in the middle."

"Aye-aye, sir," said Admiral Tim, selecting three prime specimens. "Sir! The target approaches!"

Dennis peeked over the top of the fort. Yes, there she was, ready for extermination. He hoisted the various snowballs in his hands, testing the weight, and decided to begin the assault with the rock snowball.

Target Patti was almost in range.

Almost...

Almost...

Fire!

Dennis flung the snowball, and his aim couldn't have been better. It struck her directly in the face, knocking off her glasses and making her drop her books. She screamed, threw her hands to her face, and ran crying down the sidewalk.

"Excellent shot, Captain!" said Tim.

Dennis bit his lip nervously as he watched her run away. He was pretty sure he'd given her a bloody nose. He hadn't meant to hit her in the face—well, yeah, he had, but he'd expected to feel better about it.

《《 — 》》

"Why would I want to do that, zit-boy?" asked Patti.

Dennis rolled his eyes and scratched at one of his pimples. "I'm not asking you to do anything big, just find out if she likes me."

"She hates your guts. All of 'em, even that long gooshy one under your stomach."

"She does not. She doesn't even know me. Look, all through fifth and sixth grade I passed out love notes to all those boys for you."

"But you refused to hold them down when I wanted to kiss them."

"C'mon, I just want you to find out if she likes me."

"Oh, all right."

"But don't let her know that I'm the one who wants to know."

"Well who *else* would want to know?"

"Just make her think *you* want to know."

"Why would I care?"

"Patti!"

"Okay, okay. I'll find out what I can. But I bet she hates your guts."

«« — »»

"Just leave me alone, okay?"

"Are you gonna be all right?"

Patti shook her head, sniffled loudly, then blew her nose again. "How come he had to be so *mean*?"

"'Cause he's a jerk." Dennis sat down on the floor next to her, leaning against the lockers.

"All I did was ask him to dance. He didn't have to be so mean about it. He could have just said no."

Dennis clenched his fists. When he'd seen Ted and his stuck-up friends laughing and pointing at Patti, he'd wanted to rush right over there and start throwing punches. Unfortunately, that would've been a good way to get killed.

Patti blew her nose once more. "Do you have another tissue?" she asked. "This one's full."

Dennis hurried over to the bathroom to get some paper towels. When he returned, Patti had stopped crying, though her face was still red and blotchy.

"Are you ready to go back in?" he asked.

"No. They'll just laugh at the fat girl again."

"You're not fat. They're just jerks."

"And I've got ugly hair."

"I'm not going to lie to you. You do have ugly hair. Don't comb it that way anymore."

Patti returned his grin and got to her feet. "I'm just going to walk home, I think."

"I'll dance with you, if you want."

Now her grin became an actual smile. "No way. I've seen you dance. But thanks for the offer!"

««—»»

"Dennis," said his mother, wearily, "will you *please* tell Patti that ringing the doorbell once is sufficient?"

Dennis got up from the dinner table and walked through the living room as the doorbell rang another dozen times. He swung the door open, and Patti burst inside, waving a piece of paper.

"I got accepted too! I just got the letter!" She shook the letter. "This one! This letter right here!"

"That's fantastic!" Dennis gave her a huge hug. "We should be roommates."

"Yeah, right," said Patti.

"Yeah, right," his mom agreed.

««—»»

"That was weird," said Patti, breaking the kiss.

"What was so weird about it?"

"I've always just sort of thought of you like a brother, y'know?"

"Well, yeah, when you say something like that you're sure making it weird."

Patti smiled and kissed him again. "It's a good weird. How long have you wanted to admit how you felt?"

"I dunno. Months. Years."

"That was silly. You passed up on years of kissing." She kissed him once more, letting it linger.

"When do we get to do more than kiss?"

"Soon?"

"When's soon?"

"When we're alone."

"Will you two horndogs please go someplace else to make out?" cried Patti's roommate. "I'm trying to study!"

««—»»

"How many times have you thrown up so far?"

"Three," Dennis admitted.

His brother Lee adjusted the tie on Dennis's tuxedo. "Three today, or three since I've been in town?"

"Three today. Seven since you've been in town."

"You don't have to go through with this, you know. I've got your escape route all planned. There's no shame in cold feet."

"It's not cold feet. I'll be okay. I'm just nervous."

"You know, marriage is a serious commitment. If you go through with this, you won't be able to get a divorce for at least six months, to avoid humiliating our family."

"I'm sure we can make it work for at least seven."

"There'll be a getaway car all fueled up and waiting outside the chapel, engine on, just in case. If at any point during the ceremony you're ready to bolt, give me the signal. Tap your nose with your thumb, then your index finger, then your pinky, three times each. We'll kill the lights and get you out of there before anybody knows what happened."

"You're a good brother."

"I know. This would be the part where I'd make some sappy comment about how lucky you are to have somebody like Patti and how I'm sure you'll be happy together forever, if I were the kind of guy who would make sappy comments like that, which I'm not and never will be. But I will say this: If you play your cards right, you'll probably get laid in Hawaii this weekend."

«« — »»

"So what does it do after you pee on it?"

"If I'm pregnant, it'll turn blue."

"Okay. How long does it take?"

"A couple of minutes."

"Okay."

"Should we do this?"

"Yeah. Do I need to be in there with you?"

"No, I can pee on my own."

"I know, I'm just...you know, showing support."

"We'll be fine either way, Dennis."

"I know. Okay."

Patti stepped into the bathroom and closed the door. Dennis tried not to fidget. Then he tried not to pace. Then he tried not to whimper.

The door opened.

"It's not blue."

"Are you sure?"

Patti held up the test. "See?"

"Oh, thank God. All hail the pregnancy test! I'd kiss it but I won't for obvious reasons. Wow, that was a close one, huh?"

"Yeah."

"Are you okay, honey? You look upset…"

««—»»

"Hey! I like that song!" Patti protested.

"Yeah, well, I'm driving, so it's my option to turn off crappy music."

"And it's my obligation to inform you that you have crappy taste in music."

"Duly noted. Are you sure we shouldn't have turned yet?"

"It says six miles."

"We've gone six miles."

"Right before the turn we should see a—*Dennis watch out!*"

There wasn't even time to swerve. Dennis slammed on the brakes an instant before the loud *thump*.

"Oh my God! Oh shit!"

"*You hit her! You hit her!*"

"Stop screaming!"

"*Stop the car!*"

"I *am* stopping the fucking car! Stop screaming at me! What the fuck was she doing out here?"

Dennis got out of the car and nearly collapsed as his knees went weak. He'd only taken his eyes off the road for a second. Not even a second. Oh God…

Patti threw open the door, got out of the vehicle, and let out a howl.

"Shut up!" Dennis shouted. "Don't make so much fucking noise!"

"*You killed her!*"

"*Shut up!*"

««—»»

"Oh, crap, the alarm didn't go off! I'm gonna be late for work!"

"Do you have any more sick days left?" asked Patti, opening one eye.

"No! I've got nothing! I'm gonna get *so* chewed out when I get there. Oh, jeez, I hope Stevens isn't in yet!"

«« — »»

"You okay?"

"Yeah."

"You sure."

Patti shrugged.

"It was six years ago."

"Could've been yesterday."

"Well, it wasn't yesterday. We never got caught."

"That's not the point."

"We can't let this destroy our lives."

"You don't even seem upset. You never seemed upset."

"I think about it every day! Every single day!"

"She was only five."

Dennis sighed. "We didn't do it on purpose. She shouldn't have been out there! It's not like I'd been drinking or was speeding or anything."

"Then why didn't we tell anyone?"

"Shit, Patti, we've been through this!"

"I know."

"Do you want to go to the cops now? Is that what you want? I'll do it! I'll call them right now!"

"No."

"Then what's wrong?"

"I'm allowed to be upset that we killed a little girl! You might have gotten over it, but I haven't! So I apologize if it inconveniences you that sometimes I feel sad about it!"

Dennis sat down next to her on the sofa. "Oh, Christ, honey, I'm so sorry. Let's talk about it, okay?"

«« — »»

"This show sucks," said Patti.

"So why are we watching it?"

"I dunno. Nothing better on."

"You're right. There's nothing good on TV these days."

"That's a sign of getting old, you know."

"What is?"

"Complaining that there's nothing good on TV."

"Crap. I'm old."

"Yep."

"Fetch me my colostomy bag."

"Fetch your own, Oldie."

«« — »»

"What were you doing?"

"I wasn't doing anything! Who said you could just barge in my office without knocking?"

Patti grabbed the faded newspaper clipping out of his hand. "Why do you have this? Why the hell did you keep this?"

"I...I don't know. I just did."

"I saw what you were doing!"

"I don't know what you're talking about."

"You most certainly *do* know what I'm talking about!"

"No, I don't. I was just sitting here looking at it."

"While you fondled yourself!"

"What? What are you talking about?"

"I saw you, Dennis."

Dennis shook his head. "Maybe I had my hand in my lap. So what? I have my hand in my lap all the time. Jesus Christ, what kind of sicko do you think I am?"

"That's what I want to know."

"Look, honey, yes, I kept the newspaper article without telling you. I'm sorry for that. It's just...it's just the worst thing I've ever done in my life, and I need to remind myself about it sometimes."

"You need to *remind* yourself? The last thing in the goddamn world I need to do is remind myself! Are you scared that you'll actually *forget* what we did? The memory isn't enough for you?"

"You don't understand."

"No, I don't."

"Just calm down. I apologize for keeping this from you. But I swear to God, whatever you think you saw me doing, you imagined it. You're really distraught. Why don't I get you a drink?"

"I don't need a drink! I need an explanation!"

«« — »»

"Oh, yeah! Oooh, that feels great. Oh, damn, it feels *too* great—slow down!"

"Mmmmmmm-mmmmm."

"I can't hold out any more...this is it, baby..."

"Mmmmmmmmmmm."

Dennis collapsed onto the bed, gasping. "Wow. That was...wow."

"Happy 40th birthday, stud."

"Thanks."

"Does Patti ever do that?"

"Not anymore."

"Too bad for her."

"Can we not talk about Patti?"

"It's your money. We can talk about whatever you want. What do you want to talk about, birthday stud?"

《《 — 》》

"This is the best spaghetti you've ever made."

"Is it?"

"Yeah. Did you use a different kind of sauce?"

"No, same stuff as always. But I bought the ground beef from that new place next to work."

"That must be it," said Dennis, taking another huge bite. "It's delicious."

Patti beamed. "Well, thank you!"

《《 — 》》

"Where were you today?" Patti asked.

"At work. Where else would I be?"

"They said you called in sick."

"I didn't call in sick; I had an offsite meeting. Who did you talk to?"

"A couple of people."

"Who?"

"It doesn't matter. Where were you?"

"At a meeting in the other building! What are you doing checking up on me?"

"I wasn't checking up on you; I was calling you."

"Well, I don't know who gave you incorrect information, but you need to be less paranoid."

"I know about the other one."

"What?"

"I found the pictures."

"I don't know anything about any pictures. There's nobody else, honey. I love *you*."

"You know what I'm talking about. And I know about the car you stole. Please don't lie to me."

Dennis was silent for a long moment. "Are you going to call the police?"

"I don't know what I'm going to do."

««—»»

Dennis lay in the motel room's uncomfortable bed, eyes closed.

He smiled as he remembered the sound of the car hitting the little girl. He'd been horrified, but excited at the same time.

And then the little boy.

Only two. That's all he'd killed.

He could've killed more. He could've killed a lot more. Didn't she understand that?

I love you, but if I ever see you again, I'll call the police. Bitch. He could call the cops on her. She'd kept the first one a secret, just like he had. Nice surprise she'd get, if the cops showed up at her door asking about poor Bethany Taylor.

He relived Bethany's final moment over and over, thanking God that his bitch wife wasn't around to walk in on him.

««—»»

"Fifty isn't too old to be a new bride!"

"I'm fifty-one."

"You're barely fifty-one. Do you love him?"

Patti nodded.

"Then reel this one in, fast!"

"I'm still not sure."

"Well, I'm sure, and as your best friend I know what's best for you. Say yes. He's a total sweetie and he treats you great."

"But he's fifteen years younger than me!"

"So what?"

"It's weird!"

"He's thirty-five years old! It's not like you're marrying a kid! It's time for you to be happy again, Patti."

"You're right."

"Of course I'm right."

"I'll call him now."

"Don't call him. Invite him over. I'll leave."

«« — »»

Dennis wiped the blood from his nostrils as he looked through the shattered windshield. The little boy was running off to get help.

Shit...

Dennis had swore he'd never do it again, both to Patti and to himself. And he meant it. He had his memories.

But he'd been driving, and the little boy rushed onto the edge of the road to grab the basketball, and—

One quick swerve.

The boy had been quicker.

Dennis had been going about thirty miles per hour when he struck the parked truck, and he wasn't wearing a seatbelt. He'd bashed into the steering wheel with his chest and the dashboard with the forehead.

He'd live.

Maybe.

But he sure wouldn't stay awake much longer.

He reached for the glove compartment. It would be bad, real bad, if the cops saw the pictures inside.

He lost consciousness before he could open it.

«« — »»

Patti sat on her bed, staring at the newspaper clippings. Dozens of them. The oldest was from six years ago. The newest was from this morning's edition.

Dozens of children.

Dennis had been in prison for the past seven years. She never visited him. She'd barely left the house since the trial.

Charles begged her to seek help, but she couldn't.

She didn't deserve help.

Dozens of innocent children she should have protected.

"*All my fault...*" she whispered, running her fingers over the newspaper clippings.

Children from all over the country.

Children she'd never even seen.

When Charles came home from work that evening, she was still staring at them.

COMMON SENSE

There were a million good reasons why I shouldn't steal the Idol of Trychen, the legendary cursed voodoo relic that had gruesomely taken the lives of all who dared touch its bloodstained surface.

So I didn't.

GROSS-OUT!

Story notes for the other tales in this collection are at the back of the book. This one, on the other hand, requires some up-front discussion...

Each year, the World Horror Convention features a gross-out contest, where classy folks share the most disgusting, depraved, putrescent, vile tales imaginable. The whole event is foul beyond compare, but it's, y'know, a *good* kind of foul beyond compare. Unless, of course, you're one of those whiners who's all like "It's casting our genre in a negative light! It's casting our genre in a negative light! Waah! Waah!"

Anyway, in 2005 I had no plans to participate in the gross-out contest. I figured I'd just watch, see what it was all about, and participate the following year. But famous author Brian Keene, who was hosting that year, *forced* me to participate. I didn't have anything gross prepared, so I simply read my non-gross story "Really, Really Ferocious" and added the following coda: "And then the old man went back into his house, where he slurped a quart of pus from Brian Keene's open mouth."

I did not win. But the audience loved the story.

In 2006, I was actually prepared, and I read the following tale...

<<< — >>>

Your teenage years are awkward enough without discovering that you've acquired a taste for vomit. But that's what happened to me. While I was kissing my first true love, Melissa Pacione, my freakishly long tongue danced across her uvula, and suddenly I had myself a mouthful of regurgitation.

"Don't swallow it! Don't swallow it!" Melissa cried out, but it was like getting a second helping of the scrumptious meatloaf we'd eaten for dinner. I gulped it down and thanked her. Melissa ran away as if *I* had barfed in *her* mouth, and I never saw her again.

Having discovered this new element of my personality, I became an enthusiastic consumer of upchuck. I'd fill a wheelbarrow with cheap liquor, push it down under the bridge where all the homeless people lived, and just let them drink themselves into a puking frenzy. I had to be quick to get my mouth under the foamy spew in time, and sometimes choice chunks got away from me, and sometimes I had to suffer the indignity of lapping it up off the ground, but still, I was content.

But after a couple of weeks, I realized that an addiction to homeless wino puke just wasn't what I wanted out of life. I tried vomiting into a beer mug and drinking that, and with a touch of garlic salt it was actually pretty tasty…but I knew deep inside that drinking your own vomit is kind of sick.

So I hung around bars, and doctor's offices during stomach flu season, and this Greek restaurant that had a generous expiration date policy on its meat, but while it was tasty, none of it gave me the rush as when I'd drank from Melissa. And then it hit me: I enjoyed puke the most when it came from somebody I loved.

I loved my mother.

"That's so sweet of you to pick up dinner," she said, opening the take-out Chinese food container. She took a quick whiff. "Oooh, this smells kind of rancid."

"It's a new recipe," I said.

"What's that green stuff floating in the egg-drop soup?"

"Green eggs. It's a Dr. Seuss promotion."

We had a lovely dinner, and I waited for the precious moment when I could gulp down some mom-vomit from the point of origin…but nothing happened! For dessert I gave her a mixture of spoiled milk, Listerine, and ancient tuna, and then I waited and waited but the bitch didn't even belch!

Now, you're probably going to judge me on this, but you would have done the same thing in my situation. I bashed her over the head with a crowbar, ripped open her belly with the tuna can lid, and thrust my face into her stomach to slurp away at the slightly digested meal. I dove so deep that stomach fluids seeped into my ears. I guzzled that unpuked puke like it was a cold beer on a hot summer day, and when I'd drank my fill I gargled a mouthful, spat it back into her gut, and then blew bubbles in it, mainly to lighten the mood and ease the post-matricide guilt trip.

After it was over, I felt…unfulfilled.

That's when I discovered that a) incest was overrated, b) necrophilia was underrated, and c) going at it with the lower intestine doesn't require lubrication.

But that, my friends, is another story.

«« — »»

It's worth noting that this charming saga was about .007% as gross as the average gross-out contest entry. The 2006 winner, Cullen Bunn, had more grossness in one sentence than I did in my entire story. There's something very wrong with Cullen. Avoid him.

Still, I came in third place and won a banana-flavored gummi slug, which I still have. If you ever come over to my house I'll let you lick it. (It's still in the original packaging, so that's not as much fun as it sounds.)

For 2007, I was determined to finally win the gross-out contest but—*spoiler warning*—I didn't. In fact, I came in third again. And I was still .007% as gross as the other participants when I read this story...

«« — »»

T'was a fine summer eve as I knelt behind my betrothed, making love to her in the style of the canine. It was a celebration of sorts, commemorating the one month anniversary of my providing oral pleasure without a dental dam, and because of this, I'd been allowed to enter the "special occasions" orifice.

As I thrust away in a most merry manner, I noticed that the pleasurable tightness this orifice previously offered was lacking. I also questioned the quantity of moisture therein, which seemed to be a substantial increase from previous sessions.

I gazed downward at my engorged phallus in motion, and let out a gasp of astonishment at the sight that met my eyes. The orifice that I was so gleefully boning, and the lower, more traditionally used orifice, had become one and the same!

"Gracious!" I cried, so startled that I was almost compelled to stop thrusting. "What madness is this? Instead of your typical division of feminine entrances I see but a gaping, glistening gorge!"

"Don't stop!" she pleaded.

My pelvis complied with her request. A foul discharge with the appearance of bloody egg yolk and the scent of mayonnaise past its prime squirted out of her, splattering all over my wooly mat of pubic hair.

"What has happened here?" I inquired. "Am I to understand that you've been afflicted with crotch rot?"

My beloved gazed back at me. "Harder!"

I thrust harder. A fountain of milky brown fluid sprayed into the air as if she'd sprung a leak. I clutched at her cheeks of passion and recoiled as they split apart, accompanied by a jettison of thick sticky feces-tainted love juice that covered my body. I spat out that which I hadn't swallowed, and tried to withdraw.

"No! You mustn't!"

"This is no longer pleasurable!" I insisted. "My erection drips with matter both runny and in chunks, but yet encounters no resistance while inside your body! It is as if I am penetrating a large leaking echoing tube! I shall never attain my climax in this fashion!"

"Give it to me, bitch!" she demanded.

And so I did. With my next powerful thrust, her buttocks burst in an explosion of yellow fatty blobs. I thrust repeatedly, ignoring the bones and organs that broke apart in my wake by thinking about baseball. As I fornicated my way through her body, my knees slipped on some intestine and I nearly lost my balance, but I kept going like the man that I am. Finally, my penis protruded from her open mouth, in the opposite direction to which we were accustomed.

I stared at the remains of the woman in my life, which soaked the bedsheets, and felt great sorrow. But at least she came first for once.

«« — »»

That ending was a last-minute addition, because my original plan was to end the story with "...and felt great sorrow...and great shame...and great misery...and great woe..." and so on until my time was up and the bouncers forcibly dragged me from the stage. But two other contestants who went before me also used the trick of being dragged off-stage against their will, so I needed an actual ending.

I'd write a better one for this collection, but then I'd be compromising the integrity of my gross-out contest entry, and I'm sure you'd want no part of that.

BAD COFFEE

As Richard sipped from his mug, he noticed that the coffee was a bit...off. Not off in a "Dear God, what wretched vile cretin brewed this foul sludge?" way, and not off in a way that would cause him to make obnoxious gagging sounds and spit the coffee out onto a household pet, but just...off.

He ventured another sip. Nope. Not good coffee. Still, he'd cheerfully slurp peat moss if it had enough caffeine, so he wasn't going to complain. In the future, he'd simply avoid buying ridiculously inexpensive coffee beans from sinister looking people on the street.

As he gulped down some more, a small pink tongue flicked out of his reflection at the bottom of the mug.

With a loud gasp, Richard pulled the cup away from his mouth. He spent a few moments nearly choking to death, spent a few more moments recovering from nearly having choked to death, and then spent some additional moments convincing himself that he had not, in fact, seen a tongue in his mug.

He peeked again. The tongue protruded from his reflection and splashed around in the coffee. As he watched in horror, it rolled itself up lengthwise and blew bubbles in the liquid. Then, with a fast licking motion, it flung some of the coffee into his eye.

Richard dropped the mug, which struck the kitchen floor but did not break. He dabbed at his eye with the bottom of his shirt as he tried to figure out how to handle the situation. Running around the house letting out girlish shrieks was the most appealing option, but Richard decided to try something a bit more masculine.

The mug rested on its side. Richard crouched down on the kitchen floor and peered into the mug from several feet away. From here, he could vaguely see his reflection...

…and the tongue shot out like that of a frog, sticking to the center of his forehead. The mug followed as if attached to a rubber band, flying across the floor and smacking him in the face. The tongue licked Richard's nose and then retreated back into the mug.

Richard let out one of the girlish shrieks.

He hurriedly got to his feet and kicked the mug as hard as he could. It flew against the oven and shattered, spraying drops of coffee and shards of glass everywhere. The tongue squirmed through the wreckage, moving toward him.

Richard ran forward and slammed his fuzzy-slipper-covered foot down but missed.

The tongue flapped at him.

Richard decided that after he squished the tongue, he'd say something like "How did *that* taste?" He stomped several times but the tongue continued to wiggle out of the way.

Finally he got the tip of it under his slipper, and then crushed the rest of it with his other foot, smiling at the satisfying *splat*. Instead of his witty comment, he settled for a primal scream of victory.

He'd learned his lesson. He would never, ever buy cheap coffee again.

«« — »»

And deep beneath the city of Seattle, in a luxurious bunker, Starbucks executives laughed and laughed and laughed.

WEREWOLF PORNO

"Fluffer!"

Carl watched the silicone-enhanced blonde let out an annoyed sigh, shove a bookmark into her copy of *Women Who Do Too Much*, and walk across the set. Without a word she knelt down in front of Teddy "Third-Leg" Tracer and went to work.

This was Carl's first time on the set of an adult motion picture, and he was still getting used to the fact that people could be standing around looking bored while an attractive woman performed oral sex. Most of them weren't even watching! He wanted to shout "Hey, you jaded idiots, there's a hot chick in a thong bikini giving a blowjob here! What the hell is your problem? Gape, already!"

Even Teddy didn't seem all that interested in what was happening below his waist. Carl, who had never gotten oral pleasure that didn't receive his 100% undivided attention, wanted to slap the guy with one of the strap-ons that had been used in the previous scene.

"Let's go, let's go!" shouted the director, Garry Ecks. "Time is money!"

The fluffer pulled her mouth away from Teddy, which took a moment. "If you're in such a big hurry, *you* suck it."

Garry ignored the comment and turned his attention to the lead actress. "Darla, dammit, if you don't quit moving I'm going to weld your knees to that mattress! We're on a tight schedule here!"

Darla Duncan was one of the rising stars of the adult entertainment world. She was nineteen years old and had skyrocketed to fame after starring in the incredibly popular reality porn series *Darla Dares*, where she'd pick up random guys off the street and perform whatever acts they dared her to do (they were usually naughty). Less than half an hour ago, Carl had learned that the "random" guys were in fact paid actors and that the entire series was completely scripted. A little bit of light had faded from his world.

Darla was currently on her hands and knees on the bed. She shifted positions long enough to give Garry the finger. He glared at her, glared at a few random crew members for no apparent reason, then glared at Teddy. "Are you ready yet?"

Teddy gave him a thumbs-up sign. "Hard as molten steel, baby."

"Molten steel is melted steel, dipshit," said the fluffer.

"No, it's not. It's rock-hard steel."

"No, it's steel in liquid form. In times of yore, blacksmiths would pour it into molds to create weapons and tools for use by the populace."

Teddy frowned. "Huh?"

"Goddammit, stop confusing my star!" Garry shouted.

"Since when the fuck is *he* the star?" Darla demanded.

"Enough!"

"It's my name selling DVDs, not his!"

"I said enough!"

Teddy put his hand on the fluffer's head and chuckled. "Here, babe, create my weapon for use by the...uh..."

"Put your hand on me again and I'll gnaw your dick off."

"Enough! Enough! Enough! Enough! Enough! Enough! Enough! Enough! Enough! Enough!" Garry's face looked almost fluorescent red and Carl worried that his brains might pop out of his head like a money shot. "We're on a tight schedule here and we don't have time for this! Teddy, are you good to go or not?"

"My weapon is ready, baby."

"Then get on the goddamn bed! You need to get in there, come, and get out so we can set up the orgy! Is everybody ready to go? You all damn well better be ready to go! *Action!*"

Teddy climbed on the bed behind Darla, grabbed her by the hips, and thrust his extremely ample manhood into her. They went at it for a few moments until Garry shouted "*Cut!*"

"Cut? What do you mean, cut?" asked Darla.

"Could you please try to pretend that you're getting some pleasure out of this? He's not defragmenting your hard drive, he's screwing you! Act like you're getting screwed! Put on your 'I'm getting screwed' face, for fuck's sake!"

"Should I pull out?" asked Teddy.

"Yes! Pull out! We're gonna start over!"

Teddy withdrew and got off the bed. Darla gave Garry the finger again.

"Keep it up and by this time tomorrow you'll be turning twenty dollar tricks at the geriatric ward," said Garry. "Are we still taping? Let's go, let's go, let's go! Teddy, are you ready?"

"Hell yeah. I'm gonna defragment her hard drive, baby."

"You are *such* a dumbass," the fluffer informed him.

"Shut up, everyone! *Action!*"

Teddy got back on the bed and re-entered Darla. Carl didn't notice any real change in her demeanor, but Garry seemed satisfied and stopped shouting for a few minutes.

Jeez, he's good, Carl thought as Teddy pounded into her over and over at a staggering pace. God, and he had at least three inches on Carl, possibly four. (Carl didn't have a ruler handy, nor was he willing to endure the socially awkward situation of asking Teddy to submit to a measurement, particularly when his penis was busy.) The first tremors of performance anxiety started to form in the pit of his stomach.

Garry had assured him that his lack of a gargantuan phallus was okay, and that he wouldn't be expected to go at it like a seasoned porn star. "You'll just lie there; she'll do all the work," the director had explained. "As long as the moon does the trick, we'll have ourselves the ultimate porno flick, a bestiality masterpiece beyond anything the world has ever seen!"

Carl was a werewolf. Once a month, on the night of the full moon, he'd lock himself in his basement, transform into a snarling, howling beast, scrape the hell out of the concrete walls, and then return to human form by morning. He always took precautions and he'd never killed anybody, not even the neighbor's cat. He'd been bitten three years ago, during a camping trip that had been rather pleasant and relaxing until the gory werewolf attack. Though the first few months had been kind of rough, these days it was really not much more than a minor inconvenience, sort of like menstruation.

Of course, referring to menstruation as a "minor inconvenience" was why he was single these days. Still, he stood by his comparison.

Several weeks ago, he'd been laid off when his job at the insurance company's call center was outsourced to India. He'd been working there seven years, since he was eighteen, and it was the only full-time job he'd ever held. Devastated, he'd wandered around the city for a while, hoping that upbeat music on his iPod would lift his spirits. It didn't, so he decided to get really drunk instead.

In the bar, he'd met Garry Ecks. They'd chatted for a while about how much life sucked. Carl had never met a genuine pornographer before, but was too embarrassed to ask most of the questions on his mind, though he did inquire if the cameramen ever had to wear protective raingear (no).

As Carl officially drank one more beer than he should have, he said "Did I tell you I'm a werewolf?"

"Are you, now?" Garry looked amused.

"Yep." Carl held up his palm, revealing the pentagram.

"Damn. You carve that yourself?"

Carl shook his head. "It's real."

"So did they fire you for being a werewolf?"

"Nah, nobody at work knew. It only happens on the night of the full moon, but they'd probably have gotten all paranoid about me transforming during work hours and mauling the other employees and stuff."

"That could be a definite Human Resources issue."

"Not that it matters now, anyway," said Carl, shoving his half-empty bottle of beer aside. "I didn't even get a good severance package."

"I'm sure there are plenty of job opportunities for a lycanthrope," said Garry. "Maybe you could endorse a brand of hairball medicine."

"You don't believe me, do you?"

"Do you mean about the werewolf thing? Not really."

"Why would I lie about something like that?"

"You're drunk and desperate for attention."

Carl got off the wobbly stool and stood on wobbly legs. "I taped it once. I set the camera down in the basement and made a video of the whole thing. Well, not the *whole* thing—I sorta smashed up the camera after my transformation—but I salvaged the tape and I've got it at my apartment."

"Is that so?"

"Wanna see it?"

Garry stared at him for a long moment. Technically, three Garrys stared at him for a long moment with their six eyes, but Carl figured this was a side-effect of the alcohol.

"Sure."

They'd gone back to Carl's place. Carl popped the tape into the VCR and pressed play. An image of Carl kneeling on the floor of the basement appeared on the television screen. He was wearing a t-shirt and white boxer shorts.

"Usually I'm naked," he explained. "It doesn't make sense to put on clothes that are just going to get shredded when I transform. But I didn't want to be naked on the tape, you know, in case I ever sold this to television or anything, I didn't want them to have to blur out anything, and I also thought that it would, you know, be kind of embarrassing to have lots of people watch a video where you can see everything. Not that you would mind—I mean, you see naked guys all the time, I guess, not that I'm hitting on you or anything, I'm just babbling because I'm intoxicated, but anyway—"

"Let's just watch the video," Garry said.

"Yes, sir."

Carl fast-forwarded through a few minutes of him just sitting there, letting the tape resume when he began to twitch on-camera. "See, that's where the full moon is starting to affect me."

"Moonlight doesn't need to shine right on you?"

"Nope. It happens right at midnight."

"Ah. Good to know."

Garry frowned as the tape showed Carl falling into the fetal position. As the first strands of black fur formed on Carl's chest, Garry flinched. Carl grinned an inebriated grin as the pornographer leaned closer to the television screen, watching every detail of Carl's transformation. He thrashed around, screaming in pain as fangs grew, bones changed shape, and body hair sprouted like puberty gone terribly wrong. Within two minutes he was a full wolf. The last image was of his jaws closing over the camera lens.

"Holy shit!" said Garry, jumping to his feet. "That wasn't CGI! I know CGI, and that wasn't it! You're a werewolf!"

"Duh, that's what I said."

"Oh my God, oh my God, oh my God, this is incredible! This is amazing! You're not going to mutilate me, are you?"

Carl shook his head. "Full moon's not for another two weeks."

Garry began to pace around the room. "I'm gonna make you a star. Forget the Paris Hilton and Pamela Anderson videos—this will be the greatest porn sensation of all time! Picture it: We get the hottest porn star in the business, and she fucks you—yes, you—while you turn into a werewolf!"

"I beg your pardon?"

"It will be the ultimate event in adult entertainment! The 'chicks doing dogs' audience will freak out over it, but the crossover potential is astounding!"

"I'm not a porn actor," Carl explained.

"Oh, but you will be!"

"I don't think I can do that."

"Yes, you can. You have a dick, right?"

Carl nodded.

"And you've inserted it into a vagina before, right?"

"I guess so."

"What do you mean, you guess so? That's an event that most people remember. It's one of the first things you see when you go south of the belly button. You can't miss it. You a virgin?"

"No, no, I've been with a couple of girls; I just don't have a lot of experience."

"A couple? Two?"

"Yeah."

"Just two?"

"Yeah."

"That's it?"

"Sorry."

"That's inhuman. You'd think you'd screw more women than that just by accident."

Carl shrugged.

"Are we talking two insertions total, or two long-term girlfriends? Or are you divorced?"

"Two sort-of long-term girlfriends."

"All right, I guess that makes sense," said Garry. "Well, no it doesn't, but whatever. This is gonna be fantastic. One unbroken shot. First you're inside her as a man, then you're inside her as a wolf!"

"We can't do that," Carl insisted. "When I turn into a werewolf, the animal part completely takes over. I try to kill things."

"We probably shouldn't have you kill anybody; that's a whole different sub-genre. We'll just strap you down. Muzzle you. It'll play to the BDSM audience."

"I don't know…"

"You're unemployed, aren't you?"

"Yeah, but I was thinking about applying at Prudential or something."

"Prudential won't squash Darla Duncan's tits against your face. We are going to make adult film history, Carl. Werewolf porn. How the hell can you top that?"

And now Carl was on the movie set, waiting nervously for his big scene. He'd turned Garry down that night, and the following day, and the day after that. But Garry kept increasing the money offer…and it was Darla Duncan! Carl had spent many a lonely night over the past year pretending that his hand was Darla's mouth, and now he'd be with her for real.

"Ooooooooohhhhhhhhhh," Teddy moaned, pulling out and proving that his orgasm was the work of a method actor.

"Cut!" shouted Garry. "Teddy, good job. Darla, get yourself cleaned up for the next scene."

"Yeah, yeah, whatever."

"All right, let's get Carl in his restraints and get the orgy people in here! Let's go, let's go, midnight is approaching!"

Suddenly Carl felt like he was going to throw up and wasn't sure if he could really go through with this. He wasn't a porn star. His pelvis couldn't thrust as rapidly as Teddy's.

"Right here," said one of the stagehands, beckoning him over. Carl reluctantly walked to his spot, wishing that he'd never gotten drunk, had never shown off the werewolf tape, had never agreed to appear in a porno flick, and had never walked over to the spot where the stagehand beckoned him.

A line of attractive and extremely naked people, five men and five women, walked onto the set. Carl wasn't entirely sure of the plot significance (it was not a tightly constructed screenplay), but they'd all be having sex in the background as part of some sort of ritual, while Darla rode him in the foreground during the transformation.

"Strip 'em off," the stagehand said, pointing to Carl's boxers.

"Now?"

"Uh, yeah. These days, they try to include nudity in porn films."

"You don't have to be sarcastic." Carl removed his boxers and stood there naked, hoping that nobody was staring at his inferior genitalia. He listened for telltale snickers but heard none.

"On your back," said the stagehand.

Carl lay on the mattress, which was covered with red sheets that in some way figured into whatever the ritual was (again, the screenplay was not totally clear on this issue). Three more guys joined the stagehand, and they quickly chained Carl's arms and legs to the floor. The wrist and ankle bands were made out of some kind of rubber that would stretch to fit his werewolf proportions at the appropriate time, but would not allow him to pull free.

"Are you sure that's tight enough?" asked Darla, poking at one of the restraints with her toe.

"Don't worry, he's not going anywhere," the stagehand assured her.

"Orgy people! Start screwing!" Garry shouted. "We're ten minutes away!"

As the naked people began to touch, nibble, lick, and penetrate each other, the stagehand slid the protective mask over Carl's head. It was clear plastic, sort of shaped like a lopsided astronaut helmet, and would allow everybody to see Carl's head transform into a werewolf head while preventing him from biting Darla's face off.

"He's good to go," the stagehand announced.

"Perfect!" said Garry. "We've got five minutes! Darla, do your thing!"

"He's not hard."

"Carl, get hard!" Garry shouted.

"I'm not sure I can," Carl admitted.

"What the sweet fuck do you mean you're not sure you can? *Fluffer!*"

The fluffer sighed, marked her spot again, walked over, and knelt down next to Carl. She put her face in his lap and took him into her mouth.

Carl was so nervous that he could barely feel it. *Think hard thoughts. Steel towers. Concrete blocks. Guns. Anvils. Bananas...no, no, bananas are soft, you idiot! Think of marble statues. Trains.*

Or, perhaps—here was a novel idea!—he could think about the blowjob-in-progress. That seemed like a much more efficient course of action.

"Goddamnit, I'm not seeing any bulges in your cheek!" Garry shouted.

The fluffer opened her mouth, and Carl's limp penis flopped back against his testicles. "Nothing's happening."

"So suck with more enthusiasm and skill! What the hell are we paying you for?"

The fluffer rolled her eyes and resumed her head-bobbing.

Relax...just relax...enjoy the way her tongue swirls with expert precision, despite her surly attitude...

"We're running out of time!" Garry screamed. "Get that thing in a fuckable state in the next thirty seconds or you'll never fluff in this town again!"

"You can't build the Empire State Building out of wet noodles," said the fluffer.

"It would actually kind of help if you didn't say things like that," Carl pointed out.

"Darla! Get down there and help out!"

"That's *her* job!"

"I don't give a rat's ass! We need a goddamn erection here! Orgy ladies, get over there! Everybody take a quadrant!"

Carl lay there, not quite able to believe that he now had several hot

naked women running their tongues over him…and he couldn't get it up!
He should have suspected that this would turn into a cruel joke. His penis
had always hated him, and now it was wreaking its penile vengeance.

"What can I do?" Garry asked. "Would it help if Teddy went down
there, too?"

"Hey!" Teddy protested. "I'm not queer!"

"You'll be queer if I tell you to! This is more important than your
homophobia! We're making cinematic history here! Get over there and
suck his cock!"

"I won't do it!"

"The hell you won't!"

"That won't help!" Carl insisted. "It'll make things worse, I promise.
Lots worse."

He closed his eyes. *Relax…imagine that you're on a desert island,
surrounded by naked women…*

He opened his eyes so he could better see the naked women that were
right there. God, this was dumb.

"I felt a twitch!" one of the orgy ladies proclaimed.

"You mean it?" Garry asked.

"A definite twitch!"

"I felt it, too!" said the fluffer.

"Keep doing what you're doing! Don't lose the momentum!"

"It's growing! It's growing!"

"Perfect!" Garry rubbed his hands together in glee. "Orgy ladies —
back to your original spots! It's almost midnight!"

As Darla and the fluffer continued to vigorously work on him, Carl
grew and grew. Yes! Nothing cured impotence like seven female tongues!

"Fluffer! Get the hell out of the shot! We're gonna start filming!"

The fluffer left. Darla squatted on top of Carl and eased herself onto
his mighty erection. It felt pretty darn good.

He'd expressed concerns about the upcoming size increase, but Garry
had assured him that Darla could handle it. "Are you bigger than a fire
extinguisher?" he'd asked.

"No."

"Then it's cool."

Carl lay there, watching Darla bounce, thinking that maybe he could
get used to the porn star life, even without the whole werewolf angle.

"It's midnight!" Garry announced.

For a moment, Carl was too distracted by the feeling of being inside
Darla Duncan to notice the familiar tingles. But then the tingles quickly

turned to pain, and he helplessly watched his chest become much more hairy.

"Ooooh, baby, if I have to shave, so you do," said Darla, reading off a cue card.

Carl's nails extended and there was the usual agony as his bones began to change shape. Darla bounced faster.

She giggled as his penis transformed inside of her.

The band holding his right wrist snapped.

Oops...that's probably not good...

The band holding his left wrist snapped.

Bad...really, really bad..herpes bad...

He tried to call out a warning, but it came out as a growl.

Shit!

Darla was gasping with pleasure and thrusting so hard that she didn't seem to notice the major safety issue.

Is nobody paying attention? Any second now the wolf is gonna take over and—

Carl slammed his paws against Darla's head, jamming five claws into each side. She stopped bouncing as he twisted his paws, giving her a makeshift facial reconstruction. Blood poured onto his furry chest and he could smell it even through the plastic mask.

Hungry...so hungry...

He released his grip on her head. Darla, still impaled upon him, slumped forward as Carl tore off the mask. Jaws free, he took a great big bite out of her face.

Lots of naked people screamed.

《《 — 》》

Garry figured his career was pretty much fucked as the werewolf pounced onto the orgy participants. The men's erections had all vanished, and within a few moments so had three of the five penises. He stared in shock as the werewolf rapidly mauled them, sending blood, chunks of flesh, and silicone implants flying into the air.

"Do something!" Teddy cried.

"What the hell do you want me to do?"

"Kill it! You're the director!"

"With what?"

Carl the Psycho Werewolf bit off somebody's arm, which looked like it really hurt. He swallowed it in two gulps.

"A silver bullet!"

"Did you bring one?"

"No! Why would *I* bring one?"

Garry cringed. One of the cutest asses in the porn business wasn't quite so cute anymore.

"I don't know! Foresight, maybe?"

"How could you be so irresponsible as to bring a live werewolf in here with no way to kill it?"

"It wasn't supposed to get away!"

"Well, it did!"

"I know that!"

Carl was dining on the intestines of one of the actresses. Garry thought of a really funny "eating her out" joke, and then felt guilty about it.

"So why weren't you prepared?" Teddy demanded.

"I was prepared! Just not prepared enough!"

"I'm gonna sue your ass!"

"Why are *you* gonna sue? You're not the one getting devoured!"

"Mental anguish!"

"Screw you!"

Garry had to admit, he did feel rather foolish for setting up this film shoot without bringing a way to terminate the werewolf if things got out of hand. But that was neither here nor there at this point.

"Did you even have insurance for this?" Teddy asked.

"Of course!" Garry lied.

Carl stepped over the corpses of the orgy participants, then rushed across the room and took down one of the stagehands. The stagehand wailed in terror and agony, but stopped when the werewolf tore out his throat.

BANG!

The werewolf howled and turned around, snarling.

BANG! BANG! BANG!

The fluffer fired three more shots into the creature. It let out a loud whimper and then flopped over on its side. Garry, Teddy, the fluffer, and the remaining living crew members stared at it for a long moment.

"Is it dead?" Teddy asked.

"Go kick it and see," the fluffer said.

Teddy did so. The werewolf wasn't dead. The fluffer fired a shot into its heart, and then a mercy shot into Teddy's forehead, knowing that he wouldn't want to live without his leg.

The werewolf transformed back into human form. Carl lay dead on the floor, riddled with bullet holes. Garry couldn't help but feel a little bit sorry for the poor kid, but at least he'd gotten laid before he died. That's how Garry would've wanted to go.

"Well, that sucked," said Garry.

The fluffer sighed. "You think?"

"We...we don't have to spread word about my negligence, right? I mean, how was I supposed to know he was telling the truth about being a werewolf? I thought he was some whacko off the street."

"I think we can work out a deal," said the fluffer. "But you're cleaning up the mess."

«« — »»

Blood Orgy Rampage of the Werewolf, featuring the farewell performance of Darla Duncan, was the #1 bestselling underground DVD of the year.

AN ADMITTEDLY RATHER POINTLESS BUT MERCIFULLY BRIEF STORY WITH ALIENS IN IT

"AAAAAAAHHHHHHHHH!!!" I remarked, as the aliens began to take over the world. I knew I was being less than macho, hiding behind a trash can while dozens of people became extremely disintegrated, but I'd spent countless hours in therapy coming to terms with the fact that I was a pathetic little coward, and I wasn't about to let that time go to waste.

Suddenly, I heard the unmistakable sound of a Deadly Fatal Ray of Doom, and the trash can vaporized, spilling its less-than-pleasantly-fragrant contents all over me. Fortunately I'd stopped saying "AAAAAAAHHHHHHHHH!!!" just moments ago or I would have gotten a mouthful of very, very, very old scrambled eggs.

"Surrender, human weenie!" said the alien standing in front of me. Well, that was the basic gist, anyway. They communicated by inhaling and exhaling streams of mucus, so I'd never taken much of an interest in learning their language.

But then I felt something deep inside, sort of like when I'd tried to gargle dish soap (bad idea, don't do it), but more dramatic. I was not going to let this alien scum push me around. This was *my* planet, and no snot-speaking invaders from another world were going to take it from me!

It took me about two seconds to get over that particular delusion of grandeur, and I held up my arms in surrender. So, the aliens have taken over the world, and the ultimate fate of the human race is to spend eternity being dressed up in silly, gender-inappropriate clothes and dancing for their amusement. At least we still have computer games.

MUNCHIES

[*SCENE: A restaurant. Cindy and John are seated, looking over the menus.*]

CINDY: Have you ever come here before?

JOHN: Actually, about once a week. It's very good.

[*The waiter approaches.*]

WAITER: Are you ready to order?

CINDY [*to John*]: I'm still looking. You go right ahead.

JOHN: I'll have the ten-layer lasagna.

WAITER: Very good, sir.

CINDY: I have a question about the spaghetti.

WAITER: Yes?

CINDY: The meat sauce…is it made with human flesh?

WAITER [*long pause*]: No, ma'am.

CINDY: Oh good. I'll have that then.

WAITER: Excellent choice, ma'am.

CINDY: Because if there's anything I'm not, it's a cannibal. [*to John*] A disgusting practice, don't you think?

JOHN: Uh, yeah.

CINDY: It's horrible, just horrible. Those people should be locked up.

[*The waiter leaves.*]

JOHN: So...what do you like to do in your spare time?

CINDY: What are you implying?

JOHN: Nothing.

CINDY: You're implying that I'm a cannibal in my spare time, aren't you?

JOHN: No, no, it was just a question.

CINDY: Well, I'm not. Cannibalism is illegal and morally offensive, and human flesh has never entered my stomach. Never. So you can just quit giving me that "You're a cannibal" look.

JOHN: I wasn't giving you that kind of look.

CINDY: Whatever you say.

[*Long, uncomfortable pause.*]

CINDY: Okay, once.

JOHN: What?

CINDY: I ate human flesh once. Are you happy?

JOHN: Not really.

CINDY: I was in a cave with a tour group. The exit collapsed, we were trapped for two weeks, we drew straws, my ex-husband lost...you know the drill.

JOHN: You ate your ex-husband?

CINDY: Yes. Stop that.

JOHN: What?

CINDY: You're giving me the "You're a cannibal" look again.

JOHN: I'm sorry.

CINDY: It was a long time ago, and quite frankly I don't care to dredge up such unpleasant memories.

[*Another long, uncomfortable pause.*]

CINDY: Okay, he didn't really draw the short straw.

JOHN: He didn't?

CINDY: And we weren't really trapped in a cave.

JOHN: You weren't?

CINDY: We were at home. I found out he was cheating on me, shot him dead, and ate the body to dispose of the evidence.

JOHN: You ate all of him?

CINDY: Yes.

JOHN: Even the bones?

CINDY: What are you implying?

JOHN: I'm not implying anything, I'm just asking.

[*Yet another long, uncomfortable pause.*]

CINDY: The diet wasn't going well, okay? I'd been eating nothing but rice cakes for a month and I wasn't losing any weight and I

was getting frustrated and one night I just lost it and went
down to raid the refrigerator but I hadn't gone shopping that
week so I grabbed the electric carving knife and ran back
upstairs to our bedroom and ate, ate, ate!

JOHN: Did you ever go back on the diet?

CINDY: Yeah.

JOHN: Well, that's to be admired, at least.

CINDY: Thank you.

JOHN: Yo-yo dieting is a major problem in today's society, and
though we're all human and everyone makes mistakes, it's
good that you gave it another shot and refused to give up.
And sure, you may have devoured your husband, but that's in
the past. You succumbed to weakness, but you learned from
your experience, and I would never think of holding that
against you.

CINDY: You're so sweet.

JOHN: Well, it's always been my belief that... [*He trails off, suddenly
realizing something.*]

CINDY: What's wrong?

JOHN: When I picked you up at your apartment, you squeezed my
arm.

CINDY: I don't remember that.

JOHN: You did! You squeezed my arm. And you asked me to stand on
that scale. And you had me take that body fat test. You were
planning to eat me!

CINDY: No, that's ridiculous!

JOHN: I can't believe your nerve! If you want to practice cannibalism, that's your own business, but don't expect me to offer myself for your deviant appetite!

CINDY: I wasn't going to eat you! I promise! [*A very short pause.*] Okay, I was. Raw. Are you happy now?

JOHN: You're sick! This blind date is over! [*He stands up.*]

CINDY: Fine! You're probably all stringy anyway!

[*John sits back down.*]

JOHN: I am not.

CINDY: I bet you are. You're probably kind of gritty, too.

JOHN: Hey, I'll have you know that my flesh is like filet mignon.

CINDY: You wish.

JOHN: I'm serious.

CINDY: Prove it.

JOHN: All right, you can eat my left arm. But that's it.

CINDY: That sounds fair enough.

JOHN: Shall we go?

CINDY: Sure.

[*They leave, hand in hand. Right before they exit, Cindy addresses the audience.*]

CINDY: There'll be nothing left when I'm done.

[*Curtain close.*]

ROASTING WEENIES
BY HELLFIRE

Every Friday afternoon of the school year, to celebrate the arrival of another weekend of freedom, Charlie Summers blew up a frog. He just liked doing it. He'd upheld this tradition all through fifth and sixth grade, and though his parents discouraged the activity and occasionally took away his firecrackers, they'd never been able to find his entire stash.

This is why, when a limo driver was distracted by the fornicating octogenarians in his back seat and squished Charlie like a wad of Silly Putty, nobody would have been particularly surprised to learn that the little shit went straight to Hell.

Except for Charlie. He'd been meaning to clean up his act somewhere around age sixteen, which he assumed was when the afterlife could try him as an adult. He couldn't quite believe he was standing in the brimstone cell, with the background noise of wailing souls in torment serving as the ultimate in annoying Muzak. Hell was supposed to be for serial killers and rapists and transvestites, not eleven year-old amphibian exploders.

The cell door swung open and the Devil entered, dressed in trendy scarlet. He grinned at Charlie and pulled the door closed. "So, Mr. Summers," he said, "we've been a naughty boy, haven't we? It would appear that your soul is mine to torment for all eternity."

Charlie backed into the corner and stared at the floor, trying to avoid the Devil's piercing, glowing-eyed gaze. "Give me another chance...I'll be good..."

"Oh, no, no, no, no, no," said the Devil with a chuckle. "You're mine. And your punishment for frog killing will be delightfully ironic. For the rest of your endless existence you are going to burn in a pit of searing flames listening to 'It's Not Easy Being Green.'"

Charlie buried his face in his hands and began to cry. The Devil watched him for a moment, annoyed, then let out a long, sulfur-scented sigh.

"Oh, knock that off. Take eternal damnation like a man."

"It's not fair," whimpered Charlie. "I'm just a kid."

"Hitler was a kid once. Moody little bastard."

"I want to go home…"

The Devil rolled his eyes. "Look, you can't go home. You're dead. Your old body is being scraped off the limo tires as we speak. This is your home now."

"I don't like it!"

"Well, tough titties said the kitties when the milk went dry. You're here forever, and to be completely honest I don't give a flying f—" The Devil's eyes narrowed. "You know," he said, "maybe there *is* a way out of this. Do you know what it means to be reincarnated?"

"I think so."

"Well, forget it. It's a crock. But here's what I can do." He snapped his fingers and an image formed on the wall of a small blonde-haired boy, a couple of years younger than Charlie, walking by a river. "This is Hector Wrench. Nice little tyke, kind of a nerd, *very* squeamish. Hasn't committed any mortal sins yet, so I can't hurt him, but I *can* have some fun."

The Devil snapped his fingers again, and the image burned away. "How would you like to come back to life and play a little joke that will scare the unholy piss out of our friend Hector?"

Charlie nodded. Whatever the Devil had in mind had to be better than burning in Hell.

"Good, good." The Devil cracked his knuckles. "Now, your old body is pretty much useless, so we'll have to get you a new one. And darned if a boy about your age didn't drown in that very river two months ago. He didn't kill any frogs, so you know where *he* got to go. Anyway, if you're willing, I'll zap your soul into the corpse and let the fun begin. Are you willing?"

"Yes!" said Charlie, nodding with wild enthusiasm.

The Devil's grin darkened. "Excellent."

«« — »»

Charlie gasped as he suddenly found himself beneath the surface of a freezing, fast-moving river. The gasp involved a painful intake of water, and he struggled violently to free himself from the large branch that pinned him to the bottom. The water was cold enough on its own, but after getting used to Hell it was all but unbearable.

The branch snapped, sending Charlie moving swiftly along with the current. His head bounced against several large rocks on the bottom, and he got the distinct impression that scraps of it were being left behind. He flew past another pointed branch, which ripped open a disconcertingly large portion of his stomach but freed a minnow that had swum into the drowned boy's mouth.

Finally, the water became more shallow, and Charlie washed up onto the river bank. He just lay there for a few moments, cursing the moment he'd discovered the joys of firecrackers.

"Are you okay?" a voice asked.

Charlie looked up and saw Hector peering at him from the top of the river bank. Then Hector let loose with a high-pitched shriek and took off running into the woods.

After the boy disappeared from sight, Charlie pushed himself into a kneeling position. His hands, purple and swollen, were not his own. He was wearing shreds of a blue shirt and shorts—the alligator on the pocket was still intact, but not much else. Though he figured it was probably a good idea to push his stomach back into the cavity from which it was starting to dangle, he didn't much want to touch it and left it alone.

Now what? The Devil hadn't given him any instructions. Was he just supposed to shamble around, stretch out his arms, and moan? Maybe he was supposed to shout "Brains!" like in that movie. He wondered if he ought to be chasing Hector; after all, he didn't want to disappoint the Devil and find himself back in Hell.

Hector peeked out from behind a tree, went "Eeeeeek!!!" (actually pronouncing both the "e" and "k" sounds) and ran off again. Charlie stood up, fought off a dizzy spell, then glanced to his left to see the Devil standing next to him.

"You look splendid," said the Devil, "but suck in that tummy." The Devil reached over and shoved his torn stomach back where it belonged.

"Did I do okay?" asked Charlie.

"You haven't done squat yet. Now, our wee little friend is currently rushing back to his home. Mommy and Daddy are off trying to convince Aunt Sylvia not to divorce Uncle Frank until after the sanity hearing, so they won't be around. What I want you to do is burst in, chase him all over the house, give him the scare of his life, and once you have him cornered, place both of your rotting hands on his face, look deep into his terrified eyes, and say 'Booga-booga.'"

"Booga-booga?"

"Booga-booga."

"Oh."

"Like I said, he's not a mortal sinner yet, so that's the worst we can do." The Devil pointed to a path at the edge of the woods. "Follow that path and it'll take you right to the house. Good luck."

The Devil vanished in an impressive burst of flame that warmed Charlie right up. Charlie wiped some of the dirt from the riverbank off his face and walked over to the path. There was no sign of Hector. He tried to hum a merry tune as he walked through the woods, but "It's Not Easy Being Green" kept playing in his mind.

It took him about ten minutes to emerge from the woods into a small clearing where the two-story, desperately-in-need-of-painting house stood. Charlie considered scoping out the place first, but decided that he didn't really want Hector's parents coming home to the sight of a bloated, stomach-impaired prepubescent walking corpse, so he went straight to the front door.

He opened the door and stepped into the foyer. Hector, who was waiting at the top of the stairs, released the metal bucket he'd been holding. It was attached to the ceiling by a thick rope, and began its rapid downward arc toward Charlie's face.

Charlie was surprised enough that he didn't think to duck. The bucket struck him in the face, removing a healthy portion of chin as well as sending the nails that had been inside the bucket flying everywhere. He stumbled backwards, eight or nine nails protruding from his face, and smacked into the wall.

"Yes!" said Hector, making a gesture of victory.

Hector ran around the corner as Charlie stood there, thinking about the fact that having nails stuck in his face kind of hurt. How had Hector been able to get that bucket set up so quickly? This must've all been prepared beforehand, in case of incompetent burglars.

He took a deep breath to calm himself, then cautiously moved up the wooden stairs, plucking out his facial nails along the way. A couple of them were rusty. Wonderful. He certainly didn't need a case of tetanus on top of all of this.

Turning the corner, he saw Hector standing at the end of the hallway, in front of a large window. Dozens of marbles were on the floor in front of him.

"I'm not going to hurt you," Charlie insisted. "I just want to say 'booga-booga'!"

"Come and get me," said Hector.

Charlie quickly stepped forward. He'd been distracted by the marbles, and so the thin layer of clear grease on the floor came as quite a surprise. As Hector stepped out of the way, Charlie began to slide, arms wind-milling, and let out an undignified yelp. Then he hit the marbles, slipped on them as well, let out another yelp, and went flying through the window.

At that moment, time conveniently seemed to slow down. He registered the fact that the broken glass had left some nasty cuts on his chest and face. Then he registered the even more unnerving fact that he was falling toward a picket fence around a doghouse.

He hit the fence, slicing his body neatly in two at the waist. The top part of him dropped to the ground, his face landing in a half-eaten bowl of Alpo.

Grrrrrrrrrr…

It wasn't necessary for Charlie to lift his head to discover what that sound meant, but he did so anyway. Perhaps it would be a nice Chihuahua.

It was not a nice Chihuahua. It was a very large Doberman with white foam around its mouth and a collar that read "Blood Hunter." Charlie would have wet his pants had his groin still been attached. Instead, he settled for screaming.

The dog pounced, digging its teeth into his arm and shaking its head back and forth, growling all the while. Charlie let loose with several cries of "Nice doggie!" but they didn't seem especially effective.

As the dog began to drag Charlie back to its doghouse, Hector emerged from the house and hurried over to the fence, his eyes wide with shock.

"Help me!" Charlie pleaded. "Don't let him eat me!"

The boy just stared at him.

"I'm here because the Devil sent me!" Charlie shouted. "If you let me die, he's going to come and get you!"

If he hadn't already been condemned, Charlie knew he'd get in some serious spiritual trouble for saying that. But the dog was hurting him, and he was desperate.

"What should I do?" Hector asked.

"Feed him something!"

"I don't have anything!"

"Use…" Charlie frantically glanced around for something, "…my legs!"

Hector looked over at the severed lower half of Charlie's body with some displeasure.

"Do it now!"

Hector lifted the legs and dangled them over the fence. "Here, Blood Hunter! Here boy! Come and get it!"

At the sight of the fresh drumsticks, the Doberman released its hold on Charlie and bounded over to the legs. It grabbed the left leg by the ankle then dragged the pair to a corner, snarling as it began to feast.

Charlie pulled himself toward the fence door, pain shooting through his savaged arm. His hand came down on a freshly placed and not very firm pile of dog shit.

He wanted to go back to Hell.

"Son, what are you doing?" demanded a loud, male voice in the distance. Charlie looked over and saw a man, probably Hector's father, striding towards the dog pen.

Hector rushed over to the man. "Look!" he shouted. "There's a thing in there with Blood Hunter!"

"Son, I'm getting a little tired of your stories. And I damn well better not find out that you fixed up the house again while we were gone."

Then the man noticed Charlie. Charlie forced a grin and tried to give him a friendly wave.

"What the *hell* is that thing?"

"He says the Devil sent him here!"

"Devil, my foot! That thing is a zombie! Hector, go get my rifle!"

As Hector ran off, the man swung open the door to the dog pen and stepped inside. He grimaced as he saw the dog chewing on the legs.

"Sir, I can explain," said Charlie.

"You shut up," the man told him. "I don't talk to unnatural beings."

A minute later, Hector returned with the rifle. The man took it from him and motioned for him to stand back. "I thought that zombies were all made up," he said. "Should've known that those Hollywood people couldn't come up with anything original. Now when you've got a zombie, son, the only way to get rid of it is to shoot it in the head."

He pointed the barrel of the rifle at Charlie's head and fired. Charlie's forehead exploded, filling the air with stuff he didn't even want to think about. He worked his mouth back and forth, but couldn't find his voice.

"I'll be damned," said Hector's father. "Didn't work."

"Maybe you should shoot him in the heart instead!"

"That'll do it. Thanks, son."

He pointed the rifle at Hector's chest and fired again. Charlie managed to locate his voice and used it for the express purpose of shrieking at the top of what remained of his lungs.

"Damn. Missed."

The man fired once again, this time hitting the heart. Charlie continued to scream.

"Okay, this isn't working," said the man, setting the rifle aside. "I think in this other movie, they just chopped the bastards up. Son, go get my axe."

Ten minutes of hard labor later, Charlie was lying in twenty-six pieces, excluding the gnawed lower half of his body. He wondered if the drowned boy's soul was getting pissed.

"Know what?" asked the man. "I forgot that in the movie the zombie pieces kept moving, too. You've got to burn them. Son, go get my can of gasoline and some matches."

«« — »»

Charlie had been a pile of ashes for about an hour when he finally reappeared in Hell, seated on the edge of an enormous pool of fire. He had returned to his soul body, and rubbed his head just to show how much he'd missed it.

"Tsk, tsk, tsk," said the Devil, who was seated next to him, cooking a hot dog over the flames. "A shoddy performance on your part."

"What's going to happen to me?" Charlie asked.

The Devil thought for a long moment. "Despite the rumors, I'm not a total cretin. I must say that I rather enjoyed watching you being mangled beyond recognition. Perhaps we'll try it again sometime."

"I think I'd rather just burn," Charlie admitted.

"Yeah, that's what they all say," the Devil remarked. "Well, that can wait. You hungry?"

"Starved."

"Good," said the Devil, handing Charlie a stick with a fresh hot dog stuck on the end. "Let's just relax for a while. Spend some quality time together. What would you like to accomplish during your time in Hell...?"

The hot dogs were delicious. Charlie and the Devil talked and sang blasphemous campfire songs into the wee hours of the night, as the tormented souls around them howled in their ceaseless misery.

Quite a Mess

It started, as usual, with a severed head flying through the air. The head was soon accompanied by two more. They were newly decapitated and, one assumed, blissfully unaware of their projectile status.

Most of a left arm sailed across the room, followed closely by a right arm, although they belonged to two different people. What little remained of a foot was also airborne, four of the toes skeletal, a silver ring on the still-fleshy big toe.

It was when the intestines started flying that things really got out of hand. Moments after the first length of bowel struck its target, the air was instantly filled with lungs, stomachs, livers, and whatever other guts were handy, along with more than a few bones.

Everybody was laughing, but Henry shook his head and sighed. Once, just once, he'd like to enjoy a cannibal feast that didn't turn into a food fight.

I Hold the Stick

I wipe my perspiring hands on my pants, not wanting to get sweat on the Stick. The Stick is the source of my power, and I want it kept immaculate. Perhaps it does not look truly impressive, as it is nothing more than a wooden rod, exactly forty inches tall, the diameter of a quarter. But the Guests know its purpose, and to meet my stare is to realize that there can be no argument.

I watch the Guests with a mixture of disdain and anticipation. They walk past me, sweltering in the savage heat, filled with desire to satisfy a thirst that must go unquenched for much longer than they expect. Many of them have excitement in their eyes, believing their journey to be near its completion.

But I know the truth.

I stand in front of the Great Deception, the false cathedral. The entrance seems to lead into a cave of treasures, with sparkling jewels adorning the walls, but once the Guests have crossed the threshold they will find that the path they follow is but half-over.

That is, if I allow them to pass.

I continue watching the Guests, desperately seeking out those unworthy to proceed. Though I know it is not true, to my eyes the Stick seems to glow with an almost otherworldly white light. I have not been able to use my power all day, and am desperate for release.

Then I see one. She will not reach me for another ten minutes, but I am certain she is unworthy. She yawns sleepily, as do many of the unworthy at this point in their journey. I guess her age to be six. Her father, thin and bearded, also appears weary.

The Guests proceed forward. I wait, never removing my gaze from the child.

She will not pass. I am certain of it.

I want to grin, but control myself, as I have done so many other times.

By the time they reach me, I am clutching the Stick so tightly that my hand aches. I stare directly into the girl's innocent eyes and place the Stick next to her.

She is unworthy. In fact, the Stick exceeds her height by a full inch.

"I'm sorry," I say, keeping my ecstatic giggle in check. "You're not tall enough to go on The Hidden Treasure Ride. You'll have to exit through the door to your left."

"What?" the girl's father exclaims, his eyes flaring with fury. "We've been waiting forty-five minutes!"

I give the man a false sympathetic smile. "The sign at the beginning of the line clearly states that you must be as tall as Pirate Pete to ride. You should have checked."

"But...but...can't you just let us through this one time?"

I love the pleading. I shake my head slowly. "If she isn't as tall as my stick, she can't ride. It's as simple as that. Please use the exit to your left. You're holding up the line."

The man starts to say something else, then curses loudly and drags his daughter through the exit. I feel warm. Sated.

The Guests continue moving past. Those who witnessed the exchange have varied reactions. Some smile as well, some give me dirty looks, and some whisper uncomfortably amongst themselves.

But they all know who has the power.

They know who holds the Stick.

SCARECROW'S
DISCOVERY

Completely shredded.

Arms and legs torn from the body, leaves scattered everywhere, the burlap head impaled on a wooden stake—the scarecrow had been mangled beyond repair. Ray stared at the mess for a moment and sighed.

"Guess some crows were kinda ticked," Hank said, grinning. Hank was his best friend, though Ray had no idea why.

"Shaddup." Ray shook his head in frustration. "Lousy kids. No respect for a man's property. Third one this week."

"What kids? Haven't seen any kids around here since your Johnny started serving his five-to-ten."

"Shaddup." Ray bent down and yanked the scarecrow's head off the stake. "Look at this twisted stuff they did. Like one of them pagan ritual sacrifices or something."

"Those pagan ritual sacrifices are always getting in the way of crow control."

Ray tossed the head back on the ground. "It's not losing the scarecrows that bugs me; it's that these kids need to learn respect. Between the ages of twelve and seventeen, might as well just lock them in the basement."

"I know. Darn kids."

"They need punishment."

"I know. Darn kids."

Ray glared at him, and Hank grinned again. "So how're you planning to teach these whippersnapper rapscallions a lesson?"

"Charlotte's got an unstuffed scarecrow inside that she made to replace the first one. Tonight I'm gonna wear it like a costume and just wait out here. Once those kids show up, I'll jump out at 'em and scare the livin' pee out of their rotten little disrespectful bladders. They won't be back."

Hank chuckled. "You're actually going to stand out here all night?"

"If that's what it takes."

"What if they go after one of the other scarecrows?"

"I'm takin' the others down first."

Hank shook his head in mock sadness. "Ray, I hate to be the one to tell you this, what with us being best friends and all, but you're an idiot."

"Shaddup. Now take your lazy butt over to the barn and let's finish up for the day."

«« — »»

After three hours, Ray was starting to get really sick of waiting. The scarecrow costume was itchy and uncomfortable, his back was getting sore from leaning against the wooden post, and he was falling asleep. Since he had a perfect view of the road from here, there was no need for him to be completely motionless, but nevertheless his muscles were starting to stiffen.

But it would all be worth it if those kids showed up.

He estimated it was around midnight when they finally did. He saw them off in the distance, two figures, probably young children, both carrying flashlights. As they got close enough to be illuminated by the streetlight he saw that they *were* children—a boy and a girl, no older than six or seven. Far too young to be doing stuff like this. If this was the future, society could kiss itself goodbye.

They headed right for him, the boy carrying a small grocery sack. They stopped about five feet in front of him, and the girl wrung her hands together in excitement.

"Give me the drill," she said.

"You got the drill last time," whined the boy. "It's my turn."

"Fine, be a big baby. Give me the cleaver, then."

The boy took a large, shiny meat cleaver out of the bag and handed it to her. She smiled, and then took a step toward Ray.

He suddenly lurched forward, arms outstretched, and let out a horrific moan. *"Leave me alooooooooooone!"*

Their first reaction, terrified shrieks, was exactly what he had expected. Their second reaction, the girl slashing his leg with the meat cleaver, was not. Ray dropped to the ground, gritting his teeth in pain but forcing himself not to cry out. He quickly pulled off the scarecrow mask.

"Wait!" He winced loudly. "It was just a joke. Just a mask, see?"

The children stood there, staring at him as if unsure whether to run or not. Ray tried to stand up but the pain in his leg was too great.

"I need you to do me a favor," he said. "Go over to my house and knock on the door—get my wife, okay?"

The children were silent.

"C'mon, hurry up! I'm really bleeding!"

Finally, the girl's face broke into a wide grin. "This is great! Tonight we don't have to practice on those stupid scarecrows! We can do it with a real-live person, just like Mommy and Daddy showed us! Won't they be *proud*?"

The boy nodded, the drill started to whirr, and Ray began to scream.

A Double Feature of Shamelessly Silly Holiday Nonsense!
"Howard, The Tenth Reindeer"
Followed Immediately by
"Howard Rises Again"

You know Dasher and Dancer and Prancer and Vixen, Comet and Cupid and Donner and Blitzen, though you'd probably mess up the names and embarrass yourself if somebody asked you to list them. And of course you know the mutant. But there is another reindeer whose story has yet to be told.

This is the tale of Howard, the tenth reindeer.

Howard lived up in the North Pole, and had just barely missed the final cut for Santa's team. During try-outs, he'd choked and let three presents fall out of the sleigh, including a Snotty Susie doll, the second most popular toy that year, which could say one whole sentence if you squeezed its nose for thirty seconds ("I'm calling social services on you, buster!") Fortunately he hadn't dropped the most popular toy, a Hurt Me Elmer, which said "Thank you sir, may I have another?" when you spanked it, or he might have been banished altogether.

So he'd been given a job as Comet's understudy, which meant he'd never get to pull the sleigh. Every once in a while Blitzen would overdo it on the eggnog and be incapable of fulfilling his duties (thus his name), but Comet was always ready for action. The only reindeer who couldn't be accounted for with any regularity was Vixen.

This was a terrible disappointment to Howard, because there wasn't much for a reindeer to do if he wasn't on Santa's team, besides watch *Bambi* for the 79th time. He could give rides to the elves, but they had an annoying habit of tugging on his antlers and shouting "Faster, horsey, faster!" All he wanted was to help make Christmas special, but he didn't know what he could do.

«« — »»

Though legend would have you believe otherwise, the truth is that almost all little girls and boys receive presents from Santa every year. This is because Santa grades behavior on a very generous curve, so even little boys who run over their sisters with tractors generally receive their share of gifts. For a child not to get anything from Santa means that he or she was a terrible, rotten, thoroughly despicable person that year.

Edward Stinkwater was eight years old and had never received a single present from Santa. He was a truly wicked little boy who took great pleasure in breaking other children's toys and saying mean things to kittens. His parents loved him very much, but they were delusional. Everyone else ran when they saw him coming.

He kneeled on his bedroom floor, playing with his coal soldiers. Though breaking their arms and legs off was fun, he had something even more fun planned for Christmas Eve tomorrow night. For the past three weeks he'd been working on the roof, setting a trap for Santa's reindeer. When Santa came to deliver presents for his brother and sister, Edward was going to hijack the sleigh and ruin Christmas for everyone.

He smashed the solider with his fist, then laughed and laughed. For he was truly a wicked little boy.

«« — »»

"Guess what!" said Cosmo, one of Howard's fellow reindeer. "Cupid has gone on strike demanding more vacation days per year, and Santa is letting me be a scab worker!"

"Aw, that's no fair," pouted Howard. "It's my dream to pull Santa's sleigh, but I'll never get to!"

"Well, you didn't hear it from me, but we could perhaps arrange for Comet to meet with an…accident. Those roofs can get pretty slippery, if you know what I mean."

"No! That wouldn't be in the holiday spirit! I'll just stay here and mope, I guess."

"Well, suit yourself. I'm off to do some calisthenics. Have fun with the elves, horsey."

Cosmo hurried off, leaving Howard alone to feel sorry for himself.

And then it was Christmas Eve.

"Allllll right!" shouted Santa. "It's *Oreo* time! Gimme gimme gimme!"

"Now, dear, your suit isn't ready yet," said Mrs. Claus, looking up from her ironing. "And there's still a few minutes until you have to leave. Have you double-checked your Excel file?"

"I'm all set," said Santa, holding up the hard copy. "No other holiday figure brings as much joy as me! Does the Easter Bunny receive millions of letters a year? Does the Arbor Day Druid? I think not!"

"That's nice, dear. Now, I hope you've learned your lesson from last year and won't drink any milk that an overzealous child put out a few days too early."

"Yeah, yeah. Margie almost won herself a spot on the naughty list for that one."

"Here's your coat, dear," said Mrs. Claus, handing him the newly-pressed garment. "Now go make this the best Christmas ever!"

Santa took hold of the reigns in his fully-loaded sleigh. "On Dasher! On Dancer! On Prancer and Vixen! On Comet! On Cupid—"

"Cosmo!"

"Sorry. On Cosmo! On...dang, I lost my place. On Dasher! On Dancer! On Prancer and Vixen! On Comet! On Cosmo! On Donner and Blitzen! Rudolph, quit that sniffing and lead us forward! Merry Christmas to all!"

Much, much later that night, Santa arrived on the rooftop of Edward Stinkwater's house. He parked the sleigh and used his magical Time-Ceasement ring to freeze the flow of time, which was a remarkably convenient item to have when one had to cover the entire gentile world in a night, especially when one was drinking plenty of liquids along the way.

"Ho ho ho," he said, in that jolly ol' voice of his as he walked toward the chimney. "Walt and Yoko Stinkwater have been very good this year. There will be lots of presents for them! Too bad Edward was naughty again, but I guess he'll just—"

Suddenly a rope tightened around Santa's ankles, causing him to fall onto his back with the kind of loud thump that comes from way too many cookies in one night. The Time-Ceasement ring popped off his finger and rolled off the roof. The reindeer rushed forward to help, but another large noose tightened, tying them together in a bunch.

Edward heard the clatter arising above and giggled with maniacal glee. He rushed out of the house, climbed his father's ham radio antenna to the roof, and waved his fist at Santa.

"Hahahaha! I've got you now, Nickie!" he laughed. "I'm going to crash your sleigh into a 747 and then make Rudolph's nose into a shiny red necklace! There'll be no Christmas this year! It won't be long before your ratings plummet, and the Easter Bunny takes over the top slot! Hahahaha!"

"Must...reach...emergency...beacon..." groaned Santa, trying to work his hand free.

"Nobody can help you now," snarled Edward, snapping out the blade of his pocketknife as he walked forward.

«« — »»

"Look!" shouted Mrs. Claus, pointing at the sky. A circle of light shone brightly, with the image of a candy cane inside it. "Something awful must have happened!"

"Santa's in trouble! Santa's in trouble!" the elves began chanting.

Howard felt a momentary rush of relief that he'd let Snotty Susie fall, then realized that this was his chance to save Christmas! "We have to do something!" he said.

"But what? But what?" chanted the elves.

"We have to help Santa!" Howard declared.

"No duh! No duh!" chanted the elves. "But how? But how?"

"We're useless," said Cupid. "We can't fly without a sleigh, and Santa has the only one!"

(Storyteller's note: This saga takes place in an alternate history where a sleigh is required for reindeer to fly properly. And the Nazis won World War II, but fell out of power due to poor public relations.)

Howard thought for a moment. "That's not true! There's a spare sleigh behind the tool shed!"

"No, no." Cupid shook his head. "That one was built years ago by illegal immigrant elves using lumber we bought cheap from the Mexican government! It'll never hold up!"

"We have to try!" Howard insisted. "All the good little boys and girls of the world are counting on us! We can't let them down!"

"It *will* give me some bargaining power in next year's labor negotiations," Cupid said, thoughtfully.

"That's the spirit!" said Howard. "Let's go!"

«« — »»

Edward cut Santa free of the ropes, but kept the knife pointed at him. "Just stay cool and nobody gets hurt for a while," the wicked little boy said. "Now, tell me how to drive that sleigh."

"You'll never be able to," Santa informed him. "It's a stick shift."

"I'm presently not in the mood to play games, so don't toy with me!" Edward warned.

"You are truly evil," said Santa.

"It's a gift."

«« — »»

"AAAAAAAAAHHHHHHHHHH!!!" said Cupid. "The sleigh is breaking apart!"

Howard and Cupid were just about to cross over the Canadian border. The other understudy reindeer had chosen to stay at the North Pole so that Santa wouldn't punish them for malpractice if the rescue operation went awry.

"Keep moving!" Howard shouted. "We'll make it!"

"The whole bottom just dropped out! Uh-oh, I think it's going to wipe out that old lady sitting in her backyard...no, wait, it missed her...squished the heck out of her roses, though..."

"We have to move faster!" said Howard.

"Oooh! Side stitch! Side stitch! We need to stop for a minute!"

"Never! I'll save Christmas, or die trying! Oops, I hope that rudder misses those carolers." Suddenly the last bit of sleigh broke apart. "Oh no! Without a sleigh, we're—"

"Prisoners of the force of gravity!" screamed Cupid. "We're going down! We're venison! I regret that I have but one life to giiiiiiive..."

«« — »»

"*Silent night, holy night, all is calm, all is bright...*"

Tyler Grinchdirt got out of bed and threw open his window. "Will you shut up out there? I'm trying to sleep in heavenly peace too!"

"You hear that, guys? We've got a Scrooge!" shouted one of the carolers.

"Let's egg him!" shouted another.

Tyler pulled the window closed as the rotten eggs began splattering against it, just like last year. He walked out of the bedroom and into the den, where the cookies he'd baked with Ex-Lax rested by the fireplace.

Suddenly there was a huge *thump* on his roof. He scurried up the chimney lickety-split to see what was wrong.

"You crushed my TV antenna!" he cried out.

"Sorry," Howard said, getting back on his feet.

"Oh my God, it's a talking moose!"

"No, no, I'm Howard, one of Santa's reindeer. This crumpled heap next to me is Cupid."

"Hi," said Cupid, weakly.

"We need a sleigh! Quickly! Do you have one?"

Tyler thought for a moment. "A couple, actually. But why should I help Santa? He never brought me that Momma Helga's Fruitcake Deluxe With Extra Green Chunks I asked for when I was five! It's all I ever wanted! One lousy fruitcake! Curse you, Santa! I work for the IRS because of you!"

"I'm sure it wasn't Santa's fault," Howard insisted. "Those elves— you have to keep after them every second. Do you realize how many kids got gypped during the Captain Hocker (With Super-Spitting Action) Doll craze? Lots."

"All right, all right, you've convinced me. The sleighs are in the garage, next to the harem of maids and dancing ladies my true love got me last year. There'll be some well-dressed guys jumping around, so be careful."

"Thank you so much!" said Howard. "Let's go, Cupid!"

《《 — 》》

"All right, Santa," snarled Edward. "This is your fourth-to-last chance to cooperate! Either you fork over the instruction manual to the sleigh, or—"

"Stop!" shouted Howard, his voice echoing dramatically through the moonlit skies. "Let Santa go!"

"My hero!" said Santa.

"Hahahaha!" Edward remarked. "You think two puny reindeer can stop my nefarious plot to ruin Christmas? Nothing can stop me! Because while the good little boys and girls were going to school and learning the state capitals, *I've* been gathering the supplies and doing the research and receiving the government funding that has enabled me to construct the Fearsome Death Ray of Doom! Hahahaha!"

"Well, *I'm* pretty darn bummed," Santa remarked.

Edward pressed the button on a remote control. Some roof shingles slid out of the way, and the Fearsome Death Ray of Doom rose from the hidden panel. "This ray has the power to disintegrate anything! It can disintegrate tissue paper! It can disintegrate butterflies! It can disintegrate Q-Tips! And unless you cooperate, I'll use it to destroy Santa's sleigh!" He thought for a moment. "Actually, with all the hassle that went into making this death ray, it's kind of dumb to make using it contingent upon Santa's lack of cooperation. Say goodbye to your sleigh, Kris, and thus goodbye to Christmas! Hahahahaha!"

"Wow," said Cupid. "That concept earned *five* 'ha's. We're in deep ka-ka!"

Edward pressed another button. The Fearsome Death Ray of Doom began to glow with a most un-Christmasy light.

"Noooooooooo<pause for breath>oooooooooo!!!!" screamed Howard, rushing forward.

The death ray fired, just as Howard leapt in front of it. Human and reindeer alike gasped as Howard was instantly transformed into a small pile of ashes.

"Dagnabbit!" snarled Edward. "I only had enough firepower for one shot! That does it!" He raised the knife, let out a horrific battle cry, and began to run toward Santa, his eyes wild with psychotic glee.

At that moment, a miracle happened. The wind changed, blowing Howard's ashes into Edward's eyes. "I'm blind!" he cried out, losing his footing on the slippery roof. With a dramatic "Aaaaaaaahhhhhh!!!" he slid off the roof and smashed into the snowman he'd built that very afternoon. But since Edward was truly a wicked little boy, he'd filled this snowman with nitroglycerine, which blew the little twerp into itty bitty teeny weenie pieces.

"Howard's ashes saved Christmas!" Santa declared. "He's a hero! He's the greatest reindeer who ever lived! His ashes will be placed in an airtight urn, and from now until forever, Howard will ride at the head of my sleigh!"

"Hooray!" cheered the other reindeer. "Hooray for Howard!"

It took them about two hours to find the Time Ceasement ring in the snow, but it still turned out to be the greatest Christmas ever. Howard's dream had come true at last.

And so, boys and girls, when you're hanging your stockings by the chimney with care, take a moment to grab a handful of ashes from your fireplace and sprinkle them over the Christmas tree, to help honor Howard, The Tenth Reindeer.

$$\ll\!\!\ll - \gg\!\!\gg$$

[Intermission]

$$\ll\!\!\ll - \gg\!\!\gg$$

Edward Stinkwater was truly a wicked little boy. However, since he'd been blown to bits two years ago after falling off the roof onto a nicroglycerine-filled snowman (as you probably forgot from "Howard the Tenth Reindeer"), he wasn't causing many problems anymore.

But he had a cousin, Rufus Sludgegrass, who was even more wicked. He was selfish and whiny like other teenagers, but he also drop-kicked squirrels, strangled boll weevils, mocked rhinoceri, and ran over information technology professionals with his tractor. He was so mean and vile that even Tom Brokaw didn't like him. (If that statement seems a bit pointless, you have my permission to replace it with the originally-intended trite "Barney the Dinosaur" reference. But I do not expect to see a published review complaining about trite Barney the Dinosaur references, got it?)

Rufus had one goal in life, and that was to destroy Christmas. He'd already destroyed Groundhog Day by feeding shaving cream to the official groundhog and screaming "Run for your lives! It's got rabies!" at the ceremony. He'd also destroyed Sweetest Day by publicly theorizing that it was merely created to sell more greeting cards. Now he wanted Christmas out of the way. And where his cousin had failed, he would succeed, oh yes. He had a dastardly plan in mind, a plan he would implement right after he finished his obscene phone call.

He wiped his sweaty hand across his forehead as he tightly clutched the phone. "What are you wearing?" he panted.

"What would you *like* me to be wearing?" purred the sultry-voiced woman on the other end.

Rufus licked his lips. "A size eleven yellow and orange frilly blouse, preferably bought on sale from Target. A pair of blue jeans that fit snugly but comfortably, with some minor fading. Tube socks. Any kind of tennis shoes except those dumb ones that you pump up. And glasses...ohhhhh yes...wire framed glasses that have been recently cleaned with a tissue, not a rag."

"Pervert!" shouted the woman, and slammed the phone down in his ear. Rufus grinned and hung up. Now that his fun was over, it was time to begin his evil scheme to destroy Christmas.

《《 — 》》

"I don't know," remarked Becky. "It doesn't look much like a snowman."

"Sure it does," Hector insisted. "It's just a snowman that goes to special schools."

"Maybe it would look better if we didn't live in sunny Florida," said Becky. "And if it weren't July."

The children continued staring at the grape and blue raspberry Slurpees they'd poured out onto the sidewalk. Hector swirled his toe around in it, trying to make a smiley face. "I bet he'll look just perfect if we give him a hat."

Becky's expression brightened. "Remember that magician who threw all his stuff away after those Fox specials destroyed his career? I think his magic hat landed in that garbage can over there."

They retrieved the hat, and Becky dropped it onto the melting slush. About thirty seconds later, nothing happened. Thirty seconds after that, the same thing happened. But then, one minute and thirty seconds after the hat was dropped, a man in a passing car shouted "Hey, you stupid kids! Quit staring at those spilled Slurpees and get a life!"

Unbeknownst to the man, he had spoken the words that activated the magic in the hat. There was a dramatic "aaoogah!" sound from the heavens, and suddenly Slurpee the Snowman rose from his sidewalk slush pile to stand proudly in front of the children.

"Hey, you stupid kids!" shouted another man in a passing car. "Quit transforming spilled Slurpees into mutant freaks of nature and get a life!"

"Wow!" said Becky. "He's alive! Our snowman is really alive! The hat *was* magic, after all!"

Slurpee the Snowman smiled happily at the children. Then he ate them. After that, he spent a few moments thinking about what to do with his newfound ability to be alive, and decided on a good old-fashioned homicidal rampage. He outstretched his arms, practiced saying "Kill, kill..." a couple times, then began.

《《 — 》》

"This is Channel 8 news, coming to you live from a city we won't name in the interest of not having to worry about geographical accuracy! Slurpee the Snowman, a formerly un-alive pair of delicious fruity ice beverages, has gone on a rampage, devouring dozens of people! I have with me Mayor Snortweather. Mayor, what is your opinion of this crisis?"

"Well, in the snowman's defense, at least he's not a necrophile."

"That is certainly true, sir."

"As you'll remember, I promised the people of this fair city that when elected, I would not tolerate necrophilia in any way, shape, or form. And I have kept that promise. Anyway, I'm confident that the snowman will be captured within the next few weeks and this whole incident will merely be an unpleasant little footnote in history, like Hitler."

"Thank you sir. We now return you to *Wiener Jokes*, joined in progress."

Rufus shut off the television and cackled with maniacal glee. Oh sure, everyone had laughed when he told them his evil plan. "What a dumb plan," they'd said. But he'd been sure that the best way to destroy Christmas was to sit around watching television all summer until a news story came on about someone going on a homicidal rampage, and then convince that person to do his bidding.

Soon Slurpee the Snowman would be his servant, and together they would ruin the holiday season, once and for all!

«« — »»

As a special treat, this next section of our holiday tale will be told to you by guest narrator James Earl Jones:

Hello, this is James Earl Jones. I've been asked to relate the following piece of "Howard Rises Again" because my booming, manly voice adds dignity and dramatic impact to any project I'm involved with. I was the voice of Darth Vader, you know. And I was in *Soul Man* with C. Thomas Howell.

Of course, since this is print and not audio, my presence here is pretty much wasted. Especially since if any of you are reading this aloud, it's just going to sound like I have some squeaky, annoying voice. This whole idea is kind of stupid, isn't it? My check better not bounce, that's all I have to say.

Anyway, the part I was supposed to tell you had the wicked Rufus convincing Slurpee the Snowman to become his evil servant, after which they chartered a carrier pigeon to the North Pole. It really wasn't up to the level of quality you've seen in other paragraphs of this story, so you didn't miss much by listening to me complain. Thank you.

Ladies and gentlemen, let's have a big hand for James Earl Jones! And now back to our story, joined in progress:

«« — »»

"—ing little brat?" asked Santa, standing outside of his newest toy factory while his chickens (acquired in the controversial Easter merger six years ago) fled in terror.

"I'll tell you why you should be scared," snarled Rufus. "If you don't surrender immediately, there will be wreaked a havoc like no havoc you've ever seen wreaked."

"Wreak...wreak..." said Slurpee.

Santa folded his arms. "I think not. I've survived accusations of over-commercialization. I've survived psychological testing that suggests I have a God Complex. What makes you think I'm going to be defeated by a wormy little twerp like...*whoa*, I didn't see that ravenous snowman behind you! Does he bite?"

Rufus nodded.

"Ummm...okay, you win. But I won't go quietly." Santa turned and ran, screaming "AAAAAAHHHHHHH!!!" in his loudest voice.

"Victory is ours!" Rufus declared. "But it's only July, and the fruits of my labors won't be noticeable until decorations start going up in late September. So, Slurpee...destroy! Destroy! Destroy! Make it fall, wreck it all, make them faint, scrape the paint...gooooooo team evil!"

"Wreak," said Slurpee, as he began to destroy.

«« — »»

A Special Note To Younger Readers: I know that the idea of a killer snowman destroying Santa's workplace is kind of scary. Which is okay, because scary things happen in the world, and it's best to learn to cope with them. But this is supposed to be a fun little story, and I don't want to upset you by making you wonder whether or not Santa will survive. So I just want you to know that there's no reason to be concerned, because Santa Claus doesn't exist. He's just a big lie your parents told you. See, there was nothing to worry about. Now back to the story, joined in progress:

«« — »»

"—wearing a dress of hardened Play-Doh while licking the toenails of a plummeting lemming."

"That's sick, Mrs. Claus," said her favorite elf, Spike, as he opened the door to the Hit The Fan Contingency Room. They quickly entered, and looked with the proper reverence at the pedestal upon which rested the urn containing those most heroic of disintegrated reindeer ashes.

The ashes of Howard, the Tenth Reindeer.

"He gave his life saving Christmas from the evil Edward Stinkwater," said Mrs. Claus, lifting the urn. "And now, if all goes well, he'll be able to die for Christmas once again. Spike, recite the incantation."

"Rise," said Spike.

The urn began to tremble, the ground began to quake, the house began to shake, and suddenly the ashes rose and began to take form. There was some swirling and churning and bubbling and skeedaddling and snorkling, and suddenly there he stood, in all of his dramatic glory.

Howard, the Tenth Reindeer.

At that moment, the snowman burst into the room. Howard spoke his very first word since he'd made the ultimate sacrifice two long years ago: "Huh?"

And then Slurpee ate him.

"Well, damn," said Mrs. Claus.

"Foolish woman," laughed Rufus, stepping into the room. "I've defeated your pitiful elves and even your multi-class halflings! I've destroyed your toy factory and have strewn Beanie Baby parts all over the North Pole! The children of the world will all be weeping come December 25! Now, Slurpee...get her!"

"Stop!" shouted Santa, entering the room with his candy cane revolver. Rufus spun around, pulling out the coal pistol Santa had given him years ago. Mrs. Claus whipped out her tinsel gun. Spike yanked out his ornament boom-stick. Slurpee ate Spike.

Santa fired, hitting Rufus in the chest. Rufus fired, hitting himself in the chest. Mrs. Claus fired, hitting Rufus in the uvula. Had Spike not been eaten, he would have fired, hitting Mrs. Claus in the left earlobe.

As Rufus dropped to the floor in slow motion, Santa and Mrs. Claus opened fire on Slurpee, filling the air with a cacophony of glorious bang sounds and reducing the snowman to a melted Sno-Cone. Then they started shooting at the ceiling, overcome with firepower dementia.

Soon it was all over, and they stood victorious over the dying Rufus. "Thought you could beat us, didn't ya?" asked Santa. "Thought you were soooooo tough, but gosh, if I look around the room I only see one person who's mortally wounded, golly, whoever could it be, I wonder…oh, it's *you!*"

Rufus forced a grin. "You may have beaten me, and my cousin Edward before me. But there's one thing you haven't beaten, and that's the small nuclear device Slurpee and I brought along with us as a precaution against just this kind of situation. It's going to explode in thirty seconds. Good night." And he died, bringing the official body count to eighty-seven, a new record for a story that was originally published as a Christmas card.

Santa and Mrs. Claus hurried outside, where the nuclear device lay waiting, with a red digital readout conveniently informing them that 23 seconds remained. "Hand me my clippers," said Santa, opening the access panel. "The question is, do I cut the red wire, the blue wire, the yellow wire, the green wire, the white wire, the orange wire, the pink wire, the chartreuse wire, the periwinkle wire, or the wire with 'Cut Me' written on it?"

"The orange wire," said Mrs. Claus, "because it looks most like the ball of flame that will engulf us if you get it wrong."

Santa took a deep breath, positioned the clippers over the orange wire, and cut.

"Thank you for cutting the orange wire," said a perky recorded voice from within the nuclear device. "Armageddon has been averted."

"You did it!" shouted Mrs. Claus. "Christmas is saved!"

"We *all* did it," said Santa. "Well, I guess the people who got eaten by the snowman weren't all that helpful, but everyone who survived did their share. Merry Christmas!"

Yes, once again, evil was defeated and the spirit of Christmas lived on. And so we bring to a close this tale.

The tale of Howard, the Tenth Reindeer.

(*Note: Slurpees are a registered trademark of some business, and have never been known to magically transform into psychotic snowmen. They have, however, been shown to cause irreversible kidney damage.*)

BrainBugs

My name is Charlie, and there are bugs in my brain.

They're crawling around in there, eating through my grey matter and doing Lord only knows what else.

I'm not sure what kind they are. Spiders, I'm guessing, but I didn't see them go in so I can't be certain. It sort of feels like spiders, the way they dance around.

Scientists will tell you that the brain doesn't have nerves, that it doesn't feel pain, but they're wrong. I can feel everything. I can feel every time the bugs take a bite.

They've probably eaten about half of my brain so far. I'm still doing okay, though, because you really only use a small percentage of it. But I'm scared that they'll eat through an important part.

If they *are* spiders, I wonder if they've spun webs in there?

Every once in a while I'll stick a Q-tip really far into my ear, as far as it will go, but it never comes out with webs on it. So maybe they aren't.

I wish I knew how to get them out.

What would you do, if you were me? Don't say go to the hospital. They won't help me there. I went to a hospital for something else that I don't want to talk about, before the bugs, and they didn't help me at all.

I hate doctors.

Do you think that maybe the bugs crawled in through my nose? I do get nosebleeds sometimes. Bad ones. That could be it, I guess.

Sometimes I think I want to name them. I don't know how many there are, so it's not a very practical idea, but it might be nice to be able to say "Ah, that's Hector taking a bite right now," or "Winslow seems to be especially frisky this morning."

What kind of names do you think I should give them?

You want to hear something strange? I wouldn't kill them if they crawled out. You probably think I would. They've hurt me a lot, and you probably think I'd smash them with my fist if I got the chance, but I wouldn't. They're not *trying* to hurt me. They're just hungry, like any other living creature. I'd catch them in a piece of Tupperware and then release them onto my front lawn.

I do wish they'd leave, though.

They're really, really hurting me.

You would? Seriously? For free?

I don't know. What kind of medical training do you have?

Yes, I know that enthusiasm counts for a lot, but there should be some kind of formal training before you try to remove bugs from somebody's brain, right?

No, no, you're absolutely right. They could devour an important part any moment now. Beggars can't be choosers.

One is eating in sort of a spiral shape. I think I'll name him Farley.

What the hell are you doing? You can't slice through the cranium with a pair of haircutting scissors! You clearly have no concept of proper surgical procedure. Put that down.

See, you cut yourself. You have to be more careful.

My hand hurts.

Maybe I should just learn to live with them. I don't even remember how long the bugs have been there. Maybe they've been there since I was born. I might need them. I might die if they leave.

Look, you don't have to be sarcastic about it. I know I'm in danger.

Stop it.

Oh, you have *got* to be kidding me.

Stop it. You're just trying to scare me.

I said, stop trying to scare me.

A chainsaw is not the answer. It's an imprecise tool.

Ow! You're stressing me out and I think it's making Farley hungry!

Leave me alone.

No, you're right, I don't want to die.

I'll go get it.

I wish you could come with me.

I'll be back.

I've got it, but you know what, I can't even feel the bugs right now. Maybe they've left. Yep, I bet they're gone for good. Whew, that's a relief.

I know, I know, self-delusion is not an attractive personality trait. I just think that maybe if we try this I'm going to be injured or something.

Shut up.

Now you're just being mean. If *you* had bugs in your brain, you wouldn't be talking like this.

I'll punch you.

I swear I'll punch you.

Shut up!

Look at what you made me do. Now my other hand is bleeding. I can't see you anymore. Are you still here?

You promise?

Okay, I'll let you do this, but you have to be careful. I mean it.

I won't move, but you have to be very, very careful.

I don't think you're supposed to be using these things indoors. It's so loud. I hope the neighbors don't come over to see what we're doing.

Let me find something to bite down on.

This towel will work.

Please be careful.

I'm not moving I'm not moving I'm not moving I'm not moving I'm not OH IT HURTS IT HURTS!

Stop it! Just turn it off!

You promised you'd be careful and you slipped! A doctor could have done a better job than this!

My eye is ruined!

What?

You did not.

Don't play with me.

I don't see them. No, I don't see them swimming in the blood on the floor. I just don't! I'm looking where you're pointing, but I don't see them!

Are they? Really? You mean it?

Maybe they went in through my eye in the first place. I don't know how they fit, but maybe they crawled under my eyeball.

You're not just kidding around, are you? Please tell me you're not just kidding around.

Wow.

I'm sorry I yelled at you.

No, I don't feel any better, but I'm sure I will soon.

Thank you. You're a real pal.

But I think I've changed my mind. I'm feeling faint from loss of blood and I probably should go to the hospital. Will you drive me?

CAP'N HANK'S FIVE ALARM NUCLEAR LAVA WINGS

"These wings are for pussies!" Vincent announced, shoving the basket aside. "I could force-feed one of these to my three year-old granddaughter and she wouldn't even break a sweat. Atomic wings, my ass!"

That skinny bastard had come in every weekend for the past couple of months, and all he ever did was gripe about the Buffalo wings. We were all getting a little sick of it, especially Bernard, who'd owned and ran the place going on twenty years now.

"Those are the hottest wings in town," Bernard said, leaning over the bar and speaking in a much calmer voice than I ever would've been able to manage. "We've been voted hottest wings six years in a row, and we'll be voted hottest wings this year, the next year, and the year after."

"By who?" Vincent asked. "Pussy Wing Eaters of America? I'm barely even getting a tingle out of these things. Hell, the bleu cheese and celery is hotter than the sauce. I want my money back."

Bernard patted the side of the cash register. "Your money is staying right here."

"Then at least give me a free beer."

"I'll give you a free kick in the butt, right out the door."

Vincent sighed and half-heartedly picked another wing out of his basket. "I guess I'll finish these since I paid for 'em, but I want it known that these are Girl Scout wings. Naw, *Brownie* wings. Brownies are the smaller Girl Scouts, right? These sissy wings wouldn't have even disrupted my grandmother's flow of oxygen when she was on life support, God rest her soul."

There were only four others in the bar: Randy, Sam, Terrence, and me. We were pretty much the only ones *ever* in the bar, and that's just how we liked it. We hung out at Bernard's place nearly every night, and we didn't much like new people coming in to piss and moan about the food.

Bernard made a damn good Buffalo wing, every bit as good as what they made in New York. At least I assumed that was the case, seeing as how I'd never been to New York.

Bernard glanced at each of us, and then he smiled. "Tell me, Vince, buddy, have you ever heard of Cap'n Hank's Five Alarm Nuclear Lava Wings?"

Vincent shook his head. "Nope."

"It's a special recipe. They are, and I kid you not, the hottest wings in the world. One bite and you'll be bawling in the restroom like a little girl who got spanked by her daddy."

"Yeah, right."

"You'll beg for dry ice for your tongue."

"I doubt that."

Bernard looked Vincent directly in the eye and held his stare for a long moment. "I'm not kidding. These wings will make you their bitch."

"Well, hell, whip up a batch then," said Vincent. "What are you waiting for?"

"I don't keep the sauce in stock. It doesn't store well, and I don't need to lose my bar because of some lawsuit over somebody burning their mouth. But I'll special order a jar if you want, and we'll see how much of a man you really are."

"Sounds good to me."

Bernard smiled again. "Sounds good to me, too."

«« — »»

The next weekend, we all looked up as Vincent strut into the place. He sat down at the bar and folded his arms over his chest. "Hey, Bernard, why don't you bring me a great big order of those special wings that you mentioned? And a teeny tiny glass of water to go with 'em. I don't expect that I'll need anything more."

"Sure. Give me a few to heat up the sauce," said Bernard, heading into the back room.

About five minutes later he returned, holding a basket of about a dozen wings. Those things were such a bright orange color that I thought they might glow in the dark. If you had a Geiger counter, which none of us did, I'll bet that thing would've showed more radioactivity than if you waved it over Godzilla's feces. It practically burned my nose just to smell them.

Bernard set them in front of Vincent and gestured with dramatic flourish. "Here you go. Cap'n Hank's Five Alarm Nuclear Lava Wings."

Vincent took a quick whiff. "Mmmm. Tangy."

Bernard grabbed a clipboard and set it in front of Vincent. "I'm gonna have to ask you to sign this waiver that absolves me from all responsibility and proves that you're consuming these wings of your own personal accord."

"Sure, sure," said Vincent, scribbling his signature on the form. "I've signed waivers on hotter-smelling wings than these hundreds of times."

We all watched in silence as Vincent picked a drumstick up out of his basket. He inspected it from all angles and then took a bite. He chewed, slowly and thoughtfully.

Finally he swallowed, took a sip of water, swished it around in his mouth for a moment, and then spoke.

"These," he said, "are pussy wings."

That's all we needed to hear. Everybody sprang into action, pulling Vincent off his stool, lifting him up, and slamming him on top of the bar. I held his shoulders while Bernard lit up a blowtorch.

While Vincent screamed, Bernard touched the flame to his mouth. Vincent's lips blistered, cracked, blackened, and after a while just weren't there anymore. Then Bernard started on his tongue. That took a lot longer, but none of us had anything better to do that evening.

We would've liked to leave him that way so he could think about perhaps being less rude in the future, but though Vincent couldn't speak anymore, he could still report us. So we had to kill him. It was easy; we just shoved those wings down his throat until he choked to death. Terrence drew the short straw and had to bury him.

And so things went pretty much back to normal at Bernard's bar. After a few days we quit talking about poor Vincent, and after a few weeks I don't think any of us even thought about him much.

Of course, when Bernard served me a hamburger that was way too overdone, I didn't complain.

A Call For Mr. Potty-Mouth

"Piss!" shouted Margie. "Piss, piss, piss, piss!"

"Margaret Anne Fulmer, you watch your language!" said her mother as she walked into the bedroom and put her hands on her hips. "Who taught you to talk like that?"

Margie shrugged. "I dunno."

"Well, that's not a nice word, and I don't want to hear that kind of talk from you, do you understand?"

"You've said it. You've said even worse."

"I'm not seven years old, now am I? And anyway, Mommy shouldn't talk like that either. It isn't polite."

"But I can't find my other shoe!"

"That's no reason to curse. Do you know what happens to little girls who use naughty language?"

"No."

"They get a visit from Mr. Potty-Mouth, and he washes their mouths out with soap."

"Yuck."

"That's right, yuck. So think about that the next time you want to say a bad word. And your shoe is right there next to that piece of cake you snuck into your room."

«« — »»

That night, after she'd brushed her teeth and said her prayers, Margie sat in bed playing a handheld video game. It was hard to concentrate, because it was a school night and she had to listen for Mommy's footsteps in the hallway or risk having the game taken away. But she was still doing pretty well, and was almost in the top ten scores.

Then her spaceship exploded.

"Dammit," she said, shutting off the game.

"Now, now, that's no way to talk, is it?"

Margie gasped. A man stood next to her bed. He wore purple-and-white striped pajamas and an orange pointy hat that almost looked like a traffic cone, and he had a black mustache that curled up on both sides.

"Who...who are you?" asked Margie.

"Why, I'm Mr. Potty-Mouth, of course!" he said, winking at her and politely tipping his hat. "Little girls shouldn't talk the way that you do. Oh no, no indeed. It's very naughty. I think I'll have to wash your mouth out with soap."

Margie pulled the covers over her mouth and shook her head. "I'll be good," she insisted, though the blanket muffled her words. "I won't talk like that anymore."

"Do you *promise*?" asked Mr. Potty-Mouth.

Margie nodded.

"Oh, no, I think you're a wicked little girl who tells lies." He yanked the blanket and sheets away from her and tossed them across the room. Then he grinned and showed her his bar of soap.

It was black, greasy soap, and the surface bubbled like boiling water. Some of it oozed between Mr. Potty-Mouth's fingers and dripped onto the carpet.

Margie tried to scream for her mother but the words didn't come out. "I'm the only one who can hear you," said Mr. Potty-Mouth. "Nobody else will listen to such a foul-mouthed little girl."

He grabbed her arm with his free hand and pulled her to the edge of the bed, then pushed the soap against her mouth. Margie expected it to burn, but it was freezing cold, and it smelled a hundred times stronger than the yellow soap she'd used during her bath that evening.

She gagged as he rubbed the bar in small circles. Black bubbles floated past her eyes as the thick, slimy soap got all over her lips and teeth and into her mouth. She wanted to throw up. The black ooze ran down her chin and when one of the bubbles popped in her eye it stung worse than the time Bobby next door almost poked her eye out with a stick.

"All nice and clean," said Mr. Potty-Mouth, stepping away from the bed. "I know you've learned your lesson. You'll be a good little girl from now on, won't you?"

He tipped his hat with his free hand and vanished.

Margie jumped out of bed and ran into the hallway. She still couldn't speak, so she hurried into the bathroom to wash off that horrible black stuff.

She grabbed the good guest towel from the rack and looked in the mirror as she scrubbed it over her face. No matter how old she got, she would never use bad words again. Never ever ever. No matter how mad she was, no matter how bad she did at video games, no matter what, she'd never—

Margie dropped the towel in the sink and stared at her reflection. As tears poured down her cheeks, she tried desperately to cry out for Mommy…but she couldn't because her mouth was gone.

THE BAD MAN IN THE BLUE HOUSE

In the blue house, there lives a man.
He is a bad man.
A very bad man.
In the red house next door, there lives a woman.
She has done some bad things, but she is a good woman.
She is a happy woman.
A very happy woman.
The bad man watches the happy woman.
He thinks bad thoughts while he watches her.
He loves her, but he hates her even more.
He does not want to hurt her.
Every day he tells himself that he does not want to hurt her.
The bad man lies.
Sometimes he watches her all night.
He giggles while he watches her.
Or he cries.
Or he covers his mouth and screams.
He hates the happy woman.
Sometimes she closes her curtains at night.
Then he can not see her.
But he can see her in his mind.
She looks better in his mind.
And he can hurt her better in his mind.
Over and over and over.
The bad man thinks that tonight he might leave the blue house.
He might visit the happy woman in her red house.
He might visit her bedroom.
The bad man will giggle.

The happy woman will cry and scream.
It will be fun.
The bad man has a shiny knife.
His father gave him this knife.
It might not be shiny after tonight.
The bad man watches for the happy woman.
She won't be back in the red house until it is dark out.
The bad man will watch until then.
The bad man is almost happy as he watches.
When it is dark out, the happy woman comes home.
He can see her inside the red house.
She will not be asleep for a long time.
The bad man can wait.
He giggles while he waits.
He loves the knife his father gave him.
He does not get tired while he waits.
When the happy woman gets in bed, he is more awake than ever.
The bad man leaves the blue house.
He likes the dark.
People laugh at him in the light.
Nobody laughs at him in the dark.
He walks over to the red house.
The bad man doesn't giggle.
The bad man is scared.
He tests the doorknob.
It is locked.
He knew it would be locked.
But the bad man has a key.
He has had this key for a long time.
He has always wanted to use it.
He unlocks the door.
The bad man walks inside the red house.
He is very quiet.
He looks around the happy woman's kitchen.
He stands there for a long time.
He hates the happy woman.
The bad man walks up the stairs.
He does not giggle.
He looks at the happy woman's bedroom.
The door is closed.

The bad man wants to go back to the blue house.
He wants to cry.
But he wants to hurt the happy woman more.
The bad man opens the door.
The happy woman is in bed.
Her eyes are closed.
The bad man can hear her breathe.
He moves closer.
He can smell her.
He is ready to hurt the happy woman.
He is ready to hear her cry and scream.
Her eyes are open.
The bad man drops the shiny knife.
The happy woman screams.
The happy woman scrambles across the bed.
The bad man grabs her leg.
Her skin is warm.
He digs his fingernails into her warm skin.
But she pulls her leg free.
The happy woman is off the bed.
The bad man picks up the knife his father gave him.
He giggles.
The happy woman opens a drawer beside her bed.
The bad man runs toward her.
He can not wait to hurt her.
He can not wait for her to cry.
Maybe the happy woman will even beg.
The bad man hears a loud noise.
He drops the knife again.
It is still shiny.
The bad man wants to leave the red house.
But he falls onto the bedroom floor.
He hurts.
He cries.
He picks up the knife.
He presses it to his chest.
He loves the knife his father gave him.
It is not shiny anymore.
He closes his eyes.
He can not see the happy woman anymore.

Not even in his mind.
The happy woman is safe.
But she still cries.
She still screams.
Later, the happy woman moves out of the red house.
She cries even after she has left.
Sometimes she screams in her sleep.
Sometimes she is scared.
Not always.
But sometimes.

ABBEY'S SHRIEK

The front door opened, and Abbey cringed.

"Stephanie, Abbey...go downstairs," said Dad as soon as he entered the living room.

"But Dad—!" Abbey protested.

"Are you arguing with me?" Dad walked over to shut off the television. "I thought we'd already worn out the lecture about you arguing with me, but I'll be more than happy to repeat it."

"No...I'm sorry." Abbey hurriedly began to gather up his comic books. "I'm going."

"*Now!*"

"Yes, sir." Abbey picked up the small stack of comics, then went over to the basement door. Stephanie, who at ten was three years and a month older than him, had already turned on the light and was walking down the steps. She never put up a fight.

As Abbey followed her, Dad shut the door and locked it. There were probably much worse places to be than down in the basement. They had lots of board games, some drawing paper, and plenty of books to read. But Abbey was always frightened to be down here, even when his sister was with him.

Stephanie sat down on the couch and pulled the blanket over her shoulders. The basement was cold even when it was warm outside. In the winter it could become unbearable. Abbey sat cross-legged on the floor and began to read *The Fantastic Four*. Dad called his comics "worthless trash," but, surprisingly, didn't forbid him to read them.

After a few minutes, there was a giggle from upstairs. Abbey glanced over at Stephanie, who was reading some stupid girl book. "What do you think they're doing?"

"You ask that every time."

"I do not."

"Yes, you do."

"Well, tell me anyway."

"You're too young to know."

"I am not!"

"Yes, you are. If you weren't too young you'd already know what they were doing."

"Please, pretty please tell me?"

"When you get older."

"Tell me *now*! I'll give you some of my Starburst!"

"Give me the whole pack and I'll tell you."

That was a painful demand. Dad didn't let them have candy very often, and it might be forever before Abbey got another pack. But he had to know.

"Let me have half of them, and you can have the rest," he offered.

"You can't keep any cherry ones."

Abbey frowned. He'd meant to take all of the cherry ones. He slipped the pack out of his pocket and drummed his fingers along it. "Tell me first then I'll give you them."

"No way, Jose. I know you. After I tell you you'll just shove them all in your mouth like an orangutan."

"I will not!"

"Then you'll scratch and drool all over yourself and spray snot all over the place, 'cause that's what orangutans do. Your mother was an orangutan, you know. It was supposed to be a secret. You were born out in the jungle. We have pictures."

"Shut up!" said Abbey. "Mom's in hell! Dad said so!"

"Fine, believe whatever you want." Stephanie made "oo-oo-ee-ee-aa-aa!" noises at him.

Abbey pouted for a few moments, but then opened the pack of Starburst and removed the strawberry and orange ones. He tossed the rest of the pack to his sister, spilling them everywhere.

"You retard!" Stephanie got up off the couch and began gathering up the candies.

"Now tell me what they're doing up there."

"Foreplay."

"What's that?"

"It means they're getting ready to have sex."

"So what are they going to do?"

"You retard, don't you know anything?"

"How am I supposed to know anything if nobody tells me? I'm not magic!"

"Well, I know all about it. I found some magazines in Dad's closet one day when he accidentally left the door unlocked, and I know everything."

"So tell me."

"It's really gross."

"Cool!"

"Dad's up there with some lady. Pretty soon they're going to be on the couch or in his bed completely naked."

"Really?"

"Uh-huh. Except the lady might be wearing high heels. Then they're going to lick each other, all over. Even the penis and vagina."

Abbey's stomach lurched. "Why would they want to do that?"

"Because, that's what you do in foreplay. Then he's going to stick his penis in her vagina."

"He is not!"

"Yes, he is."

"What if they have to go pee?"

"They hold it."

"Eeewwww."

"And then, after they do that for a while, slimy white stuff is going to come out of Dad's penis, and then guess what happens?"

"What?"

"The lady licks it up!"

"You liar!" Abbey said, giggling.

"I'm serious! I saw it in the magazine!"

"How come they do that?"

"They *like* it!"

"No, really, how come they do that?"

"I don't know. Grown-ups are weird."

«« — »»

Craig Powell grinned and poured more champagne into the whore's glass. The whore—Lisa—tried to take a drink but laughed in mid-sip, spraying the champagne all over the front of her shirt. She set the glass on the coffee table and wiped her face on her sleeve.

"Oh, God, you must think I'm drunk already," she said, trying desperately to stifle her laughter. "I just love this story."

Craig forced a good-humored chuckle. "Well, get to the punchline already so I can laugh too!"

Lisa clamped her hand over her mouth and kept it there for several seconds. Then she cautiously removed it, ready to replace it if a giggle escaped. "Okay, okay, I'm fine now. Anyway, we get up to the guy's bedroom, and I ask him if he's got a condom. He says that he doesn't. Well, of course I'm not going to do him without a condom, I mean, I'm not a total idiot, so I tell him no shower cap, no beaver slap. So then..." her voice began to tremble with laughter again, "...so then, he takes out a piece of gum..."

She went into convulsions of laughter, tears streaming down her cheeks. Craig was starting to become much less amused, but he smiled anyway. "I think I can guess the rest."

Lisa was now laughing so hard that she was pounding her hand against the back of the couch. At least she had a pleasant laugh, not like that hyena woman he'd been with last month. And she was nice and young, no more than nineteen. After she calmed down, she wiped the tears from her eyes and placed her hand on Craig's knee. "Do you want to get started?"

"Absolutely."

She looked at him expectantly.

"Oh, yes, sorry about that." He reached into his back pocket and dug out his wallet. "A hundred, right?"

"Yep." Lisa took the bill he offered, and then began to lick the corner of it in a gesture that some mental condition must have convinced her was seductive. She folded the bill and shoved it into her purse, then put her arms around Craig's neck.

"No, wait. Not here." Craig freed himself from her arms and stood up. "Upstairs. In the attic."

"The attic? Oooh, kinky."

"You don't know the half of it."

Lisa's smile disappeared. "This is just supposed to be vanilla sex, right? I mean, for a hundred bucks I don't do any of that weird stuff."

"No, no," Craig assured her. "The attic has a great view of the mountains. I like to stare at them while I make love. It's a beautiful experience."

"Sounds hot! Lead the way."

He took her hand and led her into the kitchen. He unlocked the door to the attic, and then shut and relocked it after they'd both stepped onto the staircase. It was completely dark.

"The light switch up here's broken," he explained.

"How come you locked the door?" asked Lisa, traces of tension appearing in her voice as they ascended the stairs.

"My kids are down in the basement. You never know when they might get curious and come see what I'm up to."

"Your kids are in the house?"

"Yes. It's all right, their mother's dead."

«« — »»

They reached the top of the stairs. Lisa didn't realize she'd passed through another doorway until she heard the creak of the door being pulled shut and the click of the lock. There was no more light up here than on the staircase. No window.

"Please," said Lisa in a soft voice, "let me go."

"Let you go?" Craig sounded genuinely amused. "What are you implying?"

"Nothing. Just let me go home. I'll give you your money back, okay?"

"Now, Lisa, I want to know what you're implying. Surely you're not implying that I might be, oh, I don't know, planning to handcuff you to the bed and then very slowly torture you, bringing untold agony until I finally decide to cut out your heart and let you die?"

"Please—"

"Because you'd be wrong. I'm not going to cut out your heart."

Before she could react, Craig put his hand over her mouth and violently slammed her onto the bed. Her shriek was muffled and she felt a cold metal handcuff bracelet snap shut over her left ankle. Followed by the tip of a knife pressing against her neck.

"Feel that?" Craig asked.

Lisa managed a small nod.

"Like how it feels? No, probably not. I'm going to take my hand away, and if you scream or make any noise, I'll rip your throat open with it. Understand?"

She nodded again.

"Good girl. Now you just keep quiet, and everything will be fine."

He lifted his hand from her mouth. Lisa didn't scream, but she was unable to stifle the sobs that emerged. She could feel Craig's presence hovering over her, and then he pulled back.

"Good enough."

He walked a few steps away and flipped on the light switch. The illumination, provided by a small, weak bulb in the center of the attic, was barely even enough to let Lisa see the walls. But it allowed her to see more than enough to scare the hell out of her.

«« — »»

"Why does Dad always make us stay in the basement?"

Stephanie looked up from her book. "Retard, can't you see I'm trying to read?"

"How come he always puts us down here? Can't they just do foreplay in his bedroom with the door closed?"

"He probably doesn't want us to hear."

"Hear what?"

"Just forget about it."

"It isn't fair!" Abbey complained noisily. "I never get to know anything! If Dad would let us have friends, I bet they'd tell me all kinds of stuff!"

"Shhhh! Don't talk so loud!"

"I can talk loud if I want to!"

"I mean it, Abbey. You're gonna get us in trouble!"

"So?" Abbey wasn't quite sure why he was getting so riled up, but it was like something inside him had exploded. He was practically shouting. "I don't care if we get in trouble! This isn't fair! I hate it down here! *I wanna see the foreplay and the slimy white stuff!*"

«« — »»

Craig tied a gag around Lisa's mouth, and then went over and shut off the light. "Be right back," he said. "There seems to be a problem with my son."

He unlocked the door and quickly went down the staircase, leaving Lisa alone in the dark.

«« — »»

Abbey's anger abruptly turned to fear as he heard Dad unlock the upstairs door. "Now you're in for it," said Stephanie. Her tone of voice was much less smug than it was frightened.

Dad came down the stairs, his face dead serious. "What is going on down here?"

"Nothing," said Abbey, avoiding his eyes.

"Nothing? All that shouting was nothing? What did I tell you?" His voice was calm, but there was pure fury in his expression.

Abbey bit his lip.

"Look at me. What did I tell you? What have I told you time and again?"

"Not to make noise." Abbey's voice was barely audible.

"That's right. When I tell you to come down here, you do so without whining, and when you're down here, you stay quiet. How old are you?"

"Seven."

"How old did you say? Three?"

"Seven."

"Really? Are you sure you're not three? Because if you were three, maybe you wouldn't understand me when I said to be quiet. But if you're seven, I have to assume you understood me. Now isn't that right?"

"Yes, sir."

"So, if you understood me, that means you were disobeying me on purpose, right?"

Abbey hesitated. "I guess so."

"You're in a lot of trouble, young man. I have a guest right now, but after she's gone you're going to be punished."

Abbey felt like he was about to cry, but forced himself to hold the tears in. Crying would only make Dad even angrier. "Yes, sir."

Dad turned his attention toward Stephanie. "Stephanie, what was that your brother was yelling?"

Stephanie's face began to turn red. "I don't know."

"I think you do know. What was it?"

She let out a sob. "I don't know."

"Stephanie, what have you been telling your brother? And how are you learning these things? Have people been telling you this?"

Stephanie shook her head.

"You've been in my room, haven't you?"

"No, sir."

"You're lying to me. Do you know what happens to liars?"

"Daddy, I—"

"Don't interrupt me." Dad was still speaking in a relatively calm tone of voice. "You've been in my room, and you're telling things to your brother. Instead of protecting him, you're hurting him. Am I right?"

Stephanie buried her face in her hands.

Dad sighed. "We're going to have a nice little talk tomorrow, just you and me. You've messed up in a big way, young lady, and this isn't going to go away for a long time. A *long* time." He scratched his chin. "Are you scared?"

Stephanie didn't look up. "Yes, sir."

"Good. Stay scared. One way or another you *will* learn to obey me. Both of you. Now if I have to come back down, it will *not* be pleasant. Understand?"

"Yes, sir," Stephanie replied.

"Abbey?"

"Yes, sir."

"Good." Dad turned and headed back up the stairs. As he shut and locked the door from the other side, Abbey looked over at his sister, wanting to apologize. But she still had her face in her hands and was crying soundlessly.

«« — »»

Lisa frantically struggled against the chain that bound her to the bed, but neither the chain nor the bed would give way. She reached out as far as the chain would allow, but it wasn't far enough to grab something to use as a weapon.

Craig entered the attic. "I'm back," he announced.

In the dark, he opened a cabinet and retrieved something. Seconds later Lisa felt a sharp pain in her arm.

"Don't worry," said Craig, "you won't be out for more than a couple of minutes. I just need time to restrain you more thoroughly. Can't have you thrashing around like a fish about to be gutted, now can I?"

Lisa closed her eyes, and then opened them immediately. No, it couldn't have been immediately, because now she was chained spread-eagle to the bed. A leather gag was strapped over her mouth. And the light was on, revealing two shelves that were filled with children's playthings, mostly stuffed animals.

But they weren't playthings that any child would ever use. A teddy bear with blood around its mouth had been enhanced with sharp metal teeth. A stuffed rabbit had its ears lined with razor blades. A porcelain doll had a small knife tucked into its revealing black leather outfit. A large colorful rattle was covered with bloody spikes.

Craig smiled at her, and then furrowed his brow, trying to decide which of the toys to use. After a full minute of deliberation, he picked up a stuffed monkey. "This is my good friend Banana," Craig said. "Would you like to give Banana a hug?"

He outstretched the monkey's arms, revealing a chest covered with dozens of tiny needles. "Oh, yes, I think you two will be the best of friends," Craig said, tenderly wrapping the monkey's arms around Lisa's neck. Lisa could feel the prick of the needles, though they didn't puncture her.

"Ah, there's nothing like a good hug, is there? Maybe Banana will give you a tighter hug later, if you really need it." Leaving the monkey in place, Craig returned his attention to the shelves, then selected the teddy bear. "Lisa, meet my friend Bernard the Bear. He likes to bite." The teddy bear snapped its jaws together under Craig's control.

Oh, God, no! Lisa thought. She tried to scream, to plead for her life, but the leather gag muffled most of the noise. She struggled desperately against the chains.

"Don't struggle," Craig said. "Just try and think of all the ways it could be worse."

The teddy bear opened its jaws wide. Craig brought it down next to her ankle. "Now, where should I start?" He moved the bear's mouth along the length of her entire body, feinting bites a few times, until it was even with her face. He began rapidly opening and closing the jaws, like chattering teeth. "Are you scared?"

Lisa nodded and cried.

"Do you like being scared?"

Lisa was having trouble breathing. Her nose was uncovered, but it wasn't sufficient to get all the oxygen she needed to deal with this horror. There had to be a way out. She'd survived her lifestyle by being strong; she couldn't possibly die completely helpless. If only she could talk to him, distract him.

"Well, no need to answer. It was a rhetorical question." Craig moved the bear's mouth over to her throat, right over the monkey's arm, and opened the jaws. "I could bite you here, but that would be too easy. Too quick. No, I paid for a full hour; I want my money's worth."

He placed the bear on Lisa's left arm, right below the elbow. The fangs pressed into her flesh without breaking the skin. "This looks like a good place," Craig remarked. "Nice, soft muscle to rip through, plenty of nerves, but nothing that will kill you before I'm ready."

Then he removed the bear. "But where would be the surprise? Let me ask you a question, Lisa. Have you ever had sex blindfolded?"

Lisa didn't respond until Craig put the bear back against her arm. Then she nodded her head.

"Exciting, isn't it? Not knowing where the next touch is coming from. Not knowing what your lover is going to do next. It adds a whole new dimension to the experience."

Craig walked over to the switch and turned off the light. Then he walked back to the bed and stood there, completely silent.

Lisa waited.

She could feel his presence, but couldn't hear him. Since there was absolutely no light in the room, her eyes weren't going to adjust to the dark.

He moved.

Nothing for over a minute. Then a light bite on her toe. But not by the metal teeth. Not yet.

His tongue slid across her ankle.

More silence. More waiting.

And then terrible pain.

«« — »»

The next morning, as the sunlight streamed into his bedroom and reflected off his Marvel Super Heroes poster, Abbey came to a decision. He was going to steal the keys and see what was in the attic. He'd always given a great deal of thought to what might be up there, but he'd never dared to satisfy his curiosity. Last night had changed everything. If Dad was keeping secrets such as foreplay, what other secrets might be up there?

If he got caught, that was it; he was going to be punished like never before. But he was in lots of trouble already, and it was worth risking more to finally solve the mystery. Hopefully Stephanie would stay in her room—she was so scared of being punished that she might tell on him just to avoid being blamed for his actions.

Fifteen minutes later, his door swung open and Dad poked his head in. "Time to get up," he said.

Abbey yawned. "Okay."

"Do you have to go to the bathroom before I get in the shower?"

"No, I'm fine."

"I want you dressed and ready to go into town by the time I get out. Understand?"

"Yes, sir."

"Good boy. I've decided to give you and your sister one more chance to behave. Don't disappoint me."

After Dad left, Abbey got up and dressed himself as quickly as he could. He listened carefully until he heard the water start running in the shower, and then walked over to the bathroom door and knocked on it.

"What?" Dad called out.

"I was wrong. I have to go pee."

"All right, come on in."

Abbey opened the door and walked into the bathroom. The shower curtain was dark blue, so Dad wouldn't be able to see him. Dad's clothes were neatly draped over the sink, and there was a bulge in his pocket that was probably the keys. Abbey started to reach for them.

Dad peeked out from the side of the curtain. Abbey instantly pulled his hand away, praying he hadn't been caught.

"What are you doing?" Dad asked.

"Nothing."

"Hurry up and go. By the way, you're seven, I at least expect you to know if you have to go to the bathroom or not. You're not a baby anymore."

"I'm sorry."

Dad pulled his head back into the shower. Abbey grabbed the keys and stuffed them into his pocket, and then lifted the toilet seat and quickly peed. He hurried out of the bathroom, heart pounding.

He glanced over at Stephanie's room. Her door was still closed. Dad always took long showers, at least ten minutes, so Abbey would have enough time to see what was in the attic and then return the keys to the sink. He could say he wanted to brush his teeth as an excuse to get back in the bathroom.

The attic door was at the end of the hallway. Abbey tested four keys in the padlock before he found the right one. He removed the lock and kept it with him as he opened the door, stepped onto the staircase, and pulled the door closed behind him.

Now he was terrified. He was going to get caught—he knew it. Stephanie would tell. Or Dad would peek out through the curtain and see that his keys were gone.

He slid his hands along the wall, trying to find a light switch. Failing that, he proceeded up the stairs in the dark, wincing as each step creaked beneath his feet. How come things always made noise when he was trying to be quiet?

He reached the top of the stairs and once again felt around for a light switch. There had to be one around here *somewhere*. Dad didn't just wander around here in the dark, did he?

Abbey walked forward with his hands straight out in front of him so he wouldn't crash into anything. After a couple of steps, he touched a bed.

It felt wet.

The white stuff?

Stephanie was right, he thought. *This is where Dad does those things. But why doesn't he just use his own bed?*

He continued to feel along the bed, and then felt something soft.

Somebody's leg.

He sucked in a scream.

Oh my God she's still up here asleep I'm gonna get in trouble Dad's gonna kill me oh my God...

Abbey pulled his hand away and stood there in silence, praying the lady wouldn't wake up. He had to calm himself down. If he took off running for the stairs, he'd wake her up for sure.

He just needed a few seconds to catch his breath, and everything would be all right.

But something was wrong.

The lady wasn't breathing.

He held his own breath and listened close. Nothing.

He reached out and touched her leg again. But this time it didn't feel like a leg. It wasn't smooth. It was wet and rough. Abbey began to back away, until he hit a string dangling from the ceiling. He pulled it to turn on the light.

It was definitely a woman lying on the bed. But the sheets were soaked with blood. And the woman had chunks torn out of her body — dozens of them. There was even blood on the floor. Fortunately, Abbey hadn't stepped in any of it.

But then he threw up.

He shut off the light so he wouldn't have to look at the horrible sight, then half-walked, half-ran back to the staircase, trying to choke back a scream.

Despite his fear and panic, Abbey managed to keep from tumbling down the stairs as he went down them, moving faster than before but not quickly enough that the noise would alert Dad. Stephanie, maybe, but not Dad.

Then Dad spoke: "Abbey?"

Abbey was at the bottom of the stairs, right in front of the door. He couldn't hear the water running any more.

"*Abbey!*"

Dad's voice sounded like it was coming from the bathroom. Abbey hurriedly opened the door and stepped out into the hallway. The bathroom door was closed.

"Yeah, Dad?"

"Get in here!"

Abbey quickly snapped the padlock back into place and re-locked it. He was dead. Maybe as dead as that woman up there. Slowly, he began to walk toward the bathroom, shoving the keys into his pocket.

But his right hand was covered with blood! He *couldn't* go in there! It was too late to enter his bedroom and wipe it off on an old shirt or something.

He stopped outside the bathroom door. "What?"

"I said get in here."

Feeling like he was about to throw up again, Abbey used his left hand to turn the doorknob and pushed open the door. He walked into the bathroom, keeping his bloody hand behind his back in what he hoped looked like a natural position. Dad was peeking out from behind the curtain.

"Did you forget something?"

"I don't think so." Abbey's voice was trembling.

"When you go to the bathroom, you flush the toilet, all right? How many times do I have to tell you? Your sister and I don't want to look at an unflushed toilet every time we come in here, and you're more than old enough to remember. So flush it."

Abbey nodded, and then stepped over and flushed. Dad gave him a strange look. "What's wrong with you?"

"Nothing."

"That's a lie. Don't lie to me. Something's wrong with you. Why's your hand behind your back?"

Abbey shrugged.

"What have you got behind your back?"

"Nothing."

"Let me see your hand."

There was no way around this. Abbey held up his blood-covered hand and began to cry.

"What happened?"

Suddenly, he realized a way out. "I—I was using one of the knives in the kitchen and I cut myself."

"Well then it serves you right. You know not to play with knives. Wash your hand off and have Stephanie put a Band-Aid on it."

"I can do it."

"Whatever. I hope you learned your lesson."

"Yes, sir."

Dad turned the shower back on, and Abbey immediately went to the sink and turned on the faucet. As he held his hand under the stream of warm water, he put the keys back in Dad's pocket. He scrubbed some soap on his fingers, but traces of blood still remained under his fingernails. It didn't matter. He took a Band-Aid down from the medicine cabinet and stuck it to his palm. If he was lucky, Dad wouldn't ask to see the cut.

But, then again, that wasn't the real problem.

He'd left a big pool of puke next to where his Dad had murdered a woman.

And even if he managed to get back up there and clean the mess up, what was he supposed to do about the fact that Dad was a killer?

«« — »»

Dad sometimes took them out for ice cream if they behaved while he ran his errands. Today was one of those days, but Abbey just couldn't enjoy the treat. As he sat in the booth, chin smeared with chocolate, Dad set down his root beer float and stared across the table at him.

"What's the problem, son?"

"Hmmm?"

"You're acting like I'm going to smack you or something. What's wrong?"

"Nothing."

"Don't tell me *nothing*. Stephanie, what's wrong with your brother?"

Stephanie shrugged and averted her eyes.

"Okay," said Dad, folding his arms over his chest, "there's something going on that I don't know about. I want to know what it is, right now."

"Nothing," Abbey insisted.

"Abbey, regardless of what you'd like to believe, I'm not completely stupid. Now, all day you've been scared to look me in the eye, I can see you flinch whenever I make a move, so what's wrong? What did you do that you're worried about getting in trouble for?"

Abbey felt tears begin to well up in his eyes. *No! You can't cry! If you act like a baby, you'll get yourself in big trouble!* God, he was scared. He was only seven, how was he supposed to deal with something like this?

"Look me in the eye."

Abbey did so, silently praying that no tears would spill. Dad stared at him for a long moment, and then stood up. "Let's go home now," he said.

«« — »»

"All right, kids," said Dad as they walked through the front door. "In the basement."

Abbey had to fight back a scream. Couldn't Dad wait until tomorrow to go into the attic?

It occurred to Abbey that faking an upset stomach might buy him some time, but faking it was unnecessary because his stomach already felt like it was being wrung out like a wet cloth. He wrapped his arms around his belly and moaned softly. "Dad, my stomach hurts."

"There's Pepto-Bismol in the medicine cabinet."

"Could you get it?"

"I *could*, but you're old enough. Hurry up—I have work to do."

"What kind of work?"

"Work that's none of your business, and you know that already. Now stop playing around."

"Can't we just stay up here a *little* longer?"

Dad chuckled, but there was no humor in it. "You'll never learn, will you? We're going to have this argument every single night for the rest of our lives. Get down in the basement."

Stephanie hurried down there, but Abbey refused to move. No matter how much trouble he got in now, it couldn't possibly be worse than if Dad went into the attic before he had a chance to clean up. "No," he said.

"*What?*"

"No. I'm not going down there."

"Young man, you are getting yourself in more trouble than you know what to do with. You march down those steps, right now, or I'll throw you down there myself."

Abbey backed up. "No."

Suddenly Dad grabbed Abbey's arm, holding tight enough that it hurt. He yanked Abbey over to the basement door and down onto the first step, then slammed the door shut. Abbey began pounding wildly against the door with both fists. "Let me out!" he screamed. "Let me out of here, you shithead!"

The door opened. Dad looked more furious than Abbey had ever seen him. "What did you call me?"

No sense lying about it. "A shithead."

"Where did you learn that word?"

"I don't know."

"Did Stephanie teach you?"

Abbey shook his head, and then lunged forward to make a break for it. Dad caught him by the collar and pulled him back onto the top stair. "If I ever hear that kind of talk from you ever again, I'll smack you sense-less. Got it?"

"Got it, shithead."

The slap almost knocked Abbey down the stairs. It stung like crazy, but that didn't matter. All that mattered was keeping Dad from going up into the attic. Maybe this would get him so mad that he'd forget about it.

But then Dad slammed the door once again, and there was nothing more Abbey could do. He sat down on the steps and began to cry.

«« — »»

That kid was going to snap out of this phase *real* quick. Craig unlocked the door to the attic and headed up the stairs, trying to decide upon a severe enough punishment. Probably a week down in the basement would straighten him out. And if it turned out that Stephanie was teaching him to swear, she'd stay right down there with him. It was just ridiculous how—

He stopped. The smell was wrong. Not the scent of death, but the scent of...vomit? He flipped on the light, saw the mess, and sighed deeply. Abbey had been up here. He'd seen everything. No wonder he was acting so strangely.

And now Craig was going to have to deal with him.

He went back down the stairs, heart pounding. Eventually he had known something like this was going to happen, but that didn't make things easier.

«« — »»

The basement door opened again. Abbey wiped the tears from his eyes as Dad looked down at him.

"Are you all right, son?"

"Yes, sir."

"I'm sorry I hit you. I shouldn't have done it. Do you want to come upstairs with me so we can talk about this?"

"No, sir."

"That wasn't supposed to be a question. Come on." Dad reached out his hand to help Abbey to his feet.

"I don't want to go back up there."

"Well, sometimes we have to do things we don't want to. I'll explain everything, and we'll both feel a lot better."

He's going to kill me.

Abbey had learned the secret, and now Dad was going to see that nobody else found out. He was going to die just like that woman. Or maybe his death would be even worse.

He let Dad take his hand and got to his feet. As he stepped through the doorframe, Dad closed the basement door, and then put his hand firmly on Abbey's shoulder and led him down the hallway towards the attic door, which was hanging open.

Right in front of the door Abbey hesitated. "Please don't make me go up there."

"Abbey, you were snooping around where you shouldn't have. Where you *absolutely* knew you shouldn't have. And you got caught, so what happens next is out of your hands. You gave up your freedom when you invaded my privacy. Now get up there."

"I'm scared."

"You should be."

"You go first."

"She's not going to bite you."

"I don't care. I want you to go first."

Dad removed his hand from Abbey's shoulder, and then went up the first three steps. He glanced over his shoulder and saw that Abbey hadn't moved. "Come on, hurry up."

Abbey slammed the door and quickly snapped the padlock shut just as Dad kicked the door from the other side. The door shook on its hinges. It wouldn't take long for him to break out.

"Abbey! You open this door right now! If you don't, I'll kill you! You hear me?"

There wasn't time to run over to his room. If Abbey wanted to get away, he was going to have to leave all his possessions behind. He'd have to leave Stephanie, too, not that she would have come along even if she had the chance.

Tears flowing freely, Abbey dashed into the living room, out the front door, and onto the driveway, where he mounted his bicycle. He pedaled down the street as fast as he could, not thinking about where he was going, not thinking about how he was going to survive on his own, only thinking about getting away before Dad came after him.

«« — »»

The door flew open, shaking in its frame, as the jamb plate that held the padlock broke from the wood. Craig ran to the front door and peered outside. No sign of Abbey. He went back to the basement door, unlocked it, and called for Stephanie.

"Hurry up," he said to her as she approached the steps. "We're going after your brother."

«« — »»

Abbey had gone less than half a mile when his front tire struck a large rock, flipping the bike and sending him hurtling into the air. He landed on his chin and his teeth smacked together on the side of his mouth, drawing blood. He lay there for a moment, and then rolled over on his back, eyes filled with tears. His arm hurt, both of his legs hurt, and his chin hurt so bad that he thought he might have tore it right off. He touched it and his fingertip came away bloody.

He wasn't going to cry though.

Seconds later, his resolve broke, and he began sobbing. Sobbing so loudly that he barely heard the car as it drove up next to him. Dad and Stephanie got out, and Dad quickly bent down over him.

"Abbey, are you okay? Can you hear me?"

"Yuh-yes," Abbey managed to reply.

"How many fingers am I holding up?" Dad held up his index, middle, and ring finger.

"Three."

"Good, you're fine. Just a little banged up. Well, a lot banged up, but you'll heal."

Dad and Stephanie helped him to his feet, and Abbey didn't struggle as they put him into the car, even though he wasn't sure Dad really *was* going to give him a chance to heal.

«« — »»

The dead lady hadn't been moved. Stephanie was down in the basement, with no complaints, of course. Dad didn't even feel the need to lock it with just her down there. Abbey stood trembling as Dad put a reassuring hand on his shoulder. Dad's other hand held a magazine, folded in half so Abbey couldn't see the cover. Abbey was still in a great deal of pain, but Dad had promised to fix him up as soon as they took care of this business.

"I was trying to shield you from this," Dad said, softly. "I was trying to shield you from everything like this, because I was afraid you'd end up like me. And your grandfather. Stephanie won't turn out this way, but I had to protect her from it to keep her from telling you things you weren't supposed to know."

Abbey was silent. His chin was so badly swollen that he probably couldn't have spoken even if he wanted to.

"I know Stephanie got into the magazines in my room. What did she tell you?"

Abbey shrugged.

"I know it's hard to talk about. I'll explain everything to you, starting tonight. And then I'll explain what makes us different. You see, to do what Stephanie told you about is easy for most people, but not for us. I don't know why, it just turned out that way."

He removed his hand from Abbey's shoulder, then gave him the magazine. Abbey unfolded it and glanced at the cover, which showed a naked lady lying on a bed.

"Open it."

Abbey hesitated, but then opened it to a page in the middle. It showed a man and a woman, doing exactly what Stephanie had described. Abbey felt sick.

"You don't have the feelings now," said Dad, "but pretty soon you will. And they'll be different from the feelings that most other people have. If you want to do *that*—" he tapped on the picture in the magazine—"you'll have to do *this* first." He pointed to the dead lady.

Abbey dropped the magazine and shook his head. "No…" he said, his jaw aching with the effort of speaking just that one word.

"I'm sorry. That's the way it is. Your mother and I were happy for a few years together, but we only did the thing in the magazine to make you and Stephanie. One day I couldn't take it any more."

"You killed her?" Abbey was incredulous. He no longer cared about the pain in his jaw.

"Someday you'll understand. You can't tell any of this to Stephanie, though, because she won't. You have to promise me. Absolutely none of this is to be mentioned to your sister, do you hear me?"

Abbey nodded slowly.

"Good. You have a few more years left, Abbey, but then I'll teach you exactly what to do. I'll even bring you the girl."

"I don't want to do this," said Abbey.

"You will pretty soon. Trust me."

Abbey took a step away. "I'm *never* going to do that!"

"Yes, you will. Someday."

"*NO!*" Abbey lunged for the shelves, grabbing a porcelain doll. He flung it at Dad, striking him dead center in the face. The doll shattered and Dad fell to his knees, clutching at his nose.

"Abbey! Stop it!"

Abbey grabbed a fire engine with a knife poking out of its front hood. "You killed Mommy!" he screamed, throwing it. This one also struck dad in the face, and he fell backward, his head slamming against the floor. But he quickly sat up again.

Abbey snatched two stuffed animals, throwing each of them, but only hitting with one. It struck Dad in the forehead, leaving gashes where the fangs bit into his flesh. Abbey had no idea he could throw so hard.

"*Abbey!*"

"I hate you! I *hate* you!" Abbey shrieked, throwing more toys at Dad, one after the other. Dad's scream of pain scared him more than any shout of rage he'd ever heard.

Abbey stood there, gasping for breath. Dad lay on his back, clutching at his throat, blood seeping through his fingers. He was still alive, but Abbey knew that he was no longer a threat.

Not that he would get too close. Yet.

The door leading to the attic swung open. "Daddy?" Stephanie's voice called out. "What's going on?"

Abbey didn't reply. He felt strange, tingly. His body didn't hurt any more.

He heard Stephanie take one step up the staircase. "Daddy?"

"Don't come up here!" Abbey called out.

"Where's Daddy?"

"I said don't come up here!"

More footsteps. She was coming up anyway. Abbey glanced over at the dead lady, and then back at Dad. Dad had been right. It *did* feel good.

Stephanie stepped into the basement and screamed at the top of her lungs. Abbey picked up the teddy bear with the fangs.

Maybe it could feel even better.

THE SOCKET

The day Quincy lost his left eye was the best day of his life.

Oh, sure, it didn't seem that way at first. Certainly not as he staggered home, hand clenched around the switchblade that jutted out of his face, blood trickling through his fingers. In fact, at this point the situation seemed to fall squarely into the category of "unpleasant."

"Kiss my ass, you zit-ridden mommy-rammer!" had perhaps not been the wisest response to the demand that he hand over his wallet, but Quincy was never one to back down from a fight. Even after the mugger held the tip of a knife up to his iris, Quincy had stood firm. But then the mugger had made good on his threat, stabbing the blade an inch and a half into the orb. Quincy hadn't stood quite so firm after that.

So not only had he lost his eye, he'd lost his wallet. Sure, he didn't have any cash or credit cards inside, but he *did* have his frequent diner card at Tanglen's Deli, and he'd only been two stamps away from a free sandwich. That hurt.

He burst into his apartment, having walked the entire fifteen blocks without anyone offering to help. Good. He didn't want anybody's help, anyway. He hated owing people. And he especially wasn't going to a hospital...hospitals killed people for their internal organs. Nope, the only person Quincy was going to trust was Quincy, and he'd take care of this little problem lickety split.

Lickety split? He'd never even *thought* the words "lickety split" before. Maybe the tip of the switchblade was poking his brain or something.

He hurried into the bathroom and stared into the mirror with his good eye. Lots of blood. Enough that he couldn't tell how bad the damage was. He took a deep breath, bit down on the sides of his mouth, and then wrenched the blade out of his eye. A gout of something clear and slimy sprayed onto the mirror, making him cringe.

The eye was going to have to come out—that much was certain. Equally certain was the fact that it was probably going to be a rather uncomfortable experience. But, hey, he was just going to have to take a couple/three aspirin and tough it out.

He could do it. He had willpower.

He wet a towel under the faucet and then wiped his face as thoroughly as he could. The eye was still oozing, but not as badly as before. He wished he had a good set of surgical tools to perform this little operation, but a kitchen knife was going to have to suffice.

Quincy went into the kitchen and opened the freezer door. He still had most of a tub of lime sherbet, so he pressed that to his eye and held it there for about ten minutes until he felt sufficiently numb. Then he went to the silverware drawer and selected the sharpest knife he owned, which really wasn't all that sharp, and returned to the bathroom. He stuffed a washrag into his mouth to muffle the inevitable screams and blasphemies, then raised the knife to begin the surgery.

«« — »»

He had shrieked a great deal during the procedure, but felt no personal shame over this. After all, he had been severing the stalk that kept his own eye from falling out of its socket. Many people wouldn't have been able to do that at all, much less in silence. He'd been brave, and now the job was done.

The blood continued flowing and Quincy grew tired of constantly wiping it off, so he stuffed the washrag into the socket—just a little, not enough to do any damage—and let it dangle.

After a while, all of the fluid leakage stopped. As there was no reason that Quincy could think of for keeping his ruined eye around, he flushed it down the toilet like a dead goldfish. Then he removed the washcloth and thoroughly cleaned out the socket with antiseptic. This should have hurt like hell, but for some reason it didn't, possibly because he was getting used to pain.

He glanced at himself in the mirror again and frowned. Well, he certainly could look worse, but he was still going to have to do something about his appearance if he wanted to keep his job waiting tables at Momma Helga's Diner. Business would not be helped if rumors were spread about frequent customer regurgitation.

He searched through his dresser drawers until he found his old black t-shirt with the grease stains. He took it into the living room, along with scissors and a needle and thread (well, fishing line), and made himself a sturdy eye patch. There. That would take care of any problems caused by his physical appearance, and he could entertain young children with pirate talk.

Quincy slept well that night.

«« — »»

The next day, with a few hours before he had to be at work, Quincy went grocery shopping. His socket—the emptiness there—was beginning to bother him. It just felt too vacant. Not to mention the fact that his depth perception was all screwed up, causing him to knock over a display of gummi bears.

He stopped at the produce section, and stared at the grapes for a very long time.

Some of them looked big enough...

No, that was ridiculous.

Of course, he *did* like grapes, so if it didn't work he wouldn't have wasted his money, would he?

«« — »»

Since Quincy was a careful sort, he first cut out part of a gallon-sized milk container and wedged the plastic near the back of the socket, just to keep anything from rolling back where it shouldn't. Then he inserted one of the grapes, after drawing an iris on it with white-out and a felt-tipped pen.

It looked hilarious.

He wished he could show somebody.

Unfortunately, the grape still felt too light and off-balance compared to his real eye.

But there were other options.

«« — »»

Tips had been stingy that night, and Quincy began to wonder if the eye patch was making people uncomfortable. Martin, his boss, hadn't been treating him especially well, either, showing little concern for the "infection" Quincy claimed to have developed.

"And how was everything?" Quincy asked the family of four: two parents, a boy, and a girl.

"I think the bread was stale," the father muttered. "And you never did bring me the extra mustard."

Quincy noted with a bit of annoyance that the man hadn't used up the mustard he *had* brought, but didn't say anything.

"My mom wants to know what happened to your eye," the boy said. His mother nudged him in the ribs, hard.

Quincy smiled. "The Easter Bunny took it."

"Really?" The boy seemed frightened by such a concept.

"Uh-huh. He took it while I was asleep. Know what he left me?"

The boy shook his head.

Quincy lifted the eye patch, revealing the melting chocolate-covered cherry he'd inserted into the socket. The mother gasped, and the little girl covered her mouth with both hands to stifle a scream. Enjoying their horrified expressions, Quincy stuck out his thumb and jammed it into the socket, squirting white goo and sending melted chocolate dripping down his cheek. He pulled out his thumb with the cherry impaled on it.

"What's that nursery rhyme?" he asked, barely able to control his laughter. "You know, the one with the kid sticking his finger into a pie and getting a plum?"

The father threw up all over his unused mustard. Quincy popped the cherry into his mouth and chewed happily. The mother screamed, and the boy and girl immediately joined in as concerned patrons turned from their meals to see what the ruckus was all about.

《《 — 》》

After cleaning the excess chocolate out of the socket, Quincy lay on his bed, pounding his fist against his pillow, his entire body shaking with laughter. That had been *great*! He couldn't remember ever laughing so hard in his life.

He wondered if there was money to be made from this.

See Quincy and His Amazing Stuffed Socket!

Maybe he could even get on television.

But first he'd have to practice.

《《 — 》》

For the next week Quincy wandered the streets, surprising unsuspecting pedestrians with whatever object he'd currently wedged in his socket. Quarters went over well, and so did cherry tomatoes. He wanted to put a Mickey Mouse head in there but was afraid he might get sued. His favorite was the balloon, which he inflated as far as he could within the socket, then popped with a needle just as the victim began to gape at him.

Quincy was having an absolutely wonderful time. He had no idea that freaking people out could be so much fun!

Near the end of the week he walked all over the city with a celery stalk protruding from the socket. Not one person was willing to ride in an elevator with him for more than one floor.

The reaction at the day care center was *incredible*.

«« — »»

"And were you ever enrolled in college?" the young woman at the employment office inquired.

Quincy shook his head, and scratched at the eye patch. "Nope. High school was more than enough for me."

"And all of your job experience has been waiting tables?"

Quincy continued scratching. "Not exactly. I spent some time as a dishwasher, too. Say, do you mind if I make myself a little more comfortable?"

The woman gave him a blank stare for a moment. "Uh, no, of course not."

"Thanks." Quincy tore off the eye patch. The live beetles he'd packed into the socket spilled out and began racing around the woman's desk. Her screams and the repeated *thuds* as she slammed a telephone book down upon the insects were well worth the fact that without a job, Quincy was probably going to be kicked out of his apartment at the beginning of the month.

«« — »»

He sat in his dark closet, laughing maniacally. The socket was beginning to show signs of rot, despite his frequent applications of the antiseptic, but he didn't care. The gangrene made his appearance all the more effective.

«« — »»

Finally, the call came.

"Excuse me," said the low, male voice on the other end, "I'd like to speak with...uh...the eye guy."

Quincy set down the artificial rat he'd been trying to cut down to socket size. "That's me!"

"I'm from *Seriously Disgusting*, the television show…maybe you've seen it?"

"Yes!" Quincy exclaimed. "I have! You guys do a great job! You want to do a segment on me, right?"

"Well, we'd at least like to speak with you, get the back story. Are you going to be available tomorrow?"

"Hell yeah! I'm ready right now, if you want!"

"No, tomorrow will be fine. We'd like to conduct a short interview at your place of residence, and perhaps follow you around town for a while. Is this okay?"

"It's great!"

"All right, how does tomorrow around noon sound?"

"Perfect!"

He gave the man his address and hung up. Yep, this was his big shot at stardom. He wondered how they'd found out who he was. Probably asked at Momma Helga's Deli. Quincy danced around the apartment for a while, singing the *Seriously Disgusting* theme song at the top of his lungs.

«« — »»

But when he woke up the next morning, he was very disturbed.

He was going into the big-time now. He couldn't just show them the same old stuff. He didn't want people yawning at the eye guy.

He needed a new twist.

«« — »»

Quincy entered his apartment, holding a bag from the toy store. He emptied the contents onto his bed, and then went into the kitchen to retrieve the metal spoon he'd sharpened just before he left.

«« — »»

Darren Taylor gave his cameraman an annoyed look as he knocked on the door a third time. He hoped this guy Quincy was legit.

"Come in!" said a voice from within the apartment. Christ, the guy sounded insane.

Darren turned the knob and pushed the door inward. Quincy stood in the center of the room, naked save for a pair of boxer shorts. His entire body was slick with blood. He had gouged out chunks of flesh along his arms, legs, and chest, and wedged large plastic eyeballs in each of them, at least forty in all. A lit cigar protruded from his eye socket.

"See?" Quincy said, making a wide, sweeping gesture toward himself. "I compensated for the empty socket!" He began to cackle with mad laughter as he fell to his knees, cracking two or three of the eyeballs in his legs as he did so.

Darren backed away, appalled. Quincy's smile disappeared. "Wait...where're you going? This is my big chance!"

He grabbed a toy pinwheel from the coffee table and plunged the stick end of it deep into his good eye. Something that looked like bloody gelatin splattered against his fist. "How about this? We can tell the viewers at home that I can see them with the eye gook on my hand!"

As Darren and the cameraman broke into a run, Quincy giggled and slurped up the eyeball residue. "Now I'll get to see the inside of my stomach! It's Must See TV!"

He gave the multicolored, metallic wheel a generous spin and staggered around the living room, laughing hysterically.

ONE OF THEM

"Come and see the freaks!" shouted the carnival barker, holding his wooden cane with a palsied hand. "For a mere fifty cents you can observe human oddities like nothing your innocent eyes have ever witnessed! See the most nightmarish and bizarre examples of human aberration and misery, right behind these very curtains! You will not soon forget the twisted and ghastly sights that will greet you upon admittance to this gallery of the macabre, for but fifty cents, a half-dollar, two quarters! Who has the courage, the constitution, to brave the horrors contained within? Anyone?"

"I want to see them," said a young boy, holding out his palm.

The barker looked at the quarters in his hand and sneered. "I'm afraid not, young man. How old are you?"

"Eleven."

"Eleven? An eleven-year-old mind is far too fragile to cope with the frights behind these curtains, I promise you that. Come back in about seven years and I'll let you in." He chuckled. "Remind me that you were here today and I'll let you in for half price."

"But I want to see the freaks."

"Ah, the persistence of youth. Shouldn't a young lad like you be in school?"

The boy shrugged.

"Do your parents know you're here?"

"No."

The barker grinned, and then glanced to his left and to his right with exaggerated caution. He gestured for the boy to lean in close and spoke in a whisper. "Well, well, well, far be it from me to refuse admission to one who has risked so much to get here. Perhaps for seventy-five cents I'll let you in. We'll call it an extra quarter for insurance purposes."

188 - ONE OF THEM

The boy hesitated, but dug into his pocket. "I don't have another quarter."

"An even dollar then."

The boy reached into his other pocket and pulled out a dollar bill. "Excellent!" said the barker, snatching the money out of his hand. "Come with me, young man, and I'll show you sights that will haunt you until your dying day!"

He held open the curtain and beckoned with his cane. The boy walked through the opening and the barker followed, letting the curtain close behind them.

"Not afraid of the dark, are you?" asked the barker, putting his hand on the boy's shoulder.

"No."

"A brave boy. Don't worry, the freaks will be well illuminated. You won't miss a thing."

They walked forward through the complete darkness for a moment. "Stop right here," said the barker. "Are you certain you're ready for this?"

Silence.

"If you're nodding, I can't see you in the dark."

"Yes."

"Good. Behold...*the freaks*!"

The lights came on. They were surrounded by cages, four on each side. Most were occupied. The boy quickly turned in a circle, looking at all of them, and frowned.

"Those aren't freaks!"

"Is that so?"

"They're just normal people in cages! There's nothing scary about them!"

"Ah, but you're wrong." The barker walked over to the first cage, which contained a grey-haired middle-aged man sitting in the corner. The barker tapped the cage with his cane. "This man has not spoken in six years, not since his wife put a handgun in her mouth and pulled the trigger in front of him and their five-year-old daughter. They say that suicidal women rarely use violent means, preferring pills or poison, but his wife was an exception. God only knows what thoughts ravaged his mind as he watched her brain matter stain their kitchen wall, and God only knows what thoughts ravage his mind at this very moment."

He tapped the next cage, which contained a young woman trembling in the corner. "This fine specimen has a fear of snakes. Having dozens of them slither all over her naked body was more than her fragile psyche could handle. She continues to brush at imaginary serpents; refuses to speak for fear that one might slide into her open mouth. One can only guess what reptilian horrors lurk in her dreams during her rare moments of sleep."

The woman looked at the young boy and then hid her face.

"Next in my gallery of freaks is this gentleman," said the barker, tapping the third cage. "An empty husk of a man. Lobotomized, though his hair has grown over the scar. He lives, and yet he does not live." The barker twisted his head at the young boy and smiled. "Imagine that. To be physically alive and conscious, and yet see nothing, feel nothing. Does that frighten you?"

"I want my money back!"

"I delivered what I promised. You expected physical deformities and grotesque mutations, but I gave you something infinitely more chilling! Why see a bearded lady when you can see a man haunted by bloody acts of violence he doesn't even remember? Why see a two-headed cat when you can see a woman who cries endlessly over the death of a son who never took his first breath? Why see the human spider when you can see a human whose grip on reality was lost for absolutely no reason at all? I have given you the freaks of the mind!"

"This isn't any fun!" said the little boy. "This isn't what I paid for!"

"It's rarely fun to catch a glimpse of your own future."

"I want my dollar back."

"There are no refunds."

The little boy turned and ran back the way they'd come. The barker smiled with satisfaction, and then rapped on the cages a few more times just to torment the occupants.

«« — »»

What a rip-off. And now he didn't have enough money left for a funnel cake. The little boy scowled as he continued walking through the carnival. His mom would probably find out that he'd played hooky, and he'd get in trouble without even having seen anything good.

As he walked through the carnival, he thought about his grandfather, who had gotten that disease where you couldn't remember anything, not even to feed yourself. In the last few months before he died, Grandpa had shouted a lot and called him by the wrong name.

Grandpa had been really nice before that.

Normal.

The little boy quickly headed for the exit, wondering if it was just his imagination that the bright lights of the carnival seemed to have dimmed a bit.

SECRET MESSAGE

Gzqudx eqnvmdc zr gd nodmdc sgd kdssdq. Otqd fhaadqhrg. Vgzs vzr sghr, z bncd?

Gd zkvzxr dminxdc rnkuhmf sgd czhkx bqxosnfqzl hm sgd mdvro-zodq, ats gd'c mdudq gzc nmd lzhkdc sn ghl adenqd. Sgdqd vzr mn qdstqm zccqdrr nm sgd dmudknod, itrs z knbzk onrslzqj. Hs vzr oqnazakx nmd ne ghr atcchdr okzxhmf z injd.

Vdkk, gdx, hs lhfgs ad etm. Gd bgdbjdc ghr unhbd lzhk (nn ldrrzfdr) zmc ghr d-lzhk (mnsghmf ats rozl), sgdm rzs cnvm zs sgd szakd zmc vdms sn vnqj.

Sgd gzmcvqhssdm kdssdq ehkkdc sgd dmshqd rgdds ne ozodq, ats sgd vqhshmf vzr udqx kzqfd zmc hs nmkx rddldc sn ad nmd rdmsdmbd knmf. Sgzs vntkc lzjd hs z ahs lnqd cheehbtks, rhmbd rnkuhmf z bqxosnfqzl cdodmcdc nm hcdmshexhmf ezlhkhzq ozssdqmr ne kdssdqr, ats sgd czhkx mdvrozodq gzcm's rstlodc ghl rhmbd ghfg rbgnnk zmc mdhsgdq vntkc sghr.

Zesdq z bntokd ne ezkrd rszqsr, gd ehftqdc nts sgzs mns nmkx vzr hs z rsqzhfgsenqvzqc rtarshstshnm bhogdq, ats hs gzc z rhlokd ozssdqm: dzbg kdssdq qdoqdrdmsdc sgd kdssdq chqdbskx zesdq hs. Gd pthbjkx adfzm ehkkhmf hm sgd qdrs ne sgd ldrrzfd...zmc qdzkhydc vgzs hs rzhc adenqd gd'c dudm ehmhrgdc.

"Vghkd xnt'ud addm cdbnchmf sghr, xntq bzs gzr addm rteenbzshmf hm sgd eqddydq."

Gzqudx bgtbjkdc. Gd chcm's gzud z bzs, nq zmx odsr. Hs vzr itrs ghlrdke zmc ghr rhwsddm xdzq-nkc cztfgsdq Shmz.

Ghr vhed vzr knmf fnmd. Sgdx'c knbjdc sgzs orxbgn to enq fnnc vgdm Shmz vzr itrs entq.

Ne bntqrd, Knthrd *gzc* knudc sn bzkk Shmz "lx khsskd jhssdm..."

Gzqudx gtqqhdc sgqntfg sgd jhsbgdm hmsn sgd fzqzfd. Gd chcm's dudm sghmj Shmz bntkc ehs hm sgd bgdrs eqddydq, ats ghr otkrd vzr qzbhmf zmxvzx.

Gd sgqdv nodm sgd khc.

Shmz vzrm's hmrhcd.

Mns zkk ne gdq, zmxvzx.

Zkk ne sgd ennc gzc addm qdlnudc. Kxhmf nm sgd anssnl ne sgd eqddydq vzr zm dxdazkk. Mdws sn sgzs, z gdzqs. Zmc sgdm z snd. Ehmzkkx, rodkkdc nts hm hmsdrshmdr, vzr sgd vnqc "jhkk."

Dxd gdzqs snd jhkk.

Gd gdzqc Knthrd'r ezlhkhzq bzbjkd eqnl sgd nodm cnnqvzx sn sgd jhsbgdm, rzv sgd atsbgdq jmhed hm gdq gzmc, zmc pthbjkx chrbnudqdc sgzs sgd ldrrzfd vzr, hmcddc, pthsd zbbtqzsd.

MR. SENSITIVE

Aw, jeez, don't let her start bawling. Jake Triben watched Melissa's (or was it Margaret's?) eyes start to well up with tears. He'd almost successfully made it out of her bed and now he was going to have to deal with this crap.

"I thought this meant something," Melissa/Margaret said, pulling the blanket up over her breasts as if he hadn't already seen them from every conceivable angle.

"Look, I didn't say it wasn't fun," Jake insisted. "Let's just not make this into more than it is, okay?"

"You said you loved me!"

Something about the pathetic tone of her voice made Jake grin. Maybe he could get some entertainment value out of this. "Okay, let me share a little secret with you. When the words 'I love you' are followed by 'Oh, yeah, baby, do it just like that,' they aren't necessarily sincere."

She angrily wiped a tear from her cheek. "You said it before we even slept together."

"Right. Well, pre-coital 'I love you' doesn't count, either. But if I come a second time and *then* say it, hey, I might mean it."

I need to save that line for future use, Jake thought, quickly getting out of bed. Toying with a recently deflowered virgin's emotions was enjoyable, but he didn't want to push it to the point where his penis became a target of violence.

She just stared at him silently as he pulled on his underwear. "You have nothing to be ashamed of," Jake told her. "You did damn good for your first time, aside from that little gagging incident. Now that the cherry popping is out of the way, you can make up for lost time."

She had a lot of lost time to make up for. Melissa/Margaret (or was it Maggie?) had still been a virgin at twenty-five, which was seriously messed up. Jake had practically gone through a woman a week since he was sixteen, and he was twenty-nine now.

He finished getting dressed, ready to make a run for it if she suddenly went nutzo, but she just continued to stare at him, sniffling. "I'll let myself out," he said.

"Jake?"

"Yeah?"

She gave him a sad look. "You should really be more sensitive."

"I'll work on that and get back to you."

Jake left her apartment and walked down the hallway, whistling. He'd gotten laid and showed some needy bitch who was boss. Another great Friday night. He wondered if he could go back, beg for forgiveness, do her again, and then dump her again…but no, even he probably couldn't pull that one off.

He went home and got some much needed sleep.

«« — »»

Jake got up just before noon. His only plans were to hit the clubs late that evening, so he sat around in his underwear and watched cartoons on television most of the day. He kept waiting for Melissa/Margaret/Maggie to call, but she never did. Of course, he'd given her a fake phone number, but sometimes these chicks could turn into stalkers. He probably should have checked for somebody tailing him on the drive home.

As he watched television, he absent-mindedly scratched his balls.

They felt…weird.

Immediately concerned, he checked them out individually. The right one seemed okay. So did the left one.

It was the new one in the middle that made him nervous.

He gasped and sat up straight. What was it? A tumor? Could this be cancer? He played with his balls all the time…how could a lump like this appear without him noticing?

Now in a state of panic, he called his doctor for an emergency appointment.

«« — »»

Dr. Nicholas McLaughlin entered the examination room, frowning as he looked at his clipboard. He shut the door behind him, sat down next to Jake, and sighed.

"Is it bad?" Jake asked.

"Ummm, I'm really not sure how to tell you this," said Dr. McLaughlin. "The good news is that it's not cancerous."

"Oh, thank God."

"It is, we believe, a third testicle."

"It's *what?*"

"A third testicle."

"How the hell did I grow a third nut?"

"It seems unlikely that you grew it, so to speak. You've probably had it all along and just didn't notice."

"Didn't notice? Didn't *notice?* Doc, I may not notice somebody's new hairstyle or new dress, but a third nut I'm gonna notice!"

"My guess is that this third testicle simply hadn't descended into your scrotum until now."

"So where the hell was it hanging out? My belly button?"

"A third testicle in males is not an unheard-of occurrence. However, we'll want to do more studies."

"Studies? You mean like studies where I appear on the cover of one of those science magazines? Jake Triben, the Amazing Three-Nut Boy?"

"I understand that you're confused and upset. Rest assured that we'll have it removed with no risk to—"

"Whoa! You're not removing a damn thing. No scalpels near there. If I have to be a three-nut mutant, I'll be a three-nut mutant, but no way are you cutting me open."

Dr. McLaughlin shrugged. "I don't see any danger in retaining the third testicle. But I do recommend that you undergo further tests, just in case."

Jake shook his head. "You said it's not cancer, and that's good enough for me. Go poke somebody else's gonads. I'm outta here."

«« — »»

Jake didn't much feel like hitting the clubs, so he stayed home and watched more television. Maybe he *should* let the doctor do some kind of nut-removal surgery…after all, he didn't want the ladies thinking he was some kind of freak, did he?

Still, what if the surgery went terribly awry? What if the doctor slipped with his scalpel? What if he removed two testicles by accident? What if Jake awoke to find himself completely penis-free? Or what if the doctor filmed the entire surgery? Dr. McLaughlin would gain fame and fortune for discovering this medical marvel, and Jake would have to go live as a hermit to escape the shame of being a tri-balled aberration.

Woe and misery.

Misery and woe.

His social life was over. There'd be no more sex with regular women. He'd have to start dating fat chicks, or transsexuals, or girls with three tits.

He walked into the bathroom, stripped out of his underwear, and stared at himself in the mirror. Actually, just standing here like this, you couldn't really tell that he had fifty percent more testicles than a normal human being. As long as the ladies didn't do too much manipulation down there, he might be okay.

He gently rolled the bonus testicle between his fingers. It was just as sensitive as the other two. Maybe it would bring him to heights of sexual pleasure that he'd never before imagined. Maybe it was truly a blessing. Maybe he was a god among mere mortals!

No, it was a freaky-ass third ball, and it creeped him out.

He went back into the living room and watched some more television, but he wasn't able to concentrate. He searched the TV listings for an infomercial about an easy-to-use third testicle removal spray, but didn't find one. Depressed, he went to bed.

«« — »»

He dreamt of being crushed by a giant boulder. He woke up in a cold sweat, lay awake for about three hours, and finally went back to sleep, where he dreamt about being crushed by a giant marble.

«« — »»

Jake woke up around six in the morning, which was normally when he'd be staggering back home. He immediately touched his scrotum, praying that the third testicle had sucked itself back into his abdomen or wherever it had been hiding before it decided to descend.

Nope, still there.

Along with a fourth one.

Jake let out an audible gasp. That wasn't possible! A recount was in order.

One. One was good. That was expected. He was happy to find the first one.

Two. The perfect number of testicles. This was just how he wanted it. Two was great. Two eyes, two ears, two arms, two legs, two nuts. That was nature's way.

Three. Three sucked, but it was the same degree to which things had sucked yesterday. He could live with three if he had to. Three was okay.

God, please don't let there be...

Four.

He had four freakin' balls.

«« — »»

"I have four freakin' balls!"

"Jake, please, calm down," said Dr. McLaughlin. "I assure you, there's a reasonable explanation."

"Like what? Aliens gave me a testicle implant? What's wrong with me, Doc? Why is this happening?"

Dr. McLaughlin sighed. "I wish I knew. Spontaneous generation of testicles is a medical impossibility. The only thing I can tell you is that you must have had two undescended extras."

"What if this extra pair of balls is from a partially formed twin brother I was supposed to have? Do you think that's possible? Aren't there stories about people who have arms poking out of their back or extra eyeballs in their leg from a twin?"

Dr. McLaughlin frowned. "I wouldn't rule out anything at this point, but I'm guessing 'no' on that one."

"I'll be okay, right? I'm not going to die or anything, am I?"

"You're not going to die. If you get kicked in the groin, it will probably hurt twice as much, but apart from that I don't see any health risks."

Jake sighed. "But you can remove them?"

"Yes."

"Safely?"

"Yes."

"Do you swear that you won't slip and slice off my dick?"

"You have nothing to worry about. Just think of it as a slightly more involved vasectomy procedure."

"Okay, that's not even one little bit reassuring."

"Again, I don't see any health risk, so you're welcome to take the time to think about it."

"I'm gonna take the time to think about it."

«« — »»

Usually when he was feeling bad, like if he missed a chance to score with a hot blonde because her jerk boyfriend was dancing with her, Jake drowned his troubles in a nice thick chocolate malt from Mr. Milkshake. Using chocolate to make one feel better was supposed to be strictly a chick trait, so he never admitted to this activity, but it did work.

Usually.

Not today.

In fact, as Jake sat in the booth sucking on the straw, he felt like he might cry. He sniffled, his shoulders began to quake, and then the tears began to flow. Humiliated, he wiped his eyes with his chocolate-stained napkin as he let out an involuntary sob.

A cute brunette with cute breasts looked over at him. Jake forced a smile and turned away.

Great. Here he was bawling in an ice cream shop. This is what his life had become. He looked out the window and tried unsuccessfully to make the weeping stop.

"Are you okay?" asked the brunette, who looked about 21, as she slid into the seat across from him.

"I'm fine," Jake insisted.

"Are you sure? Is it something you want to talk about?"

Jake looked at her. Damn, she was hot. But yet she was also chilly, as he could tell through her t-shirt. He'd sure love to rip that off of her and…

No, he couldn't. The whole quadruple-ball thing.

Then again, she didn't have to be *facing* him, now did she?

"It's my mother's puppy," Jake said. "She's very sick."

"Oh, that's horrible!" said the brunette. "The poor puppy."

"Yeah. My mom lives in Alaska and I've never seen the dog, but the thought of a sick puppy just rips a hole in my heart…you know what I mean?"

The brunette nodded.

"What kind of world do we live in where puppies get sick? Poor little guy. I'm just a mess." Jake sniffled. "You must think I'm being silly."

"No, not at all," said the brunette, shaking her head. "I think you're being lovely."

"I just wish there was something I could do. I sent her a check to take care of the vet bill, but I just don't trust those Alaska vets, you know? I wish I could take the puppy to Paris with me—they have the best vets in the world there—but I'm not leaving until next weekend."

"I've never been to Paris."

"I try to make it there every couple of months, just to clear my head from the pressure at work. It's not easy being the boss, you know? Poor little puppy."

"Is there anything I can do to make you feel better?"

«« — »»

Jake admired the Betty Boop tattoo on the brunette's back as he knelt on the bed behind her, tightly gripping her waist as he thrust into her. He'd thought that concealing his overpacked scrotum would be a problem, but oddly enough, by simply not asking for oral sex or trying to push her head in that direction, he'd avoided any lingering gazes.

At least his penis was functioning without any problems. In fact, he was giving a darn good performance, as evidenced by the brunette squealing and praising his mighty tool. Although he was getting close to release much sooner than normal...he'd have to think of something to distract himself.

Hey, I've got four nuts!

That worked for another few seconds, but then he could feel the imminent eruption again. The brunette hadn't finished (as far as he knew), but oh well, it wasn't like he'd be seeing her again.

The orgasm hit him with such force that it knocked him onto his back, sending the condom flying across the bedroom. It splattered against a framed photograph of an old woman.

"Grandma!" cried the brunette.

Jake just lay on the bed, barely able to move. Wow. That was freakin' incredible.

The brunette scurried off the bed and into her bathroom. She returned a moment later with a wet cloth, which she used to wipe off the photograph. "I've never seen anything like that before," she said. "Is that normal?"

"Only if you're all man," Jake replied, grinning.

«« — »»

Jake woke up with the brunette lying next to him, her arm draped over his chest. He'd been too exhausted to make his usual break for the exit, but after a good night's sleep he felt nice and refreshed. He gently moved her arm out of the way, rolled over, and—

Holy shit!

He rolled onto his back again and grabbed his scrotum. It felt like a bag of marbles!

He screamed.

"What? What's wrong?" asked the brunette, snapping awake.

"Uh...uh...uh...I wish my mom's puppy wasn't sick!"

"Oh, sweetie, I'm sure the puppy will be okay." She gave him a kiss on the cheek and then rolled onto her side.

Okay, don't panic. You're going to be fine. There has to be a reasonable explanation for this. Whimpering, Jake very, very, very, very carefully slid out of bed, walked bow-legged into the bathroom, and shut the door.

He looked at himself in the full-length mirror. His scrotum was the size of a grapefruit. He ran his fingers over the surface—there had to be twenty or thirty testicles in there.

He screamed again.

"It's just a puppy, for God's sake!" the brunette shouted back.

Jake turned on the faucet and splashed some cold water on his face. What in the world was happening to him? He didn't work around radiation, and he'd never taken any drugs that counted, so why was his nut sac filling up like a gumball machine?

He had to get out of here. He returned to the bedroom and picked up his white briefs from the floor, but he'd never be able to fit his scrotum into that. He certainly couldn't wear his jeans. Maybe she'd let him borrow a dress.

"Are you leaving?" asked the brunette, not looking over as he hurriedly pulled on his shirt.

"Yeah, babe. Sorry."

"S'okay."

"Could I borrow one of your...um, garbage bags?"

《《 — 》》

Jake hurried over to his car, feeling like a complete jackass in his garbage bag pants. He jostled his balls getting into the driver's seat and let out a wince of pain.

He started the engine and sped to the nearest emergency room.

《《 — 》》

Jake lay in the hospital bed, holding an ice pack to his crotch. He'd been mercifully unconscious during the operation (as was the first nurse to examine him) but they'd successfully removed...

...his entire scrotum.

He was a man without balls.

A castrated bull.

A joke.

He closed his eyes and wallowed in silent misery.

«« — »»

They released him the next day. He decided to go home and wallow in silent misery some more. Though he might've been able to keep the four-testicle problem concealed from a sexual partner, the complete lack of a scrotum was going to be a tough one to hide.

Damn, I'm going to have to get a strap-on ball sac...

He wished he'd died on the operating table. They should've at least provided him with a cyanide capsule after an operation like this. Or a helpful pamphlet like *So You've Lost Your Testes and Your Will to Live.*

He walked upstairs to his apartment, collapsed into bed, wallowed in silent misery for a while longer, and then proceeded to sleep for the entire afternoon, night, and most of the next morning.

«« — »»

He opened one eye. Darkness.

Not because the room was dark. Because something was blocking his vision.

He pushed it away, but it was attached to his forehead.

Attached, soft, and contained two balls.

He sat up. His whole body felt completely freaky. His left eye was uncovered, and as he threw aside the blanket he let out a cry of unrestrained horror.

His entire body was covered with scrotums, hundreds of them, like a demented form of chicken pox. He had scrotums dangling from his arms, his chest, his legs...everywhere but his freakin' crotch!

He stroked the one that dangled from his chin as he trembled in fear.

He needed to get to the phone and call for help. He very slowly eased his way out of bed, crying out as he accidentally squeezed two of the ball sacs on his leg. The pain brought tears to his eyes, and he had to sit motionless for a few minutes until it subsided.

He gently swung his legs over the side of the bed, thanking every deity known to mankind that he didn't have testicles on the bottom of his feet.

Slowly, ever so slowly, he padded across the bedroom floor. The scrotums were surprisingly heavy, and most of them itched.

He took a misstep, and for a terrifying moment he thought he was going to fall to the floor, but he regained his balance and continued out of the bedroom, down the hall, and into his kitchen.

He bashed three sets of balls against a chair and vomited onto the floor. He braced himself against the table, eyes closed, and just waited for the unbearable pain to go away.

It took a long time.

When he could finally walk again, he slowly made his way to the telephone. He lifted it out of its cradle and—

—the phone rang, scaring the hell out of him. It fell out of his hand and smashed against the tile, breaking apart.

Damn! Damn! Damn!

Where was his cell phone?

In the car. He'd forgotten it there because he'd been so upset over the operation.

Damn! Damn! Damn!

Okay, he'd just have to get one of the neighbors to call 911 for him. He was obviously in need of medical attention, so they wouldn't protest.

He walked into the living room, balls perspiring heavily, and then tripped on the remote control that he frequently tripped over but had never quite found the willpower to actually pick up off the floor.

He fell forward.

His life flashed before his eyes six or seven times.

But, miraculously, he threw out his hands and stopped himself from landing face-first on the carpet. Instead, he found himself in the middle of the floor in a push-up position.

Okay, this was awkward.

He supposed that he could gently ease himself onto the carpet, but there were a lot of balls on his chest to crush. He was pretty sure he didn't have the physical strength to give a mighty push that would spring him back into a standing position.

Yeah, this sucked.

He stayed in that position for a while, trying to figure out what the hell he was going to do, besides cry.

This was *not* how Jake Triben was going to die. He summoned his strength, and walked on his hands and toes across the living room over to the sofa. He gripped the arm of the sofa and pulled himself to a squatting position, enabling himself to stand up again.

Problem solved.

He walked over to the door, took a deep breath, and then opened it and stepped out into the hallway of his apartment building.

Through his free eye he saw Ms. Duncan stepping out of her apartment. She was a heavyset woman in her late fifties who, judging from her facial expression, had never seen a man completely covered in scrotums before.

She gaped at him.

"It's a Halloween costume!" Jake insisted. "I'm going as...balls!"

"It's June!"

"I know, but I'm getting an early start. But I got caught in my costume. Could you call an ambulance?"

Ms. Duncan walked over to him. "Jake, that costume is obscene!"

"I know, I'm sorry."

"What are those made of?" she asked, flicking one of the sacs on his arm with her index finger.

Jake howled in pain. Ms. Duncan flinched as if she'd been struck.

"My God, are those...are those real?" Ms. Duncan asked, seconds before she dropped to the floor in a dead faint.

Ms. Duncan's six-year-old granddaughter, who really should have been in school, peeked out the doorway and shrieked.

"It's okay, it's okay!" Jake insisted, but she slammed the door. Jake turned and hurried down the hallway, quickly but not so quickly that he could take a tumble. The balls were jiggling and jostling against each other, not quite hard enough to hurt.

He reached the top of the stairway, and there she was.

Melissa/Margaret/Maggie/Mildred/whatever the hell her name was.

"Hello, Jake," she said. She didn't seem surprised at all by his appearance.

"What do you want?" he demanded.

"Are you feeling more sensitive?"

"*You* did this to me! You cast some sort of spell on me, didn't you?"

"Kind of," she said, holding up a voodoo doll with dozens of miniature scrotums glued to its surface. "You weren't very nice, you know."

"I *said* you were good for your first time! What more do you want?"

"I just want you to be nice. Can you be nice?"

"Nice? After you've done this to me?" He waved his arms, flapping around several nut sacs. "You stupid psycho bitch, I should break your neck!"

"You're not being sensitive to my needs."

"Okay, okay, I'm sorry," Jake insisted. "I'm just in a weird place right now, y'know? If you could help me out, that would really be swell."

"Do you think you deserve it?"

Jake nodded.

"How do I know?"

"Whenever a puppy gets sick, my heart aches for—"

"You're not being sincere, Jake. Sincerity is important in a relationship. If I can't trust you, how is our marriage going to work? How can we raise our children?"

"Aw, c'mon, don't do this to me! Just fix the nut problem, okay? I'll be the most sensitive fucker on the planet, I swear!"

"Prove it."

"How can I prove it when I'm standing here like a Christmas tree decorated with testicles? Give me a break here!"

"Just answer me one question."

"Ask me anything!"

"What's my name?"

Jake froze. He could feel several of his testicles tightening up in fear. "Melissa?"

"No."

"Margaret?"

"No."

"Maggie?"

"No. It's Joan, asshole," she said, tossing the voodoo doll at him.

Jake lunged for it, momentarily forgetting that he was standing in a location where lunging for a flying object was a poor idea. He realized this very quickly as he fell forward.

Time seemed to stand still, which gave him plenty of time to think about how much it was going to hurt when he hit those stairs.

He finally struck them and bellowed with the combined agony of every male who had ever been kicked in the groin since the beginning of time. The pain was beyond devastating. He tumbled down the stairs, crushing testicles beneath him, his vision filled with a blinding white light.

As he struck the corner of one of the steps, the testicles above his right eye burst.

Jake hit the bottom and lay there, bloody sacs covering his body, sick to his stomach, the pain so intense that he couldn't breathe. He wept silently, praying that his suffocation would be quick.

Moments (years?) later, he could sense Joan standing over him.

"*Guh...*" he managed to say.

"What's that?"

"*Guh.*"

"I don't understand."

"*Gun.* Need a gun."

"Oh, now, you don't want to kill yourself, do you?"

"God, yes..."

Joan crouched down next to him. "There's no need for that. Just say you're sorry."

"I'm so sorry," Jake said, a second before he vomited.

"Say you'll bring me flowers."

"I promise."

"And candy."

"Yes."

"And you'll serenade me underneath my bedroom window, when I move into a place where I have a bedroom window."

"Yes."

"Good. Let's get those nasty things off the voodoo doll, shall we?"

«« — »»

Jake lay with his head between her legs. His tongue felt like it was going to fall off, but she wasn't ready for him to quit yet, and he knew the penalty for stopping early.

"A little more to the left," Joan said.

"Yeth, ma'am."

The chains were uncomfortable and the collar chafed his neck, but Jake didn't complain. Tending to her each and every need was a hell of a lot better than living life as a scrotum creature.

He was Mr. Sensitive now, and he was going to please his woman.

THE BAD
CANDY HOUSE

I don't get how the whole "razor blades in apples" thing is supposed to work. I think it's an urban legend. How could you get a razor blade in there without leaving a big gash in the side of the apple? I mean, yeah, kids are morons, but they're going to notice an inch-long cut in the side of their apple. I guess you could come in from the bottom, but using that technique I don't see how you could wedge the blade in far enough that somebody would actually bite into it. And there's really no set biting pattern for an apple, so unless you lucked into a direct hit the best you could hope for is a little nick on the lips—barely even worth the trouble. Most importantly, kids are going to remember the cheap bastards who handed out apples instead of candy (granted, an apple costs more than a Fun-Size candy bar, but that's not the way they see it) and they'll bring the police right to your front door.

It just wouldn't work.

That's why I used arsenic, injected with a hypodermic needle into name-brand chocolates. Even if parents checked the candy, they were unlikely to notice the holes, and the little cretins were sure to just pop those things into their greedy mouths whole. Dead kids. A Halloween present to myself.

I wasn't ignorant; I knew I wouldn't kill all of them. As soon as the first one croaked, there'd be mass hysteria all over town and parents would be yanking the bags of candy away from their screaming brats. But I figured I'd probably knock off a few of them before people started freaking out, and in a worst case scenario where I only killed one—well, hell, at least I'd be responsible for everybody else's candy being taken away. Heh heh.

Obviously, the candy would eventually be traced back to me. But that was fine. My Mildred had died two months ago, and I really didn't have anything to live for. I would've blown my brains out the same night the stroke took her, except that it occurred to me that if I didn't have to worry about any consequences to my actions, I could have one hell of an enjoyable Halloween.

I was downright giddy. I even carved a jack-o-lantern for the first time in thirty years. A jack-o-lantern was actually the source of my very first journal entry about the holiday:

October 31, 1975. Those little bastards smashed my jack-o-lantern. I hope they choke on their taffy.

I had something for pretty much every year after that. Some samples included:

October 31, 1985. Those little shits toilet-papered my entire front yard. I saw them running away and laughing, and I went for my shotgun, but Mildred talked some sense into me. I sort of wish she hadn't.

October 31, 1995. Those little fuckers put a burning bag of dog crap on my porch. I'm not an idiot and I wasn't going to just stomp on the thing, so I turned the water hose on it and put out the fire. It left burn marks on the wood that those little fuckers are going to pay for, believe me. Then when I picked it up to throw it away, the wet bag broke and spilled shit all over. I went for my shotgun, but Mildred had hidden the bullets. I saw the kids watching from across the street, and I gave them a verbal beating that they won't soon forget. I hate kids.

October 31, 2005. Those little satanists egged the whole goddamn front of my house. Where the hell did they get all those eggs? One of them threw a fuckin' ham and cheese omelet at my window. Can you believe that? A ham and cheese omelet! I swear to God, if Mildred hadn't pawned my shotgun, I'd just sit down on my porch and start picking those little demons off one by one. Boom! Splat! Boom! Splat! Boom! Splat! I hate Halloween.

But I didn't hate Halloween this year. I couldn't wait to see what they tried. Eggs, toilet paper, burning bags of crap...bring it on! This might be the last Halloween our sleepy little shithole town ever enjoyed.

At 6:44, the doorbell rang. Trick-or-treating was supposed to officially start at 7:00, but those greedy bastards didn't care.

I opened the door. Two kids were standing there, holding their candy bags out in front of them expectantly. One was in vampire makeup and the other wore a Spider-Man mask.

I stared at them. They just stood there, too lazy to even say "trick or treat!" Why don't kids say "trick or treat" anymore? Was the process of securing Halloween candy so difficult that they had to figure out a way to cut down on the manual labor? These rotten kids today have such a feeling of entitlement that they can't even be bothered to say those three words to get their damn candy bar.

They didn't even say "Hi." They just looked at me, slack-jawed, as if they didn't have two brain cells to rub together. (To be fair, I couldn't see the kid's face under his Spider-Man mask, but I don't think it's unreasonable to assume that he looked like his vampire buddy.)

"Yeah?" I asked.

"Trick or treat," said the bloodsucker, as if annoyed that I was making him fulfill his part of the bargain.

I picked two chocolates from the bowl next to the door and dropped one into each of their bags. "Enjoy," I said, wanting to add "your upcoming death" but wisely withstanding the temptation.

The vampire muttered "thank you" under his breath and they left. I smiled, which was not something I did often. I wondered if they'd realize that the chocolate tasted funny, or if they'd gobble it down too fast to even notice.

"*Oooooh, Mommy, I don't feel so good.*"

"*You've just had too much Halloween candy, sweetie-dumplings. Let me tuck you under the covers and give you a kiss and you'll be just fine in the morning.*"

"*But my tummy hurts.*"

"*Maybe you've learned a little lesson for next year. You shouldn't eat so much candy. It's not good for you.*"

"*Bleaaarrrrrgggghhhh.*"

"*Oh my God! You're vomiting blood! You're vomiting blood! Mike, come quick!*"

"*[Various frothing at the mouth noises.]*"

"*Good Lord, Tracy, what did he eat? What did you let him eat?*"

"*It wasn't my fault, you son of a bitch! If you'd helped teach our children some respect, this wouldn't be happening! I hate you I hate you I hate you I hate—AAAAIIIEEEEE, his tongue just fell out! His tongue just fell right out of his mouth!*"

"*Gagghhhrrrruuuuummmmppphhhhh...*"

"*Speak to me! Speak to me, little vampire! He's dead! He died a horrible and agonizing death! Noooooooooooo!!!*"

"*Noooooooooooo!!!*"

Hee hee hee.

Nine minutes later, the doorbell rang again. Two teenage girls were there. They looked way too old to be trick-or-treating, and were probably just collecting candy to sell for drug money. Not only did they not say "trick or treat," but the spoiled debutantes weren't even wearing costumes.

I shook my head. "You can't have candy without a costume." Yes, it was poisoned candy, so their lack of proper attire shouldn't have been a concern for me, but this was just ridiculous.

"We *are* in costume," said the blonde on the left.

"What are you supposed to be? Teenage girls scamming candy?"

"I'm Paris Hilton," said the blonde on the right. "She's Jessica Simpson."

"Paris Hilton? Shouldn't you be having sex in Night-Vision?" The computer and Internet connection had been Mildred's thing, not mine, but after she died I'd discovered the convenience of internet porn.

"You are such a pervo," said the one who was supposed to be Jessica Simpson.

"I'm not the one dressing up in slut gear," I said.

"Well, thank God for that," said Paris.

"I'm going to tell my parents about you," Jessica threatened. "They lock away creeps like you."

"All right, all right, here's your candy," I said, giving them two pieces each. "Great costumes. You look just like them. Now go away."

The girls exchanged a disgusted look and then left. I chuckled. I probably shouldn't have harassed them—if their parents did come over and cause problems I might not get to distribute enough of the chocolates—but it was fun.

The flood of kids started a few minutes after that. I smiled politely, complimented their costumes, and enjoyed merry thoughts about their deaths. I fantasized about horrified parents having to walk around the bodies littering the streets, unable to cross the street without accidentally stepping on a youthful corpse. I knew it wouldn't happen like that, but it was fun to pretend.

A mother showed up, holding a baby in her arms. The baby had kitten whiskers drawn on its face and wore a pair of fake feline ears. It was too young to even hold the plastic pumpkin by itself—the mother held it instead. Did she think a baby could appreciate the holiday? I dropped a poisoned chocolate into the pumpkin. A mother stupid enough to give chocolate to a baby deserved whatever happened.

I'd given out about half of the bowl when three kids showed up at my door. They were all tall enough to be teenagers, although their identical skeleton masks hid their faces.

"Gimme candy, old man!" they said in unison.

"Oh, that's real clever. You make that up yourselves?"

"You gonna give us the candy or what?"

"Yeah, I'm gonna give you the candy," I said, dropping one in each of their bags. "Happy Halloween."

Suddenly, all three of them pulled out squirt guns. Before I could react, they squirted me in the face.

I slammed the door and cursed loudly. I cursed even louder as the smell made it abundantly clear that the squirt guns weren't filled with water.

"Damnfuckin'bastardhellspawnmonsters!" I shouted as I rushed to the kitchen sink and turned on the faucet. If I weren't planning to kill myself tonight, I would've gone to the police station first thing in the morning and demanded DNA testing on the urine.

This was exactly why they all needed to die. You couldn't shoot a man in the face with bodily fluids and expect to live through the night.

Rotten bastards. Rotten twerps. Rotten brats. I hated them all. I wished that I could just walk through their homes, spraying piss-scented arsenic into their wide-open mouths.

Maybe I wouldn't kill myself tonight. I'd stay alive long enough to enjoy their fatal reaction to my treats. Hell, maybe I'd go on the run for a few days, but return to laugh and point during their funerals. Walk up to their dead bodies in the open casket and squirt them in the face.

Good times.

I ignored the next couple of doorbell rings while I thoroughly washed my face with soap. My left eye stung a bit, and a drop or two seemed to have gone up one of my nostrils, but at least none had made it into my mouth.

Nice and clean, I returned to my door-answering duties. The next kid actually said the magic words and politely thanked me for his chocolate, so I hoped that he'd hear about the other deaths before he ate the piece I'd given him. I gave out chocolate to Elvira, Freddy Krueger, another vampire, a toddler clown, a Mexican wrestler, some *Star Wars* character (I think), and two separate kids dressed as M&Ms, which I wouldn't have expected to be a popular costume choice.

I was almost out of candy and ready to shut down for the night when somebody rang the doorbell over and over, getting in about fifteen rings before I could answer. Officially, trick-or-treating was supposed to end at nine o'clock, and it was nine o'three, so I felt that I'd be justified in punching this little shit in the face.

I opened the door and saw a kid in a skeleton mask. The same mask those other three kids had been wearing. I wasn't sure if he'd been part of that group, but I hated him anyway.

"Trick or treat!" he said in a monotone.

"Yeah, yeah, whatever," I muttered, watching his hands carefully to make sure he didn't whip out a squirt gun. I dropped one of the last pieces of candy into his bag. "Happy Halloween."

The kid nodded but didn't move.

"Something you want?" I asked.

The kid just stood there, staring silently at me. I don't mind admitting that it was more than a little creepy.

"You've got your candy," I told him. "Go on, get back home, it's late."

More silence. More staring.

I put my hand on the edge of the door so I could slam it in his face. "Do you know who I am?" he asked.

"No. Who are you?"

"I am the one under the mask. I am the one who sees all. I know your secrets, Raymond."

"Get the hell off my porch."

"You cannot escape what you have done."

"I haven't done shit."

"Do you wish to gaze under my mask, or do you fear the visage that hides beneath?"

"Go away, you little freak."

He shook his head, slowly and deliberately. "You must confront what you have done, Raymond. Remove my mask. Look upon that behind the disguise."

What the hell is going on here? Something about this kid (it *was* a kid, right?) made me extremely uncomfortable. I didn't want to touch his mask, I just wanted him to leave, and yet I felt myself reaching out and touching the cool plastic.

I started to lift the mask.

And then a warm stream of piss got me right on the fucking lips. I stumbled backwards, sputtering in surprise and fury, as the son of a bitch squirted me again.

"*Sucker!*" he shouted.

I'm an old man, but unspeakable rage does a lot for one's ability to move fast. I rushed forward, ignoring the third squirt that got in my hair, and grabbed the kid by the collar. I dragged him inside, threw him to the living room floor, and slammed the front door.

"It was just a joke!" the kid insisted.

"A joke, huh?" I asked, wiping my mouth off on my sleeve. "Then shouldn't at least one of us be laughing? Isn't that part of what makes a joke a joke?"

"I—I don't know!"

"What if I made you squirt yourself in the mouth? Would that be funny? Would you be slapping your knee over that little joke?"

"No!"

"Are you sure? I think it would be hilarious! I'd bust a fuckin' gut! Give me the squirt gun."

The kid quickly tossed me the squirt gun. I pointed it at him and pulled the trigger, but it was almost empty and only a few drops trickled out, landing on my shoes and carpet. This did not improve my mood.

"I bet you helped egg my house last year, didn't you?" I asked.

The kid shook his head.

"Take off the mask!"

He quickly pulled off the skeleton mask and threw it aside. He was one terrified looking kid. I approved of that. He looked about sixteen and was making a valiant but ineffective attempt to grow a mustache.

"Did you egg my house last year?"

"No!"

"Liar!"

"I didn't!"

The kid started to get back up, but I pounced upon him. I was pleased with my own strength as I grabbed him by the ears and slammed his head against the floor, over and over, until he stopped moving.

I checked his pulse. Not dead.

Good.

I hurried into the kitchen, opened the drawer where I kept random junk, and got a roll of duct tape. Quickly, before he could regain consciousness, I taped his wrists together and his feet together. The doorbell rang during this process, but I ignored it.

I woke him up with a slap to the face.

"What's your name?" I asked.

"Gary."

"Gary, why did you make the decision to squirt me in the face with urine? Did you think that was a nice thing to do?"

"It wasn't my idea!"

"Was it your urine?"

"No."

"Okay. I'm sure you wouldn't lie about such a thing. I'll be right back."

I returned to the kitchen and got a carton of eggs out of the refrigerator. Then I walked back into the living room, set the carton on the coffee table, opened the lid, and held up one of the eggs to show Gary.

"For true revenge, this thing should be rotten. But I don't want to keep you in my house long enough for these to go bad."

I threw the egg at him, as hard as I could. It splattered on his chest. I'd been aiming for his face, but that was okay. I pelted the rest of the eggs, feeling a rush of adrenaline with each throw. He lay there, covered with yolk and egg shells, and it was one of the most beautiful sights I'd ever witnessed.

Next, I grabbed some spare rolls of toilet paper out of the closet. I wrapped him up like a mummy, kicking him a few times when he struggled too much. I held the last roll under running water for a minute, then smushed it against his face.

I didn't have any dog crap handy. In theory, there was no rule saying that a dog had to be involved, and I briefly considered another option, but then I decided that I had too much dignity. Besides, I figured that the kid himself was nothing more than a piece of crap, so why not treat him that way?

Oh, he screamed good when I lit him on fire.

Even though it was Halloween and people were used to kids screaming, I knew he'd attract unwanted attention before too long. As he flailed around on the ground, burning and shrieking, I noticed that his head bore a striking resemblance to one of my old jack-o-lanterns that kids had smashed.

A few blows with a baseball bat and he resembled it even more.

I sat down on the couch to relax, and got so caught up in staring at his body that the arrival of the police took me by surprise. They carted me away and put me under twenty-four hour surveillance, so my whole plan to kill myself was botched.

Sadly, I hadn't planned for police intervention this soon, and so I hadn't really covered my tracks. They discovered the syringe and arsenic, and quickly went door-to-door telling people not to eat any Halloween candy. The only casualty was the baby in the kitten costume.

I have to admit, knowing that I'll spend the rest of my life in prison is nowhere near as appealing as suicide. I keep trying to get rope or a knife or something, but the guards are watching me good. I guess I won't be seeing Mildred anytime soon.

The worst part is that, as a prank, the guards keep toilet-papering my cell. They've also hung up Halloween decorations, and the worst of them, Steve, just *loves* to knock on the bars and say "Trick or treat, asshole!"

That said, I'd do it all over again if I could. It was still the best Halloween of my life.

DISPOSAL

- 1 -

Okay, first things first: I'm a complete prick.

A scoundrel. A scumbag. A sleazy reprehensible immoral bastard…and I'm cool with that, thank you very much. But if you're one of those touchy-feely people who requires a sympathetic storyteller, you may want to find something else to read, because trust me, I suck.

My name's Frank. Last name doesn't matter. Hot thirty-one year-old body, black hair, goatee, muscular build that drives the chicks wild, and hung like a T-Rex. That's pretty much all you need to know.

Oh, I'm also an armed robber.

I don't knock over banks or convenience stores or anything like that. Those places have security cameras. Me, I'll do the occasional dark alley mugging, but I'm big on robbing places that don't normally get robbed. Comic shops, delis, pet stores, the occasional nursing home—joints like that. It's not like you can retire to a desert island with a harem of nubile nymphos on that kind of score, but it's really not about the money. It's about the thrill of pointing your gun in somebody's face and scaring 'em shitless. It's fun. You should try it.

On the night when everything in my life turned to absolute frozen-crap-on-a-stick, I was down to two bucks and fifty-three cents. Though my needs in this world are minimal, they do include an Extra Value Meal every once in a while, so I walked into a twenty-four hour dry cleaning service. I'm not sure why anybody would need a twenty-four hour dry cleaning service, but I guess they were catering to the "drunk husband who puked all over his clothes and needs an emergency cleaning before going home to his angry wife" market. It was almost eleven o'clock and the place was empty except for the woman behind the counter. Perfect.

I pulled the pistol out of my inside jacket pocket and pointed it at her. "Open up the register, bitch!" (You pretty much have to say "bitch" in these situations.)

Her mouth dropped open and she looked like she was going to wet herself. I've always enjoyed seeing that facial expression. However, she didn't move toward the register.

"I'm not playing around here, bitch! I *will* shoot you if you don't start handing over some cash!"

"We don't have much," she insisted.

"I didn't ask for your fuckin' financial history! You lookin' to die tonight? Is that it? Got some terminal disease? *Open it now, bitch!*"

She nodded and opened the register. She was a cute one. Tall, stacked, red hair, freckles, maybe twenty-five or twenty-six years old. She wasn't dressed suggestively, but her tits were definitely trying to make their presence known. Hopefully I'd score enough from this robbery to pick up a hooker on the way home.

The woman grabbed the bills out of the register and slid them across the counter. I grabbed them and did a quick count. "Twelve bucks? That's all you've got?"

"I said—"

"I know what you said! But twelve bucks? How can you even make change with twelve bucks? What if somebody paid with a twenty?"

"We don't get a lot of business."

"Well, hell, I guess not! Give me the coins, too. All of them."

She scooped out the quarters, dimes, nickels, and pennies. I used the gun to scrape them off the counter and into my hand, then shoved the change into my pocket.

"Do you have any checks in there that you could sign over?"

"We don't accept checks."

"Dammit! How do you even stay open?"

She shrugged.

I thought about stealing some laundry, but I didn't want to weigh myself down and this place probably only washed clothes for nerds or fat chicks. Oh well. At least I got enough for the fast food meal.

"You stay right where you are, hands in the air, and count to a hundred," I said. "I don't know if your twelve bucks was insured, but if I find out you called the cops on me, I'll hunt you down and shoot you in the back of the head, execution-style. Got it?"

The woman nodded.

"Good." I turned and headed for the door. Next time I'd hit a library. Even twenty-five-cents-a-day late fees had to add up to more than this.

"Wait!"

"What?" I asked, not turning back.

"Can I ask you a question?"

I immediately had a really bad feeling about this, like her question was going to be something ironic like "Did you know there are eighteen cops waiting outside with helicopters and a tank?" I sure hoped there weren't eighteen cops waiting outside with helicopters and a tank. That would suck.

I pushed open the door. "No, you can't."

"Have you ever killed anybody?"

I stopped, took a step back, and let the door swing shut. What was this chick's deal? When some guy robs you at gunpoint and doesn't shoot you, you don't turn it into social hour. You cheerfully let him exit your place and then thank God you're still alive.

It could've been a trap, but she seemed genuinely interested. And, like I said before, she was stacked. Perky, too. Fear does wonderful things to nipples.

"You serious?"

"Yes."

I gave her my most winning smile. "You bet your sweet ass I have."

"How many?"

"Eight."

Okay, officially it was two, and only one was on purpose. The accidental one was during a mugging. This jackass in a business suit handed over his wallet like I asked, no problems, but then he tackled me. I mean a literal tackle, like he thought he was a football player or something. My gun went off. Too bad he wasn't wearing a football helmet. Heh heh.

The one on purpose was this guy Jason who ripped off some of my DVDs. I wasn't planning to commit murder, just get back the DVDs (or at least the pornos) and beat the shit out of him, but he kept mouthing off the whole time and finally I got sick of it and popped him. I felt kind of guilty watching him writhe around on the floor, clutching his chest, but I'm not the kind of guy to hang on to feelings of remorse for very long and I shot him twice more.

If you want to get technical about it, I did throw a guy off a bridge once, and I beat another guy so badly with the handle of my gun that he wasn't moving anymore when I left, but for all I know they all lived and went on to fulfilling careers in the clergy, so I don't count them.

"Eight?"

"Yeah, eight. Why? You looking to make it nine?"

"Maybe."

Great. I'd robbed some whack-job with a death wish. "Sorry. I don't do assisted suicides."

"No, no, I didn't mean me! I thought that maybe you could kill...somebody else."

"Who?"

"My husband."

"You're kidding me, right?"

"No."

She sure *seemed* sincere. Of course, I've never been any good at reading women. Ask my ex-girlfriends. "Sorry, babe. Not interested."

"I could make it worth your while."

"What're you gonna do? Dig through your couch cushions for spare change?"

"I know I can't offer you any money, but I can offer other things."

"What kind of things?"

"Use your imagination."

Suddenly I was more than a little interested. (Remember: Stacked. Perky nipples.) "I'm not very imaginative. Why don't you spell it out?"

"Kill my husband, and you get one night with me, anything you want to do that doesn't leave permanent marks. No cameras, spectators, or other participants. Protection at all times. Aside from that, anything goes."

I whistled. "Wow. That's quite an offer."

"Oh, and we're defining 'night' as 'eight hours'. Consecutive hours, so if you decide to sleep for six of them, that's your call."

"You seem to have this pretty well thought-out."

"I need my husband dead."

"Why not kill him yourself?"

"I've tried."

"So why do you need to waste him? He screwing around on you?"

"Something like that."

"You probably should've offered him that 'anything you want to do' deal."

She glared at me. "Do you want the job or not?"

"The way I figure, this is like a big cocaine deal. You sample the wares before you purchase."

"You're really sleazy, you know that?"

"Know it. Like it. Don't plan to change."

She sighed. "Fine, fine. Let me lock up the place first."

Now I'm not one to kiss and tell, but that's okay, because there's no way I was kissing those lips after what they did. This chick was amazingly talented. I mean, that sort of thing is always enjoyable unless they scrape you with their teeth, but this was exquisite. She even let me grab a handful of her hair while she worked.

Believe me, I'm not exactly hurting for female attention, so the fact that I was actually considering killing her husband was proof that she was *mmm-mmm* good. I know what you're wondering—*hey, Frank, you've got the gun, why not just take what you want from her?*—but I don't play that way. I'm scum, but I've got a moral code tucked away somewhere.

So, yeah, it didn't take all that long for me to decide that I definitely wanted to indulge in her offer. I already had at least five or six ideas for ways to test her "anything goes" attitude.

"When do you want to do this?" I asked her, when it was convenient for her to speak again.

"Tonight. Now."

"Now?"

"Do you have a problem with that? The sooner we do this, the sooner you get paid."

I shrugged. "Your call. I kind of assumed that there might be some planning involved."

"This isn't going to be some elaborate Agatha Christie scheme. I just want you to come to my place and kill the bastard."

"Works for me. Why make homicide into a big deal?"

"Exactly. I only live three blocks away."

"Question for you," I said. "You got a name?"

"Call me Gretchen."

"Call me Frank."

"Hi, Frank. Let me close up shop and we'll head off."

- 2 -

I guess I'll be honest with you: I was sweating like a morbidly obese kickboxer as we walked those three city blocks. This would be my first premeditated murder. I was okay with the guy biting it, but this was a pretty big crime to be committing with so little prep time. I didn't want to end up in prison over this or have the husband blow me away with a shotgun or something. I'd just have to be careful.

She unlocked a graffiti-covered door, and we walked up three flights of stairs to her apartment. She unlocked that door as well.

"So, what, I'm just supposed to walk right in with you?"

"Yeah."

She opened the door and stepped inside. I hesitated. This was too weird. Maybe it wasn't worth it. If I ditched this idea and went bar-hopping, there was a chance I could pick up some skank who'd do at least one of the things on the "anything goes" request list.

Gretchen dropped her keys, then bent down to slowly pick them up. This was clearly for my benefit in case I was thinking of backing out. The sight of that fine ass got rid of those feelings real quick. If you'd seen it, you'd have been willing to kill her husband, too. (If you're a straight chick or a gay guy, imagine that it was Brad Pitt's ass or something like that.)

I closed the door behind me and looked around the living room. The place was nicer than I'd expected. I wouldn't invite the Queen over for high tea or anything like that, but I'd been thinking "shithole" for sure, and that wasn't the case.

The television was on, the volume low. A commercial was playing for one of those phone numbers where you could spend $4.99 a minute to talk dirty to a fifty-three-year-old hag pretending to be a hot eighteen-year-old slut.

"He's right there," said Gretchen, pointing to the blue recliner facing the TV.

There was clearly not going to be a hell of a lot of subtlety involved here. Staying on the opposite side of the room, I walked forward so that I could get a good view of the guy.

"What the *fuck*?"

I'd figured he was sleeping or something, but this bastard was dead. He was slumped over to the side, eyes open, skin drained of color, his pajamas covered with blood. He looked about sixty (how the hell did he end up with such a hot young wife?), and his mouth hung open. A thin line of bloody drool had dried on his chin.

I quickly noticed two other very important details: his throat was slit, and the left side of his head looked like it had been bashed in with a sledgehammer.

"You have to kill him for me," Gretchen said. "Please."

"There's nothing left here to kill! Jesus Christ, he looks like he's been dead for days!"

"He hasn't."

The only stiffs I'd ever seen were freshly killed, but her husband had *clearly* croaked, and had been in that state for a while. This crazy bitch had brought me here to murder a dead body.

"I'm outta here," I said. "This is too messed up for me. Your ass ain't *that* nice."

Gretchen stepped in front of me to block my way. "Please. You have to help me."

"Can't. Don't have any prescription meds to share."

"He's not dead!"

"He's a rotting corpse!"

"But he doesn't stink."

I took a whiff. She was right. He didn't reek, though he did sort of have that old man smell. "What'd you use, Febreze?"

"He's alive. Check his pulse."

"I'm not touching that nasty thing."

"He's breathing."

I watched him for a moment. "No, he's not."

"He is. It's hard to see, but he's still breathing."

"Babe, your husband isn't doing anything but waiting for the maggots. Hell, it was probably maggots moving around under those PJ's that made you think he was breathing. The guy is dead. I'm not judging you for killing him, I'm just saying that you may want to join our little piece of reality."

Gretchen almost looked like she was going to cry. Fortunately, a woman's tears have never affected me. The lunatic could bawl all she wanted. I wasn't hanging around.

"Why won't you check his pulse?"

"One, because he could have diseases. Two, because I don't feel any great need to put my fingerprints on a murder victim. Three, because it's fuckin' gross. Do you need more reasons?"

"I'll prove it to you," she said. She walked past me and down a hallway.

I stared at the body. That was one dead dude. As far as I could tell, in addition to the slit throat and bashed-in head, she'd also stabbed him in the chest about a dozen times. I guess it made sense that she'd go insane after doing something like that. She was probably hearing his voice, whispering into her ear. *"Gretchen...Gretchen...you'll pay for this atrocity, you skanky tramp!"* Or she was hearing his heartbeat like in that thing where the guy kills the old man with the weird eye—I think it was a Shakespeare play.

Why was I even still here? The obvious course of action was "step away from the looney." It's sort of like when a chick tells you she's pregnant. You don't hang around, waiting for her to start whining about child support; you get the hell out.

Then I realized that I was being a complete idiot. This would be the easiest kill ever! Poke him with a stick, let him flop over onto the floor, and call it a job well done. I had no moral issues about taking advantage of an insane woman. I'd just make sure I didn't fall asleep afterward and that I went home before she started to get clingy.

Gretchen walked back into the living room with one of those stupid little mirrors women use to check their makeup. She pressed it underneath his nose.

Nothing happened.

"Maybe his dainty breaths are light as a feather," I said.

"Shhhhhh."

The mirror fogged up just a bit.

I leaned closer, pretty sure I hadn't seen that. It fogged again.

"See?" she said. "He's breathing."

"Well, dip me in hot fudge and roll me through a Weight Watchers meeting," I said. Or maybe I said "holy shit." I forget which. It was probably "holy shit."

I would've never believed that the old guy could look like that and not be dead. To be honest, I still wasn't totally convinced, but I supposed it was possible that he had some tiny little flicker of life left in him. I had to admire this guy. A dozen stab wounds to my chest would probably be the end of me, and I'm no sissy.

"Now do you understand why I need your help?" she asked.

"Uh, no."

"What do you mean, no?"

"I mean, uh, no. Look at him! This guy is about two or three heartbeats away from giving up the ghost as it is. You don't need me for this. You could finish him off by throwing a Tic-Tac at him."

"Try it."

"I don't have a Tic-Tac."

"I mean try to kill him." She grabbed the old man's hair and yanked his head forward, revealing a nasty, deep gash on the back of his neck. "I'm not stupid, Frank, and I'm not insane. I've been trying to murder him for the past week. I've sliced him, stabbed him, and beat him, and he *won't die!*"

"You just didn't stab him hard enough," I said. "Or hit him hard enough."

"I also used poison."

"Or poison him hard enough."

"Right. So you can see why I need your help."

"Yeah, yeah." I figured that a good bullet between the eyes would keep that mirror from fogging. Unfortunately, if I fired a gun in an apartment, I'd probably have to kill all of the neighbors who overheard the shot, and I wasn't that motivated.

"What'd you hit him with?" I asked.

"A rolling pin. It broke."

"Do you have a baseball bat?"

"No."

I looked around the living room. There were a couple of ugly vases, a lamp, and a figurine of two piglets getting it on (or maybe snuggling). I picked up the figurine, but it turned out to be cheap plastic.

"Don't you have any good, solid bludgeoning objects?" I asked.

"It wasn't usually a bludgeoning type of household."

"What about the TV?"

"I need the TV."

"Do you have a microwave?"

"What about a book?"

"I need something heavier than a book. I want to do this in one blow."

"What about a chair?"

"Show me what you've got."

She led me to the dining room table. The wooden chairs looked kind of flimsy. "Got anything better?"

"We have a metal folding chair for guests."

"Well, obviously that would be better than the balsa wood shit you've got going on here, don't you think?"

"You don't have to be a jerk."

"You're asking me to kill your husband! Do you expect me to be Miss Manners?"

"I'm just saying."

"Well, don't say."

She opened a closet door, pushed some crap out of the way, and pulled out a folded metal chair. I took it from her and returned to the recliner.

Her husband still looked pretty damn dead.

"All right, slump him forward," I said.

"Why?"

"So I have a straight shot at his head! Why are you asking dumb questions? I'm not asking you to wiggle your tongue in his slit throat, I'm asking you to slump him over."

"I was just making sure you had a plan of action." She pinched his shirt collar between her thumb and index finger and tugged. Her husband's head dropped to his knees.

I hoisted the chair over my head, accidentally smacking the ceiling.

"Careful!"

"Shut up, bitch!"

"You can stop calling me bitch. You're not robbing me anymore."

"I'll call you bitch as many bitching bitch times as I want, bitchy bitch bitch."

"No, you won't. Use that word again and I'm going to ask you to leave my house."

"You won't let me murder your hubby?"

"That's right. And then no reward."

"Can I call you a wench?"

"No. In fact, you need to stop disrespecting me altogether. You're not the only man who would commit murder for me, you know."

"Uh-huh."

"I'm serious."

"Yeah, well, I'm already here, so I might as well do it." I hoisted the chair over my head again, being more careful about the ceiling this time. "Now you're *sure* you want me to do this, right?"

"I'm sure."

"I don't want to hear any whining after I hit him."

"You won't."

I took a deep breath, then swung the chair as hard as I could, and let me assure you that it's pretty goddamn hard. The back of the chair connected perfectly with his skull, knocking his body right onto the floor. He lay on the carpet with a brand-new dent in his head and his neck at a really fucked-up angle.

"Hubby's dead," I announced.

She crouched down next to him and held the mirror next to his nose. I thought this was pretty stupid, considering that his head and his body weren't quite facing the same direction anymore.

"He's still alive," she said.

"Bullshit."

"Look at the mirror."

"I don't care about the mirror. If the mirror is fogging up, then you've got funky A/C in here. That guy is dead."

"Check his pulse."

"I already said no."

She pulled up the corpse's sleeve and pressed her fingers against his wrist. "He still has one."

I crouched down next to her and grabbed the dead guy's wrist. It felt cold and creepy. "Nothing."

"Your fingers aren't in the right place."

"Yes, they are."

"Don't you know how to check for a pulse?" She pushed my fingers into the proper spot. "Feel it?"

Yep. There was a definite pulse. A strong one.

"How is he still alive? I broke his neck!"

"I told you! He won't die!"

"That's impossible!"

"Apparently it's not."

"This is crazy! What the hell kind of vitamins does he take?"

I stood up. No way should he have survived that hit. At least not when he was 97% dead already. Unless…

"Did he have a metal plate in his head?" I asked.

"No."

"Damn."

Once again, a big red neon sign was flashing before my eyes: *Get The Fuck Out. Get The Fuck Out. Get The Fuck Out.* But now it had become a personal challenge. I mean, how dare that decrepit prick not die when I bashed him over the head? If I couldn't kill him, then I was a complete loser of a human being, and I just wasn't willing to walk out of there without my dignity intact.

Her husband was *toast*.

"What've you got in the way of butcher knives?" I asked.

- 3 -

"I already tried stabbing him," said Gretchen.

"I don't want to stab him. I want to cut his head off."

"I already tried that, too."

"I'm going to try with more skill."

She went into the kitchen. Her husband was resilient, all right, but a little decapitation would keep him from fogging up that mirror. He'd never done anything to me personally, but man, I was ready to kick his severed head out the goddamn window and try to hit a dog with it.

"Here," said Gretchen, holding out the knife.

"Don't hand it to me blade-first, wench."

"I said you couldn't call me a wench."

"Fine. That's not how one properly hands a sharp instrument to another human being, *Gretchen*." My British accent sucked, but she got the idea.

"Much better." She flipped the knife around and handed it to me. I took it by the handle and rolled her husband onto his back. Then I decided that I didn't really want to look at his face while I was cutting his head off, and re-rolled him onto his stomach.

She'd already made a pretty decent groove in the back of his neck, so I pressed the blade of the knife into the groove and gave myself a mental pep talk.

I want to make it perfectly clear that I'm not a wuss. Remember how I told you that I beat that guy to possible-death with a gun? You can't do that kind of thing if you're a wuss. I've never been squeamish. Bring on the *Faces of Death* movies. Give me good seats to an open heart surgery. Shred some old lady with a cheese grater on my dining room table while I'm trying to eat lasagna. No problem. Honestly, the only thing that has ever bothered me is when I was a little kid, and my friends would do that thing where they pulled on their lower eyelid and turned it inside out. Holy fuck, is that ever disturbing! But aside from that, nope, not squeamish at all.

But you have to keep in mind that I was about to cut off somebody's head. Oh, sure, for all I know, you might be the Havana Head-Chopper and whack off people's heads every other Tuesday, but most people would have a problem with the concept.

So I hesitated.

"What's wrong?" asked Gretchen.

"Nothing."

"Then do it."

"Don't even think of giving me orders. I'll do it when I feel like doing it and not a second sooner." I removed the knife from the neck groove.

"What are you doing?"

"Waiting."

"For what?"

"For enough time to pass that I'm doing this of my own free will." I set the knife down on the floor.

"Are you kidding me?" Gretchen asked.

"Nope."

"How childish can you be?"

"I'm not being childish. But I don't take orders from anybody, especially some chick I just robbed, and even more especially when I've got a gun and a butcher knife. I'll cut his head off for the sex, but I'll do it when I'm good and ready."

Immediately after saying it, I hoped that the phrase "I'll cut his head off for the sex" would never be taken out of context.

"Okay, whatever. I take back what I said. You may decapitate him at your leisure."

"I will."

We were silent for a long moment.

Gretchen sighed.

"I'll take that sigh as a signal of impatience," I said. "Keep it up and we'll be here all night."

"Being impatient isn't the same as telling you what to do."

"It's close enough."

We waited for an even longer moment.

"Do you think he knows we're hovering over him ready to cut his head off?" I asked.

"I'm not sure. I assume so."

"That would suck."

"Yes, it would."

"Bummer for him. I guess I'm in the mood to cut now. Thank you for your patience." I picked up the knife, pressed it into her hubby's neck, and pushed down.

I didn't seem to be making any progress, so I pushed harder.

And harder.

And even harder until I felt compelled to say "Dammit!"

"What's wrong?"

"This knife won't go through the bone."

"I know! That's the problem I had!"

"Then why did you give me this crappy knife?"

"Don't blame the knife."

"Of course I'm going to blame the knife! A Ginsu would get the job done. I can't cut through bone with this dull-ass piece of shit."

"It's not dull. It's a great knife."

"His non-severed head says that it's not."

Gretchen grabbed the knife out of my hand, which pissed me off but I decided not to make an issue of it. She walked into the kitchen, opened the refrigerator, and took out a cellophane wrapped t-bone steak. She held it up. "See this?"

"Yeah."

She slammed the steak down on a cutting board. "Watch."

I stood up and walked over to see the exciting demonstration. She pressed the blade of the knife against the meat, pushed down, and with only a little bit of effort sliced through the steak, bone and all.

"It's a good knife," she informed me.

"Well...maybe it's harder to cut through human bone than cow bone."

"Maybe, but we're not trying to cut through his leg here! We're cutting through his neck! And it's not working! He's unkillable!"

"We just need a better tool. What have you got that's better than that knife?"

"Nothing!"

"What about a hacksaw?"

"I told you, this knife is the best I've got!" she said, practically screaming.

"Gee, why not shout that a bit louder so all of your neighbors can hear? Hey, actually, do you think any of your neighbors have a hacksaw we can borrow?"

"I'm not going to ask anybody for a hacksaw in the middle of the night."

"Then how about I come back tomorrow?"

"How about you go get a hacksaw and come back?"

"I don't own one."

"So buy one."

"Where?"

"Wal-Mart. There's a twenty-four-hour one."

"Let me try something else first. How many times do you think you stabbed him?"

"Ten or eleven. Maybe twelve."

"Give me the knife."

She handed me the butcher knife. I clutched it in my fist and returned to her husband. I crouched down next to him, raised the knife, and *slammed* it into his back. The knife went in deep. I wrenched it out and stabbed him again.

Gretchen, still in the kitchen, leaned over the sink and gagged.

I stabbed him three more times. There was some blood, but not as much as I would've expected and there wasn't any spurting.

"Do a breath check," I said.

Gretchen, who now looked positively sick to her stomach, hurried over. I lifted the back of his head by the hair, and she placed the mirror under his nose.

"Still alive."

"Shit!"

I rolled him onto his back and stabbed him another five times in the heart. Again, a little blood, but not much.

"Breath check."

Gretchen checked. "Alive."

Okay, *now* we had issues. Killing a human being is a lot more difficult than it looks in the movies, but at the same time, when you get stabbed in the heart five times, you're pretty much supposed to die. And you're supposed to bleed all over the place.

"Was your husband into black magic?" I asked.

"Yeah, a little bit."

"Did he ever say anything about spells or rituals or anything that could grant him eternal life?"

"Not that I remember."

"Is this something he might have kept from you?"

"I wouldn't have thought so, but I also didn't think he'd be cheating on me with some slut."

"Okay. I thought I'd ask because it looks like we've got something supernatural going on here."

She frowned and nodded.

I stayed calm, but I was absolutely furious. How could she be so irresponsible as not to warn me that there might be otherworldly elements involved? That should've been the first goddamn thing out of her mouth: "Hey, could you help me murder my husband, who by the way might have struck a deal with Satan for eternal life?"

"I'm leaving," I said.

"What? No, you can't!"

"You should've warned me."

"We don't know for sure that it's black magic."

I stabbed him in the heart again and left the knife sticking out of his chest. "Black magic."

"Okay, it's probably black magic. But I still need your help!"

"I'm not questioning that you need my help. I'm saying that I'm done helping you."

"I'll call the cops."

"Huh?"

"You stabbed my husband almost ten times with a butcher knife. You also bashed him in the head with a chair and broke his neck. Those are both felonies."

"I'm not the only one who stabbed and hit him."

"They won't know that."

"Actually, they would. Autopsy results would show that the second set of injuries came a long time after the first."

"They wouldn't do an autopsy. He's not dead."

"But they'd look at his injuries."

"He's not bleeding like a normal person. The tests they use to determine time of injury might not give accurate information."

"They'd figure it out."

"I'll change our deal to twenty-four hours."

"No deal. I didn't even plan to use the full twelve."

"How about three eight-hour sessions?"

"How about forty-eight half-hour sessions?"

"Four six-hour sessions."

"Six four-hour sessions, and you bring a friend."

"Guy or girl?"

"What do you think?"

"No deal."

"You bring a girlfriend for the last session."

"No. The deal was no other parties involved."

"We're renegotiating."

"Not gonna happen."

"Four six-hour sessions, with a quickie in advance."

"No."

"Why not?"

"Because I said no. Four six-hour sessions, and you have to use them up within a week. That's my final offer."

"What if I find a friend for us?"

"No."

"Prude."

"Then leave," she said. "You're clearly not interested, so just get out of here. You probably couldn't get it up anyway."

I chuckled. "You think that insulting my manhood is going to change my mind?"

"Yes. I think it's going to make you feel threatened, and when you walk out that door I'll always think of you as somebody who couldn't *handle* six hours with me. I'll have mental images of your poor little penis shriveling into a tiny nub, and I'll tell my hot girlfriends all about it. We'll laugh and laugh and laugh. You'll never hear about it, probably, but deep in the back of your mind you'll always know that I think you're not up to the sexual task."

Wench.

"I'm not that easily manipulated," I said.

"Then go."

"Nah, I'll stick around."

I want to make it perfectly clear that I did *not* agree to stay because I was worried about some imaginary women laughing about my dick. I stayed because this was still my only real opportunity to experience a golden shower.

"So what next?" she asked.

"Hacksaw. No, chainsaw. We'll get both."

"I can't run a chainsaw in my apartment."

"You will if that's what it takes to cut off hubby's head. Look, I don't know much about witchcraft, but I can't imagine that he'd keep breathing after we cut off his head with a chainsaw. It just doesn't happen."

"It's not witchcraft."

"Huh?"

"He wasn't Wiccan. Leave witchcraft out of this. Wicca is a very misunderstood lifestyle, and I really get offended when people think—"

"I don't give a sloppy shit if this is witchcraft or Satanism or fuckin' *Dianetics*! His head needs to come off! Are we agreed on that?"

"Yes."

"Good. *Jesus.*" Then a rather obvious idea occurred to me. "Did your husband have any black magic books or scrolls or anything like that?"

"Not in the house."

"Are you sure? Maybe hidden under the mattress next to the Playboys?"

"I'm sure. I looked."

"Maybe in his closet, in a shoebox or something? That's where I kept my porn when I lived with this one chick. Now I just leave it out on the floor and in the bathroom."

"I don't care about your porn."

"You should. It's good porn."

"I'm sure it is. Now why don't you head over to Wal-Mart?"

"Are you giving me orders again?"

She closed her eyes and lowered her head.

"What are you doing?"

"Counting to ten."

"All right, all right, we'll go."

"You mean you'll go. If my husband turns up headless, it's probably best if I don't have a recent chainsaw purchase on my credit card."

"Well, I don't have enough money for a chainsaw."

"How much is a chainsaw?"

"Dunno. More than the twelve bucks I got from you. Anyway, even if I had the money, I wouldn't pay for this stuff. That's your problem."

"Jerk." She stormed off into another room. What did she think, I was going to purchase hardware for her? Give me a break. I once dated this chick, and she asked if we could stop by the convenience store for a Coke, and I said sure and went in with her, and when the clerk said that it would be a buck-nineteen she looked at me all expectantly, as if I was supposed to buy her Coke. It's not even like I was getting one for myself. I made her buy her own damn Coke. No way in hell was I going to buy Gretchen a saw with my own money. Screw that.

She returned with some cash. "This is a hundred and sixty-five dollars. It's all the money I have in the world." She handed me the wad of bills. "I want change."

"Not a problem."

"Be back in an hour or I'm calling the cops on you."

That did it. I reached into my jacket, pulled out the revolver, and shoved it in her face. "If I'm not back in an hour, you'll wait another fuckin' hour. If I'm not back then, you'll kiss your hundred and sixty-five bucks goodbye and be glad you're still alive. You got that?"

"Yeah."

"Say 'yes.' It's more polite."

"Yes."

"Thank you." I was tempted to bash the barrel of the revolver against her nose, but then she probably *would* call the cops. And besides, I didn't feel like screwing some chick with a swollen nose. I hoped that the gun-in-the-face would be enough to remind her that she wasn't the boss of me.

I tucked the gun back into my inside jacket pocket. "I'll *try* to be back in an hour, but I can't help it if people try to go through the 'twelve items or less' line with thirteen items."

She nodded without much enthusiasm. Clearly this little reminder of who was in charge had bummed her out. Good. It actually made me kind of horny.

"Feel free to keep trying with the butcher knife," I said, as I headed for the front door.

"I think I'm just going to watch some TV."

"Whatever. Seeya in an hour or so."

- 4 -

As I walked down the sidewalk, I wondered if I was a complete dumbass for going through with this. I quickly decided that yes, I was indeed a dumbass, a big one, but that it would be worth it in the end.

I wasn't scared of prison. I mean, I certainly didn't want to *go* to prison, but when you live like I do, it's pretty much a given that at some point you're going to end up doing time. I figured, worst case scenario, even if I got life in the slammer I'd be clever enough to figure out a way to slit my wrists or hang myself.

Live fast and die young. Take risks. I didn't even like to wear condoms.

Now I had to figure out what to do. I was definitely going to keep Gretchen's cash for myself, but that meant I'd have to figure out some other way to get the necessary saws. I've never been skilled at breaking-and-entering, so stealing one from somebody's home wasn't an option. Neither was stealing one from Wal-Mart, since not only would a chainsaw not fit down my pants, but I wouldn't put one down there if it did.

Maybe I could pick up one for cheap at a pawn shop.

Hmmmmm.

One thing was for sure: I was going to be back in an hour. Yeah, yeah, I put Gretchen in her place, but I still couldn't trust that she wouldn't call the cops on me. Though it wouldn't be in her best interest to do so, I had to keep the whole "insane woman" element of the situation in mind.

I found a pawn shop pretty easily, but sadly they didn't have either a hacksaw or a chainsaw. They did have the latest Alice Cooper CD for five bucks, so I picked that up.

I resumed walking down the sidewalk, trying to figure things out. What else could be used to separate a stingy head from its body? Perhaps we'd given up too easily. If I bashed at his neck with a claw hammer, over and over, the bones would have to separate before too long, right?

Made sense.

Or maybe the brain itself was the issue. Yeah, we'd bashed his skull in, but we hadn't actually gone after his grey matter. If we got the skull open, we could stab his brain a few times with the butcher knife. That might work better than stabbing the heart.

Hmmmmm.

The problem with being lost in thought is that I wasn't paying as much attention to my surroundings as I normally would. For example, under normal circumstances, when I walked past an alleyway, I'd notice if there was a pair of young thugs hiding in the shadows, waiting for a victim to approach. I'd be certain that my gun was ready to draw at a moment's notice, do my I'm Pretty Sure You Don't Wanna Fuck With Me walk, and they'd leave me alone.

Instead, I was doing my Lost In Thought Trying to Figure Out Where The Hell I'm Gonna Get a Chainsaw At This Late Hour walk. So I was *really* unhappy when I saw the gun pointed at me.

"Get in here!" said one of the young thugs, grabbing me by the collar of my jacket. He pulled me into the alley while his buddy kept the gun pointed at me.

Both of the assholes looked about eighteen or nineteen. The one with the gun had a shaved head and a Swastika tattooed on his forehead. The one who had dared to touch my jacket was holding a switchblade knife and he had a green mohawk.

Mohawk Boy slammed me against the wall. "Give me your wallet, bitch!"

"Whoa, whoa, hold on," I said. "I'm in the business. How about showing some professional courtesy?"

"I'll professional courtesy your ass!"

"I don't even get what that means."

"He said, hand over your wallet!" said Mr. Shaved Head.

I dug my wallet out of my back pocket and handed it over. Mohawk Boy opened it and quickly flipped through the contents. "Two bucks?"

"The economy's crap, man."

"Turn your pockets inside-out!"

I reached inside my jacket pocket.

"No, your pants pockets first!"

"What difference does the order make?"

"Pants pockets first!"

Damn. I reached into the pocket of my jeans and took out my earnings for the night. I could've easily knocked the knife right out of his hand and then fed him his own mohawk, but I didn't own any Kevlar leotards so I had to think about his buddy with the gun.

I handed over the money. Mohawk Boy grinned. "Thanks."

"Anytime. Don't mention it."

"What else ya got?" asked Mr. Shaved Head.

"You just took almost a hundred and eighty bucks from me! What the hell else do you need?"

"Maybe we need blood."

"Yeah, okay, whatever. So how come that Swastika hasn't gotten you killed yet?"

"'Cuz I know how to take care of myself."

"Yeah, but doesn't it keep you from being served at restaurants and stuff?"

"No."

"I can't imagine that. I mean, your friend can wear a hat when he doesn't want to look like a complete retard, but you don't even have any hair to comb over your forehead. Do you slap on a wig?"

"You need to stop talking."

"What's gonna happen when you're middle-aged? Some Jewish kid will kick your ass. Aren't you thinking about the future?"

"I'm serious. You need to keep that mouth shut."

"Sorry. I'm just wondering why somebody would want to make it so they can't even walk into a McDonalds without some sort of conflict. Seems like social suicide to me."

"Kiss my ass."

I looked at him more closely. "That's a temporary tattoo, isn't it?"

"Fuck you!"

"It is! I can tell from here!"

"So what?"

"Wow, you must be quite a badass. Did you get that at Hot Topic or Claire's?"

"I said shut the fuck up!"

Okay, I promised myself that I would be brutally honest when I wrote this, which means that I can't talk about using his anger as a distraction, reaching into my jacket, pulling out my gun, popping a bullet right into the middle of his ridiculous Swastika, and then taking out Mohawk Boy a split-second before he lunged at me with the switchblade.

No, the truth is that they beat the shit out of me.

Don't get me wrong—I put up a good fight. I think I broke Mohawk Boy's nose and I rubbed off part of Mr. Shaved Head's tattoo. Still, I was outnumbered. In the movies, the hero can beat up dozens of opponents, but in real life, fighting two guys at once generally means that you're gonna get your ass kicked.

They ran off with my money and wallet, leaving me lying on the ground with a bloody nose, split lip, cut arm, headache, earache, stomachache, groinache, broken toe (I think) and about eighteen billion bruises.

And then I lost consciousness for a while.

- 5 -

I awoke to a warm, pleasant sensation on my legs. When I opened my eyes and saw that it was wino taking a piss on me, the sensation became less pleasant. I cursed, sputtered, and scooted away.

"Sorry, din't seeya dere," said the wino, giving me a rotten-tooth smile.

I reached into my jacket pocket to grab my gun so I could shoot his dick off.

It wasn't there.

"Lookin' for dis?" he asked, pointing my gun at me. The safety was off.

"No, I was looking for something to wipe off your goddamn urine."

"Urine. Dat's funny. Urine." He chuckled. The wino looked about eighty years old and had a thick grey beard. He was wearing raggedy clothes that looked like they hadn't been washed in six weeks, and he'd done a lot of vomiting in those six weeks.

"Give me back my gun," I said.

The wino shook his head. "Uh-uh. *My* gun. Guess I lied when I said I din't see ya dere, huh?" The wino's belly shook as he laughed, like a bowl full of Jell-O shots.

I pushed myself up to a sitting position, which really, really hurt. "I mean it. Give me back the gun, old man."

"I'm 'onna sell dis gun, an' get me some boooooooze. My belly's gon' be full tonight! Boo-ya!"

"That gun was used to commit a crime today. You try to sell it, you're going to jail."

The wino threw back his head and laughed. "I ain't 'fraid of jail. Dey got booze in jail."

"No, they don't."

"Dey sure do! Dey got booze an' poontang an' biscuits."

"You're thinking of the magical jail in the land of fairy dragons."

"Boooooooooooze."

I almost liked this old guy, except that he'd stolen my gun and taken a leak on me. "Just give me my gun. I don't want you to hurt yourself with it."

"Ain't goin' hurt myself. Goin' hurt *you*."

"I don't think so."

"Goin' make you *bleed*!"

At this point, it was time to make the situation with the wino go away. I kicked him in the shin as hard as I could. He let out a loud yelp and fell to the ground, howling in pain. I plucked the gun out of his hand and turned it on him.

"*Oh, sweet Jesus!*" he cried out. "*Don't shoot me! Please, please don't shoot me!*"

"I'm not gonna shoot you," I said, getting to my feet.

"*Don't kill me! Don't kill me! Oh, Lord, I'm not ready to die! Please don't call me home! I don't wanna die! I don't wanna die! Oh, please, show some mercy, kind sir! I'll do anything! No, no, no, no, no, don't kill me!*"

"I'm not gonna kill you. Shut up."

The wino grabbed my right leg with both hands. "*You are! You're gonna kill me for what I done! Oh Jesus God Christ Buddha I don't wanna die! Why won't you have sweet mercy? I wasn't goin' hurt you wit' da gun, I swear it on my dead momma's life! I was goin' let you go! Oh, please, please, please, can't you find it in yourself to let me and my children live?*" Tears streamed down his face.

I tried to shake him off my leg. "Knock it off. What the hell's the matter with you?"

"*I'll do anything! Anything at all! I'm too young to die! I got too many unresolved issues in my life! Want my shirt? I'll give you my shirt!*"

"I don't want your shirt."

"*Take it! Take da shirt off my back!*" The wino hurriedly unbuttoned his filthy shirt, took it off, and thrust it at me. "*Take da shirt in exchange for my life! Please!*"

I thrust the shirt back at him. "I don't want the shirt or your life. Go away."

"*You're goin' kill me!*"

"I said I wasn't."

"*You're goin' shoot me in da back of my head!*"

"Jeez, get some self-respect," I told him. I turned and tried to walk out of the alley, but the wino wouldn't let go of my damn leg. I turned back and pressed the barrel of the gun against his head. He shrieked.

"*I don't wanna die don't wanna die don't wanna—*"

"Let go of my leg!"

"*—die don't wanna die don't wanna die don't wanna—*"

"Stop blubbering! I'm not gonna kill you. Get your hands off my leg so I can leave!"

He let go of my leg, then clawed at the zipper of my pants. "*I'll suck your dick! I'll suck it good so you won't kill me! We won't have to tell no one 'bout it!*"

I came pretty close to shooting him then, but I settled for kicking him in the chest. He fell onto his side and then scrunched up into the fetal position, sobbing.

I shoved the gun into my inside jacket pocket and hurried out of the alley, wincing at the pain that seemed to be in every joint in my body. I hurt enough from my beating that I didn't notice the cop until I walked into him.

"Uhhhhh," I said.

"What's going on?" the cop asked. He was a big guy with a bad complexion, and he looked like the kind of person who really enjoyed using his billy club.

"Nothing, sir."

"Oh, Lord, he's goin' come back to kill me, I just know it! He's goin' crack my teeth on the pavement and shoot my brains out! Please, please, please heavenly Allah don't let him come back! I need a drink!"

"A homeless man tried to mug me," I explained. "No big deal. He seems kind of mentally disturbed; you may want to check him into a soup kitchen."

"Looks like he beat you up pretty bad."

I nodded. "Yeah, yeah, I did take a few punches. I've always tried to live a life of peace, so it's hard for me to defend myself against physical violence. God gives me strength, though. I forgive the homeless man for what he did."

The cop narrowed his eyes. "Why don't you wait here?"

"Yes, sir."

The cop walked into the alley. I tried to decide if I should make a run for it or not. Technically, I was the victim here, but I don't think it will surprise you to discover that I didn't have a concealed weapons permit for the gun in my jacket, nor was it even registered in my name.

Unfortunately, I was sore as hell, and staggering away from the scene in a pathetic half-limp wouldn't get me far. I was going to have to talk my way out of this one. I'll admit that I did think about popping the cop, but purely in a "Gosh, it sure would be stupid to pop the cop" sense. They don't stop looking for cop killers.

I stepped back to the entrance of the alley so I could watch. The wino kept begging for his life, although by now it was pure gibberish, while the cop tried to calm him down. I sort of hoped that the wino would offer to fellate him, which would've been pretty funny.

The cop pulled the wino to his feet, pushed him against the wall, and handcuffed him. The wino shouted something that I couldn't understand but that was most likely a request that the cop not kill him.

"Nobody's going to kill you," said the cop, who had obviously learned to speak Incoherent Wino during his training.

"You takin' me to jail?" asked the wino.

"I'm taking you to the station, yes."

"*All riiiiight! Poontang! Poontang!*"

The cop led the wino out of the alley. "You stay put," the cop told me as he passed. I nodded. The cop took the wino to his squad car, which was parked alongside the sidewalk not too far past the alley, and put him in the back seat. Then he returned to me.

"You say he attacked you?" asked the cop, taking out a notebook.

"Yes, sir."

"Start at the beginning."

"I was on my way home, and I passed this alley here. He asked me if I could spare a dollar. I felt badly for him, because here I was on the way to my heated home, while he clearly didn't have a home, so I agreed."

"Go on."

"I took out my wallet, which was a mistake, I know, but I've always been trusting and naive. I forget that not all human beings follow God's path. As soon as I did so, he began to strike me."

"Did you fight back?"

I lowered my head. "I've always been passive."

"So may I ask why he thought you were going to kill him?"

"Oh, he didn't mean me."

"Who did he mean?"

"Lucifer."

"Lucifer?"

"As he was striking me, I informed him that his sins were putting him in the path of Lucifer, and that Lucifer would most likely kill him and drag his soul to Hades. He got upset."

"I see."

"I don't know if that's true or not. I just wanted him to stop the physical violence."

The cop stared at me for a long moment.

"Are you trying to bullshit me?" he finally asked.

"No, sir. Is it standard practice to use that kind of language around civilians? I've just been through a traumatic experience, and I don't appreciate the sting of your profanity."

He stared at me for another long moment. I wondered if I'd pushed the act just a bit too far.

"I'll drive you to the hospital," he said.

"I'm fine."

"He beat you up pretty bad."

"I don't have medical insurance. And nothing seems to be broken. All I need is a relaxing hot bath and my waterproof bible."

"I at least need you to come in to the station to press charges."

I shook my head. "I don't want to press charges. Just give him a warm place to sleep off his intoxication. The best thing you can do for that poor man is check him into a rehab program. I don't need revenge. He'll burn in Hell anyway."

The cop continued to stare at me. It was making me uncomfortable. I was starting to think that maybe I should casually reach into my inside jacket pocket and...

"Fair enough," the cop said. "You sure you don't want a ride somewhere?"

"No, no, I'm fine. I'll use the walk for silent reflection."

"All right. Try to be more careful next time. You could've been killed."

"Thank you, officer. I'll remember that." I walked away, unsure if I was a brilliant actor or if the cop was really dumb. Most likely it was a combination of the two.

Now what? I still didn't have any kind of sawing instrument, but thanks to my unconsciousness, I'd been gone much longer than planned. I was a lot less horny after getting the crap beat out of me, so I considered just calling it a night and letting Gretchen deal with her homicide problems herself.

But I couldn't.

It wasn't because I was scared that she might call the cops on me. Well, okay, that was part of it. I'd done my share of the attempted murdering, and as a woman scorned she may very well have tried to blame the whole thing on me. Because I'm a complete dumbass, I'd certainly left behind fingerprints and DNA evidence and all that stuff, so it was not in my best interest to leave that loose end untied.

And...I dunno...I kind of liked her.

Don't worry, I wasn't in love or anything retarded like that. I wasn't gonna make goo-goo eyes at her or hold her hand or make babies. I just kind of realized that I liked her a little bit more than simply wanting to bang the hell out of her.

So I went back.

- 6 -

Through some sort of amazing miracle, I made it back to her apartment building without getting beat up or soiled. I pushed the buzzer.

"Yes?" her voice crackled through the speaker.

"It's me."

"Where the hell have you been?"

"Getting hurt. Let me in."

"Don't you know I've been worried sick?"

"Just let me in."

"I want an apology first."

"Say what?"

"Apologize and I'll let you in."

I couldn't believe this. "I don't owe you an apology."

"Then you can stay out there for all I care."

"I'm here to help you!"

"You need to start thinking about other people besides yourself. For all I knew you could've been lying dead in a ditch somewhere."

"I was unconscious in a fuckin' alley! Is that good enough?"

"Apologize."

"Screw that!"

"Then I guess we have nothing to say to each other. Good night."

"All right, all right, I'm sorry! Jesus!"

"That's not an apology."

"Yes, it was!"

"Not said in that tone of voice, it wasn't."

"Bitch!"

"Okay, then you can *really* stay down there."

"I got *mugged*! I almost got killed!"

"Uh-huh. Likely story."

"It's the truth!"

"You were out drinking with your buddies, weren't you?"

"No I wasn't out drinking! This is ridiculous! Open the door!"

"After you say you're sorry."

At this point, I wanted to throw back my head and let out a primal scream of misery that would rattle the windows, crack the pavement, and echo throughout the heavens.

Instead, I'm said: "I'm sorry."

"Apology accepted."

The buzzer sounded, and I opened the door.

I stomped up the stairs, not caring about how much it hurt. Then I twisted my ankle and started to care again.

Who did she think she was? Apologize. Yeah, right. I was helping her! I was putting myself at risk to assist her with her problems, and I deserved a little bit of respect. If she didn't appreciate all that I was doing for her, well, then it was over between us.

The door was already open when I got to the top of the stairs. Her pissed-off expression immediately changed to one of concern as she saw me. "Oh my God! What happened?"

I told her the whole story, leaving out the embarrassing parts. I tried to leave out the part where I got pissed on, but I had to explain the scent.

"Oh, you poor dear," she said. "Did you get the saw?"

"No."

"Isn't that why you went in the first place? What, did I need to make you a shopping list for two items?"

"There were distractions!"

She sighed. "Men."

"Don't blame my gender! If you got mugged, you sure as hell wouldn't have come back with a chainsaw!"

"Well, lucky for us, while you were out playing with the boys, I went to Wal-Mart." She pointed to a plastic sack that rested on the dining room table. "Brand-new hacksaw. Have at it."

It took us a while to get the hacksaw out of the packaging, but I don't feel like sharing the details. I mean, c'mon, let me retain some shred of dignity, okay?

Oh, yeah, I also changed out of the pants that the wino pissed on, and into a pair of her husband's dork pants. No dignity for me.

Then I knelt down beside the poor guy and pressed the hacksaw against the back of his neck.

"Do it," Gretchen urged.

Instead of requesting that she please shut the fuck up, I began to saw. The saw went through the already-cut part pretty easily, and then I encountered resistance.

"Ow," said her husband.

I yelped. Thrice. Then I scooted away from him. "Shit shit shit shit shit!"

"What's wrong?" Gretchen asked.

"Shit!"

"What's wrong?"

"He said ow!"

"Well, you're cutting off his head!"

"I thought he was comatose!"

"He didn't say it loudly!"

I closed my eyes and took a deep breath. This decapitation was definitely not worth it.

"Saw off his head and he'll stop saying ow!" Gretchen said.

I scooted back over to him. I could do this. *Become one with the saw. The saw is my buddy.*

Once again I placed the blade in the groove, and pulled the saw back toward me. It made sort of a...I'm not quite sure how to describe the sound. I don't wanna say it was *crunchy*, but that's sort of what it was like. I gave the saw a few more back-and-forth strokes. It was definitely working. This fucker's head was going bye-bye for sure.

Fresh blood started to trickle from the wound. I turned my head away and kept sawing. It was becoming more difficult, but I was still making progress.

Then the resistance stopped. The saw cut through the remaining throat-flesh with no problem.

"Don't scrape up the floor!" Gretchen said.

"Do you wanna be next?"

"I'm just saying, I'll lose my security deposit."

"You'd be amazed how little I care about that. Really. You'd be astonished. One of those astrophysics scientists or whatever they're called couldn't even measure how little I care about your stupid floor using one of their molecular scales."

"What are you babbling about?"

"Fuck your floor." I did one last slice, and that was it for hubby's head. It rolled onto its side, no longer attached to his body.

"Wanna try your mirror *now*?"

Gretchen nodded and went to get it.

"I was joking!"

"I know you were. But we're still going to check."

"If it's still breathing, I'll french kiss that head," I told her, knowing that if the head was indeed still alive, I'd do no such thing.

Gretchen returned with the mirror. "Roll the head over."

"You roll the head over."

She looked like she wanted to start our four hundred and ninety-seventh argument of the evening, but settled for muttering something under her breath (I detected traces of "bastard" and "asshole") and rolling the head so that it was face-up. She placed the mirror in front of his lips.

We waited.

Nothing.

After a couple of minutes, Gretchen set down the mirror and checked his pulse.

"He's dead," she announced.

"Woo-hoo!"

"Thank goodness."

"So let's go fuck," I said, suddenly horny again.

"Are you for real?"

"What? That was the deal, right?"

"Yeah, but not with his headless corpse bleeding all over the place! We need to saw up the rest of it and get it out of here."

"You just said to kill him. You didn't say that I had to perform disposal services."

"I can't believe you want to have sex right after you've chopped off somebody's head. What does that say about you?"

"I'm a stud."

"It says that you're sick. You're a sick man."

"You'd better not be thinking of backing out of our deal," I warned her. "I'll fuckin' kill you."

"I'm not backing out. I just thought it was understood that I wouldn't be pleasuring you until my husband's body stopped oozing! Jesus, you're foul!"

"You make that sound sexy."

"We'll finish slicing up my husband's body, *then* we'll get rid of the chunks, *then* we'll take a long shower, and *then* we'll get some sleep—and no, you can't spend the night—and *then* I'll pay you."

"That wasn't the agreement."

"That's the agreement now."

I know what you're thinking: "Damn, Frank, why didn't you just backhand the tramp and make her pay up?" I considered it. I mean, yeah, I was still in a lot of pain from earlier, but that didn't mean I couldn't give her a good solid slap across the face.

I'm not sure why I didn't. On one hand, I guess I was worried that she might go absolutely apeshit berserk on me and start screaming and freaking out and hollering for help and then my only option would be to get the hell out of there and spend the rest of the night making sweet, sweet love to the artificial vagina I got as a gag gift one year, and that thing chafes. On the other hand, I simply didn't want to hurt her.

It was mostly the first one.

So I sawed. I cut off his arms and his legs, wrapped them in old issues of *Entertainment Weekly*, and stuffed them into garbage bags. I sawed his torso into quarters (not exact quarters, but close enough) and we wrapped and bagged those as well. Gretchen mopped up the floor, and then used her Swifter Wet to get up the last spots.

"That wasn't so hard," I said. "Shall we hit the shower?"

"I'm going first."

"Not together?"

"Do you know what the most overrated erotic experience is?" Gretchen asked. "Showering together. You spend half the time shivering because you aren't getting any of the water, and the spray off the other person gets in your eyes, and the only things the guy is ever interested in helping you wash are your tits."

I nodded. "Yeah, you're right. And it's not really sexy to watch the other person washing their ears and that kind of shit."

"Not at all."

"Fine. I'll go second."

"Thank you. I'm glad to see you're not always a jerk."

I had a pretty funny jerk-style comment to make, but decided against it. I wish I could remember what it was. Now that's gonna bug me for the rest of this story until I think of it. Damn.

She headed off for the bathroom, and I stood around in the kitchen, itchy in my gore-stained clothes, looking at the garbage bags.

"I hope the extramarital snatch was worth it," I told the bags.

The bags did not answer.

I opened up her refrigerator and looked through the contents. Lots of nasty stuff, like soy milk and veggie burgers and apples. At least they had a couple of beers. I grabbed one, popped it open, and chugged most of the can.

"Don't touch my beer," somebody said.

I glanced around. There was nobody there.

I finished off the can and let out a nice long belch.

"That's not your beer!" The voice was muffled. It kind of sounded like it was coming from one of the garbage bags.

I tossed the empty beer can in the sink, then took the second can out of the fridge. I waved it at the garbage bags.

"You don't drink another man's beer!" the voice said. One of the garbage bags—the one I was pretty sure contained the head—shifted a bit.

I stared at it.

Nah.

I popped open the beer and took a tentative sip.

"You're buying me another one," the voice warned.

I kicked the bag. "Shut the fuck up," I told it.

"I don't care if you screw my wife, but leave my beer alone! I'm warning you."

I set the mostly full can of beer down on the counter. "Gretchen! Your husband's head is talking!"

She didn't answer. She probably couldn't hear me over the shower. I hurried out of the kitchen and knocked on the bathroom door.

"What?" she asked, annoyed.

"Your husband's head talked to me."

"What did he say?"

"Not to drink his beer."

"So don't drink his beer!"

"The important part isn't the beer! The important part is the talking head!"

"Let me finish my shower, for God's sake! I'll be out in a minute!"

I walked back into the kitchen. I picked up the beer can.

"Put it down," the head said.

"How can you even see me through the bag?"

"I'm not seeing you through the bag."

"Then why is the bag moving?"

"Because I'm *talking* to you through the bag. I'm not *seeing* you through the bag. Why would my eyes make the bag move? You really are an idiot."

There'd been plenty of indicators this evening that I should leave the apartment and go home. The talking head was the biggest one. But I was more curious than scared.

I took a defiant sip of beer. "So what are you gonna do to me, head?"

"I'm going to send your soul straight to Hell."

"Bullshit."

"I am."

"You're bluffing."

"Don't test me, mortal."

I took a big swig of his beer and swished it around my mouth just to piss him off. "One, if there is indeed a Hell, then I've already damned my soul about seven hundred times. Two, I don't believe that a severed head has that kind of influence."

"You're wrong."

"Uh-huh." I finished off the beer and turned the can upside down to make sure he knew there wasn't any left. "So send my soul to Hell."

"In time."

"You're so full of shit. If you could do it, you'd do it now." I gently kicked the bag. "Does that bug you?"

"You're sealing your fate, mortal."

I kicked the bag a few more times. "Is that annoying you? It would sure annoy me. Why don't you make me stop? Huh? Why don't you curse my toes or something?"

The head didn't respond.

"What's the matter? Is my foot in your mouth?" I knelt down and untied the garbage bag. I reached inside and pulled out the wrapped-up head.

"You'll pay for this."

"You keep saying that, and yet has my soul been sent to Hell? I don't think so." I set the head in the sink and unwrapped the magazines.

Hubby's face was completely smeared with blood. He opened his eyes. "You've sealed your fate," he said. His mouth moved, but not quite in sync with his words, like a bad dub job.

"Oooh, I'm trembling."

The head glared at me. "You know not what you do."

"You mean like this?" I pinched its nose.

"I don't need to breathe anymore, dumbass," said the head in a slightly nasal voice.

"I'm not trying to suffocate you. I'm trying to annoy you."

"Knock it off."

"Go on, send my soul to Hell. You chicken?"

"You don't understand the powers you're dealing with."

I let go of his nose and poked him in the right eye. Not enough to puncture the eyeball or anything; more like a Three Stooges poke.

"Ow," said the head.

"So you can feel that?" I poked him in the other eye.

The head opened its mouth and tried to bite me. I moved my hand out of the way and slapped it in the face.

"Don't do that again," I told it.

"I'd advise you not to touch me anymore."

I slapped it on the other cheek.

"You little punk!"

I pinched it again. "Got your nose!"

Hubby's head made another attempt to bite me. This time, his teeth scraped against the back of my hand. I grabbed the revolver out of my inside jacket pocket and pressed it against the head's forehead.

"You want some of this?" I asked. "Huh? You want a piece of this?"

"Go on—threaten a severed head! Does that make you feel like a big man? Ooooooh, you're *so* tough!"

"I'll pop you! I mean it!"

"Does it boost your male ego to threaten a head? Why don't you drag out the rest of my body so we can compare penis size?"

"That's it, you're dead!" I shoved the barrel of the revolver into its mouth.

"What the hell are you doing?" asked Gretchen. Her hair was wrapped in a towel and she was wearing a light blue bathrobe.

"He was mouthing off," I explained.

"Put the head back in the bag."

"But it's not dead yet!"

"I can see that! That doesn't mean you need to put a gun in its mouth! What's the matter with you? It's not like you're gonna really shoot it!"

"Well, don't tell *it* that!"

"Put the gun away, moron."

I pulled the gun out of the head's mouth, then poked it in the forehead with the barrel.

"Put the gun away," Gretchen said.

"I am!" I stuffed the gun back in my jacket pocket.

"Now put the head away."

"Are you sure we should do that? There could be money in this."

"Put it away, Frank!"

"We could make the talk show circuit or at least hit a few carnivals. We don't have to tell people how he got decapitated."

"*Frank!*"

"All right, all right."

Her hubby's head glared at me as I wrapped it back up in the magazines. I dropped it back into the garbage bag and tied it closed.

"He can't really send my soul to Hell, can he?" I asked.

"Sure he can."

"You serious?"

"Yeah. Don't piss him off."

I decided not to kick the garbage bag again. "I thought you didn't know if this was black magic or not."

"Well, Frankie, it's entirely possible that I know more about the situation than I let on. If you weren't a complete idiot, you might have figured that out by now."

"So what's the next step?"

"Next you get in the shower and wash off that gook so that you can get rid of the body without people saying 'Hey, where's that blood-covered asshole going with those bags?' Make it quick. It's going to be light soon."

I took a shower. Bitch used up all the hot water.

- 7 -

After the shower, Gretchen gave me some more of her husband's dork clothes to wear. I see no need to describe them.

Then she outlined the plan. We were going to very casually take the garbage bags down to the Dumpster, as if disposing of traditional weekly refuse, and then get the hell out of there. It was not exactly the scheme of a criminal mastermind, but it was nice and simple.

"What if he talks to somebody?" I asked, as Gretchen picked up the bag containing the head.

"He won't."

"How do you know?"

She held the bag up to her face and spoke loudly and clearly. "Because if he does, I'll smash him like a pumpkin."

"Yeah, but wouldn't that be better than festering away in a garbage dump?" I asked.

She gave me a dirty look, as if to say *ix-nay on the estering-fay away in an arbage-gay ump-day.*

"Well, it *would* be," I insisted. "I sure wouldn't want to live for eternity as a disembodied head in a garbage bag. A jar in a lab, maybe, but not in a garbage bag."

"Okay, fine, you're right," said Gretchen. She slammed the bag down on the kitchen table.

"Why are you getting pissy? You're lucky I thought of that."

"I just want this over." She took a dishtowel out of a drawer, then quickly opened up the garage bag and unwrapped the head. "Pry his mouth open for me."

"Hell no."

"Do it!"

"Remember a half-second ago when I said 'hell no'? That still stands."

She looked at the head. "Open your mouth."

The head did not open its mouth.

"Open your mouth, or so help me I'll set your hair on fire."

"Oooh, can we do that anyway?" I asked.

Gretchen ignored me. "I mean it. I'll cut your fuckin' lips off and start ripping your teeth out with a pair of pliers."

The head opened its mouth and she shoved the rag inside.

"Wow," I said. "You can be one unpleasant chick."

"Shut up."

"That was a compliment."

She wrapped the head back up and once again tied the garbage bag. "Are we ready to go, or do you have anything else to complain about?"

"Nah, I'm good."

And so we headed off. I carried two bags and she carried one, which I assure you was me being chivalrous and not pussy- whipped. The Dumpster was right around the back of the apartment building, and we managed to *almost* reach it without everything getting fucked up.

A dumb-looking little kid, maybe...hell, I can't tell kids' ages, I guess he was about five or so, was sitting in front of the exit, playing with a couple of dolls. And by "dolls" I don't mean "action figures," I mean "dolls," as in "dolls that even a five-year-old deserves to get the shit kicked out of him for playing with."

"Hi!" said the kid, smiling at Gretchen.

"What are you doing here this early in the morning, sweetie?" Gretchen asked. "It's not even light out."

"Waiting for my mom. She's taking me to visit Gramma."

"That's nice."

"Did you two make babies last night?"

"Charles! That's not a nice thing to ask," said Gretchen.

I shook my head. "All she did was perform oral—"

Gretchen elbowed me in the ribs, hitting right in an especially sore spot from my earlier beating. I winced, gritted my teeth, and politely refrained from traumatizing the youngster by beating a woman to death in front of him. Gretchen walked past him and pushed open the door to the outside. I followed her.

"What the hell is the matter with you?" she demanded as the door swung closed behind me.

"What? He asked a perfectly legitimate question."

"You think you were being funny? You don't say stuff like that to a little kid when you're trying to be inconspicuous."

"Better that I said it than the head."

"Moron."

"Actually, it would've been a lot funnier if I'd made a joke about you giving me head. Damn. Any chance we can go back in there and try again?"

"Just throw away the bags."

I set down one of the bags and raised the lid to the Dumpster with my free hand. "This is your last chance to reconcile with your husband. Don't you think he's earned a second chance?"

Gretchen gave me a look that indicated that she was not fond of my sense of humor. That only made me want to be funnier. "I could probably recommend a good therapist for you two," I said. "Or you could go on Dr. Phil. Make that smug fucker work for his money!"

"Are you done?"

"Almost. I have one more Dr. Phil joke. No, wait, I forgot it. Yeah, I'm done."

"I can't believe I asked for your help. Let's just throw this stuff away so we can get some sleep."

As I lifted the bag to throw it into the Dumpster, the door opened and the dumb kid stepped outside. "Hi," he said.

I tossed the bag into the Dumpster. "Hi," I replied.

"Sweetie, you should go find your mom," Gretchen told him. I noticed that her bag was beginning to squirm.

"She's putting on makeup."

"Then you should wait in your apartment."

"My Playstation doesn't work."

"Still, it's not safe out here. You shouldn't be out here by yourself."

Suddenly the little brat's mouth dropped open and his eyes widened. "Puppies?"

Gretchen noticed that her bag was squirming. "No, no, not puppies!"

"Kitties?"

"No, nothing cute! It's a broken blender. I can't shut it off."

"Can I pet the puppies?"

"I told you, they're not puppies."

"Woof! Woof!" said the head.

The door opened and some hag wearing a shitload of makeup (and yet, somehow not enough) walked out of the building. "Charles! I told you to stay inside!"

"They're throwing away puppies," Charles said, pointing at the bags.

The head whimpered in a most puppyish way.

The brat's mother looked absolutely horrified. "That's terrible! Charles, come with me!"

"I want a white one like Snoopy."

Mommy grabbed Charles' hand and glared at me. "That's evil! You're both evil. I'm calling the police."

I pulled out my gun and shot her in the face.

You're probably going to judge me for that, but what would you have done? Just let her call the cops? I bet you're thinking that you never would have gotten involved in this mess in the first place, but I don't believe that for a second. It's one of the basic rules of survival: If the bitch is gonna call the cops, you waste her.

Okay, I'll admit that the cops might not have come speeding out to the apartment, sirens blaring and lights flashing, just because they thought we were going to toss some puppies in a Dumpster. We might have had time to find another suitable dumping location for the dismembered corpse. But it's not like I had time to sit around, sipping cappuccino and mulling over my options. She said she was gonna call the cops, I didn't want her to call the cops, so I popped her in the face. Done. No use getting all upset over things that you can't take back, right?

It *was* a pretty good shot considering how little time I'd taken to aim. Got her in the left eye. (Well, my left, her right, so I guess that would make it her right eye.) There was plenty of blood, but those of you who think I'm a total dick should know that none of it got on the kid.

Her body dropped to the ground.

Gretchen just stood there in shock.

The little brat also stood there in shock.

Only the head spoke: "Jesus Christ! What the hell is the matter with you?"

I punched the bag in Gretchen's hand. "Quiet! I thought we gagged you!"

"Oh God…oh God…oh God…" Gretchen whispered. I couldn't wait to hear her say that later that day, in a different context.

The brat looked as if he weren't sure if he should run, cry, or tug on the sleeve of his dead mother. I don't want to get all gooshy here, but I do have to admit that I felt sort of bad for the poor guy. Not *too* bad—I mean, the little shit was playing with dolls—but if I ever became an orphan, I'd probably be kind of sad about it, too.

Finally, the brat made his decision. He frantically tried to open the door to get back into the building, but he was too scared and pathetic to do anything more than turn the doorknob back and forth without success.

"What should I do about him?" I asked.

Gretchen closed her eyes and let out a sob. "Make the problem go away."

"Done."

Okay, you know what? I'm starting to sense a little hostility coming my way. I guess you just obey those Ten Commandments every chance you get, huh? You're probably one of those people who sits at home on your comfy couch and watches *Survivor* and thinks "Gosh, if I were on that show, I'd never complain about the harsh conditions like those whiners," while you gorge yourself on a double pepperoni pan pizza with extra cheese. Well, in this situation, I didn't have the extra cheese. I did what needed to be done.

But to keep you from getting your panties in a twist, I won't describe it. How does that sound? We'll just skip over that whole part. I didn't have to use my gun again, though, which I happen to think is pretty impressive.

So: One gunshot. Dead mom. Dead kid. Blubbering Gretchen. All caught up? Good.

By now she was sitting on the ground, with her face buried in her hands. But like I've already said, crying women don't really bother me all that much, so I mostly just wanted her to shut up.

"What's the new plan?" I asked.

She looked up at me and gave me a look of pure hatred. It actually creeped me out a little. I was glad that most of my "anything goes" activities involved her facing the other way.

"Fuck you," she said.

"There's no reason to be impolite. You're the one who said to make the problem go away. I would've let the little rugrat go."

She gave me the finger. I blew her a kiss.

Then she stood up. "We have to get out of here."

"Should we dump the bags?"

"No, we shouldn't dump the bags! It's a murder scene now! They'll check everything for clues! Hurry up and get the one you already threw away."

"Who cares if they find the bags of body parts now? Two murders, three murders…what's the difference?"

"The difference is that my dismembered husband will be traced back to me, you fucking idiot!"

"Well, so will Mommy and the tyke."

"I had nothing to do with that!"

"Methinks you're self-deceptive."

"Okay, asshole, I had nothing to do with that that anybody can prove. Happy now?"

"Gleeful."

"Now get the other bag out of the Dumpster so we can get out of here."

I shook my head. "I'm not carrying these things around. We're dumping 'em here like we planned." I picked up the bag with the head and tossed it into the Dumpster.

There was an "*oooof*!" from inside.

I was pretty sure it wasn't the head.

"What was that?" Gretchen asked.

"Nothing." I tossed the third bag into the dumpster.

"Seriously, what was that?"

"How should I know? Probably a rat. Probably lots of rats. Who cares?"

"Get the bags out of there."

"Screw that. Help me carry the dead chick."

"I said, get the bags out of there!"

"Uh-uh."

"If you don't get those bags this minute, you don't get to so much as touch a nipple. Not one nipple."

To be honest, I was surprised that our deal was still on. I shrugged. "Fine. I'll get the bags."

I peered over the top of the Dumpster. It was too dark to see anything inside except for vague shapes. I hoisted myself up onto the edge, so that I was bending over the side at the waist, and then reached down to retrieve the first bag.

Cold hands grabbed my arms.

I said "*Aaaiiggghhh*!!!" (approximately).

The hands pulled me inside the Dumpster. I landed on something that didn't feel very good to land upon. I struggled and flailed around as the hands clawed at my arms. A third hand grabbed my ankle.

The smell was absolutely putrid. We're talking dirty diapers mixed with rotten cantaloupe mixed with last week's salmon mixed with uncooked chicken mixed with a dozen instances of corpse flatulence. (I'm not saying that I identified those specific scents, but rather that the mix of aromas in the Dumpster was comparable. Just in case you were wondering how I could make note of all those smells during such a stressful experience.)

Another hand punched me in the leg, hitting me on one of my juiciest bruises. I screamed and kicked. Something crunched. I yanked my arm away and jabbed it on something really sharp. I screamed again. I tried to grab my gun but it seemed to have fallen out of my pocket.

Gretchen's head popped into view.

"Help me!" I screamed, reaching out to her. "Get me out of here!"

"Asshole," she said. And then I was cast into total darkness as she pulled the Dumpster lid closed.

- 8 -

I spent about two seconds thinking unkind thoughts about Gretchen, and then returned to my blind panic. I punched and kicked and screamed and bit. Most of my punches hit garbage bags. A couple of the kicks seemed to connect their targets. My screams made me feel better. The biting accomplished little of consequence.

My attackers—Dumpster bums, of course—began to giggle.

Finally, one of them spoke in a low, gravelly voice: "You're in our house."

"You pulled me in here!"

"We want food," the second bum whispered in my ear. I could feel his thick beard brush against my skin.

"I don't have any food!"

"Sure you do," said the first one. He pushed up the leg of my jeans and bit down on my calf. Except that he apparently didn't have any teeth, so he just gummed it.

His friend gummed my shoulder.

I tried to throw another punch, but my fist slammed against what felt like a steel girder but most likely wasn't. I doubt that I actually broke every bone in my hand, but that's the sensation I got, and *something* broke for sure.

This pain, combined with all of my supplementary pain, was so intense that I'm ashamed to admit that I just gave up. I couldn't struggle. I couldn't scream. I couldn't bite. I simply lay there and wallowed in silent misery.

The bums continued gumming my leg and shoulder. I'm not sure exactly what they hoped to accomplish, but it was freaky as fuck.

The bum at my shoulder started to gum my neck. He had a pretty solid jaw grip for a guy with no teeth. I could feel a big blob of his slobber still on my shoulder.

It would take a long time to be eaten alive under these circumstances.

I closed my eyes and listened to the disgusting smacking noises they made. This was how I was going to die: Gummed to death in a garbage Dumpster. Still better than the way my uncle Marcus went.

A gooey tongue swirled in my ear.

"I can help you," said a muffled voice.

"Who was that?" asked the bum, although his words were hard to understand because he kept his tongue in my ear while saying them.

"Just let me die," I said.

"You can die if you want. But I don't care to expire with my head under your ass. Let me help you."

The bum bit down on my ear, with hurt even without teeth.

The other bum dug his fingernails into my leg. I couldn't see them, but they did not feel as if they'd been recently trimmed.

And then something awakened inside of me. A sense of hope. A sense of power. I didn't have to die in this Dumpster. This was not the way I was going to go. When I died, damn it, people were going to say "Did you see the way Frank left this world? Holy shit, what a stud muffin!" They weren't going to find me lying in a pile of garbage covered with dried bum drool. I was going to *fight*!

Ignoring the pain, which was difficult because there was a lot of it, I yanked the garbage bag out from underneath my body. I tore it open, thankful that the cheap bitch hadn't used a Hefty, ripped the magazines apart, and grabbed hold of the severed head by the hair.

Then I thrust it at the bum next to my shoulder.

I heard a chomp.

The bum shrieked as the head gnawed on his face. I couldn't see clearly what was happening, but the sounds were unmistakable and the small splatters of blood on my face also provided a helpful clue.

The other bum crawled on top of me. "What *is* that thing?" he said with a gasp.

I pulled the head away from the first bum, hearing something snap off that I thought might be a lip, and slammed it against the second bum. More chewing sounds. I continued to press the head against the bum until he stopped screaming. It only took about twenty or thirty seconds.

The other bum was still moving around and making noise, so I set the head on his neck. While it went to work, I forced myself to stand up, and then pushed open the lid of the Dumpster. I picked up the head and stomped on the bum's face a few times until he shut up.

I started to climb out of the Dumpster. "Don't forget the other bags," said the head.

I was a little too disoriented and freaked out to argue, so I fished around until I found the other garbage bags and tossed them out of the Dumpster. I climbed out, fell on my ass, stayed on my ass for a moment, then got back up and stood there looking stupid with a bloody head in my hand.

"Do you want revenge on my wife?" asked the head.

"Hell yeah."

"Then work with me. Wipe this blood off my mouth, and then get those other corpses into the Dumpster as fast as you can. We don't want the cops doing an all-out manhunt if we can avoid it."

I wiped the head's face on my shirt. Hell, it was his shirt anyway, so what did I care? I set the head down and went over to get the body of the dead kid. I tried a couple of times to lift him, but I couldn't get leverage.

"What's the problem?" asked the head.

I held up my swollen hand. My pinky was bent at a rather grotesque angle. "My hand's broken."

"Deal with it. Get rid of those bodies or you're spending the rest of your life in prison. They loooove child killers in prison."

It hurt like hell, but I quickly got the kid into the Dumpster. And yes, I felt bad about what I'd done, okay?

"Now the mother."

"I can't lift the mother."

"I'd help if you hadn't chopped up my body! This is your mess, and you'd better appreciate my help and do what I say. Get the mother hidden away. The police could be here any second."

I decided not to argue and instead hoisted the dead woman over my shoulder. Fortunately I hadn't shot some fat cow, and she was petite enough that I was able to get her into the Dumpster along with her son. I closed the lid and picked up the head.

"Happy now?"

"*Freeze!*"

It was a cop. The same cop who'd arrested the wino. He didn't seem happy to see me again.

"I didn't do anything," I said.

"Put down the head!"

"It's not a real head. It's a special effects head from the movies. See, it talks and everything." I shook the head. It didn't talk.

"*Drop the head!*"

"I swear, it's not real! It's a movie prop! It's from that movie...*The Head.*" I shook the head some more. It remained silent, like that goddamn singing frog in the Warner Brothers cartoon.

"*Now!*"

I dropped the head.

"Keep your hands in the air where I can see them," said the cop, moving toward me. "I've already got backup on the way, so don't try anything."

I kept my hands in the air. The cop spun me around and slammed me against the Dumpster, which felt just delightful in my beat-up condition. A moment later I was in handcuffs.

"I swear, it's all fake," I said.

"We got a call of a gunshot being fired and a disturbance. Care to explain all of the blood?"

"It's not real blood. We were making a movie without permits. Long live independent cinema!"

The cop didn't seem convinced. If I did go to prison for the rest of my life, I hoped I'd at least get a chance to stomp that head into mush first.

"Hey," said the head.

The cop glanced around.

"This is the severed head on the ground talking to you."

The cop poked at the head with the toe of his boot. The head glared at him. "Knock that off."

"Who's doing that?" the cop asked.

"It's my partner," I explained. "He's doing it through remote control."

The cop carefully picked up the head by the hair. "You're a very handsome man," said the head. "How about a kiss?"

"Its mouth doesn't even move in sync with its words," the cop said. "It's still a pretty good effect, though." He looked around, then raised his voice. "Whoever you are, come on out! I'm not going to arrest you but we need to discuss this."

The head puckered up its lips. "Come on. Kissy kissy!"

The cop chuckled. "That might make a good picture. Think I could play a part in your movie?"

"Absolutely," I told him. "It's a religious movie about a severed head. Are you available tomorrow night?"

"I sure am." He unlocked the handcuffs and latched them back onto his belt, while still holding the head in his other hand. "I'm not going to make an issue out of this, but do try to be quieter in the future, and tell your friend to respect law enforcement officers, or I will have to make an arrest, okay?"

"Yes, sir. Praise Jesus."

He lifted up the head again. "That is really cool. How do you do that?"

"Movie magic."

"Watch this." The cop stuck out his tongue and gave the head a french kiss. I tried not to gag. The cop chuckled again and wiped some blood off his mouth. "I can't believe how real that thing feels. I commend you for going with practical effects instead of CGI."

"Thanks."

He gave me back the head and took a card out of his pocket. "There's my contact information. I won't do nudity, but I'm up for anything else."

"Sounds good. We'll be in touch."

The cop smiled and left.

"I can't believe I had to let another man tongue-kiss me," said the head. "That's just sick."

"Homophobic, are we?"

"No. You can support gay rights without wanting a man to stick his tongue in your mouth. Good thing I can't vomit any more, or I would've puked all over him."

"Well, you're not the one who almost went to jail."

"Excuse me? Are you comparing our problems? I had to become a cannibal because of you! Do you think I ate human flesh before tonight? No! But I had to in order to save your worthless ass."

"It doesn't count as eating human flesh if it doesn't go into your stomach," I explained.

"The hell it doesn't!"

"If you're a vegetarian and you chew up a piece of meat and spit it out, that's not a violation of your religion."

"You are such an idiot. Put me back in the bag and let's go someplace safe."

"Like where?"

"I don't care! Someplace safe! Why does the guy with the exposed brain have to make the decisions?"

I put him back in the garbage bag, picked up the other two, and we headed back to my place.

- 9 -

By the time we reached my apartment, I could barely move. It's hard enough to walk twelve blocks when you've merely been beaten half to death, let alone when you've got three garbage bags containing the sum total of a human body slung over your shoulder. I couldn't even switch hands every once in a while, since my left hand was now about twice its size and not much good for anything. Oh, how this sucked.

Fortunately, the head provided moral support the entire time, cleverly disguised as a continuous onslaught of insults.

I dumped the bags in my bathtub, then sat down on the toilet and gasped for breath.

"Mind letting me out?" asked the head.

"In a minute."

"No, how about now?"

"I said, in a minute. I'm still in charge here."

"Right. Because you know *exactly* what you're doing."

"Bite me."

"Look, I'm still annoyed about the cannibalism thing. You'd be well advised not to make jokes about it."

"I wasn't making a cannibalism joke. I was just telling you to bite me. It's the same as if I'd told you to fuck off. Fuck off."

"Do you want help with revenge or not?"

I sighed and stood up. I really hated this head. I tore open the garbage can and lifted it out. "Happy now?"

"No. Turn on the faucet and wash me off. I need to get the taste of blood and cop spit out of my mouth."

I turned on the bathtub faucet and held the head underneath the water. He told me that it was too hot and called me an asshole, so I cooled the water down. I rotated him until most of the blood had rinsed off, and then let him swallow a few mouthfuls. The red water trickled out of the bottom of his neck.

"Much better. Now unwrap the rest of my body."

I did as I was told. Soon I had a bathtub full of gory body parts. The pieces of his chest hadn't really held together very well. As we started to lose a chunk, he told me to put the stopper in the drain and called me an asshole again.

After I threw away the garbage bags, I sat back down on the toilet and looked at the pool of gore in my tub. "That's really gross," I said.

"And you're blaming *me*?" the head asked from his perch on top of a quadrant of his back.

"Just making an observation."

"Don't make observations. Now we need to bring Gretchen here. Give her a call on her cell phone."

"I don't know her number."

"Hey, guess what, she's my wife! You think maybe, possibly, somehow, I might know the number?"

"You don't have to be sarcastic."

"Actually, I do. It's the only way I can stay sane when I'm dealing with your almost supernatural level of stupidity. God, you're dense. You're the dumbest human being I've ever encountered, and I've met some dullards in my time, let me tell you."

"Keep it up, head," I warned. "I'll jump in there and start stomping your guts like grapes."

"Like you have the energy."

"I'd take a nap first."

"Stop talking. Gretchen isn't as dumb as you are, but she's not exactly a rocket scientist or brain surgeon, so we need to get her over here before she gets herself nabbed by the cops. Then: vengeance."

"Cool. What kind of vengeance?"

"Death."

"Sweet." I considered that for a moment. "Y'know, my payment for killing you was supposed to be in sexual favors. I know this is sort of awkward, but is there any way I could cash in one or two before we kill her?"

"Are you kidding me?"

"What? It's not like you can do anything! Why shouldn't I get a piece of that? I earned it, dammit!"

The head smiled. "Actually, as much as it disgusts me to think about it, yes, you will get a piece of that. The revenge curse requires carnal relations. So if you're the kind of man who will fornicate with another man's wife while his severed head watches—"

"I am," I assured him.

"—then you will get your reward. Hopefully you get a bonus payment of the clap."

"Is the clap still around? I thought they cured that."

"Call her."

The head told me what to say, so I gave Gretchen a call. She answered on the third ring.

"Hello?"

"Hi, babe."

"Frank?"

"Yep. Nice of you to leave me behind."

"I'm sorry. I got scared. I was on my way back to help you out when you called."

"Uh-huh. Listen up, bitch—may I call you bitch? Your hubby's head told me where the pages are hidden."

"What pages?"

"The missing pages of the tomb."

"*Tome*, dumbass," the head corrected.

"Tome, sorry. The pages that grant you eternal life."

"I didn't know any pages were missing."

I covered the phone receiver and spoke to the head. "She says she didn't know that any pages were missing."

"Assure her that they are."

I nodded. "I'm supposed to assure you that they are."

"Where are they?"

"I'm not telling. By the way, he also told me that the whole reason you asked me to help cut up your hubby is because the murder had to be committed by somebody of soft mind for the spell to work. That pisses me off."

"Well, you know what, Frank? You're not the sharpest crayon in the box. Get over it."

"I am over it. Anyway, your Sweet Babboo hid the pages after he figured out that you were going to try to off him, and if you want them back, you'll have to pay me a visit."

"And what happens when I pay you a visit?"

"You do me."

"You're such a pig."

"Hey, do you know what I've been through these past few hours? I've been beat up, pissed on, insulted, handcuffed, gummed, and my fuckin' hand is broken. I deserve to get laid. You have half an hour to get over here—without the cops—or I'm leaving town and you'll never see me or the pages again."

There was silence on the other end.

"Hello?" I asked.

Nothing.

"I think she hung up on me," I told the head. I slammed the phone down on the receiver. "Bitch! Now what?"

"She needs those pages," the head said. "She won't do anything to risk that."

"She left us in the Dumpster with the vagrants. That risked it."

"Trust me."

The phone rang. I picked it up. "Gretchen?"

"Hi, Frank. We got cut off. Bad reception. What did you say?"

"What was the last part you heard?"

"You said 'Hey, do you know what' and then the signal faded."

"Oh. I basically just said that I've been beaten up and pissed on and insulted and my hand is broken and that I deserve to get laid and that if you don't show up here in half an hour I'm leaving town and you'll never see me or the pages again."

Silence.

"You there?"

"Yeah. I'm thinking."

"There's nothing to think about. Get your ass over here."

"Sex, and then you tell me where the pages are, right?"

"Well, it has to be *good* sex. You can't just give it a few tugs and say we're done. But, yeah, that's how it's gonna work."

"Fine."

I gave her directions to my place and hung up. I was putting a lot of trust in the idea that she'd actually show up instead of calling the cops, who would then discover a pile of body parts in my bathtub, but hopefully the allure of eternal life was sufficient.

"Is there a way for me to get eternal life, too?" I asked the head.

"No."

"Why not?"

"Because you have a soft mind. You can only be used as a vessel."

"Your wife's mind is kind of soft. Why does she get eternal life?"

"She doesn't. This is a trap, remember?"

"Oh, yeah."

"You either need to quit asking stupid questions or you need to quit getting indignant over the soft mind thing."

"My bad."

Twenty-six minutes later, there was a knock at my door. I peeked through the spyhole and saw that it was Gretchen. She seemed to be alone, so I opened the door.

"C'mon in," I said, as she walked past me.

"Where's Michael?"

"Who?"

"My husband."

"Is that his name? Michael? He's in my bathtub. First door on the left."

She hurried into the bathroom. She seemed relieved when she came out a few seconds later. "So now what?" she asked.

"We get nekkid."

"Have you even looked at yourself? You're, like, one giant bruise. Look at your pinky—that's hideous. How can you be thinking about sex right now? You should be thinking about an ice pack."

"Listen, my dick is the only part of my body that doesn't hurt right now. So I can either make it happy and get one tiny bit of pleasure out of this nightmare, or I can sit around and think about how much my goddamn pancreas hurts. I don't even know where my pancreas is, but I can tell you that it hurts!"

"Okay. Where do you want to do it?"

"Bathroom."

"I don't think so."

"Bathroom or no room. I want your husband to watch."

"He's not into that. I asked about it when we were first dating."

"I don't want him to get his kink on! I want to piss him off. I want him to sit there like a helpless little head while I diddle his wife."

"That's really tacky."

"Sorry, but that's the way it's gotta be."

"I guess I'd expect nothing less from somebody who would strangle a little boy."

"Quit harping on the little boy. You'd think I clubbed a baby seal or something. Let's go."

I grabbed her hand with my bad hand, which is not something I recommend. When the tears stopped (yes, there were tears, I admit it) we went into the bathroom and got undressed. Taking off your clothes in front of a naked woman is supposed to be a pleasurable experience, but bolts of pain tore through my body with each movement, and by the time I was nude there'd been at least one more instance of tears.

I lay down on the cold tile floor. Gretchen looked damn good naked, with breasts that looked so tasty that I wanted to bring out a knife and fork. Despite the agony in the rest of my body, my soldier had no trouble whatsoever standing at attention.

"Salute it," I told her.

"What?"

"Salute my soldier."

She looked at me with disgust. "You are *such* a dipshit." She saluted my soldier with her middle finger. I decided that would have to suffice.

I put on the condom that Ms. Paranoid made me wear, and then she straddled me and slowly lowered herself onto my awesome meat. She winced a little bit, probably not used to receiving somebody of my size. Heh heh. If there was one thing I could get into, it was a hot chick making sounds of pain because I was too big for her.

I gave a sharp upward thrust to facilitate the process, which sent a roaring wave of pain through my hip. I decided to let her do all the work.

She started to ride me. It felt damn good, even though she wasn't really getting into it. I reached up and cupped her fine fake tits. After a few thrusts, she started to move a little faster, and she made some sounds that indicated that perhaps she wasn't having a completely miserable time.

Over her soft moans, I could hear Michael's head whispering something that sounded like Latin, or maybe German. I wasn't sure why he was doing that now. The chanting wasn't supposed to start until I was done.

My thumb sunk into the flesh of her right boob.

"Aw, *shit!*" I said.

Suddenly, all in one motion, the skin slipped off her body and landed on me with a loud *splat*. She looked at her glistening insides in horror and let out a silent scream.

I thrust faster. I'd be damned if I was going to go through all this shit and not finish.

A big red blob of fleshy goo dropped onto my chest. Her eyeballs leaked out of their sockets as her teeth sprung out of her bloody mouth like popcorn.

I thrust harder and harder, but she was becoming a lot less tight. This wasn't fair! "You son of a bitch!" I screamed at Michael as the bottom half of Gretchen's head splattered on top of me.

It was no use. It was like screwing a bowl of pudding. Her arms fell off and her bones turned to whitish yellowish liquid and it wasn't long before I was covered with a thick layer of slime that had formerly been Gretchen.

The head laughed.

"Real funny," I said, pushing myself up to a sitting position. "Real fuckin' funny." I wiped some of the slime off my chest. "You couldn't have waited eight more seconds?"

"Like I care about your gratification."

I stood up and grabbed a towel. I had an urge to engage in a bit of self-pleasure and finish up in a location that he assuredly would *not* appreciate, but my boner was history.

"Why'd you do that?" I asked, as I ruined one of my best towels, though to be honest all of my towels were pretty crappy.

"I needed a sacrifice."

"You never said anything about a sacrifice. You just said revenge."

The head chuckled. "There are many things I didn't share with your soft mind. And now that the sacrifice is complete, my release is imminent!"

"Oh, sure, *you* get to release. Prick."

A thin cloud of black smoke formed underneath the head. I backed away. Unfortunately, I backed away into one of the many patches of slippery slime, and I fell, bashing my head against the floor.

The head rose into the air on a layer of smoke. An arm joined it, and then another. Then the four pieces of chest came together—sort of—and hovered underneath them.

I tried to get back up, but my hands and feet kept slipping on the slime. I scooted on my ass toward the bathroom door, whimpering like a baby. That's right, a baby. There's no shame in that.

Michael stepped out of the tub. The pieces of his body were more or less in the right place, and though they didn't fit together perfectly, the smoke seemed to be holding them together like some sort of…I dunno, black smoke glue.

Slime or no slime, I was getting the hell out of there. I turned over and crawled on my hands and knees for the doorway. Once I'd reached the hallway carpet, I stood up and ran for the living room. Or at least I tried to run for the living room. Two steps and I twisted my ankle and hit the floor again.

"Don't kill me!" I begged. "Don't turn me into ooze!"

Michael floated out of the bathroom. His grin seemed to fill half of his face. "Fool," he said. It was the exact same voice, but for some reason it sounded a lot scarier now. "You mocked forces you didn't comprehend!"

"I comprehend them now! Please, let me go!"

"Oh, no, I don't think so. I have plans for you, Franklin."

I was too frightened to even tell him what happened to the last person who called me Franklin. "C'mon, I could've left you in that Dumpster!"

"You're grasping at straws."

I scrambled on my hands and knees into the living room. I grabbed a half-empty bottle of beer off my coffee table and threw it at him. He caught it in the air and crushed it in his fist, sprinkling glass shards and Budweiser onto the floor.

"Your fate is sealed, Franklin."

"I don't think so." I picked up a 3rd place bowling trophy that I'd stolen from my father. It wasn't much of a weapon, but it was the best I had. No floating pile of body parts was going to seal my fate in my own goddamn apartment.

I held the bowling trophy out in front of me as if it were a sword. Not pain, nor fear, nor blue balls was going to stop me this time. That dismembered son of a bitch was going *down*!

I let out a battle cry and rushed at him.

The black smoke abruptly disappeared and the pieces of Michael fell to the floor.

Then my legs gave out and I fell to the floor as well.

I saw stars when my chin smacked the carpet, but I blinked a few times and cleared my vision quickly in case that wasn't the end of it.

I was looking into my own bruised, slime-covered face.

What the fuck…?

My naked body got up, wiped off some more slime, and smiled at me.

It picked me up by the hair and lifted me to its face. I looked down and there was no body underneath me.

"Nice body you've got," it said in my voice. "You've treated it very badly, though. I'm going to have to find a hospital."

"You...you...you..."

"Me what? Are you trying to think of a good threat? What are you going to do to me—you're just a head!"

"It's not fair!" I wailed.

"Oh, it's fair. It's mucho fair. I think I'm going to enjoy your body. Maybe I'll go out and get laid tonight. Wanna watch?"

"Please! You can't do this!"

"Correction. I can't un-do this." He tossed me to the floor. I landed on my nose, breaking it, and then rolled onto my left cheek.

I let out a sob.

"Oh, don't worry, Franklin," he said, crouching down next to me. "As tempting as it might be, I'm not going to leave you trapped in that head. Talking severed heads attract too much attention. Sure, I could bury you, but you never know when a dog is going to dig you up or something like that."

He got up and walked out of sight. I tried to roll myself, but my cheek muscles weren't strong enough for that kind of thing.

My ex-body returned, holding a baseball bat. An autographed one, signed by Pete Rose, who had become my hero after the gambling scandal.

"What are you gonna do?" I asked.

"Exactly what you think I'm going to do. Your soul will leave the head when there isn't enough left of it to sustain life."

He hoisted the bat over his head, then slammed it down upon my new skull. A large bone chunk fell on top of my right eye.

"*Please!*"

He smashed me with the bat again. I tried to repeat the word "Please" but my jaw was broken and it came out sounding like "*uuuuuuuh.*"

"A couple more should do it," he said. "And then you'll see that I always keep my promises."

He had to slam the bat down nine more times before everything went black. But that's only because both of my eyes were squished. It took another seven hits before all sensation faded.

When I awoke, I was back in my real body. But it was covered with black, leathery, slithering things that burned as they slid across my flesh.

A rusty steel door slid open. Glowing red eyes and a leering, fanged grin greeted me.

- 10 -

Hell is the worst shithole imaginable. You'd think that after the first million or so times they flay every scrap of skin from your body, you'd get used to it, but no, it stings like crazy every single time.

Every night, three of the most gorgeous women I've ever seen dance naked in front of my spiked bed. But they're always out of reach. And when I try to at least fondle my dick, my hand passes right through it. That got old really quick.

I do get to have sex on occasion, but believe me, it's not fun.

All of the food tastes like crap. Unfortunately, there's a very logical reason that it tastes that way. The worst part is when they make me watch it being made before mealtime.

Most of my time is spent in my cell, writing this memoir. They were nice enough to provide me with a laptop computer. I've been writing this thing for centuries now, because the keyboard keeps biting off my hands, but they grow back in time.

I guess if there's a moral to be found in my little tale, it's that no good can come from associating with women. They're wretched creatures. Stay away from them.

That's all I have to say. I hope you enjoyed my story.

Aw, fuck, Attila is horny again...

STORY NOTES

Warning: These are laden with spoilers. Read the stories first. If you don't, doom will befall you and those you care about. I mean it.

REALLY, REALLY FEROCIOUS

This was written for the Charles Grant benefit anthology *Small Bites*, specifically the "Animal Attacks" section. I wanted to make sure that my choice of animal wasn't used by any other author, and a wiener dog seemed like a safe bet. So I started writing the story without having any idea where it was headed... and then I got *completely* stuck.

There had to be some kind of twist, but what? The obvious choice would be to have the wiener dog turn out to be a truly ferocious beast, either chomping off the solicitor's hand or transforming into a terrifying creature. But the "horrifying wiener dog from hell" idea just seemed lame and predictable.

So I brainstormed and rejected idea after idea after idea after idea until...hey, what if the old man used the wiener dog as a weapon, and just bashed the hell out of the solicitor with it?

Bingo. One of my most popular stories was born.

SOCIALLY AWKWARD MOMENTS
WITH AN ASPIRING LUNATIC

This was originally published as a stand-alone chapbook by Biting Dog Press. For quite some time, I'd had an idea for a humorous novel about a guy who wants to become a serial killer, but is really, really bad at it. But a full-length novel seemed like too much time to spend with this character, and I scaled the idea way down into a short story.

This is a story where "voice" is everything. A narrator who decides, for no particular reason, that he wants to become insane is not exactly a relatable concept for your average reader, and the end product could easily be inaccessible and merely weird for the sake of being weird. So it was important to write this in a conversational, friendly style (which gradually falls apart as the story progresses) to carry the reader along with this whack-job.

HIGH STAKES

This was inspired by my experience as a little kid at a theme park. I was playing this ridiculous carnival game that was virtually impossible to win, and I'd spent *way* more than the market price of the stupid little stuffed animal that I didn't even want, but dammit, I was *not* going to leave empty handed!

And I didn't. But then I couldn't afford a corn dog and was quite devastated.

SPECIAL FEATURES

I'm always amused by DVD audio commentary tracks where the participants are still in heavy-duty "ass-kissing for career ascension" mode.

Unlike many writers, I find that coming up with the basic idea for a short story is a lot more difficult than the execution, so after my moment of "Aha! Commentary track for snuff film!" I wrote this one fairly quickly.

SEX POTION 147

Believe it or not, this started out as a straightforward smut comedy. It was going to be a collaborative novel with erotica/chick-lit author Michele Bardsley, but we abandoned the project after a couple of chapters, like the slackers that we are.

I was working on "Werewolf Porno" as a chapbook for White Noise Press, and I suddenly remembered that I had "Sex Potion #147" lying around. If I could figure out a new, demented direction for it, I'd have *two* sex/horror/comedy tales for the chapbook, and an improved marketing angle!

JEFF STRAND - 271

I'd written the first section of the novel, which ended at the part where the Gypsy gave our heroine a free sample of the potion, so I got rid of everything after that, added a serial killer who keeps his penis in a mason jar, and took the story in a *completely* different direction from the original concept.

I sent it to Michele when I was done. Her response: "You are *so* weird."

THE THREE LITTLE PIGS

When I was little, my friend had a "Three Little Pigs" record, and I was horrified that the wolf actually *ate* the first two pigs. (I was only familiar with the story in its animated Disney incarnation, I guess.) The first side of the record actually faded out on the sounds of the wolf greedily devouring his prey. It was disturbing as hell.

When the editor of *Wicked Karnival* magazine asked me to write a story based on a fairy tale, I bashed my head against the wall for a few hours until my traumatic childhood memory resurfaced and I decided to write a gore-drenched version of the pig saga.

EVERYTHING HAS A PURPOSE

My algebra teacher in junior high was pure evil, and she was never able to offer an explanation for why we'd use this crap beyond "It teaches you basic problem solving skills." So does being thrown into a tank of piranha.

THEM OLD WEST MUTATIONS

This has the longest "story begun" to "story completed" gap of anything in the collection. I wrote about half of it in 1995, when a publisher was seeking cross-genre western stories for a series of chapbooks, and wrote the other half ten years later.

With almost all of my "humorous horror" short stories I try to include some element of legitimate horror, something to make the reader wince or cringe or at least say "Dude, that is messed up!" I kind of like that this particular story is simply harmless goofy fun, even though everybody dies at the end.

WASTING GRANDPA

I believe this was the first story I ever wrote with a complete prick as the narrator. Since then, writing from the point of view of scumbags and insane people has become a favorite technique. I probably do it too much. Sorry about that.

A BITE FOR A BITE

This was another story written for the *Small Bites* anthology, for the "Zombie" section. *Small Bites* had a very strict 500-word maximum for all stories, no exceptions. The first draft of "A Bite For A Bite" came in around 750 words, and I remember that it was absolute *torture* trying to get this thing down to 500. I went through the story over and over, cutting as little as a single word in some passes, cursing the editors for their unfairly stringent rules that were destroying my creative vision.

Now, a couple of years later, the story can be as long as I want, and I can't think of anything I want to put back. Weird.

GLIMPSES

One of the few "serious" pieces in this book, and by that I mean "doesn't combine the humor and horror." Like my "serious" novel *Pressure,* there's a lot of humor in "Glimpses," but the dark elements are played straight. Even though I tend to write about really horrible things, I don't usually end on a complete downer, so this one's kind of a nice change of pace.

COMMON SENSE

There is so much to be said about this 36-word epic. Themes to discuss, stylistic techniques to analyze, shocking plot twists to mull over...the sheer *richness* of this tale continues to amaze me every time I read it. If you don't think this story drips with atmosphere, then you're simply ignorant in the ways of dripping. This is my finest literary hour.

QUITE A MESS

Okay, this one's more of a joke than a story, but I think it's kinda funny. It shares thematic material with my unpublished-and-not-included-in-this-collection poem "Food Fight of the Living Dead."

BAD COFFEE

This appeared on an actual coffee mug designed by Insidious Publications. It was done in an extremely low production run of only 25 mugs, and since the "Do Not Put In Dishwasher" warning was a crucial piece of advice, I figure it's one of the rarest collectibles in my career thus far.

WEREWOLF PORNO

Though it's not *that* smutty, this is certainly my most sexually graphic story. When this appeared alongside "Sex Potion #147" in *Funny Stories of Scary Sex,* my mom elected not to purchase a copy. For that I am grateful.

I actually read this story in front of a live audience once and about three paragraphs in I really wished that I'd picked another story. That was a long twenty minutes.

AN ADMITTEDLY POINTLESS BUT MERCIFULLY BRIEF STORY WITH ALIENS IN IT

I won a $50 computer game (*Stupid Invaders*) by entering it in a contest, so it wasn't all *that* pointless, now was it? Ha!

MUNCHIES

I've written dozens of comedy skits, but I only allowed myself to include one in this book. I think a skit about cannibalism was a fine choice. This actually appeared in a humor column I used to write about computer games for the Just Adventure website, around the time that I accepted that I had nothing funny left to say about computer adventure games and didn't even try to stay on topic.

Roasting Weenies by Hellfire

Okay, okay, I'll admit it. This story (written over a decade ago) almost didn't make the cut for this book. I'm not going to pretend that it's a tightly-plotted masterpiece, but...c'mon, it's a splattery version of *Home Alone,* except with the Devil and stuff!

There were tough decisions to be made with *Gleefully Macabre Tales,* and I voted in favor of the story with the little kid using the severed lower half of his body to distract the hungry Doberman. If that's so wrong, then baby, I don't wanna be right!

I Hold the Stick

I forget which theme park I was at when I was inspired to write this story. We were waiting in a long, long, loooooong line in hot, miserable weather, and right before the entrance to the actual ride was the attendant with the stick to make sure you met the minimum height requirements. And I thought "Why would they put him at the *end* of the wait? He should be stopping too-short kids before they even get in line. What a miserable job this guy must have."

But then I thought, hey, if you hated little kids and had an inflated sense of power, it would be a dream job!

Scarecrow's Discovery

Originally this story ended with the kids cutting up poor Ray with an electric carving knife. After *Horrors! 365 Scary Stories* came out, a co-worker insisted that there was no such thing as a cordless electric carving knife. I scoffed at that idea. Of course there was such thing as a cordless electric carving knife! What if you needed to carve turkey at your dinner table and there was no electrical outlet handy? But I researched the issue and could find no evidence that there's such thing as a cordless electric carving knife. So, with much sorrow, I changed it to a drill so that whiny people like my co-worker don't complain in the future.

HOWARD, THE TENTH REINDEER / HOWARD RISES AGAIN

About twelve years ago, I wrote "Howard, the Tenth Reindeer" and sent it out as a Christmas card to my writer friends. Response was overwhelmingly enthusiastic, so the next year I followed it up with "The Little Girl Who Wished Away Christmas," which was about 4% as popular. I sent out "Howard Rises Again" the year after that, and the cards were sucked into a black hole of polite silence. That ended the Christmas card idea.

I'd be unlikely to write something like "Howard" these days (much the same way that I don't expect to write another novel along the lines of *How to Rescue a Dead Princess*) but I do enjoy the shamelessly silly, just-for-laughs tone.

BRAINBUGS

When our cat goes insane for no discernable reason, my wife and I like to say that the bugs in her brain are acting up again. So this story was inspired by my cat.

CAP'N HANK'S FIVE ALARM NUCLEAR LAVA WINGS

Buffalo wings are my favorite food, but I tend to be a "medium" kind of guy. I'm a wuss, I know.

This story is previously unpublished, but was set to be part of a magazine that went bye-bye. Tom Moran did a very cool but absolutely disgusting illustration of a guy having his lips sizzled off by a blowtorch to accompany the tale. Heh heh.

A CALL FOR MR. POTTY-MOUTH

Mr. Potty Mouth is real. Watch yourself.

THE BAD MAN IN THE BLUE HOUSE

Sometimes you write a story and have no idea if it's any good or not. This was completely different from anything I'd ever written, and I couldn't figure out if it was hilariously bad or, y'know, kind of cool.

I decided to let my test readers decide.

Most of them voted in favor of eliminating this story from the collection. Which, to be completely honest, is the way I was leaning.

But...a couple of them said it was among their favorites.

So I kept it. You decide if I made the right choice.

ABBEY'S SHRIEK

This one's kind of icky, isn't it? It appeared in the anthology *Unravelings: Beyond the Mundane,* which led to me getting reviewed by *Romantic Times* magazine: "More graphically violent and bloody stories, such as Jeff Strand's 'Abbey's Shriek,' are not for the faint of heart, or those who don't enjoy their daily dose of gore."

Does Jack Ketchum get reviewed in *Romantic Times* magazine? I think not.

THE SOCKET

Many authors have a particular "market killer" story, meaning one that destroys every market that accepts it. *Twisted Magazine* accepted it for its second issue, but died after the first. *Winedark Sea* also accepted it for its second issue, and perished as well. It was eventually published in *Deathgrip: Exit Laughing,* and that signaled the end of Hellbound Books.

So, basically, Dark Regions Press is screwed.

ONE OF THEM

Sometimes, an author must be stubborn. None of my rest readers liked this story. It was the only unanimous "Cut this one!" decision in the entire process.

Well, you know what? I like this damn story. I don't care what anybody says! Screw you all! Don't touch my baby!

This story is a complete reversal from my usual approach. I like to take macabre, unpleasant subject matter and add a sense of fun to it. "One of Them" takes something that should be entertaining and sucks the fun out of it.

If you don't like the story, blame me. The test readers are on your side.

SECRET MESSAGE

Nope, I'm not going to decode it here. I will say that as far as substitution ciphers go, this is about as simple as it gets.

However, if you don't want to write in the book or transcribe the whole thing, drop me a friendly e-mail at JeffStrand@aol.com and I'll send you a version suitable for printing out and scrawling on.

MR. SENSITIVE

Nick Cato, publisher of *The Horror Fiction Review,* e-mailed me and suggested that someday we work together on a project, maybe something called *Two Twisted Nuts*. What he meant was "Two Wacky Guys," but I e-mailed him back and said *"Two Twisted Nuts?* What's that, an anthology of scrotal terror?"

Weeks later, Nick told me that he loved the idea and had written a story for *Two Twisted Nuts: A Chapbook of Testicular Terror.* I was in no way obligated to contribute something, but he was definitely going forth with the project.

I feared the repercussions to Nick's career if he went around e-mailing authors and asking them for stories about testicles, so I wrote "Mr. Sensitive."

I cringed when I re-read this one for the collection. I think that's a good sign.

THE BAD CANDY HOUSE

One of my most mean-spirited tales, and my story of choice when I'm doing a live reading. Everybody laughs at the line near the end where we find out that the baby died. You people are sick.

DISPOSAL

Biting Dog Press originally published this as a hardcover limited edition. That version also included ten mean-spirited forewords by Mike Arnzen, MaryJanice Davidson, Christopher Golden, Rick Hautala, Brian Keene, J.A. Konrath, Gregory Lamberson, Mark McLaughlin, Jim Moore, and James Newman, where they talked about how much they despised a) me, and/or b) the book. I had several other authors in mind in case my first ten picks turned me down…but none of them did. And those bastards were *mean*. It's well worth seeking out the hardcover edition to watch them hurt my fragile feelings.

Jeff Strand is the author of enough books that if you tried to cut off one finger for each of them, you'd completely run out of fingers, and then you wouldn't have anything left to hold the knife when you started on your toes. (You would not, however, run out of toes—at least for now.) Some of those books include *Pressure*, *Benjamin's Parasite*, *The Sinister Mr. Corpse*, and *Graverobbers Wanted (No Experience Necessary)*. He's been a finalist for the Bram Stoker Award twice, and won zero times. He lives in Tampa, Florida, and thinks that it would be best for all concerned if you visited his website at:

www.JeffStrand.com

Made in United States
North Haven, CT
13 August 2022